D0794847

Would Like to Meet

Polly James

avon

This novel is entirely a work of fiction.
The names, characters and incidents portrayed in it are the work
of the author's imagination. Any resemblance to actual persons,
living or dead, events or localities is entirely coincidental.

AVON

A division of HarperCollins*Publishers*
The News Building
1 London Bridge Street
London SE1 9GF

www.harpercollins.co.uk

A Paperback Original 2016

1

Copyright © Polly James 2016

Polly James asserts the moral right to be identified as the author of this work

A catalogue record for this book is available from the British Library

ISBN-13: 978-0-00-754855-2

Typeset in Bembo by Palimpsest Book Production Ltd, Falkirk, Stirlingshire

Printed and bound in Great Britain by Clays Ltd, St Ives plc

All rights reserved. No part of this publication may be
reproduced, stored in a retrieval system, or transmitted,
in any form or by any means, electronic, mechanical,
photocopying, recording or otherwise, without the prior
permission of the publishers.

MIX
Paper from
responsible sources
FSC **FSC® C007454**
www.fsc.org

FSC™ is a non-profit international organisation established to promote
the responsible management of the world's forests. Products carrying the
FSC label are independently certified to assure consumers that they come
from forests that are managed to meet the social, economic and
ecological needs of present and future generations,
and other controlled sources.

Find out more about HarperCollins and the environment at
www.harpercollins.co.uk/green

Acknowledgements

No thanks are due to one of my next-door neighbours, whose obsession with knocking down walls and hammering the shit out of things has provided the world's most distracting soundtrack to the writing of *Would Like to Meet*.

Very fond thanks are however due to my fantastic agent, Becky Thomas, for taking calls and answering emails and texts at all times of the day and night; travelling to the wilds of Norfolk to help me restructure the manuscript, and for generally keeping me sane. (No mean feat.)

I also owe my husband and children a lot, both for putting up with my moaning about the constant hammering and for talking me out of going through with my frequent threats to "do a John Stonehouse", rather than carry on writing the book. (Mr Stonehouse abandoned his clothes on a beach and faked his own death, in case you're wondering. Probably *allegedly*.)

Finally, many other people have helped in a variety of ways: some by sharing their dating experiences; others by reading the manuscript and making editorial suggestions, and some by offering practical help such as meals, hugs or hospitality. Alex

Marsh even lent me one of his best lines, and he and others continued to believe in me whenever I ceased to believe in myself, which was probably a tediously frequent occurrence.

In no particular order, my sincere thanks are therefore due to the following people: Eloise Wood, Natasha Harding, Kate Ellis and the rest of the team at Avon; Katy Loftus; Anna Morrison; Jennifer and David Yuile; Sue Welfare; Suzanne Moore; Diana Clark; Jayne Lavelle; Phil Durrant; Simon Davis; Donna Picton; Andrew Mackey; Heather Price; Carol Okazaki; Phil and Jo Crocker; Harriet Cobbold Hielte; Marika Cobbold; Ian and Susan Dafter; Andy Hicks and Peter Black AM, as well as the men I "met" during the time I spent on dating sites. (For research purposes only, in case my husband's reading this.)

For Mark, Daisy and Jack, as always – and for Becky Thomas, without whom there would be no book.

"There is no disguise which can hide love for long where it exists, or simulate it where it does not."

François de la Rochefoucauld, 1613–1680

Prologue

Dan lets go of both oars and searches the front pockets of his jeans, looking more anxious by the second.

"Shit," he says. "Where've I put it?"

I take no notice, as I'm too busy lounging in the stern of the dinghy and trailing my fingers in the water. The sky is intensely blue and I'm as happy as I've ever been. (I'm about to get even happier, though I don't know that yet.)

"A-ha!" says Dan. "I've found it. Thank God for that."

I'm still not looking at him, because now I'm friend-spotting amongst the groups of art school students celebrating the end of finals on the banks of the Serpentine in Hyde Park. The sun's so bright, I can't see properly without the sunglasses I dropped overboard the last time Dan kissed me, so I just wave vaguely in the direction of the crowds.

Someone shouts something unintelligible across the water, at the same time as a duck squawks and Dan says something equally unintelligible.

"What?" I say. "I didn't hear you."

"Oh, for God's sake, Hannah," says Dan, his dark eyes fixed

on mine. "Pay attention, will you? I'm trying to do something important here."

The boat bobs gently up and down as he adds, "I asked you if you'll marry me."

I stare at him, wondering if I've misheard due to that infuriating still-squawking duck, and then he tries again.

"I love you, Han. Marry me?"

"Oh, my God, *yes*," I say, "Yes, please."

I jump up and hurl myself towards Dan, just as he tries to pass me the small blue ring box that he's holding, but then the boat rocks and tips me headfirst into the lake.

Thirty seconds later, Dan has already dived in to rescue me from the weeds in which I'm now entangled, and has lost my engagement ring in the process – as well as the boat, which is drifting away.

Fifteen minutes after that, we've swum to the bank and are outside the cafe, wrapped in blankets and toasting each other with mugs of hot chocolate, while being lectured on why you should never stand up carelessly in a dinghy by the owner of the one we allowed to drift away. That's the exact moment at which an off-duty press photographer takes our photograph, the one that appears in the local paper the following day, under the headline: *Loved-Up Art Students Make a Splash*.

Twenty-Seven Years Later...

Winter

Chapter 1

It's all the fault of the half-naked teenagers, or most of it, anyway. They're staggering about drunkenly on the TV screen, and Dan is staring at them as if his life depended on it.

"What the hell are you watching?" I say, as I come into the room bearing two mugs of extra-strong coffee to help prevent the hangover we'll otherwise be doomed to have.

It's 12:30am, and we've been drinking geriatric drinks all night: Aunt Pearl's way of thanking us for moving her belongings into her new retirement flat during the day. I don't think port and lemon agrees with me, and it certainly doesn't agree with Dan. It's given him short-term memory loss, judging by the fact that he completely forgot to wish me a happy New Year when we heard Big Ben strike twelve on the radio, in the taxi that was bringing us home.

Once we arrived, Dan got out of the car, unlocked the front door, and then headed straight for the sofa like a homing pigeon. One with opposable claws for operating remote controls, and a tendency to go deaf whenever wives ask awkward questions.

I try again.

"What *is* this programme, Dan?" I say.

"God knows," he says, taking the mug I pass him without moving his eyes away from the screen. "*Brits in Ibiza*, or something like that."

He must be able to sense my expression, as then he adds, "Probably the channel Joel was watching before he went out tonight."

It's so useful having a supposedly adult son still living at home whenever you need to pass the buck. I doubt Joel would be caught dead watching this idiotic programme, not when he can view similar scenes any night of the week when he's out clubbing – and in the flesh, as it were. God, there's a lot of *that* on this TV show.

I shift about in my seat, suddenly uncomfortably aware of what I'm now wearing: mismatched pyjamas, to go with my rather less mismatched face and arse. They say either your arse can look good after the age of forty, or your face, but never both. When you get as close to fifty as I now am, both are past their sell-by date.

"I can't see the appeal of half-naked teenagers, myself – not since I stopped being one," I say. "Especially not when they're vomiting everywhere like this lot will be in a minute. Isn't there anything better on?"

Dan doesn't reply. You'd swear he'd been watching this programme for at least the last two hours and it was about to reach a thrilling climax, given how hard he's concentrating. I repeat what I've just said, and then I wave at him across the room, but he doesn't react, and then I feign a coughing fit.

Still no response whatsoever – *none* – so I pull off one of my slipper socks and throw it at him.

My aim's a bit off, but I do finally succeed in getting Dan's attention. In fact, he almost jumps out of his skin.

"What the fuck, Hannah?" he says, fishing the sock out of his coffee, and making a face. "Why did you do that?"

"You were ignoring me," I say. "Too busy ogling those girls with their boobs and arses hanging out."

"Oh, for Christ's sake," says Dan, who suddenly looks quite angry. Very angry, actually. I'm not used to seeing him like that, even during the stupid arguments we've been having recently. He did get a bit cross when I complained about him and Joel never putting toilet-roll inners into the bathroom bin the other day, but nothing like as cross as this. Now he looks as if he can't stand the sight of me.

"I was joking, Dan," I say, quickly. It's only half a lie, but he spots it, anyway.

"Like hell you were."

Dan glares at me, and then he adds, "All I wanted was to chill out in front of the TV, after a bloody long day dealing with Pearl, and it didn't matter what I was watching, as far as I was concerned. But if I *had* picked this programme on purpose, then who could blame me? The only flesh I get to see these days is on TV."

Dan seems almost as shocked by what he's just said as I am, and there's silence for a moment, as we both let his words sink in. Then I swallow, and say very slowly and clearly, "You mean that's the type of flesh you prefer. You make that pretty obvious."

Did I really say that out loud? I laugh, to lessen the sting, but Dan has lost his temper now.

"You can't say something like you just did, and then laugh as if you didn't mean it, Hannah," he says. "And how exactly do I make my 'preference' so obvious?"

I wish I'd never started this conversation now. It's one thing to feel inadequate, but ten times more humiliating to admit to it, and then to explain why you do.

"I just meant," I say, keeping my head down and staring intently at a piece of fluff on the carpet, "that you make it clear that you don't fancy me any more. I know I don't look like the woman you married these days, but —"

"You don't act like her, either," says Dan. "In fact, you're nothing like her. You want me to be as miserable as you are, and God forbid that either of us should have any fun. So I don't quite get what I'm supposed to fancy about someone who's more interested in Joel and Pearl than in me, as well as in their stupid job, and who's so obsessed with losing their looks that they walk around with a face like a wet weekend the whole damn time. That's really bloody attractive."

I'm so stunned I don't know what to say, or where to start, so I just sit there, twisting my hands in my lap, and trying to ignore the tear that's rolling down the side of my nose and heading towards my mouth. Dan spots it and it seems to annoy him even more.

"I don't know why you're crying, Hannah," he says. "You started this, and normally you'd be the one with the killer line to finish it. So why don't we just get it over with? I know you're unhappy with yourself, but now you're blaming me for it, and making me feel like a useless husband, too. I'm sick and tired of you trying to push me into saying I don't fancy you, so here you are: I don't. Feel better now?"

I think it's safe to say I don't, and I feel even worse when Dan and I end up agreeing to separate. Happy New Year, Hannah Pinkman. Nicely done.

Chapter 2

Huh. Dan's still sleeping in the spare room and doing that "no-talking" thing the rest of the time, even though New Year's Eve was *days* ago. How can you have a row so bad that you decide to separate, then fail to mention it ever again? That's just bloody typical. He obviously didn't mean a word he said, which is really annoying, as I haven't slept a wink for the last three nights.

I'm like a sleepwalking zombie when I go back to work this morning, which doesn't escape the notice of my boss, the *Apprentice* wannabe better known as the Fembot. At lunchtime, she writes my stats on the whiteboard in much larger writing than she uses for anyone else's.

"Hannah's having trouble keeping up with us young ones today," she announces to anyone who's listening, at the same time as rising up on her toes and twirling around to show her arse off to its best advantage. What sort of dingbat wears hot pants to work, for goodness' sake?

"I'm sorry," I say, when it becomes apparent that eye-rolling is insufficient, and some sort of verbal response is required. "I'm not feeling well. I've got a bit of a stomach upset, to tell the truth."

"I see," says the Fembot, in the tone of voice that means, *I don't believe a word of it.*

I go to the loo four times in the next forty-five minutes, just to prove her wrong. Then, when she leans over the back of my chair to ask if I realise that I've been "spotted leaving my desk four times in the last forty-five minutes", I tell her that there's a highly-contagious bug going around.

"Joel's been ill with it for days," I say. "He looks like shit. I hope none of you will catch it."

It's only a small lie, given that Joel has had a three-day hangover since he overdid the drinking on New Year's Eve, but it serves its purpose very nicely: the Fembot moves away as if she's been electrocuted. She's got a date tonight.

"Go home, Hannah," she says. "Right this minute."

"Are you sure?" I say, standing up and following her across the room, getting as close as I can and breathing heavily down her neck. I cough a couple of times, for good measure. Now she's put the idea in my head, I really fancy an afternoon off – preferably spent sound asleep.

"Yes, I'm positive," says the Fembot, glaring at me. "You can work from home instead."

I hate modern jobs. In the olden days, when you were too ill to go into your place of work, no one expected you to work at all. Now you do everything on a computer or a mobile phone, you'd have to be dead and buried before you could get away with claiming to be unfit to work.

I particularly hate *my* modern job.

It isn't the type of thing I thought I'd be spending my working life doing when I met Dan at art school all those years ago. Then we both thought we were headed for fame and fortune, or for something creative, anyway. Instead, Dan got such a boring job at the Council that he can't even be bothered to explain to people what it is, and I ended up as a graphic designer for HOO, a question-and-answer site. (Officially, HOO stands for *Helpful Opinions Online*, but staff know it better as *Halfwits' Opinions Online*, or *Halfwits* for short.)

"Ahem," says the Fembot, who's obviously noticed that I'm no longer listening to whatever it is she's going on about. "As I was saying, Hannah, you can email me that artwork from home tonight, but don't forget it's very urgent."

Only the Fembot would use the word "urgent" to describe a stupid "thumbs-up, happy face" icon. It's not half as urgent as dealing with a husband who does his wife's head in by saying something terrible that he doesn't mean, then taking a vow of silence afterwards. I'm going to *make* Dan talk to me tonight, as soon as he gets home, and sod the Fembot's bloody icon.

★   ★   ★

Oh, my God. Dan says he meant what he said the other night. He really did. Twenty-seven years of marriage down the drain, just like that.

He comes home just as I'm waking from my nap, but doesn't say a word until Joel goes out to meet his girlfriend. Then he takes a deep breath and hits me with it. (Not the breath, obviously.)

"So," he says, turning off Netflix and putting the remote control out of reach. "I guess we should talk about what we're going to do. I'm assuming you haven't told Joel yet?"

"Told him what?" I say, annoyed at missing the last five minutes of *Breaking Bad*.

"That we're splitting up," says Dan, as if it should be obvious. "I haven't said anything about it so far, as I didn't see the point in stressing him out until we'd got it organised."

Oh, *brilliant*. Dan's worried about stressing Joel out – Joel, who's oblivious to almost everything once he's smoked a joint to celebrate finishing work for the day. And what about *my* stress levels? I could have a heart attack at any second, at my age.

I think I might be, actually. Having a heart attack, I mean. My breathing's gone all funny and now I feel genuinely sick. I've got pins and needles in both my arms as well, though I suppose that could be because my fists have suddenly clenched so tight.

Dan doesn't seem to notice there's something wrong with me. He's too busy looking down at his hands, which he's fiddling with in his lap.

"If we're getting on each other's nerves so much," he says,

inspecting his fingers as if his life depends on it, "then it seems the only sensible thing to do. Doesn't it?"

Well, if *that's* how he feels, it obviously does.

"Yes," I say.

Then I run upstairs to the bathroom, and am sick. I never believed it when people in films threw up after they'd had a shock. Now I know it happens in real life too.

When I finally come back downstairs, still shaking and clammy, Dan glances up at me, then says,

"You okay? You don't look good."

I forgot *that* was the explanation, or rather, I must have blanked it out. Dan said he doesn't fancy me any more the other night, didn't he? And you can't make someone fancy you again, once they've stopped. At least, I don't think you can ... and what's the point in being married to someone who doesn't want to be married to you, anyway?

I reach for the remote, and turn the TV back on.

"I'm fine," I say, staring back at Dan without blinking, so he'll believe I'm telling the truth.

I'm not going to cry. I am *not*. Not when the only thing left to salvage is my dignity.

★　★　★

Well, my no-crying resolution didn't last long. I'm standing by the coffee machine this morning, when the Fembot starts holding forth about her date last night.

"I don't usually fancy older men," she says, "but I think I've been missing out on something. They *really* know what they're doing in bed, and they appreciate younger women, too. Probably because the ones their own age are so bloody hideous. They give up bothering about how they look, once they've been married for a while."

She means women like me, doesn't she? And men like Dan. I hadn't thought of *that*. Now Dan's probably going to start dating a hot-panted child, while I'll be stuck on my own, consigned to the scrapheap just in time for my fiftieth birthday.

"I think your coffee's ready," says someone behind me, so I make a grab for the cup, catch it against the top of the machine, and then drop the damn thing on the floor, narrowly missing the Fembot's feet – which is a tragedy when she's wearing her favourite pair of Louboutins.

My legs are covered in hot coffee, though I'm not too worried about that. I'm more concerned about the funny noise that's just started escaping from my chest. It sounds like the beginning of what could easily end up being a full-blown sob, if I don't choke it off. I bite my tongue, hard, which seems to do the trick, though the Fembot's already noticed that something's up.

"All except you, Hannah," she says, looking a bit shocked. "I didn't mean you, even though you are a lot more mature than the rest of us. Like *Taste the Difference* cheddar, you know."

Cheddar? Now I'm like *cheese*? I can't speak, in case another one of those funny noises makes its presence felt. Luckily, I don't have to: the person behind me intercedes on my behalf.

"Hannah's fine," she says. "Though she may have scalded her legs a bit. I'll go with her while she puts cold water on them."

17

Then she takes me firmly by the arm and shepherds me out of the office.

"Thanks, er … um," I say, as we make our way along the corridor towards the ladies' loos. Who *is* this Good Samaritan?

"Esther," she says. "We met when I came for my interview, a couple of weeks ago."

I must have been on another planet at the time as I don't recall ever meeting this girl before, even though I can see her more clearly now my eyes have finally stopped being so inexplicably watery. *Girl* is a bit of a misnomer, actually, as Esther is definitely a lot older than the Fembot, at first glance. On second thoughts, though, maybe she isn't. I think it's just her clothes and hair which give that impression: she's probably only about thirty-five.

"Nice to meet you, Esther," I say, shaking her hand. "And thanks for coming to the rescue, too. I don't know what came over me."

"Listening to your boss, I should think," says Esther, pretty much hitting the nail on the head. "All the other staff seem nice, but does she really despise anyone older than her as much as she just sounded as if she did?"

"Not everyone," I say, as I finish taking off my tights, then stick one foot into the sink and turn the cold tap on. "Only older women, as far as I can tell. Older men seem to be in a different category: the lust-worthy one. Oh, sod it all to hell and back."

I've turned the tap on too far and now there's water all over my dress, as well as on my leg. The Fembot will probably assume I'm incontinent, and order a Tena Lady dispensing machine for the loo, clearly marked for my use only. Then she'll ask Dan out on a date ... or someone even younger will.

"A-a-arrhhh," I say. Out loud, despite biting my tongue again, which just makes the sob more hiccupy. Then, before I know it, I've taken my foot out of the sink and am sliding down the wall onto the cold tiled floor, where I sit wailing like a baby. In front of a brand new member of staff. I think I'd better ask for permission to go home. Again.

★ ★ ★

That's better. I've got a grip now, thanks to back-to-back episodes of *Friends* on Comedy Central, though I'll probably get fired if I take any more time off work. The Fembot made that pretty clear before she told me I could go home early "yet again".

It was worth her disapproval, though. After four hours of lying on the sofa and watching how much fun you can have when you're single, I am *fine* with this. Absolutely, completely fine. In fact, I'd go so far as to say I think it's going to be exciting, which is one thing life with Dan hasn't been for donkey's years.

All I need to do is find somewhere to live – a house-share with a few cool, fun people, preferably my age – and then Bob's your uncle! Before you can say, "hot pants", I'll be youngish, free and single, and having a ball. (I ruled out "middle-aged, free and single" because it didn't have the same ring.)

I can see my new life now, as clear as day. After work (where I'll be responsible for something that doesn't involve icons), I'll rush home to get changed into something simple and chic (but dazzlingly sexy), then I'll swig a quick glass of chilled white wine in the kitchen while my funny, affectionate new friends quiz me about whether tonight's date is "good enough" for me.

Then my taxi will arrive and I'll waft off into the night, leaving behind a trail of Chanel or whatever's cool these days, and arrive fashionably late at a little Italian restaurant: one that only the most sophisticated man would know about. It'll be *intime*, and the maître d' will not only know my date's name, but he'll give him the thumbs-up approvingly when he thinks that I'm not looking.

I suppose I might have to eat from one of those stupid wooden chopping boards with handles (the ones Dan always calls "totally pretentious"), but the food will be great, and – who knows – being single might prove so good for my cholesterol levels that I won't have to pull a bottle of Benecol out of my bag and swig it as soon as I've finished eating, for once.

And there'll be conversation, too – proper conversation, not just moaning about work, and Joel, and why he and Dan never throw toilet-roll inners into the bin – and there'll be eye contact, as well. *Lots* of eye contact, so intense it'll fire up all those neurons or whatever those things are that give you the shivers when you're filled with lust. If my neurons aren't all dead from lack of use, of course.

Afterwards, my date will say, "I don't want the night to end yet, Hannah. Your place ... or mine?"

I'm having a hot flush just thinking about it. Well, not a

hot flush, because sexy single women don't have hot flushes. It's a bit humid for January, that's all.

Where was I? Oh, yes – so while I'm playing at being Charlize Theron or Keira Knightley in one of those perfume ads, and staring deep into Mr Suave's gorgeous eyes, Dan'll just be lying on the sofa watching TV, and only remembering that I don't live with him any more when he glances across to see if I've noticed the covert nap that he's just woken from. No more watching his eyes glaze over when I tell him about the Fembot's latest idiotic idea, either, or when I ask him where we've gone wrong with Joel; no more being "mum" first, and a woman second, and no more boring Hannah without anything resembling a social life. I'll get a makeover, and become a cougar or whatever Courteney Cox is called these days. It's all going to be *better* than fine.

All I need to do to get to *Friends*-cum-perfume-advert land is take control. No more wallowing in self-pity, and no more keeping what's happening to myself, in the hope that it will go away. Dan and I will tell Joel when he gets home from work tonight – just like we agreed we would last night. Then, as soon as I've found somewhere to live, I'll move out, leaving the pair of them free to fill the whole house with empty toilet-roll inners, if they like. That's if they can spare the time to go to the loo while binge-watching episodes of *Half-Naked Brits in Ibiza*. I won't care. I'll be too busy drinking, dancing and being interesting again. Just like I used to be when I married Dan, all those years ago.

Chapter 3

By the time I wake up from another very uncougar-like nap on the sofa, Dan and Joel are both in the living room, though they're not talking to each other. Joel's too busy yelling abuse at a faceless stranger who's annoyed him by killing him when he wasn't looking. (Young guys are so rude to each other when playing *Call of Duty* online, I'm sure it's a major factor in the lack of world peace.)

I pull a disapproving face, then tell Joel to shove up and make room for me on the sofa.

"Keep quiet, Mum," he says. "I've already messed up once, thanks to Dad."

"I had the temerity to ask him what he fancied for dinner," says Dan, before he stands up and moves towards the door. He can't bear to be in the same room as me for more than five minutes at the moment.

"Hang on a sec, Dan," I say. "I thought we were going to speak to Joel together."

"But –" says Dan, as Joel throws the controller onto the

22

floor and sighs as if the world is ending. Which I suppose it's about to, in a way.

"What?" says Joel. "This had better be important."

I don't know whether it is, or isn't, actually – to Joel, anyway. Who knows what's going on in his head? Sometimes I think he can't stand either me or Dan, but then sometimes – especially if he comes into a room unexpectedly, and catches me when I'm feeling a bit tearful, or lonely – he'll say, "Mum! What's wrong? Come over here."

Then he'll give me a big hug, and tell me that everything's going to be okay, even when he has no idea what I'm sad about. It helps much more than you'd think it would – but I can't let myself think about feeling lonely at the moment. I have to get this nightmare over and then I can focus on making my *Friends* fantasy come to life.

"We've got something important to tell you, Joel," I say, "so pay attention."

"Um, Hannah," says Dan, shifting about from foot to foot, and looking extremely uncomfortable. "There's something else I should tell you first."

I take no notice, as delaying tactics are typical of Dan. He'll always put off doing anything tricky or emotional if he can, but he's not getting away with it this time. We said we'd do this together, and we said we'd do it tonight – and that's exactly what we're going to do. Even if "together" means him standing there like a spare part while I do the difficult bit.

"Your dad and I are splitting up, Joel," I say.

Joel doesn't react at all, but when I look across at Dan and catch his eye, he shakes his head and swallows, then decides he'd better help out, after all.

"Joel?" he says. "Did you hear what your mother said? We're splitting up."

Dan's voice sounds deadly serious, if a bit shaky, but Joel just laughs.

"Yeah, yeah – very funny," he says. "Pull the other one. You two would *never* split up."

It takes ages to persuade him that we would – and are – and then he's incredulous, and extremely upset.

"But why?" he says. "Why the hell would you do that?"

I suggest Dan explains, seeing as the whole thing was originally his idea, but that doesn't help at all, because he takes so long to get to the point. He starts by telling Joel about the argument, and what it was about.

"You argued about *what*?" says Joel, staring at Dan and me in turn. "A television programme? Have you both gone senile overnight?"

For a split second, I wonder if we have, but then Dan tells Joel that we haven't. He adds, "I suppose we're trying to make our lives happier, before we do."

When I hear that, I excuse myself by saying I need to make an urgent call. I suddenly can't face hearing why Dan's so unhappy with me and, anyway, it's always good to check that the Speaking Clock still exists. I give myself a talking-to at the same time as I discover it is 7:32 exactly, and then I replay the Mr Suave scenario several times in my head, just to remind myself that everything will be all right, eventually.

It almost works, until I go back to the living room, to find Dan sitting slumped in a chair with his head in his hands, and Joel pacing round and round the room in circles.

"You tell him why we're doing this, Hannah," says Dan. "I've run out of reasons, and he thinks all the ones I've already given him are 'total crap'. He says we're both going to be lonely, too."

"No, we won't," I say. "We'll be fine, Joel. We'll have our friends to keep us company – and you, of course. You can come and see me whenever you like."

"You two have ignored your friends for so long, you haven't got any real ones left," says Joel, at the same time as Dan says, "What d'you mean he can come and see you, Hannah? See you where? He'll be here – with you – every day. You'll need him to pay rent to help with the mortgage, once I move out at the end of this week."

Oh, dear God. When *Dan* moves out at the end of this week? *This* week? And Dan's the one who's moving out, not me? I don't know what to say to any of that, but Joel does.

"I've never heard such a dumbass reason for splitting up, in all my life," he says. "And I think one of you is lying, or both of you. Which one of you is seeing someone else?"

That possibility hadn't occurred to me until now, but if one of us is, it isn't me. Not when Mr Suave's not real. I think I may be about to cry again.

Chapter 4

It seems that one of Dan's colleagues had a spare room going – really cheap – so Dan says he'd have been a fool if he hadn't taken it. He also insists that Joel was wrong about him seeing someone else, though he was right about the other thing: I've got no friends. Well, I have, but even though I've rung all of them over the last few days – while Dan's been supposedly working late – they all went on so much about how long it had been since the last time I called, that I ended up not telling any of them that he and I were splitting up. They might have thought it was the only reason I was bothering to phone them now.

It was, I suppose, but that's not the point. They've all posted that thing on Facebook about it not mattering how long it's been since you last spoke to an old friend, so I'd assumed that was genuinely how they felt. Obviously, it wasn't, so things are already looking pretty desperate on the friends front by the time that Joel gets home from work.

He sits down on the sofa next to me, and kicks off his shoes while I stare in disbelief at his socks. One says, "Fuck" and the other says, "Off".

This is what you have to endure when your son refuses to go to university, and insists on working in a super-hip streetwear store instead, one where all the staff are required to talk in gangsta-speak even if they've never been anywhere near a gang. The whole thing drives Dan mad, and Joel's still in the middle of a fairly incomprehensible explanation of how he uses the socks to swear at his boss without him being aware of it, when I lose the will to listen and decide to phone Theo and Claire, instead.

They're neighbours, rather than friends, but Dan and I have probably socialised more often with them than with anyone else over the last ten years (mainly because that keeps us close enough to home to prevent Joel throwing parties while we're out). I think they're all right, though Dan's never been keen on Claire.

When she answers the phone I tell her my news straight away. There's no point giving myself the chance to chicken out, even though I know it'll make the whole thing feel much worse once someone other than Joel knows.

"Good God," says Claire, and then she repeats herself. After that, there's quite an uncomfortable pause before she adds, "I assume you won't be coming to our dinner tonight, if that's the case?"

I'd forgotten all about it, what with what's been going on with me and Dan, and I'm about to confirm we won't be there when I wonder if I'm being stupid. You're probably supposed to start as you mean to go on, when you're trying to rebuild your messed-up life.

"Well, I guess I could come by myself," I say to Claire,

after taking a few deep breaths. "Seeing as I'm still going to be your neighbour, at least until Joel decides it's time to move out."

It sounds as if Claire snorts at the remoteness of *that* ever happening, but then she pulls herself together and says, "That's great! See you in a couple of hours."

Her voice sounds a bit weird when she says it, but I don't give that any further thought, until the phone rings ten minutes later, and Joel answers it. He sounds very charming and un-gangsta-like while doing so, which is reassuring, but what happens next isn't reassuring at all. The caller is Theo (of *Theo-and-Claire*), and he's obviously drawn the short straw, given that he's the one making this call.

"I'm so sorry, Hannah," he says. "Claire asked me to tell you she was so stunned by your news, she completely forgot to mention there's been a problem with the catering, so we've had to cancel the dinner party. We'll reschedule it for another time."

"Oh, that's a shame," I say. "Seeing as it was for your anniversary, and that's today, isn't it?"

Their twenty-seventh wedding anniversary, the same one that Dan and I celebrated less than a year ago, not that Theo gives a toss about that.

"Oh, yes," he says. "It is today. Another year of the life sentence without parole done and dusted. Oh. Um. Sorry, Hannah. A bit insensitive in the circumstances."

Theo's not usually so tactless, but he doesn't sound himself at all. In fact — at the risk of sounding like the Fembot — I don't believe a word he's just said about the dinner being cancelled, and that impression's strengthened when he adds that Claire says why don't I pop round and have a quiet drink with her next week instead?

"I'll be away on business then," says Theo, "so she could use some company when she's on her own. Oh. Ah, I guess you probably could, as well."

I'm going to borrow Joel's socks and wear them during my next visit, if Theo keeps this up. Claire always makes guests remove their shoes.

★   ★   ★

When I get off the phone, Joel's even more furious with Theo and Claire than he is with me and Dan, when I tell him what's just happened. First he describes the pair of them as "tossers", and then he invites me to accompany him and his girlfriend Izzy to the cinema, but I refuse. Three's company at the best of times and, anyway, I ought to go round to Pearl's. It's not fair to tell outsiders about me and Dan when I haven't told her yet.

★   ★   ★

I drive across town, while trying to work out the best way to handle what's bound to be a tricky conversation, but I'm still clueless by the time that I arrive. However I put it, Pearl isn't going to take my announcement well. She's always been very fond of Dan, and she knows better than anyone what it's like to end up on your own after a long-term marriage, since her husband died three years ago. They'd been together for the previous forty-five, roaming the world due to Clive's job as a senior diplomat. That's why I visit Pearl so often these days, because I know how much she hates being on her own, especially in the evenings, and she's bound to be even more lonely now that she's living somewhere new.

I pull into a parking space directly outside the Elysium Retirement Home, which Pearl renamed "Abandon Hope" when Dan and I moved her in on New Year's Eve. I can't see why she called it that, as it looks like a stately home to me. The diplomatic service look after their own, unlike *Halfwits*, and I'll be lucky to afford something the size of one of the broom cupboards in a building like this when I retire.

★ ★ ★

I push open the main doors, then walk across the lobby and into a wide carpeted corridor that leads to Pearl's new ground-floor flat.

"It's open," she shouts, when I ring the doorbell. "As long as you've brought some money with you, that is. We're not messing about with buttons or IOUs tonight."

That makes no sense whatsoever, until I open the door to reveal a dozen elderly people playing poker.

The cocktails are flowing and there are already plenty of competitors for the title of drunkest OAP, though Pearl's not one of them.

"I pride myself on being able to hold *my* drink, Hannah," she says. "Unlike some people I could mention. Now let me introduce you to the *Hopeless* gang."

There are loads of people in Pearl's flat, and I doubt I'd recognise any of them again, except for Albert and Fred, who I end up sitting between. Albert looks like Pope Francis, the nice one from Buenos Aires, while Fred looks more like the Child Catcher in *Chitty Chitty Bang Bang*. I must count as a child, given the disparity in our ages, as that's the only reason I can think of to explain why I keep finding Fred's hand creeping up my leg under cover of the tablecloth.

★   ★   ★

"Bloody hell, Pearl," I say, when she shows the last guest out, then joins me in the kitchen, where I've been hiding from Fiddling Fred for the last half-hour. "That Fred's a creep, but I like your other new friends. You've made so many here, already!"

"You can't waste time when you get to my age," says Pearl. "Or yours, for that matter. You look terrible – what's up?"

I've lost my bottle while I've been waiting to spill the beans and now I can't go through with it. Telling people what's happened makes it all seem far too real.

"Nothing much," I say, swilling out a cocktail shaker and putting it aside to drain.

Pearl raises her eyebrows and says, "You've always been a poor liar, ever since you were a child, so leave the washing up and try again. And this time, make it the whole truth and nothing but."

I do as I'm told, though I don't mention that Dan said he doesn't fancy me any more. That would be too humiliating, so I just say we had an argument about a television programme that turned into something much, much worse.

"Good God," says Pearl, when I've finished. "Are you sure about this, Hannah? It's no fun being on your own, you know. Why d'you think I agreed to move in here? This place has a better ratio of men to women than every other retirement place I looked at, which is not a lucky coincidence. I did my research, because I'm sick and tired of being alone after the last few years."

So that's why Pearl was doing sit-ups when I came round the other day – she's on the pull, when I thought *I* was too old to find someone new!

"I'll be fine," I say. "I mean, I *am* fine. I won't be on my own forever, after all."

I try to conjure up an image of my fantasy Mr Suave, as Pearl looks me up and down, but he won't appear. I just keep seeing Dan's face instead, and Pearl clearly isn't too impressed with what she sees when she looks at me, given how worried she's now become.

"What?" I say. "Why are you looking at me like that? I'm miles younger than you and you're not planning on remaining single, so why should I?"

"No reason," says Pearl. "I just think you two splitting up is the most ridiculous thing I've ever heard of. And who is this colleague Dan's moving in with, anyway – do you know?"

Why do people keep asking that? I don't know *any* of Dan's colleagues, not least because he usually refuses to go to any of the few social events to which staff are allowed to bring their partners. He claims that's because I have an even lower boredom threshold than he does, so I'd probably say something to get him sacked – but now Pearl's implying that might not be the only reason, just like Esther did when I mentioned it to her the other day at work.

"I don't know," I say, "but that's not the biggest problem, is it? Dan swears he isn't leaving me for another woman, but he'll find one at some point, once he's living the single life."

That thought makes me feel sick, which must show on my face, as Pearl decides the time has come for some distraction.

"Let's go for a walk while we give this further thought," she says. "I want to show you the gardens here. The residents can help in them, if they're up to it, so I'm thinking of signing up myself. It'll keep me fit, all that physical activity in the fresh air."

★ ★ ★

Although it's dark, the gardens are illuminated and exceptionally beautiful, even now in what's still winter, and for the first time in years, I wish I'd brought a sketchbook with me. There's nothing very artistic in designing stupid icons, but I'd love to draw the view from where we're standing. It's on the top of a steepish incline (which Pearl climbed a lot faster than me), and it overlooks a large area of dense, glossy greenery, that eventually gives way to a meandering path that leads to the Elysium building itself. The silver bark of the birch trees lining the path sparkles where the lights hit it, and the effect is spectacular. Abandon Hope, my arse.

"What are these?" I say, pointing at some tiny, glossy-leaved plants peeking out through a mass of dead foliage.

"Violas," says Pearl, pointing her torch at them. "You can take one with you, if you like? Gardening's good for the soul and the staff won't notice. They rarely bother with this section."

If gardening's good for the soul, I'll try it, and I might even draw the viola once it blooms, if I can persuade Dan to get my art materials out of the attic before he moves out – and maybe I'll come back and sketch this landscape in the daytime, too.

Pearl pulls a tiny trowel out of one pocket, and a plastic bag from another, and then she digs up the plant and dumps it into the bag.

"Did I mention violas are also known as 'heart's-ease', Hannah?" she says, handing me the bag. "On which note, why don't you get off home now, while Dan's still living there? You could always try talking to him about staying, instead of wasting time discussing what you'll do without him once he's gone."

Chapter 5

Even though I take Pearl's advice and drive straight home, Dan's already asleep on the sofa by the time I get there, and I'm still dithering about whether to wake him up and talk to him about being my soulmate, when Joel turns up. He's barefoot, and carrying his trainers in one hand.

"You okay, Mum?" he asks, after peering into the living room and spotting the snoring Dan. "I'm sure you guys could get this sorted out if you still wanted to. You don't *have* to split up over something so stupid, you know."

For one wonderful moment I think he may be right, until I recall that Dan doesn't fancy me any more, and that he seemed pretty definite about moving in with that colleague of his.

"I don't think I've got any choice, Joel," I say. "Your dad seems determined it's going to happen, and anyway, who knows? Maybe he's right, and we'll both be happier once we're single."

"You won't be happier if everyone starts treating you like that bloody pair of idiots up the road just did, once you are," says Joel. "I can't believe they uninvited you from that dinner party just because you'd have been going on your own. Talking of which, that reminds me. Come outside."

It's pitch dark and freezing cold by now, so I try to refuse, but Joel insists.

"Put your coat on," he says, "if you're as cold as that. It won't take a minute and it'll be worth it, I promise. It might even make you laugh."

I seriously doubt that, though I change my mind when Joel walks me along the road to the place where Claire has parked her car.

"*Ta-da!*" he says, gesturing at the windscreen, or more specifically, at the windscreen wipers. Each now carries a succinct message – from a sock.

* * *

I still think that Joel's anonymous message to Theo and Claire was so funny that I tell Dan about it when I get up this morning and find him in the kitchen, drinking coffee, but he doesn't laugh at all. He just gives me a wan, half-hearted smile, and then makes polite conversation about nothing until the time comes for me to leave.

"Shouldn't you have left already, if you're not going to be late for work?" I say to him as I pull on my boots, then start to button up my coat.

He shrugs, then says, "I've got a few things to do before I go."

He looks at me with a really weird expression – and for what feels like a very long time – and it's as if he's trying to convey something desperately important, though he doesn't say a word. I'm going to be late myself, if I don't leave now, but I'm not comfortable going while he's looking at me like this.

"What is it, Dan?" I say.

There's a long pause, but whatever it is, it can't be that important, because then he just shakes his head and says: "Nothing, Hannah. You'd better go."

I do, in case the Fembot sacks me for poor timekeeping like the woman Esther was brought in to replace, but tonight, I'm not going to bed until I've had it out with Dan, once and for all. This whole thing's ridiculous, and it can't go on.

★   ★   ★

I can't settle all day at work, even though Esther tries her best to cheer me up. As this mainly takes the form of telling me how unlucky in love she's always been, it doesn't actually serve its purpose, and nor do the cupcakes the Fembot brings in "as a treat" – not once she announces what she intends to do with them.

"We're all going to take it in turns to bake cupcakes every evening from now on," she says. "Then we're going to photo-graph everyone holding their own cakes and upload the pictures to our social media streams. It'll help our users get to know us, and to feel they're a part of the team here at HOO."

"Well, that's our credibility shot," I say to Esther, later on. "Now the whole world will find out that *we're* part of the team at HOO – and they'll know what we look like, too. I'll never get a proper job as an artist, if prospective employers find out I'm responsible for that stupid 'thumbs-up, happy face' thing."

"I wouldn't worry about that," says Esther, with a rare flash of humour. "I should think the Fembot will find an excuse not to use *our* photos. You're too old and I'm too fat."

Esther can't be more than a size 12, so I do wish she wouldn't keep going on about her weight, but when I tell her so, she just says that, even if fat isn't an issue, her acne is. She's only got one or two spots, as far as I can see, but she's right about one thing, anyway: the Fembot isn't going to use our photos.

At the end of the day, she calls us both into her office, and says, "I know you guys are busy, and you have a lot more personal responsibilities than the younger ones, so don't feel you have to join in with the cake-baking thing. You can contribute in some other way."

Honestly, I wouldn't mind but, although I've got Joel and Pearl to think about, Esther's only got a rabbit, and just wait 'til I tell Dan about it! There's no way he can keep claiming his job's worse than mine – not after this.

Oh, I forgot, he probably won't be claiming anything, will he? Not if he's still being as uncommunicative as he was this morning when I get back home. I shall just have to keep talking to him, until he starts talking back. Meaningful looks never solved anything.

* * *

Oh, my God, Dan's moved out. He snuck out today while I was at work, the bloody, bloody coward. This whole separation thing was his idea and then he hasn't even got the nerve to face me when he's bringing our life together to a sudden end. No wonder he was giving me funny looks this morning: he must have been riddled with guilt and, if he wasn't, he damn well should have been.

"Thought it might be easier on both of us this way, Han," says the note he's left on the kitchen counter. "I'll be in touch about collecting the rest of my stuff, and money for outstanding bills, etc. Look after yourself."

He's underlined the last sentence and scribbled over something that followed it. I try scratching the ink off with my fingernails, and then with the edge of a paring knife, but I still can't tell if Dan added kisses or something, by mistake. My eyes have gone blurry all of a sudden, which is also why I don't immediately realise that he's left his keys on the counter, too.

When I do eventually spot his keyring, the one containing a photo of us on our honeymoon, my eyes get a whole lot blurrier and my chest gets tight, and I think I may be about to have a stroke. I call Joel's name, but there's no reply, not even when I shout it at the top of my voice, so he must be out and I'm all alone, which makes things even worse.

I spend ten minutes breathing into a paper bag until I don't feel quite so dizzy, and then I crawl up the stairs and spend the next three hours curled up on the floor of our – I mean, *my* – bedroom, sobbing and hiccuping into one of Dan's old shirts. I found it at the back of his wardrobe, and it still smells of him.

I don't even know why I'm crying, for goodness' sake. If Dan doesn't want me any more, I'm buggered if I'm going to want him either. I'm just being stupid and pathetic with all this crying, and I need to get a grip before Joel comes in and sees me in such a state.

I know, I'll go and plant the viola from the garden at "Abandon Hope", and see if it survives its change of circumstances.

If it can do it, then so can I.

★　★　★

Joel's just come in and woken me up.

"What time is it?" I say, completely befuddled.

"Almost midnight," he says. "Are you okay? I was in the pub with Izzy when Dad sent me a text telling me what he'd done, so I came home because I was worried about you. I had no idea he was planning to move out today. Did you?"

"No," I say, though I'm not sure if Joel hears me, as the word comes out more like a hiccup than a "no", so I shake my head, for clarity. Then I roll myself into a ball on the sofa and start to cry as if I'll never stop.

"Oh, Mum," says Joel, in an unusually quiet voice.

He sounds so sad, it makes me cry all the more, and then he tries everything to make me stop, from patting me ineffectually to pushing a large glass of neat vodka into my hand. It must have been left over from when he and Izzy were "pre-loading" before they went out tonight.

Once I've drunk the lot, wincing at the taste, Joel leans over me, slides an arm under my shoulders and pulls me to my feet.

"Come on, Mum," he says, "I'm taking you upstairs to bed. Everything will seem a lot better if you get some sleep."

"Will it?" I say, as we make our way up the stairs. "Are you sure?"

Joel doesn't answer until we reach the landing, and then he just says,

"It has to, doesn't it? It can't get worse."

Chapter 6

Well, it's been two weeks now since Dan left home and my mission to prove to Joel and Pearl that I'm coping is going well. Being single's a doddle so far, even if I do seem to have signed up for rather more weekly evening classes than there are evenings in a week. In fact, I'm so busy that Joel told me to "take a chill pill and calm down a bit" last night, when I arrived home after mistakenly going to the yoga studio when I should have been at French conversation class. He doesn't seem to realise that all I'm doing is "getting myself back out there", like the self-help gurus advise you to – and if you keep busy, there's no time to think, which is an added bonus.

The Fembot doesn't know about the lack of thinking, but she does approve of the busy part.

"You've been coming into work unusually early, Hannah," she says, first thing this morning. "I'm impressed. That's what I expect from a dedicated member of the team. Are you after a promotion or something?"

"God, no," I say, "I just can't sleep, so I thought I might as well make myself useful rather than sitting around on my arse at home."

The Fembot stopped listening at "God, no", judging by her unamused expression.

Mine is more panic-stricken than unamused, as I probably *should* be chasing promotion, in case Joel doesn't pay his new, realistic rent at the end of the month (the one he described as "extortionate" last time I mentioned it), but it's too late now. The Fembot's gone off to upload photos of her latest batch of cupcakes to the company blog. They're owls, with faces made of chocolate icing and chocolate buttons, though I'm not sure about the Fembot's claims that they denote the wisdom of our users. Most of *their* opinions aren't worth having, as I discover when I scroll through the site while eating my lunch.

An hour later, I've finished my sandwiches and written a load of answers to questions asked by women worried about ageing, such as, "I don't think my husband fancies me any more – what do I do?" It's a lot easier helping other people who are crushed by insecurity than dealing with the same thing in yourself. Even the Fembot's impressed by the shameless lies I've told, of which the most outrageous is "love conquers all".

The trouble is, I don't believe a word I've said and now I feel a bit depressed, so when Esther asks if I'd like to go salsa dancing after work, I say, "yes", even though I've never been before. It's got to be better than what I did have planned for this evening: attending a talk on the lifecycle of the electric eel. Much better, when you consider that in a couple of hours,

I'll be salsa-ing my butt off with loads of good-looking, snake-hipped men.

★ ★ ★

Esther's got two left feet, which I know for a fact because she's the only person who's asked me to dance all night. The ratio of men to women at this salsa class is 1:20, whether you're counting ones with snake-like hips or not, and I'm still ranting about why they all refused to dance with any women they weren't married to by the time Esther drives me home.

When she drops me off, I walk inside and promptly start to rant again, though this time about men in general, not just the salsa-dancing kind. Joel's broken the tumble dryer and left a mountain of wet washing inside the drum. He's also left me a note telling me that he's "just popped out", together with a totally-useless explanation of what happened to the dryer: "It started rattling like mad, so I turned it off."

My first thought is that Dan will sort it out, until I recall that he's not here. At that point I get even crosser, and then I start to cry. Once I've stopped, I watch a video about repairing tumble dryers on YouTube and then I have a go myself. It's not easy when your only equipment's a knife and fork.

Joel's obviously been raiding the toolkit I bought from Ikea after Dan moved out because, when I open it, the only things left inside are a full set of screwdriver heads without a single screwdriver to attach them to. Meanwhile, the tumble dryer's not rattling any more – now it won't turn on at all.

★ ★ ★

"Haven't you solved the problem yet?" asks Joel, when he walks in at 10pm to find me on my knees, my head virtually inside the drum.

"No," I say. "And if that's supposed to be so easy, then maybe *you* should try."

"Already did," says Joel. "Why haven't you heated this up?"

He points at a pan containing some dried-out pasta sauce he must have made before he went out. It's the only thing he knows how to make, so I probably shouldn't keep leaving the cooking to him. The trouble is that Dan always used to do it and I don't get hungry since he moved out.

I shrug, in answer to Joel's question about the sauce.

"For God's sake, Mum," he says. "You have to eat. I'll cook you some spaghetti now, and heat this up to go with it."

While the pasta cooks, Joel explains that he spent several hours trying to repair the dryer but then had to abandon the attempt because he was late to meet someone.

"Who?" I ask, though I'm not really listening any more.

I'm burrowing in the cupboard under the stairs, where the meter is. Maybe the dryer just blew a fuse.

"I met Dad," says Joel. "Whoa, be careful, Mum! Are you okay?"

No, I'm not. I've just banged my head on the shelf that holds the iron and a pile of miscellaneous household goods – all previously broken by Joel – and I banged it so hard that now I'm seeing several Joels, all at once. It's like looking at a young Henry VIII through a kaleidoscope. After he first grew his hipster beard.

"Did you say you've just been for a drink with your dad?"

I ask, a few minutes later, while Joel chucks a load of ice cubes into a plastic bag, then hammers the hell out of them with the mallet Dan bought to tenderise meat. It's the one with pointy edges, so now there's crushed ice everywhere, except inside the plastic bag.

Joel pauses, picks up the bag and holds it to the light, then nods with satisfaction. He always likes to know why things don't turn out as expected, though he never seems to retain that information long enough to make practical use of it.

"Holes," he says, as he scoops the ice up off the counter, wraps it in a tea towel, and then orders to me to press it against the giant bump that's been forming on my forehead while he's been considering the physics of the situation.

"You look like one of those body-modification loonies," he says, when he removes the ice pack ten minutes later, then stands back to admire the effect. "Except they prefer holes in their bumps, so it looks as if they've got doughnuts in the middle of their foreheads."

"Don't change the subject," I say. "Tell me about your father."

"Well, I told him about the dryer," says Joel. "And he said if you call him tonight, he'll arrange to pop round and fix it tomorrow if that's convenient for you. I said it would be, seeing as you never go anywhere, other than to boring evening classes and to Pearl's."

Honestly, that's *so* not true – and how did Dan know I wouldn't be able to fix the dryer? I'm not totally incompetent, and I can manage perfectly well by myself, thank you very much. Or I could, if I didn't have to share a house with the number one tool thief in the country. I'll prove it, now.

I attack the dryer with renewed vigour, adding a carving fork and a pair of kitchen tongs to my arsenal of tools, along with a pack of bamboo skewers. None of them succeed in removing the back of the machine, but the skewers keep snapping off inside it so that, before long, it starts to resemble a porcupine. Then the carving fork skids off the plate hiding the motor, causing a shower of sparks to fly and me to get an electric shock.

"Phone Dad," says Joel. "Please, Mum. Before you kill yourself."

He picks up my phone, keys in a series of numbers and then passes the phone over to me. I sit and fume, while I wait for Dan to answer.

"Hello," says a voice, after what seems like hours. "Daniel's phone."

Since when is Dan called *Daniel*? And, more to the point, it may be Dan's phone, but why's a *woman* answering it?

Chapter 7

It's all very well for Joel to say the sex of Dan's landlord makes no difference, but it makes all the difference in the world to me. She's one of Dan's colleagues, after all – he told me so – and I bet he only left me because he wanted to get involved with her. Maybe he didn't even wait 'til then? He could have been having an affair with her behind my back for months, or even years. I can't remember how long it's been since he stopped paying me any attention, so it could have been *decades* for all I know.

"Well, that would make more sense," says Esther, when I ask her opinion during this morning's coffee break. "I mean, if Dan was having an affair before he moved out. Seems logical to me."

Sometimes, you can go right off Esther. I preferred Joel's opinion, the one he gave me when I went a bit nuts last night after I finally managed to speak to Dan.

"Don't be stupid, Mum," he said. "His landlady's a right dingbat, and fugly too. I met her earlier on tonight, so I should know."

"Well, why didn't you tell me about her, then?" I said, "That would have saved me from sounding like a nutcase when I spoke to her."

Spoke isn't really the word, though *screeched* quite possibly is. I blame that on the shock.

"What do you mean, *Daniel's phone*?" I said to the mystery woman in the aforementioned screechy tone. "He's not called *Daniel*, and who the hell are you to be answering his phone?"

"I'm his landlady," said the woman. "And there's no need to be so rude. I can only assume you're his wife? Or *ex*-wife, should I say?"

That last bit stunned me into silence, but by the time I felt able to reply, intending to be ruder still, there was a scuffling noise and the woman said, "Oh, all right. If you're sure?"

She must have handed Dan the phone straight after that, because then he began to speak.

"Hannah?" he said. "Are you okay?"

Oh, my God, I hadn't realised how long it had been since I'd heard Dan's voice. Maybe that's why it sounded so different to how I remembered it. Different, and better, too. Dan's always had a nice voice, but last night it sounded smoother, and deeper, and – oh, I don't know – *warmer* somehow. It was hard to listen to, whatever the reason, so I made Joel take the phone.

"You make the arrangements," I said. "I've got something urgent to do."

When I'd finished dealing with the emergency – which mainly involved crying myself into a state of semi-asphyxia, due to shoving my face so far into my pillow to muffle the noise – it was past 3am, and Joel was sitting on the floor outside my bedroom door, as if he was my bodyguard, except for the fact that he was fast asleep. I woke him up when I fell over him on my way to the loo.

"She really is just Dad's landlady, Mum," he said, "so be cool when he gets here tomorrow night to mend the dryer. Please."

I agreed, but Joel looked unconvinced by my reply.

"Cool is my middle name," I said.

*   *   *

I make it home from work in a panic just before Dan's due to arrive. I don't know why, but it seems important to look my best tonight, despite the fact that he hasn't noticed what I look like for years. Even when I'd really made an effort, the best he could usually do was, "You look fine." That wouldn't have been so bad in itself, if he hadn't always qualified the compliment by adding, "for a woman of your age."

That's such an insult, isn't it? I think it's even worse than I used to now, because of a question I read at work today, from a man who wanted advice on how to save his marriage. It only needed saving in the first place because he said he couldn't face having sex with his wife any more, because her appearance now "repels" him. That was bad enough, but then loads of other men joined in, saying they had exactly the same problem, because their wives had also aged so much! I scrolled through hundreds of their horrible comments before I finally found one from a female user. "Do you guys look the same as when you married your wives?" it said.

That shut the men up, and made me laugh, but now I want to look good when I see Dan – or as good as possible, anyway – but then Sod's law ensures I don't. I haven't even managed to change out of my work clothes when the doorbell rings, and Joel shouts, "Mum! Dad's here."

There's a whooshing noise inside my head, and I suddenly feel boiling hot (by which I mean *hot* hot, not sexy hot), and my legs start to feel all funny. I've got pins and needles in my fingers, too and I'm oddly breathless, again not in a sexy way.

I wish I could lie down until I feel a bit more normal, but I've got to go downstairs straight away. If I don't, I'll look as if I can't handle seeing Dan – and then he'll have the upper hand – so I make my way down very slowly. It's not easy to appear nonchalant while you're clinging for dear life to the banister, though I do my best.

"Hi, Hannah," says Dan, at the same time as Joel says, "Well, I'm off out. See you guys later."

He makes his escape so fast that I can't stop him, and now I'm all alone with Dan.

"I brought my bike inside," he says. "Hope you don't mind, but I didn't want to risk it being nicked."

"Bike?" I say, as if I can't see a shiny new one right in front of me, blocking my path to the kitchen and the tumble dryer. The bloody tumble dryer that's the whole reason I'm having to stand here, with my sort-of ex-husband, in my grottiest dress and shiny-kneed tights. And all while my legs are wobbling and I can't seem to pull enough air into my lungs. Thanks, Joel. Thanks a bunch.

"Are you all right?" says Dan, moving the bike to allow me to wobble my way past. "You don't look very well."

That's just great, isn't it? I don't look very well, when what I wanted to do was look stunningly gorgeous, absolutely irresistible, and totally on top of everything. Especially when Dan looks better than I remembered and has obviously taken up cycling, too.

"I'm fine," I say, as I drag the tumble dryer out from under the counter. "Absolutely, completely fine."

"Oh," says Dan. "Oh, I see."

He almost looks disappointed. As well as annoyingly attractive.

"How are you?" I say, because I feel I should.

"Um, I'm fine, too ... I suppose," says Dan.

There's an awkward silence, and then he adds, "You can leave me to get on with this, if you like. If you've got anything else to do, I mean."

He can't bear to be anywhere near me, can he? Not even for a moment. I'm amazed our marriage lasted as long as it did, when he obviously finds me as repulsive as those horrible men on the internet find their wives. No wonder we hardly had sex any more, and so much for the excuses Dan made when I asked him why he thought that was, in the middle of one of our arguments. Repulsion's a much more relevant factor than my going to bed later than him, and I'm sure he didn't seriously think that I didn't fancy him any more. I only mentioned middle-aged spread once, and I was joking!

Talking of middle-aged spread, maybe I should get a bike, or do something to get myself in better shape. It looks as if that's what Dan is up to, and I really don't want to think about why he's only bothering to do it now. It's certainly not for my benefit, is it? I think he's lost some weight already.

I'm still trying to guess exactly how much when he finishes whatever he's been doing to the tumble dryer, and stands back up.

"Found the cause of the problem," he says, though he doesn't look too pleased about it. Bewildered might be a better word.

"Someone's cut through the wires to the motor," he continues, "and removed some working parts. I'll need to order replacements, so this could take a while."

I bet he thinks I caused the damage when I was trying to fix the dryer, but I know I didn't. It must have been Joel, the bloody idiot. I wondered why he'd stolen my wire-cutters, along with all my other tools, though I can't imagine why he thought cutting through wires would solve anything. Dan says he can't either, "though why Joel does most things is shrouded in mystery".

We both laugh at that and, all of a sudden, I can breathe again. This is sometimes how it used to be: we could find the same things funny, as well as finding each other irritating.

Dan's eyes meet mine for the first time since he arrived, then he smiles and says, "You can always send Joel to the launderette."

"As punishment, you mean?" I say, at which the more relaxed mood evaporates abruptly. I have no idea why, but Dan turns round, grabs his bike and starts wheeling it backwards towards the door.

"Right," he says. "I've got to go. I'll be in touch when the parts come in."

Then he opens the door, pushes the bike outside and rides off without a backward glance. Now my breathing's gone all funny again.

★   ★   ★

I'm still sitting on the sofa, trying to work out why Dan suddenly started being so frosty, when Joel finally returns home.

"Where's Dad?" he says. "Still in the kitchen working on the dryer?"

"He left," I say. "Ages ago. As soon as he found out what you'd done to break the bloody thing."

"Ah," says Joel. He looks a bit embarrassed for a moment, then treats me to the winning expression he used to rely on to get him out of trouble when he was a toddler, more than twenty years ago.

"It worked, though, didn't it?" he says, ignoring my scowl. "My plan, I mean, not the dryer, obviously."

"What plan?" I say. "Why on earth would you plan to break the tumble dryer? I've got half a ton of damp washing in the kitchen that's going to go mouldy if it doesn't stop raining soon. And most of it belongs to you."

It'll serve Joel right if all his clothes end up covered in mildew, though God knows how much he spends on them each month. Almost as much as he spends on trainers, I should think, and he's paranoid about looking after everything he owns, or about me looking after it, anyway. He went ballistic last week when I shrank one of his T-shirts by accident, so he'll go nuts if his entire wardrobe ends up going mouldy.

"My plan," says Joel, disregarding the threat of damage to his precious "streetwear" in an uncharacteristically offhand way, "was to get you guys back together again, or talking about it anyway. So, did it work?"

"No," I say. "And nor does the dryer so, tomorrow, you'll have to take everything to the launderette."

Joel looks horrified, though I'm not sure whether that's due to the failure of his stupid plan, or to the prospect of having to take his clothes to the Eezimat, then sit there for hours watching them dry. I'd find that pretty boring myself.

Oh, shit. I didn't always find it boring, though. Not when Dan and I got locked inside the art school's launderette overnight and decided to wash everything we owned, including what we were wearing at the time. *That* night was far from boring, or from being "punishment".

Chapter 8

Oh, God, this splitting-up thing must be catching: now Joel and Izzy have split up, too. He told me about it late last night when he came back from a date with her, and said it was his choice, but then clammed up when I asked him why. I try again this morning, when he finally drags himself out of bed.

"Well, you and Dad are hardly a good advertisement for long-term relationships, are you?" he says. "And anyway, I'm fine with it."

He may be, but he looks a lot more bleary-eyed than he normally does after a night out drinking.

In fact, he looks so rough that I don't feel I can ask him to go into the loft to find my painting things, so I end up doing it myself, which is not the world's most enjoyable experience. First the ladder wobbles alarmingly, and then I have to climb off it into the attic, which is so dark that I can barely see a thing, apart from all the horrible cobwebs near the hatch. I *hate* spiders – and so does Joel – so I've no idea how we're going to deal with them now Dan's not here.

"You've got no choice, so just man up," I say to myself.

(That's another thing that happens when your husband's left you: you start talking to yourself, like a lunatic.)

Luckily, my art stuff is in the box closest to the hatch, so soon I'm back downstairs, sitting at the kitchen table and drawing the viola Pearl gave me from the garden at Abandon Hope. My first few strokes of the pencil are tentative, but after that, my drawing becomes more fluid and the result is surprisingly good, given that I've done nothing but draw stupid website icons for the last ten years. The trouble is that, once the flower drawing's complete, I can't think of anything else to draw and – after a few minutes spent racking my brains to no avail – I realise I've been doodling Dan's name, over and over, by accident.

I scribble all the doodles out.

"What shall I draw next?" I say to Joel.

"I don't know," he says, which is no help whatsoever, but then I recall what I used to do whenever I ran out of ideas at art school: go for a walk in the countryside.

I pack up my sketchbook and drawing materials and then I arrange to go over to Pearl's. I may as well kill two birds with one stone, I suppose.

★   ★   ★

"You look terrible," says Pearl, as soon as she opens the door to me. "I'm surprised you've got the energy to go for a walk. Are you still not sleeping?"

"No," I say, "I mean, yes, I am. But that's actually worse – because of the nightmares I've been having recently."

Pearl raises an eyebrow.

"Nightmares?" she asks. "What nightmares?"

She makes me a coffee while I tell her about my recurring dream.

"It starts with me and Joel standing on the deck of the *Titanic*, while Joel keeps yelling at me that Dan has disappeared," I say, finding it all too easy to visualise the scene that replays itself in my mind most nights: dark water swirling round our ankles, the captain of the ship conspicuous by his total absence, and the deck tilting more and more alarmingly.

"So what happens then?" asks Pearl.

She actually seems interested, which is unusual, given how boring most of us find listening to other people's dreams. Esther tells me about hers every morning when we arrive at work, and I'm starting to wish she wouldn't bother, though I'd never dream of saying so.

"Go on," says Pearl. "We haven't got all day, so don't drag this out."

"I've nearly finished," I say, "and I was only pausing to take a breath. Anyway, when the ship's about to capsize, Joel and I spot Dan sitting in a lifeboat in the sea below, so we both breathe a big sigh of relief because we know he won't let us drown. Then we start jumping up and down, yelling, until he spots us ..."

My voice tails off again at that point, as I suddenly get a bit choked up, so I try to cover that by slurping at my coffee, which is still so hot I burn my mouth.

"Ouch," I say, getting up and heading for Pearl's kitchen for a swig of cold water.

"Don't change the subject by leaving the room," says Pearl, getting up and following me. "Not when I'm still waiting to hear how this blooming dream ends – though I don't see how you can call it a nightmare, if Dan rescues you."

"That's the thing," I say. "When he finally sees us, he waves ... but then he starts to row really fast. *Away* from us."

"Ah," says Pearl, who I've never known to be lost for words before.

She remains mute until we reach the wooden viewing seat at the top of the hill that forms the outer edge of the Abandon Hope estate, the same hill that overlooks a lake situated in a public park just outside the boundary. If Pearl thinks the sight of a large body of water is unfortunate in the circumstances, she doesn't say so, and nor do I. I just avert my eyes.

"I want to give you some advice, Hannah," she says, after a minute or two has passed. "From experience. When you find yourself on your own after a long time of being half of a couple, solitary hobbies like drawing and painting aren't enough. You need to get out and meet people. You really do. I know it's terrifying but you just have to face the fear. Take the opportunity to make new friends, whenever it presents itself, and be friendly to everyone you meet. Even people you don't like."

"Why have I got to be friendly to *them*?" I say, as I begin to sketch the view below us. (The one that doesn't involve the lake. I've got my back to that.)

"Because they may have friends you like a lot," says Pearl. "Ones they can introduce you to – oh, hello!"

She's addressing one of the men who attended her poker night, the nice one who looks like Pope Francis, not the vile Fiddling Fred. He's approaching us from the direction of the lake, dressed in a fisherman's jumper and a very natty cap. The sort that a ship's captain would wear, if he was the sort of captain who didn't abandon women and children on the deck of a sinking ship. (I know Joel's twenty-two, but to me he'll always be a child.)

The man says hello to Pearl and then he smiles at me, and says, "Beautiful view, isn't it?"

Pearl steps in before I can tell the truth about how I feel about the sight of large expanses of water at the moment.

"Hannah, you remember Albert, don't you?" she says. "He's one of my lovely fellow residents."

I'd forgotten Albert's name, but Pearl's obviously taking her own advice by referring to him as "lovely". She definitely told me she'd ruled him out as a potential new husband after the poker game, because he was "too quiet" for her taste.

The conversation between them isn't exactly flowing now, which is a bit awkward, so I escape and walk to the very edge of the hill where I sit down on the grass, and start to draw the other view – the one which does contain the lake. Face the fear, and all that self-help stuff.

"I row my boat across that lake every morning," says a voice behind me, and I turn round to see Albert looking down at my drawing. "It's become one of my favourite places in the world."

I don't know what gets into me, but – all of a sudden – my mouth opens and I say,

"Albert, would you teach me to row?"

It might be purely symbolic, but imagine how much better I'd feel if I was rowing, not drowning.

Chapter 9

It's all very well for Pearl to tell me to take up more sociable activities, but after my first rowing lesson, Albert says I'm going to need a lot more, with the emphasis heavily on "a lot". He claims he doesn't mind how long it takes because I'll get the hang of it eventually, and enjoy it once I have, but I doubt I'll ever enjoy my other new outdoor activity: this ridiculous singles' walking club.

There's mud everywhere, and I'm freezing cold and soaking wet. Turns out that Joel's super-cool "waterproof" jacket (the one I sneakily borrowed while he was still asleep this morning) is not only miles too big for me, which isn't a surprise, but isn't rainproof either, which certainly is. And the bloke running this stupid group is bossier than the Fembot, which I didn't think was even possible.

The rest of the walkers are a motley crew as well, especially the men. There are quite a few young, fit ones dressed in lycra, which is a sartorial faux pas I might consider over-looking if they weren't also so far ahead of me along the ridge that I couldn't interact with them if I tried – and the ones staggering along behind me don't look as if they'll make it to the next stopping place alive. I hope they don't, seeing as they've talked about nothing other than football and steam trains all the way so far. God knows why I ever thought this was a good idea.

"Too right," says a voice from somewhere nearby, though I can't see who it belongs to. And did I really just say what I was thinking out loud? (That's a very worrying development, especially if I do the same thing whilst at work.)

"Over to your left," comes the voice again. "Behind the tree. You can join me if you like – I'm going to make a run for it."

That idea sounds so appealing that I don't even stop to think before I make a sharp left-hand turn, and nearly send a train-spotter flying off the edge of the ridge. Then I peer around the only tree for miles that's managed to retain its foliage in the face of the high winds that are presumably the norm up here in the wilderness. (Joel's useless jacket isn't windproof, either.)

"Hi," says a blonde woman who's standing with her back pressed flat against the tree. "Finally, someone else with common sense. I spotted a pub not far from that dip we passed a little while ago – d'you fancy joining me? I need a stiff drink after this."

I need a *hot* drink, rather than a stiff one, but hopefully the pub will have a coffee machine as well as alcohol. I decide to take the risk, and follow carefully in the woman's footsteps as she steps off the path and heads towards open ground. I hope she's got a good sense of direction, though I have no idea how she's walking at all, seeing as her trainers have wedge heels.

"Iz–urgh Mu–unt," she says, when she sees me looking at her feet, but the howling of the wind obliterates most of each word, so I'm still none the wiser until we eventually reach the pub. I'm not that much wiser then, to be honest.

"I said, 'Isabel Marant'," says the woman, as we stand together at the bar.

"Nice to meet you, Isabel," I say, which proves to be an error on a par with joining this ludicrous walking group, at least as far as my companion is concerned.

"Not *me*," she says, looking appalled. "Isabel Marant's a designer, though I'm not sure these trainers are her most practical creation."

"Ah," I say.

Maybe Joel will have heard of this Ms Marant. I certainly feel I should have done.

"I'm Hannah," I say, for want of a more sophisticated topic of conversation. "Hannah Pinkman."

"Eva Fraser," says the woman, as she puts out her hand.

She pulls it back in again when she realises it's covered in mud, which she wipes off on the bar towel in front of us. The barman notices but doesn't object, which I can only put down to how glamorous Eva looks in her fur-trimmed parka, immaculately cut jeans and fancy Isabel Whatsit trainers. Even her hair looks good – as if it was intended to look wind-swept – while I resemble an ageing Afghan hound that's spent the last hour in a wind tunnel experiment.

I do my best to smooth my hair down while Eva establishes that the bar doesn't serve coffee, and orders double gins for both of us. We dispose of these with indecent haste, re-order and take our refilled glasses over to a table by the window, where we make ourselves comfortable. I may feel a bit of an idiot for not knowing much about designer footwear, but this is miles better than being outside on that bloody ridge. The weather's got a whole lot worse over the last twenty minutes, too.

"So, Hannah," says Eva. "Tell me about yourself."

Oh, I hate that question. What on earth am I supposed to say? *I have a job I hate, an adult son who's never going to leave home, but a husband who already has?* The whole thing makes me sound like a walking disaster. Talking of which, I've just spotted one of the trainspotters outside the entrance to the pub, shaking himself off like a dripping dog. He's purple in the face, and looks even less attractive than he did earlier, when I almost knocked him off the ridge.

"Shit!" says Eva. "It's the bore to end all bores. Duck – *quick* – before he sees us!"

We crash heads as we both dive under the table, and by the time we've stopped apologising to each other, the train-spotter has chosen the lounge bar, leaving us safe in the snug.

Eva clinks her glass against mine in celebration, then takes a large swig of gin before she begins telling me about herself. Apparently, she's in the process of moving back to the UK, having spent years working in the USA as the editor of a glossy magazine! It's a good job I didn't tell her what I do for a living. Designing icons for a question-and-answer site isn't going to sound too impressive to the newly appointed editor of the British edition of *Viva Vintage*, though after a few more drinks I don't care. Eva's much easier to get along with than she looks, and not quite as confident either, which is good news as far as I'm concerned. Over-confident people have a tendency to suck all the confidence out of me – the Fembot does it every day.

"I'm not worried about the new job at all," says Eva, "as it's not going to be much different from my old one in the States, but I have been worried about making new friends. It's not so easy when you're our age, and you're busy all the time, is it, Hannah?"

"No, it isn't," I say, "especially when you've let all your old friends slip away. That's what I seem to have done."

Eva clinks her glass against mine for the second time.

"Well, in that case," she says, "why don't we be friends? Anyone who hates walking-for-singles as much as I do has to be a kindred spirit. Let's arrange to meet up, as soon as poss. We can go clubbing together and see how many men we can pull."

I suspect Eva's score will outstrip mine by quite some margin, but maybe I can pick up the odd cast-off here and there. Things might be starting to look up.

★   ★   ★

Esther says that Eva sounds "intimidating", when I tell her how the walking-for-singles went, but I don't let that put me off. When I get home from work this evening, I find the business card Eva gave me and then dial her number straight away, before she can change her mind about being friends with someone as unglamorous as me.

"I've got an early start tomorrow," she says, "so I can't go clubbing tonight, but I'd love a coffee and a chat instead, if that's any good for you?"

"It's even better," I say. "I've made cupcakes."

I haven't, but I don't want to make Eva think I'm even less competent than I am. The Fembot let me have the ones she made for today's cupcake photos in return for a generous donation to the charity box.

"Great," says Eva. "I can't cook to save my life."

★　★　★

Her new house turns out to be only five minutes away from mine, so she turns up at the door before I've finished instructing Joel to be on his best behaviour, and not to mention that I design stupid icons for a living. She kisses both of us enthusiastically, which I have a feeling makes Joel blush, though it's hard to be sure due to most of his face being covered in beard. Then I make coffee while Eva pumps him for information about when he thinks the hipster beard craze will finally peak, and which vintage sneakers he considers the most desirable.

He's still holding forth about *that* by the time I join him and Eva in the living room, bearing the box of cakes in front of me like a prize. I put it down on the coffee table and open it with a flourish, only to find it contains four cupcakes, two of which are iced to look like breasts in frilly half-cup bras and the other two to resemble Kim Kardashian's naked bum.

Eva raises her eyebrows when she sees them, as does Joel,

so then I have no choice but to 'fess up that I lied. That passes off surprisingly well.

"Always fake it, if you can't make it," says Eva. "I know I do."

She takes an enormous bite of Kim's bottom and starts to chew. Then she tells me some more about herself, like the fact that she was christened Enid, but changed her name by deed poll as soon as she left home. She's also been divorced for years. Quite happily.

Everyone's divorced these days, aren't they? Apart from Theo and Claire, though if it could happen to me and Dan, it could easily happen to them – or to *anyone*. Not that we're divorced, of course. Not yet …

Chapter 10

Joel looks incredulous when I tell him I'm going clubbing with Eva tonight, so I decide to go out straight from work, rather than risk going home to get ready and having to endure his probably even-more-incredulous expression when he sees me dressed up to the nines. If I *am* dressed up to the nines, that is.

I have no idea what people my age wear to go clubbing and Esther wasn't much help when I asked her advice yesterday, so I just grab my newest dress from the wardrobe, the one I bought myself one lunchtime last week, to make up for bursting into tears in the food section of M&S. (I'd just put Dan's favourite apricot tart into my basket, by mistake.)

I shove the dress into one of his old suit bags, pick up my most impractical pair of shoes, and leave for work. Then I hang the suit bag in the staff room, hoping the creases will drop out of my dress before I finish work, and hurl my shoes under my desk.

That was a mistake, as – before you know it – the Fembot looks the shoes up and down and wrinkles her nose.

For once, she doesn't say what the wrinkled nose denotes, but then she wrinkles it again at the end of the day when she spots me sitting at my desk, trying to finish applying my make-up without anyone noticing. Then her comments come thick and fast.

"Ooh, look, guys," she says, to no one in particular. "Hannah's tarting herself up to meet a man!"

All the HOO staff dutifully turn round from their desks to look at me, and then turn back again, without saying a single word. For one delusional moment, I think the worst is over, but then the Fembot adds,

"I guess it takes a lot longer once you get to your age, Hannah. Filling the cracks, you know?"

She giggles to herself, twirls around on her toes a couple of times, then says, "There's some Polyfilla in the cupboard where the vacuum cleaner's kept, if you need it. 'Bye, everyone!"

There's a deathly silence for all of thirty seconds and then a series of dutiful grunts by way of response. (It's a mystery why the Fembot is always the first to leave when she claims the place can't run without her.)

I sit and glare at her back as she click-clacks her way out of the office on her Louboutins, and breathe a sigh of relief as the door slams shut behind her. Then Esther pops her head over the screen that separates our desks.

"Sometimes, I really hate the Fembot," she says. "The other day, she told me all my allergies were in my head."

"I sometimes think she's got Asperger's," I say. "Then, other times, I just know she's evil. Oh, shit!"

I've just looked at my watch, and I'm going to be late if

I don't hurry up. I aim some red lipstick at my mouth without bothering to put my glasses on, then freak out when I check the outcome in the mirror. By then, the lipstick has already sunk into all the tiny lines around my mouth, so I have to wash it off in the staff-room sink, which removes half of my already ill-applied foundation in the process. I dry my face under the hand dryer (which causes an immense hot flush), chuck some more blusher, eyeliner and mascara on, and then revert to my usual nude lipstick instead of the red. That seems a safer option for someone whose upper lip appears to have lost all definition overnight, but whose wrinkles haven't.

I put on my still-creased dress, my nose-wrinkling shoes and, finally, my padded coat. It's freezing cold, so I zip it up to the neck, then add a thick woolly scarf.

"Ready?" says Esther, as she comes into the staff room to collect her belongings and walks straight into the cloud of perfume I've just squirted up into the air. (I was planning on spinning around in it, but she got in the way.)

"Where are you meeting Eva?" she says, rapidly rinsing her face to get the perfume off.

"At the Habanero bar," I say. "Wherever the hell that is. We're having drinks and tapas before we head for a club. Oh, bugger, I've forgotten to shut down my computer."

"I'll do it," says Esther. "You go, in case Eva's waiting. I'll meet you there a bit later on, once I've been home to change."

My face must be a picture, as then Esther adds, "If that's okay with you?"

★   ★   ★

Luckily, Eva's fine with Esther having invited herself along – "the more the merrier", she says – but there's a reason I haven't been clubbing for so many years: it's horrible, and I am the world's most useless flirt.

It's not too bad in the pub, although the heating's broken down so we have to sit there trying to look sophisticated while bundled up in our coats. Eva pulls it off with her usual panache, but Esther and I look like rolled-up sleeping bags. I'm also starting to regret the gins I had while I was trying to think how to tell Eva about Esther, as I think they're giving me palpitations now.

"Don't be ridiculous," says Eva, when I mention my fluttery heart to her. "It's just because you're shivering. Have another drink and let's get this party started."

Esther and I look over at each other, and – although we don't say anything – I get the impression she's almost as tempted to make a run for it as I am. It's scary going out when you're not used to it, especially when everything's changed so much. Although Dan and I used to go to our local pub every now and then, the bar Eva's taken us to looks more like a nightclub. Most of the women inside are wearing barely any clothes, despite the heating problem, and they're all wearing loads more make-up than me. There are a lot of those drawn-on, squared-off eyebrows, and everyone's covered in tattoos. Some of those are spectacular, but others look as if their owners sketched them on the backs of envelopes while they were pissed.

Eva points in the direction of one girl with a shock of dyed black hair and the heaviest eye make-up I've ever seen in my life. It makes her look half-asleep, though in a sexy way, and I'd be quite tempted to slap on the make-up myself if I didn't think I'd just end up looking knackered and ancient, instead of appealing. The girl must sense I'm looking at her, because she turns towards us, revealing a large tattoo beneath her collarbones. It's a life-size (and very lifelike) portrait of her own face.

"She's going to regret *that* in another twenty years," I say, "when she looks in the mirror and spots the difference."

"She ought to regret it now," says Eva, "seeing as she looks as if she's got two heads, especially from a distance. Whatever was she thinking?"

I can't imagine, and the tattooed girl's starting to look a bit irritated by our staring now, so I suggest we go and get another drink before we accidentally cause a fight.

There are people queuing ten deep at the bar, so getting served takes forever. Most people don't even walk away when they've been served, as they're all drinking shots, so they just chuck those down their necks and order more straight away. We're *never* going to get served, and I'm beginning to feel claustrophobic. A huge group of girls has just surrounded us, most of them with the kind of voices that make your ears hurt, and they all smell strongly of vanilla.

I like vanilla in food, but not on people.

"Why do all modern perfumes smell like some sort of foodstuff?" I ask Eva, as she waves a fifty-pound note above her head in an attempt to attract the bar staff's attention. "If it isn't vanilla, it's mango or chocolate."

"It's because the EU banned all the ingredients that used

to make perfumes smell sophisticated," she says. "That's why there's such a market for vintage scents."

If only there was a market for vintage women – real ones, not the fakes. There are plenty of *those* in here, ranging from young women dressed like burlesque dancers to those who've obviously spent hours creating victory rolls with their hair. I'm starting to feel less pathetic about the half-hour I took to get dressed and made-up now, even though Dan listed "taking ages to get ready" as one of my most annoying habits.

The trouble is, the effort these young women have put into getting dressed up has (largely) paid off, whereas I'm pretty sure I've wasted my time. I *know* I have, once we walk into the club and remove our coats.

"What's this?" says Eva, pulling a face. "Have you two come as Siamese twins?"

Esther's wearing an identical dress to mine. She claims it was an accident, but when Eva corners me in the loos a little later, I have to admit I'm sure I showed it to Esther straight after I bought it.

"It's all a bit *Single White Female*, isn't it?" says Eva, as I try to work out if I can get away with wearing my dress back to front.

I can't, so Eva rummages in her gigantic bag and pulls out a selection of what she calls "statement necklaces". They all weigh a ton, but the largest one does succeed in making my outfit look marginally different to Esther's, even if its weight pulls on my neck so much that I feel like a hunchback.

"You'll be fine, as long as you don't bend forward too quickly," says Eva, as I do exactly that to check my make-up in the mirror – at which point the necklace swings into my face and almost loses me an eye. That's still weeping by the time we rejoin Esther, who's found us seats in a corner. The Siamese twins impression is now even more marked than it was before, seeing as Esther's obviously allergic to the perfume I accidentally sprayed into her face. She's covered in blotches and both her eyes are running continually, so we both sit sipping our drinks and dabbing our eyes with bits of tissue, while Eva concentrates on making eye contact with men – or boys, to be more accurate, if being Joel's age still counts as a boy.

"I'm going to circulate," she says after a while. "It's never a good idea to go hunting in packs, and you two look like wounded animals."

Apparently, we look less like wounded animals than employees of the club. As soon as Eva walks off, Esther and I are approached by five people in quick succession, who all want to know why women's handbags are being searched when none of the men's pockets are. Then some drunken bloke staggers backwards and falls over Esther's extended leg, spilling his drink onto her dress.

"Watch out, you clumsy idiot," she says, which turns out to have been the worst thing she could have said. Never insult an 18-stone man who's drunk his own body weight in beer.

Mr Flobby glares at Esther, and then looks over at me. His vision must have cleared temporarily, because – somehow – he manages to spot our matching outfits. Then he moves closer to Esther, until he's almost nose-to-nose with her.

"Well, love," he says, his mouth distorted by a sneer. "I

might be clumsy, but at least I'm not fucking ugly. You might dress like your friend over here, but with that horrible spotty face of yours, you sure as hell don't look like her. You're fatter, too."

Then he lurches off to annoy someone else, while Esther stands silently, watching him go. She looks absolutely stricken, and I feel incredibly angry on her behalf as well as horribly guilty. I know I didn't make that absolute git say what he did, but if I hadn't sprayed her in the face, she wouldn't have been blotchy. And she isn't "fucking ugly", either – or fat. She's just got a bigger bosom than me, that's all, and shift dresses were created for those of us who are flat of chest.

I tell Esther this, several times, but she just raises her eyebrows at me, and doesn't bother to reply. The whole thing's getting more stressful by the minute, especially as Eva's still on the dance floor getting up close and personal with a young guy who looks familiar – and now an attractive man has come over to ask if he can sit next to me.

I have NO idea what to say in reply – and these horrible sensations are definitely not shivers. It is *boiling hot* in here.

★   ★   ★

Well, this is going well. Eva's still dancing, Esther's disappeared, I've drunk too much and the good-looking guy keeps trying to talk to me, even though I can barely hear a word he says. Have I suddenly developed early-onset deafness or something? There's a weird roaring noise in my ears, so maybe it's my blood pressure rising.

Even when I *can* hear Mr Good-Looking, I've just realised that I have absolutely no idea how to talk to men that I don't know – or how to flirt with them, anyway. Every time Mr GL says something complimentary, I either try to laugh it off or I find myself giving him a sceptical look, as if he's taking the piss. I even say, "Yeah, like that's true" once, like a sulky teenager. I don't know why he's still bothering with me at all – or why I'm bothering with him, either, if I'm honest. I'd far rather be sitting at home in comfy clothes and watching TV, while chatting sporadically with Dan. That seems far less boring now than it did when it used to happen every evening, and being with someone without feeling you *have* to talk to them is like the Holy Grail, at the moment.

What if I *never* find anyone else I can sit comfortably in silence with? Mr GL's fine to look at, and he could be the world's most fascinating conversationalist for all I know, but he's not Dan. That thought makes me feel as if I'm going to do one of those sudden sobs that keep catching me unawares, so I clamp my lips together and concentrate on breathing in through my nose, thus rendering further conversation impossible on my part, though not on Mr GL's.

He doesn't give up easily, I'll give him that. In fact, he leans in closer and keeps up a continual stream of chatter about God knows what for the next few minutes, until the buzzing of my phone gives me the perfect excuse to move away from his arm, which has just started sneaking its way along the back of my seat. Too much, as well as *far too soon*.

"Excuse me a minute," I say, meaning "for the rest of the evening". Or even for the rest of my life.

Maybe it's suddenly become obvious that's how I feel because, as I open my messages, Mr GL stands up and says he's going to the bar.

"I'd offer you a drink," he says, "but ... well, you know."

"Yeah, I do," I say. "Sorry, but thanks anyway. It was nice meeting you."

I can't do this stuff. I just can't. And it seems Esther can't either, as the text's from her, apologising for disappearing, and saying she started to feel unwell so she walked to the taxi rank and is now on her way home. I think I'll follow her example as soon as I find Eva ... and send Dan a drunken text.

★ ★ ★

Two people complain to me about the state of the loos as I make my way across the club towards where Eva's still dancing her arse off. Another asks why there are so few bar staff on duty tonight. They might as well just come out with it and say, "You look *way* too old to be here, unless you're running the place."

That's not an attitude Eva seems to be contending with. As I push past a group of young guys who are standing watching while she shakes her enviable booty, I overhear them taking bets on "who's going to shag the cougar". I just hope it's not the one I know: Joel's best friend, Marlon, who I've always thought was such an innocent! I make a point of saying hello to him in a very disapproving voice, because I'm *in loco parentis* as his mum's not here.

Eva nearly has a fit when I tell her Esther left hours ago,

and then she demands to know why I didn't come and join her, rather than sitting on my own "like a Billy-No-Mates".

"I wasn't on my own," I say, "but I've had too much to drink and now I want to go home. You stay, and I'll call you tomorrow. Just don't sleep with Marlon, Eva – his mum would *not* approve."

Eva promises she won't, albeit with a certain degree of reluctance, and then she peers at me suspiciously.

"Are you all right, Hannah?" she says. "You look a bit tearful, as well as pissed. You're not going to do anything stupid when you get home, are you? Like drunken texting, for example?"

"No," I say.

I'll probably do *that* as soon as I get into a cab.

★ ★ ★

Dan didn't answer my texts, or his phone, when I rang that instead – which may explain why I'm now hiding behind a bush in his new back garden, watching him through a ground-floor window. I am officially going mad.

Chapter 11

I had no idea Dan's landlady had a dog! Luckily, it's one of the handbag kind, so although it snaps at my ankles and yaps when it's let out into the garden, it doesn't do any permanent damage, although it does nearly give me a heart attack. If the music Dan, Aasim (the other housemate) and the landlady are playing wasn't so loud, they'd definitely hear the dog barking and come outside to investigate, so I suppose I should count myself lucky I don't get caught in fully fledged ex-wife stalker mode. The trouble is, I don't feel lucky in the slightest *and* I'm worried I may be losing my mind.

I can't imagine what got into me, telling the taxi driver to take me to Dan's on my way home from the club, but seeing my husband enjoying himself with his new housemates when my evening's been so shitty, certainly doesn't make me feel any better – and nor does having to fend off a stupid sausage dog with chilly blue eyes and very sharp teeth.

When it first starts trying to bite me, I'm stooping down behind a large evergreen bush, looking in through the un-curtained windows of what's presumably the dining room.

Dan's in there, sitting at the table with a glass of wine in his hand and engaged in what must be a fascinating conversation, given that he's paying far more attention to what Aasim is saying than he's paid to anything I've said in years. He looks both animated and relaxed, if one of those adjectives doesn't preclude the other.

After the dog incident, I probably look even more animated than Dan does, though considerably less relaxed – especially since I've just realised who his landlady is. It's Alice, one of the more junior officers in Dan's department, the one he always describes as bonkers. I've only met her once, briefly, at one of the Council's Christmas work "do's", when she looked at me and nodded when Dan introduced us, then immediately turned her head away and carried on talking to him as if I wasn't there. While wriggling about a lot, and pulling the wide neckline of her dress further and further off her shoulder, as I recall. She kept saying, "Oops" whenever the top of the dress threatened to fall off completely, as if it was an accident.

Dan said he hadn't noticed, and he found it funny when I told him later that I thought Alice fancied him.

"She fancies anything in trousers," he said. "That doesn't mean anyone fancies her back."

I took that claim at face value at the time, but I spend my next taxi journey – this time genuinely heading for home – stewing about whether what I've just witnessed involved any flirting with Alice by Dan. I'm still undecided by the time the taxi draws up outside my house, as I can't actually remember how Dan behaves when he *is* flirting. Hopefully, he's as rubbish at it as I've proved to be tonight. On the basis of that embarrassingly shoddy performance, I'm never going to find a new man and I'm going to be doomed to sleep alone for the rest of my life. Well done, Hannah. *Fantastic* achievement. Ten out of ten for gross incompetence.

I suppose the only plus is that at least I can wear whatever I like to sleep in now, seeing as no one's ever going to notice. Joel's not usually sober late at night, so he doesn't count, as he'll either see two of me, or none at all, depending on how close to being shut his eyes are when he finally staggers in after yet another night on the tiles. I'm surprised he wasn't with Marlon at the club tonight, now I come to think of it, especially now he's single again. He's definitely out somewhere, though, as he's nowhere to be seen when I let myself into the house, so I decide to go straight to bed.

The bedroom's freezing, and so is the bed, now there's no warm Dan to curl up against, so I put on a pair of very attractive red polka-dot flannel pyjamas. After that, I add green-and-white striped socks and a hideous leopard-print fleece Claire gave me for my birthday last year. When I glance in the mirror before I get into bed, I look like one of those oscillating paintings by Bridget Riley. One she produced on a *very* off day.

My name is Hannah Pinkman, and I am sex symbol of the year.

★   ★   ★

No sooner have I fallen asleep (it seems) than I wake up again. You can't drink much during the evening when you get to my age, and certainly not enough gin and tonic to fell an ox. They say gin dries you out, but if it does, it's only because it's a diuretic. Now I'm dying for a wee.

I try to ignore the sensation for a minute or so, but then roll out of bed and make my way across the room with my eyes still shut. I'm working on the principle that if I keep them closed, I won't wake up properly, so then I'll go straight back to sleep as soon I get back into bed, instead of lying awake fretting for the next few hours. That's what used to happen every night once Dan moved out, until I developed the "eyes–shut" technique. Now there are no more piles of his discarded clothing forming trip hazards across the bedroom floor, I can usually make it safely to the bathroom without having to open my eyes at all. Note the word "usually".

Tonight, I open the bedroom door and step out onto the landing with my eyes still closed, and my arms stretched out in front of me. I'm using them to locate the banister rail that runs along the landing, in case I miss where landing ends and stairs begin.

"Arrrrgh!"

Now I'm screaming, because my hands have just touched something warm, squishy and unexpected.

"Ow," says a voice I've never heard before.

Oh, my God, it's a burglar, and I've just poked one of his manboobs.

I open my eyes, blink several times to make sure I'm seeing what I think I'm seeing, and then I close them again, out of a misplaced sense of modesty. There's a naked girl on the landing, right in front of me. For a few seconds, I try to dodge round her without looking at her, but that just leads to more accidental physical contact, so eventually I have to half-open one eye so I can work out how to negotiate my way to the bathroom without any more squishy surprises. I'm *desperate* for a wee by now.

"Um, hello," says the girl, while I stare fixedly over her left shoulder, or as fixedly as you can stare while also hopping up and down.

For one crazy moment, it looks as if she's going to offer to shake my hand, until she realises that would involve exposure of even greater indecency.

"Who *are* you?" I say, as we sidle past each other, our eyes downcast.

"Ruby," she says, as she reaches Joel's bedroom door, turns the handle and enters the room.

"Nice to meet you," she adds, before she shuts the door behind her.

I'm not sure I can say the same.

★ ★ ★

It's not just Joel and the naked girl. *Everyone* is having more sex than me, or talking about it anyway.

I wake up early, despite the hangover, and decide I'll go to see Pearl, rather than hanging around at home. It's Sunday, and I've no desire to spend the whole morning waiting to encounter Ruby again, whenever she and Joel finally get out of bed.

"Well, you can't deny your son a sex life, Hannah, just

because you don't have one any more," says Pearl, as I unpack the blueberry muffins I picked up on my way to her flat.

"I bloody can," I say, "while he's living under my roof, and especially when he prevented me and Dan from having one most of the time. We never knew when he was going to come barging in, looking for a missing sock."

Pearl's fiddling about with a fancy new coffee machine I've never seen before, so I'm not convinced she's giving the subject of Joel's inappropriate sex life due consideration.

"He obviously doesn't realise it's just as *eurgh*-inducing for parents to think of their kids' sex lives as it is the other way round," I continue. "And my heart's not up to coping with the stress of meeting naked strangers in the middle of the night."

Pearl raises her eyebrows, froths some milk, then pours it onto the coffee that she's already shared between two mugs. Then she starts farting about trying to create fancy patterns in the froth, until I lose my patience and grab my mug. I need caffeine, and I need it now.

"There's nothing wrong with your heart, my girl," she says. "Apart from being a bit broken, that is, and that will pass with time. Do you like the coffee maker Dan bought me, by the way?"

Dan's been to see Pearl? *My* Aunt Pearl? That's almost as rich as this fancy coffee.

"Why did he do that?" I ask, putting my mug down and pulling a face. "You're my aunt, not his, and it's not your birthday or anything. He shouldn't be coming to see you now we've split up, anyway. What did you two talk about?"

"I've been Dan's aunt-in-law for twenty-seven years," says Pearl, "and I am fond of him, and he of me. *That's* why he bought me a house-warming present, but as for your other question –"

She stops talking and taps her nose. One of her more infuriating habits, I've always thought.

"You'll have to mind your own business on that front, Hannah," she continues. "I'm following Joel's lead when it comes to you and Dan. I'm not telling you what Dan says to me, and I'm not telling him what you say, either."

Joel's lead? What the hell is going on? Anyone would think that Joel's the adult and I'm the child, especially now I'm the one having to stuff my fingers in my ears to avoid overhearing him having sex. The world is rapidly going mad.

I scowl at Pearl, then put the kettle on to make some tea. I've gone right off coffee now.

Pearl turns the radio on to alleviate the rather awkward silence that ensues, and picks up a magazine from the coffee table. She flicks through the pages while I sit and stew.

"Another muffin?" she says, after a while.

"No, thank you," I say. "I'm fine as I am."

It's possible that I'm undermining the effectiveness of this claim by the way my feet keep jiggling, and my fists are clenched, so I lean over to the coffee table and rummage around for something to read. Amidst the magazines, I find some of those Sunday supplement-style gadget catalogues, so I choose a few of those. If Pearl can sit there ignoring me by pretending to be absorbed in reading something, then I can do the same to her. And gadgets don't take much concentration, which is good, given how my mind's still racing.

I open the first catalogue and flick through a few pages showing incontinence aids, massage cushions and adult bibs, when something slips out and falls to the floor.

"Holy shit!" I say.

Something called "Your Free Kinky Sex Booklet" is lying at my feet. It's generously illustrated, and it almost makes me lose the will to live. If even elderly people are supposed to carry on like fetish models now, I'm never going to get laid again. Imagine having a hot flush while wearing latex!

Pearl tells me not to be silly when I ask if she owns anything rubberised, and then she orders me to be "more open to new experiences".

"You and Dan got stuck in a rut," she adds. "Not just when you were together, but in terms of who you are. You both need to be willing to try different things."

"What – like some of these?" I say, pointing to the small ads in the back of "Free Kinky Sex".

The men in the photos are ancient, but the girls look as if they've just left school.

"Of course not like *those*," says Pearl, chucking the leaflet into the wastepaper basket, "but something more daring than learning to row – though that's a start. What about internet dating? I'm going to give it a try, seeing as there aren't any good male prospects here at Abandon Hope. There are lots of men on these websites, though, so you could easily meet someone your own age instead of hanging out with oldies like me."

She pauses, but she can't resist. I *knew* she wouldn't be able to.

"You can't keep up with us," she adds.

*   *   *

I drive home from Pearl's thinking about what she said about trying new things and, by the time I get there, I've decided I'll join one of those singles' supper clubs. That'll kill two birds with one stone: it'll get me out of the house and meeting men, and save me the bother of having to cook. Joel can go and eat at Dan's new place on the nights I'm out if he misses Dan's cooking as much as he says he does. I miss it, too, though not as much as I miss some of the other things Dan used to do. Like dealing with Joel, when he's being a pain.

I pause on the front doorstep as I recall the naked girl. If she's still in the house, I hope she's put some clothes on now. I've seen enough naked people in the course of the last twelve hours to last me a lifetime – which it may have to, if I can't even get my head around flirting with someone new, let alone seeing them naked. Or them seeing me.

When I open the door and step inside, I can tell immediately that the house is empty. You always *can* tell, though I don't know why. It must be something subtle only the lizard part of your brain picks up: a lack of disturbance in the air or something like that. Joel's probably avoiding me, to give me time to calm down about last night's shock encounter, though it's going to take a while for *that* to happen, when I'm still so cross about it.

The stillness of the house is a bit depressing, so I heat up some more of Joel's ageing pasta sauce and eat it without spaghetti, but with a spoon. Then I take my sketchbook into the garden to make the most of what little daylight is remaining. I know it's boring, and solitary, and all that, but for the rest of today I'm going to do something that makes me feel good, and drawing fits the bill.

I spend an hour or so sketching – first the violas, from every angle, and then the dormant lilac tree, though that just looks like a collection of twigs. Now I'm at a bit of a loss to know what to draw next, seeing as most of the garden is still in bleak post-winter mode, much like me.

I stand in the centre of the overgrown lawn and turn around in a circle, looking for inspiration, and then I decide to draw the house. That turns out to be quite testing – getting the perspective right when I'm so out of practice – but when I stop concentrating on how depressed I am, and start concentrating on what I'm looking at, eventually I get my hand in, and the result is pretty good. In fact, the process proves so enjoyable that I feel miles better by the time the light starts to fail and I go back indoors. I haven't drawn anything for years, apart from stupid website banners and icons, and now I can't imagine why I ever stopped. Was it something about being with Dan, even though a love of art was the first thing we shared? The whole thing suddenly strikes me as so odd that, if we hadn't split up, I'd be asking his opinion about it right this minute.

But we have split up, and now I'm miserable again ... until I walk upstairs to the bathroom and find a message Joel must have left for me before he went out.

There's a large piece of paper on the floor of the landing, which looks as if it's been torn from one of my sketchbooks. On it Joel has drawn a self-portrait in charcoal, showing him wearing a very penitent expression along with an outfit that wouldn't look out of place on a rap musician. Beneath his feet, which are encased in a pair of extremely elaborate trainers, he's scrawled, "I'm sorry, Mum". It's all a bit smudged due to the charcoal, but the drawing isn't bad at all, and I'm just wondering whether to suggest Joel reconsider his decision not to go to art school when I hear the front door slam, and then him shouting, "Mum?"

I go downstairs intending to demonstrate that all is forgiven by giving him a hug, but he shrugs off my attempt.

"Have you been annoying Dad?" he says. "Or doing something stupid?"

"No," I say.

Joel glares at me, then says, "You must have done. Dad says he's taking that secondment he was going to refuse because he 'needs some space'. So now he'll be moving miles away at the end of the week."

I'm so nonplussed, all I can do is to stand there, my mouth gaping open as if I was a fish, while I rack my brains for why Dan would need more space from me. Maybe he objected to my drunken texts – unless he realised I was hiding behind the bush in his garden the other night? I should've killed that bloody dachshund, as soon as the damn thing started to bark.

Spring

Chapter 12

It's March the 21st today – the first day of spring – but I can't say I'm enjoying it, so far. It's pouring with rain when I wake up, and I seem to be pouring, too. I thought all that unpredictable crying had finally stopped after the apricot tart meltdown in M&S a week ago, but this morning I can't seem to stop because of this secondment thing. If Dan's not even living in the same town as me any more, then that must mean he's really gone for good.

Joel's still pretty fed up, too, though at least he's stopped blaming me for Dan's decision now.

"I know it's a bit shit about Dad moving away, Mum, but maybe it's for the best," he says, as he plonks a cup of tea down on my bedside table. "It isn't easy, bumping into each other all the time, not when you've split up. Izzy walked past my shop yesterday and even *that* was awkward."

He doesn't mention Ruby, so presumably Izzy only counts because she's Joel's "official" ex-girlfriend, rather than a random naked person on a landing. I don't say anything, anyway, as I don't know what to say. "A bit shit" is the understatement of the year, unless it's being used to describe this cup of tea. Joel never waits for the kettle to boil.

I sit and sip the lukewarm sludge while tears roll slowly off my nose and into my cup.

"You're in no fit state to go to work, are you?" Joel says, after a while.

I agree entirely, but I've got no choice. The Fembot was off sick on Friday, with some sort of unspecified virus, and if she's still claiming to be unwell today I've got to cover for her at the stupid strategy meeting after lunch.

Joel asks what I mean by "claiming to be unwell".

"I'm not convinced she was genuinely ill," I say. "She'd already asked for Friday off to have a long weekend at a spa, but the MD refused because we're too busy. Then she rang in sick that day."

"Well, if she's been faking it, then your problem's solved," says Joel, passing me a box of tissues. "That's the great thing about imaginary illness syndrome. You can just say you've caught it from her, and then she can't prove you're lying without admitting she was too."

I admire the genius of Joel's reasoning but go to work anyway, not only because he didn't inherit his disregard for authority from me, but also because I need to check whether Esther's got over the Mr Flobby incident at the club by now.

Her face is no longer blotchy, which is a plus, but she's still in a foul mood with that horrible man, and with me.

"It comes to something," she says, "when a man thinks someone decades older than you is more attractive, doesn't it?"

It's not *decades*, plural, it's only one and a half (if Esther's referring to me, as I assume she is), but I bite my tongue. I suppose I can't blame her for being upset, so maybe she'll feel better if I tell her about Dan's secondment? Then she won't think she's the only one whose love life most resembles a pile-up on a motorway.

"Are you serious?" she says, once I've finished speaking. "Dan's gone to Birmingham? Bloody hell, he must have been desperate to get away."

She doesn't add, "from you" but it feels implicit, and I'd forgotten how much Esther hates Birmingham, too. It's where she was living when her last relationship ended badly, though that's all I know about it, apart from the fact that she now detests anyone with a Brummie accent.

Maybe Dan will hate Birmingham as much as Esther does, and then he'll come back sooner than planned?

Esther says she thinks that's unlikely, as she walks back to her desk, humming, while I feel the tell-tale prickle of tears and head for the loo.

By the time I return to my desk, I'm in a much better frame of mind, mainly because I've just called Eva who said she's coming to see me after work.

"It's time to put *Hannah Pinkman Moves On* into action," she explained. "After that, you'll be too busy having fun to even *think* of crying."

★　★　★

Joel sends a text just as I'm leaving work to tell me to hurry home because he's locked himself out, so I power walk all the way while talking to Pearl on my mobile. I get horribly out of breath, but Pearl doesn't notice because she's too excited. She's set up her online dating profile and has already been offered loads of dates. I'm impressed, until she admits her profile photo "isn't one hundred per cent accurate".

"What d'you mean?" I ask, trying to keep *talking-while-walking* to a minimum.

"I look quite a lot like Sophia Loren in it," says Pearl, who has never looked anything like Sophia Loren in her life.

It turns out that the reason Pearl looks like Sophia Loren in her profile photo is because she used a photo of Sophia Loren *as* her profile photo. I'm so horrified that I prioritise talking over breathing when I respond.

"Won't Trade Descriptions say something about that?" I say, or rather, gasp. "It's dishonest, isn't it?"

Pearl tells me not to be ridiculous and that no man would seriously think Sophia Loren would do online dating, "so they're bound to realise it's just a talking point".

"And it's no less honest than men are about height and weight in their profiles, anyway," she adds. "Or how much hair they've got."

Joel says he never thought he'd have a great aunt who went in for catfishing, when I finally arrive at the house and let him in. My phone starts ringing before I have time to ask him to explain what catfishing is.

It's Eva calling, from her car.

"Hannah," she says. "I'm stuck in traffic but hopefully I won't be long. Oh, and seeing as you're so unsettled by the Dan thing, I'm bringing something to cheer you up."

"Hopefully not a man," I say. "I've got my second-worst set of underwear on."

I didn't realise Joel was lurking in the hallway. Wriggling out of saying that proves difficult, so I'm quite glad when my explanation is interrupted: first by the arrival of Marlon and some of Joel's other mates, and then by Eva herself. She really *is* bearing gifts.

"For you," she says, chucking a beautiful beaded flapper dress at me. "Got it from today's photo shoot. It'll suit you better than me, seeing as bosoms were a no-no in the Roaring Twenties."

That's an attitude that can't come back soon enough, as far as I'm concerned.

"Just to make it clear," Eva adds, "in case you are now confused by my apparent breach of my own sartorial rules, women our age are allowed to wear one-off, very special pieces like that dress. We are *not* allowed to wear anything our mothers would have worn, because those risk looking age-appropriate."

"Ah," I say, though I haven't a clue what Eva's talking about. She works for a magazine that promotes all things vintage, including clothes, so what's the problem?

"Clothes are only vintage if you don't look old enough to have worn them the first time round," she explains, after spotting my confused expression. "Otherwise, they're simply *your old clothes*. Now make us a coffee, and pass me your laptop. I have a plan – to get you a man."

I do as I'm told and then watch, totally out of my depth, while Eva flicks through various internet dating sites, only to rule half of them out straight away.

"Tinder's no good for you," she says. "Not just because you're at the top end of their age-range, but also because of your cack-handed inability to tell left from right. You'd keep swiping the wrong way and end up dating nothing but weirdos."

"Thanks," I say, and then I tell Eva about Pearl pretending to be Sophia Loren.

"Good for Pearl!" she says, before ruling out Match.com for some reason that I can't recall, and then something called Grindr because I'm not male or gay.

I rule out other sites myself, either because they require you to be a practising Christian or because I'm not willing to pay to be humiliated, which is what's bound to happen when no one bothers to contact me. That prospect's bad enough, but when Eva tries to take a photo for my profile picture, the result's so awful that I tell her I've changed my mind about the whole idea.

At that point, she gives way to irritation and says it's no wonder I'm such a mess when I always think the worst of myself, and am "totally unwilling to experiment".

She smiles as she says it but the accusation stings, so I give her carte blanche to do whatever she thinks best, then head for the kitchen to make something to eat. (I made the mistake of telling Joel I was a bit tired of his signature pasta dish the other day and he hasn't made a new batch since.)

By the time I return, having accidentally tipped one pizza down the back of the oven shelf and dropped the other face down on the kitchen floor, I'm wishing I'd been more appreciative of Joel's culinary expertise. I'm also starving, as is Eva, but at least she's achieved her task more effectively than I have mine.

"You now have fully fledged dating profiles on *Plenty of Sharks*, and *No-kay Cupid*," she says. "Now pass me some food. What *is* that? Pizza, or some sort of weird, lumpy pasta sauce without the pasta?"

"More to the point," I say, staring in disbelief at the screen. "*Who* is that?"

My profile picture shows a blonde woman who looks awfully familiar, though not from looking in a mirror, and my username is *PintSizedPammy*.

"It's Pamela Anderson," says Eva, who's still turning bits of pizza over with her fork and inspecting them warily. "I thought if Pearl could get away with catfishing, then so could you."

"Oh, for God's sake, Eva," I say. "You're as daft as Pearl. No one's going to believe I'm Pamela Anderson, and even if they do, they'll just be disappointed when they find out I'm not. Whatever were you thinking?"

"I got bored waiting for you to choose a profile picture you could live with," she says, "so I chose one of Pammy at random. You can change it when you next log in."

Before I can argue, she shuts my laptop down. Then she phones to order a takeaway.

★　★　★

I've corrected all the lies Eva told about me in my dating profile now, but it's hard photographing yourself, especially when your eyesight's rubbish. I've taken about ninety selfies in the half-hour since she left, but all of them are terrible. Either my eyes are looking in the wrong direction or I've caught my chin(s) at the most unflattering angle possible, despite switching to self-portrait mode. The trouble is, I need my glasses to see whether the photo will look any good before I take it, but I haven't mastered the art of keeping my head (and eyes) in exactly the same position while removing my glasses and then taking the shot.

I've tried everything I can think of to improve the results I'm getting: sideways angles (which are rubbish), pouting (even more ridiculous), and putting my chin down while peering upwards into the camera. That last one gave me at least five more chins, along with an odd, simpering expression, but the alternative (looking upwards while sucking my cheeks in, like the Fembot does) made me look demented. I can't think *what* to do now, and I'm not at all sure I want to have my face on display so that people I know could recognise me, anyway. Maybe I should try some sort of disguise?

I ask Joel if he's got any masks left over from all the Halloween club nights he's been to over the last few years, but the only one he can find is a full-face rubberised mask of a malevolent pig.

"You going to a fancy-dress party, Mum?" he says, which gives me an idea.

The last time Theo and Claire had one of their ghastly parties, the theme they chose was "Gangsters and Molls", mainly because Claire had just bought a red '30s-style dress and matching shoes, and Theo thought molls were guaranteed to wear stockings. He was disappointed, unless you count the male guests who went in drag, but I guess that's life.

Dan decided we should go as Bonnie and Clyde, so I wore one of my old berets and Dan bought a cheap fedora from our local market, which I'm pretty sure is still in a box on top of our wardrobe.

I retrieve it, and try it on. It's so big it slides halfway down my face, leaving only my nose and lips on display. Even better, if I suck my cheekbones in very slightly and then angle my head a little, I look mysterious, full-lipped and a bit like Marlene Dietrich, before she reached the age when she started yanking half her face behind her ears and taping it there. I take a quick test shot and the result's so good, I wonder if I could wear a fedora in bed?

I'll try it, once there's a realistic chance of finding another person *in* my bed. Until then, I'll just upload the photo, change my username, then go to bed and wait and see.

Chapter 13

God, I'm hot. I'm seriously fucking *hot*!

I've just got home from work and checked my emails – twice, because I thought I was seeing things the first time I did it. I've only been online dating for less than twenty-four hours and I've already got over a hundred messages in my inbox on *Plenty of Sharks*, and you should see what some of the senders would like to do to me, or rather to Pammy, seeing as I can't work out how to change my username.

No-kay Cupid's proving a bit less fruitful than POS so far, but I don't care. A hundred sharks are more than enough to be going on with, and I can't wait to tell Eva about my new status as a sex symbol. In fact, I won't. I'll phone her now.

"Hannah," she says, "how are you doing?"

"I'm hot," I say. "Really, really, mega-hot."

"Well, use that paper fan I gave you," says Eva. "They're the best thing for hot flushes. Can I call you back? I'm still at work, in the middle of something important."

Honestly, anyone would think I was past it, if the first thing my friends assume when I say I'm hot is that I'm menopausal. (I may be, for all I know, but that is absolutely *not* the point.)

And I'm too busy to chat myself, now I come to think of it. I've still got ninety-nine emails to answer before I go to bed.

⋆　⋆　⋆

I'm at work, designing yet another stupid icon, but I can't help logging into my POS account every hour or so, because the whole thing's such a buzz. My inbox is still filling up, and I had no idea I was capable of attracting so many men – or even *any* men.

It's doing my confidence a world of good, and now I'm surprised Dan managed to keep his hands off me so much of the time. He must have overlooked whatever it is about me that's so appealing to other men, unless I've improved a lot over the last few days, which maybe I have. The Fembot asked if I'd changed my beauty regime when I arrived at the office this morning, because I "looked much brighter". Not bad for someone who'd hardly slept at all because she'd been awake until 3am replying to admiring messages.

I'm only keeping half an eye on the ones that keep coming in today, not reading them, but Esther says I'm being stupid anyway. Well, first she says she wishes she had the confidence to try internet dating, and then she tells me that I'm being stupid.

"What if the Fembot's monitoring your computer?" she adds. "You could get fired. Don't forget she threatened to sack those guys last week – you know, the ones she caught spending too much time on Wikipedia."

"Well, that was idiotic of her," I say, "as I told her when she did it. In my head."

Everyone at HOO uses Wikipedia all the time. That's how we get enough information about things we'd otherwise know sod all about to answer our users' dodgier questions, like whether failing a drug test invalidates probation, but I guess Esther's got a point. I'll wait until I get home before I check my messages again.

If they keep coming in at this rate, though, I may have to give up work, as well as housework and going out. Otherwise, I won't be able to keep up.

★   ★   ★

I'm back home now, but I am *traumatised*. I've just opened a POS email to find a photo of a guy who looks younger than Joel, and who's stark-bollock-naked, apart from a tattoo of the Nike swoosh just above his crotch, and another that says, "Just do it" on his upper thigh.

"Does your mum know you're sending women stuff like this?" I type in my response. "Concentrate on your homework, instead. Just do that."

I hit *send*, then I delete Master Nike's message and turn my attention to the others in my inbox. A lot are from men who've taken their tops off in their profile pictures, though I can't think why, in the case of some of them. Their ages range from thirty to seventy-five, and their body weights vary between skinny and enormous, so let's just say some of their profile pictures are more aesthetically-pleasing than others.

Men are rubbish at choosing usernames, too, if this lot's are typical. *BertieBigOne* obviously has an extremely small appendage (as well as a freakishly small head), and *BillyFatWallet* highlights that he's a merchant banker in his one-line "About Me", in case we'd otherwise fail to grasp his point.

Dan would definitely say Billy's got one letter of the word "banker" wrong, but Dan's not here, and that's why I'm reading these cringeworthy messages, isn't it? I plough on ...

There's *abcde1234*, who sounds about as imaginative and interesting as his username, and then there's *SocratesButCleverer*, who obviously has an ego the size of one of the larger planets. Finally, I get to *PaganPaul*. He's a diamond geezer.

I work in mental health, and I'm married, but I'd like to have sex with you in every position ever documented, as soon as it can be arranged.

I have *no* idea what to reply to that, or whether to even bother, though I was brought up to reply to *everything*.

Paul's married but wants to shag me senseless, while working in mental health? I wonder what his wife's psychological state is like, poor woman. Pretty shitty, if she lives with that creep, I should think.

My mental health's not too good already, if the fact that my head often feels as if it's exploding is anything to go by, so I delete *PaganPaul* as fast as I can. Then I get to *SexyJockeyJoe*, who wants to know whether I'd be willing to dress up as a topless pony and then walk round and round in circles in a field while he shouts instructions and brandishes a whip. (Answer: No.)

I'm about to give up and log out when I spot an email

that's just come in, from someone called *RealNiceGuy*. The subject title says, "Please read this – high priority."

I'm a sucker for good manners, so I click idly on the message, start to read, and then freak out.

Hi Pammy, I can see you're new to **Plenty of Sharks**, *so you're probably only just finding your way around the site, but did you realise you'd ticked the box saying you were "up for anything"? If you didn't mean to, I should think your inbox is already filling up with dodgy stuff.*

That's understatement of the year, so I check my profile, and of course, he's right. According to bloody Eva, *PintSizedPammy* is "up for anything and everything", but you know what's even worse than that? Mr *RealNiceGuy* doesn't ask me for a date, unlike Mr Naked-in-Socks, Mr Pervert Pagan, Mr Small Head *et al.*, including the crazed fantasist with a penchant for golden showers. I had to post a question on *Halfwits* myself – anonymously, of course – just to find out what *that* was.

*   *   *

Oh, brilliant. Over the last few days since I stopped being "up for anything" on POS, I've only had five messages, and one was from someone half my age, and three were from men older than Pearl, so I ruled all those out straight away. I know that's probably being just as ageist as the Fembot, but I don't want to date someone a quarter of a century older than me. I want a man my own age, just like Dan.

Number five is only a couple of years older than me. He also doesn't have an idiotic username, or a half-naked profile photo, so once Eva's failed to persuade me that I should follow her example and date much younger men, she says I should meet this one for a date.

★   ★   ★

Esther disagrees and says I shouldn't, "as he's bound to be a conman or something", but she's been so fed up since the Mr Flobby incident that her opinion of men has become even lower than it used to be. Her judgement's even more impaired about what she looks like, too, so I draw a portrait of her at lunchtime today, to prove she's prettier than she thinks she is. She thanks me politely, then puts the drawing under a pile of folders on her desk, so I have no idea if it worked or not – and I still haven't a clue whether to listen to her advice, or Eva's, either.

I rack my brains for someone whose judgement I definitely trust, now I can't ask Dan for his opinion, but nobody springs to mind until this evening's rowing lesson, when I ask Albert what he thinks.

"Faint heart never won fair gentleman," he says, just before I drop my oar and then almost capsize the boat when I lean out to recover it. "Just make sure to meet him on dry land."

That's why, when Mr *FairandSquare* suggests we dine together at the floating restaurant, I suggest we don't. But I do agree to his alternative suggestion: drinks at the new cocktail bar in the centre of town, at 8pm tomorrow night!

Chapter 14

I have no idea whether I'm having a super-extended bout of hot flushes or whether I'm just excited – or terrified. Why on earth did I let Eva talk me into this? Okay, so Mr *FairandSquare* looks normal, and can express himself competently in an email, but there are probably serial killers who can pull off that particular combination. And why did I agree to a date at such short notice, too? I haven't got a thing to wear, and I look like shit.

If I'd thought about it, I'd have realised that I needed to leave at least two days between arranging the date and the damn thing actually taking place, if only to allow some time between shaving my legs and fake-tanning them, to avoid the rash I always get when I do both things on the same day. Now I'm sounding like Esther with her allergies, but spotty red legs are not a good look. I've got similar red lumps all over my upper lip as well, thanks to the last-minute plucking of a few stray hairs. I look as if I've got the plague.

"I can't go through with this," I say to Eva, when I phone

her in a panic with only half an hour left before my cab is due to arrive. "And I've just lied to Joel, too. I told him I was coming round to yours, so you'd better cover for me if he ever asks."

"Why did you do that?" says Eva, as if lying to Joel was the most important thing at a time like this.

"I thought he'd be upset if he knew I was going on a date," I say. "I know *I* am."

Eva instructs me to drink a large gin, and then to tell her exactly what I'm wearing.

"The dress I wore to go clubbing," I say. "Without your necklace this time, obviously. It's the only relatively-new dress I own."

Eva sighs, but then says, "Okay, well, I guess that's fine. Send me a picture of your hair and make-up. Now."

I do as I'm told, only for her to order me to change my hair, and then to put more mascara on. Lots of it, and eyeliner, too.

"Darken your eyebrows a bit, as well," she says, "then brush them flat. You've got white hairs sticking out."

She's given me so many things to do by the time she rings off that I don't have time to think of a good enough excuse to cancel my date before I end up in the taxi, still trying to pull off the "up-do" Eva described as "idiot-proof". (She tells lies.)

I finally give up on my hair, which is now in some sort of "half-up, half-down do", in order to concentrate on breathing through my nose. I overdo it a bit and let out a sudden snort, which makes both me and the driver jump.

"You all right, love?" he says, glancing at me in his rearview mirror.

"Never better," I say, as much to convince myself as him.

There follows an awkward silence, during which I find something else to worry about: what if Mr *FairandSquare* and I have nothing to talk about? Esther says she always prepares topics of conversation whenever she has a date, but I thought that was so tragic I didn't bother to do it myself. Now I'm starting to wish I had.

I rack my brains for interesting subjects to discuss, but to no avail. My mind has gone completely blank, so then I ask the taxi driver.

"What do you talk about when you go on a first date?" I say.

He glances at me in his mirror again, then starts to laugh.

"Nothing," he says. "You don't need to talk to each other when you've been married for twenty years."

Then he starts to indicate left, pulls over and brings the taxi to a halt. Oh, dear God, we're here already.

★ ★ ★

When I get out of the taxi, that's when the nerves really kick in, not helped by the fact that the cocktail bar has floor-to-ceiling windows all along its frontage, so anyone I know who just happens to be passing will spot me inside instantly – including Joel, if he's one of them. Maybe the floating restaurant wasn't such a bad idea? At least no one I know was likely to start rowing past *that* by accident.

I tell myself a date with a new man is something to look

forward to, not to get freaked out about. Then I tell myself the same thing again, repeatedly, until I've almost managed to convince myself it's true. At that point, I sidle along past the restaurant windows, trying to see if Mr *FairandSquare* is inside, but there's no sign of a lone male at any of the tables – or at the bar. It's pretty quiet in there, anyway, so it doesn't take me long to check, but I turn round and walk back in the opposite direction, just to be sure. The result's the same: no sign of Mr F&S.

I can't go inside and sit at a table by myself, I can't – so I phone Eva again, instead.

"For God's sake, Hannah, get a grip," she says. "Just go in, walk to the bar and order a drink, then sit down at a table and compose yourself. This could be the start of something great."

It could, couldn't it? I take a couple of deep breaths, rotate my shoulders forwards and back again, then raise my chin and approach the door.

Five minutes later, I'm sitting at a table, sipping my drink and telling myself, "I am attractive and sophisticated" under my breath. My legs are artfully positioned to their best advantage, and I've smoothed my half-up, half-down hairdo down. I've even taken a surreptitious look in my handbag mirror to check I haven't got lipstick on my teeth or in the lines around my mouth. I haven't, so now I'm ready for the next stage of my life to begin.

I look at my watch, so I'll know exactly when it started – it's 8:01pm.

★　★　★

It's now 8:45pm, though that's approximate. It doesn't need to be precise for me to know that Mr F&S has stood me up. Either that, or he walked past, saw me sitting alone at my table, and then concluded that I only look good when most of my face is obscured by hat, as it is in my online profile picture. I reckon everyone else in here knows I've been stood up, too, as they all keep giving me sympathetic smiles whenever I look in their direction.

I want to cry, and I also want to get out of here as fast as I can, without embarrassing myself any further, so I text Eva, and instruct her to call me asap. For once, she does exactly as she's told.

"What's up?" she says.

"What did you say?" I ask, more than loud enough for everyone else in the bar to hear. "Oh, my God, really? You're in A&E? No, don't apologise – I'll be there soon."

I hang up, just as Eva starts to squawk, "What the hell are you talking about?", then I don my coat and make my exit.

I text her while I'm walking to the taxi rank.

He stood me up. Don't want to talk about it.

I press *send*, and then it starts to rain. That's a bit of an understatement, actually. It starts to rain torrentially – in huge drops that rapidly turn into puddles, which then join together to form one large pool of oily water that spans the road from one side to the other. It reflects the lights of the pubs and bars along the high street, which seem to glimmer and shift, as the pool grows ever larger.

By now, most of the drivers of passing cars have slowed right down and are travelling through the flash flood as slowly as they can, but then, along comes the inevitable idiot. Instead of reducing his speed, he accelerates, while getting as close to the pavement as he can. Before I realise what's about to happen, I'm covered in cold, oily water from head to toe, and the tosspot driver is tooting his horn.

I'm so shocked that it takes a few seconds before I react, which means that the tirade of abuse I eventually begin to shout serves no purpose, as its target is long gone by then.

I've been stood up, and almost drowned by a complete wanker, and now all the other pedestrians are looking at me as if I'm barking mad. I can't say I blame them because I probably look insane standing there raging at no one in particular, while my clothes and my hair are dripping wet. My shoes are full of water, too, and they make a sloshing sound with each step I take as I pull myself together and make my way onward to the taxi rank.

I'm freezing cold, but at least I'll soon be home in the warm, so things can't get any worse than this tonight – except they can. The first taxi waiting at the rank turns out to be the one that brought me into town.

"That was quick," the driver says. "Run out of conversation early, did you, love?"

"Yes," I say.

★ ★ ★

I'm telling Esther all about last night's disastrous date while we're standing in the car park at work, waiting for the weekly fire alarm test to finish.

"He stood you up?" she asks, and then she starts to laugh, so loud that the Fembot looks over and glares at us. She's marching around armed with an enormous clipboard and a walkie-talkie, while yelling at the rest of us to take this fire drill much more seriously.

"Yes, he did stand me up," I say, "though there's no need to tell the world about it."

"Sorry," says Esther. "It's just the whole thing sounds so ..."

She breaks off, overwhelmed by another bout of giggling.

"So what?" I say. "Funny? I promise you, Esther, it really wasn't."

My tone is snappier than I intended, and Esther looks a bit wounded, but I don't get a chance to apologise because then the Fembot orders us all to gather round. First she informs us that the fire drill is officially over and we completed it thirty seconds quicker than we did last week, and then she makes a surprise announcement.

"I've got a treat for you all today," she says. "We've got a video guy coming in a little while and guess what? He's going to film us all dancing to Pharrell's 'Happy', to show how great it is to work here at HOO. So off you go – start practising your moves."

She does some of her special twirls to give us the general idea, while Esther asks whether participating in the video is compulsory.

"No," says the Fembot, stopping in mid-twirl. "Not if you

have no spirit of adventure. For those who have, we'll be gathering in the conference room in half an hour."

I get separated from Esther as we all move towards the fire exit ready to file back into the building in an orderly fashion, so I can't tell whether she now regrets upsetting the Fembot – or me, for that matter – but I'm too busy to go and look for her in order to find out. Even if I wanted to join in with this stupid video, I couldn't, because I've been given a "special project" to complete by the end of this week: creating an animated fluffy owl. According to the Fembot, he is to be HOO's new "brand ambassador", and will pop up when users are least expecting it, offering to help them "acquire more wisdom". Presumably that's why I've been given strict instructions to draw him wearing a mortar board.

"Bet *you're* glad I asked whether joining in was compulsory," says Esther, appearing from nowhere, like the owl.

She perches herself on my desk and knocks a large stack of books and papers onto the floor. I give her a quizzical look as she stoops down to pick them up.

"Why?" I say. "Why would *I* be more grateful than anyone else?"

Esther straightens up, dumps the stuff back onto my desk, then says,

"Well, I don't know, Hannah. I just thought you wouldn't want to do anything else to embarrass yourself this week. Internet dating at your age must feel bad enough, especially when guys don't turn up."

I take a deep breath, then ask Esther exactly what is so

bad about internet dating *at my age.* I say the last three words very slowly, which you'd think would warn her to be careful with her answer, but she isn't.

"It's undignified," she says. "I'm not being ageist – you know I would *never* be that – but it just is."

I think for a moment or two about what Pearl or Eva would say if they were here, and then decide that I won't say it. Instead, I look down at my watch. If I hurry, I can still make it to the conference room in time.

Chapter 15

God, I'm so pissed off. The *Happy Halfwits* video has gone viral – or at least, locally – and I'm not even in it. I gave the damn thing my all, only to be edited out and replaced by a dancing owl. Eva's watching the video online when I go round to hers this evening.

"That owl is really getting down," she says, hurling a pile of junk off her designer sofa to allow me space to sit. (Eva's house isn't anything like as immaculate as you'd expect it to be, given how stylish she is herself.)

"It's called *getting your rave on* these days, not *getting down*," I say, as if I knew that before Joel told me yesterday. "And I was *really* going for it when I joined in, but then they edited me out! I didn't even realise I'd been replaced by the owl until he was mentioned in the local press."

Eva gives me a sympathy hug, then pauses the video and goes into the kitchen. She comes back bearing a cake tin and two chipped mugs of tea.

"I made you a cake as consolation," she says, "though it didn't quite turn out as planned."

She opens a cake tin to reveal a brown, brick-shaped object with a gigantic hole in the middle of it. An accidental hole, apparently.

"Ah," I say.

"Yep," says Eva. "We ran the recipe in this month's edition of *Viva Vintage*, so this is a bit of a worry. The cookery editor insists I did something wrong."

"Like I must have done," I say, accepting a slice of mutilated cake against my better judgement. "Both in the video, and when I went on that stupid date. I probably should have worn Dan's hat during both, so no one would have to look at my repellant face."

"Don't be daft," says Eva. "Mr *FairandSquare* sounded dull to start with, and *Happy Halfwits* is only a stupid video. I'm proud of you for joining in with it, especially when Esther said you should be more dignified at your age."

She didn't exactly say *that*, but I was quite proud of joining in, anyway, even though I knew I looked an idiot, because it was nice to feel a proper part of the team for once. Now I just wish my dating profile would attract a small proportion of the hits *Happy Halfwits* has been getting over the last few days.

"Still no go with *Plenty of Sharks*, then, since you stopped being 'up for anything'?" says Eva, as she presses *play* again, and that bloody owl begins to dance.

"Not unless you count octogenarians or guys trying to scam me out of life savings I haven't got," I say.

Eva's searching for the original Pharrell *Happy* video now, mainly because she fancies him.

"Joel's friend looks a bit like Pharrell, now I come to think of it," she says, watching closely as Pharrell gets his rave on. "What's his name, again?"

"Marlon," I say. "And he's far too young for you, as I keep pointing out. He's only three years older than Joel, don't forget."

Eva doesn't comment, and just changes the subject back to internet dating.

"What about *No-kay Cupid*?" she says. "Is that going any better?"

It is, actually, in terms of getting emails from people who are younger than eighty, and who aren't offering to transfer millions of dollars into my account at some unspecified time in the future if I'll advance them loads of money right this minute. The *No-kay Cupid* guys are all quite impressive, though that isn't as much of a plus as you might think. They all sound so dynamic, or cultured, or well-off, or all three, they make me feel intimidated. I haven't got a clue what to talk to them about, even in an email, and as for flirting with them, I haven't the faintest idea where to begin. It's even worse than when I made such a hash of things with Mr Good-Looking at the club. At least then I had the excuse of being drunk.

Now I just sit in front of the screen, reading all the men's profiles and trying to imagine how on earth I could hold my end of the conversation up if I ever met them – if they bothered to turn up, that is. Most live in other countries, anyway, and I seem particularly popular with Italians, French and Belgian guys. They're so chic, even the ones much older than me, that I bet they take even longer in the bathroom than Joel does.

Eva says I'm being silly and asks why I don't try imagining what my life could be like if I was in a relationship with one of them.

"Just think," she says, "you could be spending your weekends wandering arm in arm along the Left Bank in Paris – also known as *La Rive Gauche* to those of us who've led more adventurous lives than you."

She continues droning on, something about visiting the Louvre, then eating at *Les Deux Magots*, but I'm not listening. The mention of *Rive Gauche* has made up my mind, as that's the perfume Dan always bought me on our anniversaries. I'm going to delete both my dating profiles as soon as I get home, because real life is where it's at, especially when you're no good at being anyone other than yourself. That's the me Dan fell in love with in the real world, so I'm just going to have to hope that someone else will, too, eventually. Probably someone blind.

★   ★   ★

Apparently, I am a "valued member of the *Plenty of Sharks* community", and my account can't be reactivated if I go. Despite this threat, I'm welcome back at any time – any time I'm willing to be "up for anything" again, I presume. That's probably what it would say if I were to click on the link that promises "great tips to make your profile more desirable", but I don't. I choose the link that says, "To delete your profile, click *here*" instead.

Now to deal with *No-kay Cupid*. I've had loads of emails from them today, and a few of the guys who've messaged me sound as if they'd be quite promising if only they weren't either totally embittered by previous relationships or still hung up on their ex-partners. (I know I am too, but I'm pretending not to be.) And what does the "match percentage" mean, for goodness' sake? I have no idea why one person's deemed a seventy-five per cent match for me, while another's only forty-five, so maybe I should read up on how the process works before I give up internet dating altogether. It's not as if my last attempt at the real-life version was a resounding success, and "keeping your options open" is probably in one of Esther's stupid self-help books, the ones she keeps offering to lend me since Mr F&S stood me up.

I type, "How *No-kay Cupid* match percentages work" into Google, but I can't make head nor tail of the answers that come up. Maybe Pearl will know? She's the internet-dating expert in the family, after all, not that she's impressed with her experience so far. Last time I saw her she said she'd given up using the Sophia Loren photo (after she got a few complaints from men who'd genuinely expected to *meet* Sophia), but now that she's using a picture of herself, all the men who contact her say they just want companionship.

She added, "I was hoping for more action than that, seeing as I'm not dead yet."

I'd happily settle for companionship myself, tonight. I feel so lonely, even though it's been less than an hour since I got back from Eva's. Joel's out with Marlon so the house is horribly quiet, and I don't feel any less alone when I phone Pearl, only to get her answer phone – at eleven o'clock at night!

There's a beep from my mobile, which nearly makes me jump out of my skin, it sounds so loud. I've got more mail from *No-kay Cupid*.

Maybe I'll just read the latest lot of messages before I cancel that account. You never know – one of them could be my perfect match.

★ ★ ★

The people at *No-kay Cupid* have great news for me. Their first email reads as follows:

From: *No-kay Cupid*
To: *PintSizedPammy*
About you, *PintSizedPammy*:

Your personality: Really great
How bad guys want you: So bad
Your profile, as of 8 milliseconds ago: Approved!

Guys want me so bad? They're having a laugh, though the Fembot obviously ought to work for a dating site. She loves this wildly-enthusiastic, less-than-honest stuff. I hate it, but I grit my teeth and carry on reading anyway, seeing as I'm still trying to be more spontaneous and fun-loving, despite the setback with *Happy Halfwits*.

The next message is even more exciting. It promises "this week's best new matches" – *matches*, plural – although it then turns out there's only one. Mind you, this guy's apparently "an exceptionally good match" and, when I scroll down, I see it's true: he's a ninety-eight per cent match for *PintSizedPammy*! That's a twenty-five per cent improvement on everyone else so far.

I keep scrolling down through the email with one hand, while keeping the fingers of the other firmly crossed. It looks as if there's a photo attached so, please God, don't let this be another tattooed naked man.

Never say that God doesn't respond to prayers, though he has a cunning way of getting back at you for praying to someone that you don't believe in. It isn't a tattooed naked man. It's a *million* times worse than that.

Chapter 16

The guy in the photo of my almost perfect match is Dan. I'm sure it's him, though I take off my glasses, polish them, then put them back on again to make sure. I even repeat the process several times, but it doesn't make any difference. *Dannyboythesaxman* remains Daniel Pinkman, unless Dan's got a doppelgänger with a hundred per cent match percentage.

I read the profile information, which makes things even clearer. Dan – *my* Dan – is on *No-kay Cupid*, so he must be dating other women.

I need the bathroom, urgently.

★   ★   ★

I haven't actually been sick yet, though I have spent ages retching miserably while my heart bangs away in my ears and my extremities feel numb and weirdly tingly. Finally, I remember the paper bag trick, so I start breathing in and out of the one Joel got with his most recent purchase of sweary socks.

After about ten minutes, I'm capable of semi-rational thought, which is not the bonus it might seem. I can't believe Dan's on a dating site already. Couldn't he wait to be rid of me? And who the hell has he been dating? Twenty-five-year-olds? I can barely stand to check the requirements he's set for the women he says he's willing to date, though eventually I do.

Ah. He's looking for someone within a ten-year radius of his own age – which is also *my* age, so I suppose that ought to make me feel better, but it doesn't. It just makes the whole thing feel more real. Here's *my* husband, father of *our* lunatic son, putting himself on public display and available to anyone whose fancy he may take. Worse, he looks so good in this bloody photo, there'll be a lot of women who meet that particular criterion. Why didn't I notice how sexy Dan still is while we were living together? Maybe he's had plastic surgery, or perhaps it's just relief at being shot of me that's given him back his *je ne sais quoi*? I don't know what to think, so I text Eva. She's the expert in being single, after all.

"Dan's on *No-kay Cupid*!!!!" I say.

"So are you," she replies. "So give the excessive exclamation marks a rest."

★　★　★

I don't think Dan has had plastic surgery, as I've been looking at his photo for hours now, zooming in on his hairline and checking his forehead for Botoxed shininess, but he still looks all-natural to me. I'm staring at his eyes in close-up at the moment, and trying to recall when I last looked into them, as opposed to just glancing at them during conversations about who broke the central heating thermostat, or why Joel leaves dirty glasses under his bed until the contents go mouldy. I can't remember, nor can I recall what it was like to be able to touch Dan whenever I wanted to, while his face and body could still have been said to "belong" to me.

The only things I *can* remember are all those times I didn't kiss him when he came in from work, or when I sat alongside him on the sofa all night without ever bothering to move closer for a cuddle. We did still hold hands when we walked anywhere together, I think, but that was probably just from habit. And as for sex … oh, God, Dan's already got a love life with someone else, hasn't he? I bet he's been on this bloody site for months, even if joining wasn't his idea, which is what he claims in the one-line summary below his profile picture: "My housemates made me do this," it says. "I am obviously easy to manipulate."

Easy or not, I could *kill* Alice and Aasim for suggesting it. And Eva, too, for calling me a hypocrite.

★ ★ ★

It's past midnight, Joel's still out with Marlon and I'm still logged on to *No-kay Cupid*. Who is Dan talking to on this bloody, bloody horrible site?

Any of the women on here, including the ones pouting furiously into the camera with their cheekbones sucked right in and the cords in their necks straining from the effort of holding their chins aloft, could end up being my son's stepmother, and any one of them could be there at every significant event in my life in future: Joel's wedding, the birthdays of his children (preferably in that order, given recent naked girl events), and *their* weddings or graduations. The list goes on and on. And if Dan's new woman is always there, then I'm going to have to smile and be polite to her for the sake of my dignity, as well as for Joel's benefit. The effort of not killing her will probably end up killing me.

And any one of these women could be in bed with Dan right now. *Ohhhh.*

I feel faint at the thought, and then – while I'm still light-headed – that's when I do something really stupid. I log out of my account and start trying to access Dan's instead. I know his email address, so that's no problem, but what the hell can his password be?

Chapter 17

It's 7:45am, Joel's been in bed for hours and I've been up all night, but I still haven't cracked Dan's password. I've tried every title of every song he's ever liked, as well as those of his favourite films, his date of birth, and his parents' names and ages, as well as Joel's. Talking of Joel, maybe I'll try Dan's favourite description of what's wrong with him: *failuretolaunch*.

That doesn't work, but then I capitalise the first letter and add the number one. Talk about inspired – I'm in at last!

Now what? Read the messages, I suppose.

I swig the remains of my latest mug of coffee and take three multivitamins for strength, along with two Kalms tablets to lessen my caffeine- or anxiety-fuelled jitters, and then I open Dan's inbox to find out how many emails he's had from other women since joining the site.

Oh, Jeesus. Oh, shit, shit, *shit*. There are loads, most from women who look miles younger than me, and way more glamorous, too. I haven't got time to read what they've got to say for themselves, though I'm absolutely desperate to. I can't be late for work, because today's the day for my big presentation, the one the Fembot ordered me to give about upgrading quality. I probably should have asked Dan for tips on that, seeing as he's obviously been planning to upgrade me for quite some time.

* * *

No one noticed that I was still hyperventilating by the time that I arrived at work, and they just laughed when I referred to upgrading "women" twice, instead of "quality", in the middle of the presentation. They *did* notice that I was wearing mismatched shoes.

I kick those off without caring where they land as soon as I get home again, and log on to my computer as fast as I can. Oh, thank God. Dan hasn't changed his password since this morning, so he can't have realised that he's been hacked. I'm just starting to read his messages from those bloody, bloody women when the doorbell rings. Eva's on the doorstep.

"You ready, Hannah?" she asks, which comes as a bit of a surprise.

With all the excitement, I've forgotten she and I are supposed to be going to the private view of an exhibition this evening: *Fashion through the Ages*, or something like that.

"Yes," I say. "Almost."

Eva gives me a sceptical look, which I can't say I blame her for, given the state of what I'm wearing, even without the mismatched shoes.

"I'll give you twenty minutes to get changed," she says.

I manage it, though I don't look anything like as stylish as the people who are already thronging around the pictures by the time that Eva and I arrive at the exhibition. They're all dressed in immaculately-cut clothes: edgy black dresses for most of the women, and trousers and cashmere polo necks for most of the men. They're also sipping Prosecco and saying, "Oh, yah," a lot.

Eva reaches out and grabs a couple of glasses from a tray being carried by a passing waiter. She hands one to me, then sips at the other one herself, a thoughtful expression on her face.

"You okay?" she says. "You seem weird. Weirder than usual, I mean. Is it this thing with Dan?"

"I feel weird," I say, as I stare at Princess Di's wedding dress. "And yes, it is."

I'm about to continue when Eva's called away by someone she knows, and I watch as she exchanges air kisses and "Hello, darlings" with a woman whose hands are covered in so many oversized rings that I'm surprised that she can raise them, let alone gesture as wildly as she is. The conversation seems set to go on for quite some time, which is fine by me as I don't feel up to meeting new people tonight and, anyway, Eva needs to mingle in her new role as editor of *Viva Vintage*. I smile at her, then get out my sketchbook and start to draw.

The rest of the evening continues in much the same vein. I've moved on to stand in front of David Bowie's Iggy costume where Eva rejoins me, only to be immediately approached by someone else. I draw another sketch and walk on to the next exhibit, at which point the same thing happens. By the time

I've seen all the clothes, I've done loads of sketches, and I've also got through a fair bit of Prosecco, too. Every time the waiter passes, I reach out and grab another glass. He's started anticipating that now, and passing me one before I've even extended my arm.

"Sorry, sorry, sorry," says Eva, when she rejoins me yet again. "I keep starting to introduce you to people, only to find you've disappeared again. Are you feeling shy or something?"

"Yes," I say, at which Eva gives me a hug.

"Let's finish up here and go to a bar," she says. "Then you can tell me properly what's been going on. But, first, show me what you've drawn."

She takes my sketchbook out of my hands, then says, "Oh, wow. These are great, absolutely fantas –"

"Yeah, thanks," I say, cutting Eva off partly due to embarrassment, but mainly because I've just realised I haven't eaten anything for twenty-four hours.

★ ★ ★

All I can think of is food, now I've realised how hungry I am, so that's why we go straight to the nearest Indian restaurant rather than on to a bar. Luckily, the restaurant has WiFi, as well as food, so once we've ordered and Eva has gone in search of a loo, I make another attempt to read Dan's messages.

Oh, God, they're bad. "Your place or mine, handsome?" says one, all pouty lips, shiny forehead and drawn-on eyebrows.

"I'm super-flexible," says another. Her hobbies include yoga, and she includes a series of photographs of her wearing very little, in what she describes as her favourite early-morning poses. They look more like illustrations from the *Kama Sutra* to me.

I take a few deep breaths, to stop myself throwing up, and then I open the next message, from a very attractive woman who's got sensible eyebrows and isn't pouting, though she's definitely standing at the funny sideways angle celebrities use when posing on the red carpet at premieres. She's also a lawyer who loves art, and culture, and travelling – and probably saving the bloody world as well, though I don't have time to find that out. Eva's back, much quicker than I expected.

I stab at my phone in a hurried attempt to turn it off, but so clumsily that all I succeed in doing is pushing it across the table to Eva's side. Now she's staring at the screen – the one displaying all the messages unknown women have sent to *Danny boy the bloody saxman* – so I've got no choice but to explain what I've been up to. It makes Eva's day when she hears that I hacked Dan's account.

"I didn't think you had it in you, Hannah," she says, once she's finished laughing. Then she picks up the phone and starts searching through Dan's profile settings, which apparently tell her he only joined the site a couple of days ago.

"He's got a better hit-rate than you've had since you stopped being 'up for anything', though," she says, a bit insensitively, if you ask me. "Though he obviously hasn't found the time to reply to any of these women yet."

I'd been trying to convince myself that was because he'd

remembered he was still in love with me, so he didn't need to bother with anyone else, though I don't tell Eva that. I just bite into a poppadom instead.

Eva helps herself to an onion bhaji and eats it absent-mindedly, while she reads the rest of the messages out loud.

"Some of these women don't believe in playing hard to get, do they?" she says. "They're *really* up for anything."

"I know," I say. "And even the ones who aren't sound ten times more interesting than me, and more successful, too."

My voice comes out sounding as glum as Marvin the Paranoid Android, but honestly, I'm doomed. Dan's going to be spoilt for choice on this bloody site, and I'm going to be on my own for good.

"He'll be asking himself why he waited so long to get rid of me, once he reads these," I add.

"Hm," says Eva, who's staring into space and chewing the side of one of her manicured fingernails. After a few seconds, she starts tapping away on my phone, though she refuses to tell me what she's doing and fights me off when I try to look. What on earth is she up to now? I'm pretty sure it isn't anything I'd want her to be doing, so I dig around in my bag for my bottle of Rescue Remedy, and tip half of it into my mouth in one go. The quantity I swallow must be fifty times the regular dose, but it makes no discernible difference to how I feel.

"Rescue Remedy's a waste of time," says Eva, putting my phone back down on the table. "It never works, because it's taking action that makes you feel better. You need to find someone new before Dan does, which you won't, if you're too busy fretting about what he's getting up to. That's why I've done *this*, to give you a head start on him."

She swivels the screen to face me, revealing Dan's inbox, which is now completely devoid of messages. I take another large swig of Rescue Remedy, which works no better than the first.

Chapter 18

I found a bottle of herbal Nytol tablets in the bathroom cabinet when I got home last night, so I took two of those to get to sleep, and then two Kalms this morning before I left for work. As a result, I've just followed Eva's advice and accepted a date with a guy called Will, aka Mr *NordicNoirFan* on *No-kay Cupid*. For tomorrow night, so I won't have time to change my mind.

I don't tell Esther about it, because I don't want any more comments about internet dating being undignified at my age, and she's too busy to listen to me, anyway. She's beavering away at something for the Fembot, which she says may earn her a promotion if she does it well. I'm surprised she wants to be promoted, as I thought she hated her job at HOO and wanted to escape as soon as possible, just like me, but now she says she's changed her mind.

"I took a demotion to come here, don't forget," she says, "to get away from Birmingham – and it's not as if I've managed to get a life outside work since I've been here. Not like you,

Hannah, gadding about with Eva to glamorous events all the time."

Honestly, that is so unfair. First of all, I hardly ever go anywhere, and secondly, I would have invited Esther to last night's exhibition if she didn't always say she finds Eva "bossy and insensitive". I'm in the middle of explaining that, as tactfully as I can, when the Fembot calls me into her office and makes her shock announcement.

"You and I are going to be on local TV on Saturday lunchtime, Hannah," she says, "to talk about *Happy Halfwits*."

"But I'm not in the video," I say. "Not since you edited me out of it."

The Fembot looks a bit embarrassed, which is a first.

"I know," she says, "and I'm sorry about how that was handled. It's just that we wanted to leave space for Humphrey HOO the owl, who is your design, after all. That's why I thought you should come with me to the interview."

Humphrey HOO the owl? Since when has he had a name? Since he needed one to be included in the credits of the video? That bloody bird is better known than his creator.

I don't actually say any of those things about Humphrey, of course, because the Fembot is still talking.

"I know it's at the weekend, Hannah," she says, "but you can take back the time in lieu. Okay with you?"

I'm so gobsmacked by the whole thing that I don't know how to react. Despite what Esther thinks about my manic social life, it's not as if any leisure time's easy to fill now that I'm on my own, which is why I've got a rowing lesson with Albert booked for Saturday lunchtime. I can cancel that easily enough, but it's the idea of being on television I object to most. I'm bound to make a fool of myself in a live interview, so that's exactly what I tell the Fembot.

"I hear you've already made a fool of yourself internet dating," she replies, "so you should be used to that by now. Now how's that revised 'thumbs-up, happy face' icon coming along? Is it looking good?"

I shrug instead of answering, and then stomp off to my desk. The face on the icon is positively homicidal by the time I finish it.

★　★　★

It only takes me an hour to get ready to meet Mr *NordicNoirFan*, partly because Joel is visiting Dan in Birmingham for the weekend and isn't around to get in my way, but mainly because I'm not expecting Mr Nordic to turn up, so I don't exactly make an effort. I just wash my hair, which needed washing anyway, then pull on a clean pair of jeans and a fitted black top, and add another coat of mascara to the one I put on this morning before I left for work. That'll have to do.

When the taxi driver texts me to say that he's outside, I glance at myself in the full-length mirror in the hallway and decide it definitely will not do – so then I hurriedly swap my pumps for a pair of heeled ankle boots and spray myself generously with Rive Gauche, before opening the front door and rushing to where the taxi's parked, while trying fruitlessly to stop my umbrella from blowing inside out. It's windy and raining tonight, which doesn't seem a particularly good omen given the soaking I got after my last "date".

As luck would have it (the bad kind of luck), it's not just the same weather, but also the same taxi driver.

"Hello, love," he says, giving me a wink as I clamber into the back seat and accidentally spray him with water droplets as I fold my umbrella up. "Got a second date?"

"No," I say. "Unless you count a second first date, that is."

The taxi driver nods sagely, then changes the CD he's playing.

"This'll help you get in the mood," he says.

Oh, dear God, he's chosen Barry White.

I sit and panic as Barry does his sexy thing. What if Mr Nordic does turn up and expects to sleep with me tonight? I know I used to complain to Dan that we hardly ever got around to having sex, but I wanted more sex with Dan – not with a complete stranger. And certainly not with a complete stranger who's never seen my body before, so he won't be inured to the gradual deterioration that's been taking place ever since I hit my forties. I'm tempted to tell the driver to turn round and drive me straight back home, but now we're already pulling into the car park of the restaurant. I must start arranging dates a lot further away from home to give me time to change my mind en route.

"Want me to wait, in case this one turns out to be a dud as well?" asks the taxi driver, whose name is Mick, according to his licence.

"Yes," I say. Then, "No."

It's time to think positive, seeing as I can't afford to lose my head start over bloody Dan.

Chapter 19

Maybe there's something in this "thinking positive" approach to life: Mr Nordic doesn't stand me up!

I spot him sitting at the bar as soon as I walk into the restaurant, which is both good and bad. It's good, because he looks exactly like his profile photo, so at least he hasn't been catfishing me, but it's bad because I was hoping to go to the ladies' and check my hair and add some more make-up before meeting him, and the entrance to the loos is on the far side of the bar. I'd have to walk straight past him to get there, while pretending I hadn't noticed him, only to come back with my sight miraculously restored along with my *maquillage*.

I loiter in the doorway for a moment, dithering about whether I can get away with it.

"Are you meeting that gentleman?" asks the maître d'. "The one waving at you from the bar?"

Oh, bugger. I've been spotted, so my options have now declined to one.

I wave back, then make my way across the room.

"Hello," says Mr Nordic, at the same time as I say, "Hi."

Then we both say, "How are you?" at exactly the same time, too.

"Fine," we both answer – also simultaneously – and then Mr Nordic stands up and goes to kiss me on the cheek, at the same time as I bend my head to undo the buttons of my coat. Mr Nordic's kiss thus ends up in thin air a couple of feet above my left ear.

"Shall we try again?" he suggests, so I stand stock-still, one arm free of my coat by now, but the other one still halfway in.

Everything goes fine with the cheek-kissing business this time, until I assume that we're stopping after two kisses, one for each cheek. Mr Nordic seems to have been planning on several more, so his third attempt results in him kissing my right ear. It's more embarrassing than erotic, despite ears supposedly being erogenous zones.

We both laugh, and then he sits back down and asks me what I'd like to drink. I'm still considering my answer when he stands back up again, to help me climb onto the bar stool next to his.

"Would you prefer to have your drinks brought to your table?" asks the barman, who's been watching the various kissing and stool-climbing attempts with interest.

"Yes, please," I say.

Bugger consulting Mr Nordic first, this stool is miles too high for me, and it's impossible to look sophisticated when your feet are swinging miles above the floor.

Once we're settled at our table, we do the names thing – *Will, Hannah – pleased to meet you* – and then we shake

140

hands self-consciously, before leaning back and covertly studying each other while we wait for the menus and drinks to arrive.

I have no idea what to say.

Luckily, Will does. He asks me a volley of questions while I sip my drink and try to work out what to order: What I do for a living? How long have I been internet dating? Do I have any children and how old are they? Do I own my own house or rent? I wonder if he's got a mental checklist and he's scoring my answers as we go along? It's definitely starting to feel a bit like an interview by the time our starters turn up – one of those interviews in which the panel are so po-faced you can't tell whether they like what they're hearing or think it's laughable. As a result, I have no idea whether I'm going to get the job of being Will's second date or not. I don't even know if I want the job, though it is nice to have someone taking such an interest in me – and ordering another bottle of wine already, too.

"Do you like sports?" asks Will, as the waiter clears our plates ready for the main course to arrive.

"Um," I say. "To watch or do?"

I'm not sure that "like" is the right word for the experience of spinning round and round in circles in a boat while looking for an oar, or for being forced to try planking by your ageing aunt, but I hate watching sport even more than I hate doing it.

"Either," says Will, who then proceeds to tell me how much he loves both. That's a lot, judging by how long he talks about it: all the way through the main course and the second bottle of wine. Land-yachting, kite-surfing, surf-surfing, road cycling – you name it, Will enjoys it.

"Well, you do look fit," I say, when he pauses, as if waiting for me to make some sort of comment.

"You do, too," he says, winking, then passing me the dessert menu. As he does so, he runs his fingers lightly along the back of my hand and I recoil, as if I've been given an electric shock.

I excuse myself and go to the loo. While there, I give myself a strict, if drunken talking-to: I am not to make any more comments that could be viewed as double entendres. Not when I don't intend them to be double entendres, anyway. I am also going to change the subject away from sport.

"What's your favourite film?" I say, buttering half the bread roll I forgot to eat earlier on. I need to give my hands something to do, other than to be fondled when they're least expecting it. "Or your favourite actor?"

Will leans back, and closes his eyes while he thinks about it. He looks very attractive, all of a sudden, so I'm really hoping he's not going to pick something like *Dumb and Dumber*.

"Actors: DiCaprio, Nicholson and Brando, of course," he says, finally opening his eyes again.

Oh, my God – I love Marlon Brando, too.

"Mm, yeah," I say. "Especially in *A Streetcar Named Desire*."

Will raises an eyebrow, as if that's an interesting choice.

"Not *Apocalypse Now*?" he says.

Never challenge the opinion of a woman who's drunk too much wine, on top of spending the last two hours off her head on a combination of nerves and adrenalin. She will be predisposed to argue with you, especially when dessert is taking a ridiculously long time to arrive.

"*Last Tango in Paris*," I say, then immediately wish I hadn't.

This is not a competition, and I am supposed to be making Will like me, not arguing with him about Brando's best films. I'm going to shut up right this minute, so – to make sure of that – I butter the other half of the bread roll and stuff most of it into my mouth in one fell swoop. I probably look like a wide-mouthed frog.

"Like butter, do you?" says Will, raising his eyebrows while doing that thing on my hand again.

"Well, these days nutritionists say it's better for you than margarine," I say, desperately trying to get back to single-*entendre* territory.

This is getting out of hand and I have totally lost my nerve. I am going back to the loo, and this time I'm going to phone Eva while I'm there.

"How's it going?" she says.

"Terrible," I say. "I mentioned *Last Tango in Paris*, and then I spread half a ton of butter on my bread and shoved a great wodge of it into my mouth. I don't know what the hell I'm doing."

"Ah," says Eva. "The notorious *Marlon with butter* scene. That was quite something, wasn't it?"

I put her on speakerphone so I can talk while also splashing my face with water. First date nerves are quite enough to cause a hot flush, let alone the *Marlon with butter* scene. (That was censored for good reason.)

"This guy Will seems a lot more experienced at the dating game than I am," I say, as I shake my head to get the water off my face. "*And* he stroked my hand! I moved it, but then he did it again, and now I don't know what to do. He's unnerving me so much I haven't got a clue what I'm saying half the time, and that's making everything ten times worse. I am seriously losing it."

"Well, no one's less experienced than you," says Eva, "so it's good you're learning from an expert, isn't it?"

I don't think it is. I'd prefer to blunder my way through this whole weird dating thing with someone who felt as clueless about it as I do, not someone who's watching me the whole time in a very knowing way.

"He works as a proper designer," I say, "so he was totally unimpressed by my stupid job. And he has young children, too. Do I want to date someone with young kids, when I'm still waiting for Joel to finish growing up? And what if he's expecting sex?"

My voice has risen to a wail by the time I get to that last sentence, which is unfortunate, as – at that moment – the woman who was sitting at the next table walks into the loos and gives me a really funny look. I turn Eva off speakerphone, and clamp the phone to my ear, just in time to hear her telling me I must calm down.

"Look," she says, "all you have to do is take this a step at a time. Eat your pudding while he does all the talking and then call a cab. Don't do anything stupid tonight, like going home with him – just leave him wanting more. Phone me when you get home so I know you're safe."

I take a few deep breaths, then walk back out into the restaurant where I do exactly as she says.

★　★　★

"Text me when you get home," says Will, as he kisses me on the cheek, and then opens the door of the taxi and ushers me in.

"Um, okay," I say, "but why? I'll probably go straight to bed, to be honest."

Will gives me a weird but unreadable look when I mention going to bed, and then he says,

"Why? So I know you got home safely, of course."

That's nice, isn't it? I'm so chuffed by what a gentleman he is, that I don't object when he leans into the cab and kisses me briefly on the lips.

"Until next time," he says, then he slams the door and raises his hand as Mick the taxi driver revs the engine and pulls away from the kerb.

"I see this one went a bit better," he says, "judging by the way he said goodbye."

I lean back against the seat and watch the streetlights as they flicker past.

"You know," I say, "I think it did."

★　★　★

I let myself into the empty house and double-lock the door behind me, and then I get out my phone and start to type.

I'm home. Thank you for a lovely evening.

Then I hit *send* and walk upstairs to bed, where I lie under the covers, thinking about Will and whether he'll want to see me again – and whether I'll want to see him too.

On the one hand, I hated having to make awkward conversation with someone I've never met before – and the sense that I was being vetted – but on the other, it's not as if I've got the option to date someone I know really well, and who doesn't make me anxious, is it? Not when Dan has left me and, anyway, Will does seem nice. As nice as anyone can be when I know next to nothing about him, other than what he's told me himself, both in person and in cyberspace.

The whole internet dating thing's nothing like the real-life kind, though maybe it *is* the real-life kind these days and I'm just hopelessly behind the times. I don't think Joel would bother trying to meet women through the internet, though, not when he can just meet them down the pub or in a club. Maybe it's just for tragic people like me. (I'm pretty sure "tragic" is the word Esther used the other day – not that she's had any luck with men in real life recently.)

Beep, beep, beep.

My phone lights up with a message from Will. Well, I say "message" but the text contains no text, if that isn't the oxymoron of the year.

There's just a string of weird icons that make no sense. God knows why a grown-up would send another grown-up cartoon pictures, instead of using words like a normal person. That's why I keep my reply short and to the point:

???

It's the only thing I can think of in the circumstances, and I'm none the wiser when Will replies with another series of icons, this time of fruit and vegetables. Wtf? There weren't any aubergines in our meals, nor any peaches or bananas. Maybe Will was drunker than I thought, unless he's insane and I just failed to notice until now. I suppose I'd better check.

I'm sorry, I don't know what you mean. Are you all right?

The answer's clear when I get Will's response. This one contains another cartoon-cum-icon thing, but this time it's a face with a sticking-out tongue.

I stare at it in disbelief for several seconds, then make my last text much clearer than any of Will's have been.

Oh, fuck off!

Chapter 20

I'm still fuming about Will's texts this morning when Eva calls.

"Can't talk for long," I say, "I'm running late. I'm on my way to the TV studio, and I've still got to cancel today's rowing lesson with Albert before the interview starts."

"Then speak fast," says Eva. "I can't wait any longer to find out what happened with your date last night."

I sigh and roll my eyes, then remember I ought to keep them on the road.

"Nothing happened," I say. "Except the idiot texted me some fruit and vegetable icons afterwards, and another one with a sticky-out tongue. So then I told him to fuck off."

For some reason, Eva thinks that's so hilarious that she's still choking with laughter when I end the call and manoeuvre into the car park at the TV studio. So much for the sisterhood.

I wave to the Fembot, who's hovering in the entrance to the building, and then I phone Albert several times, but the call goes straight to voicemail, every time. He must be on his way to the lake already, as the signal's so patchy there, so now I don't know what to do. We'd arranged to meet at the lakeside cafe this morning, instead of at Abandon Hope, so maybe he's gone there a bit early, to read his paper and observe the birdlife on the lake. He enjoys that when the weather's nice, like it is today, and he says he's also doing his best to keep the cafe going, as it doesn't seem to be getting many customers these days. He's obviously alone in this admirable endeavour, as when I try to call and leave a message with one of the staff, I discover the phone's been disconnected.

I call Pearl instead, and ask her to walk down to the cafe and give Albert my message. She seems about as un-keen on this idea as it's possible to be, but eventually she agrees, albeit reluctantly. She still doesn't find Albert very interesting, though I can't see that he's any worse than the guys she's been meeting via the internet. The last one asked her if she thought she was fit enough to be his carer, or so she says.

"That reminds me, Pearl," I say. "Have any of your internet dates sent you pictures of fruit and vegetables?"

"Don't be silly, Hannah," says Pearl. "Why on earth would they do that?"

I can't answer, partly because I still don't know, and partly because I'm so distracted by the text I've just received that I hang up on Pearl by accident. As usual, Eva doesn't mince her words.

Those cartoon vegetables were emojis, you muppet, and so was the icon with its tongue sticking out. Will was sexting you, not insulting you. The fruit and vegetables represent body parts, and the face with the sticky-out tongue indicates what he'd like to do to the peach. Look it up if you don't believe me.

I don't have time to look anything up, because it turns out that the Fembot has somehow forgotten to warn me that she and I are expected to join the presenters in dancing along to "Happy" when the credits roll at the end of the programme.

Luckily, that brilliant idea does not go well when we rehearse it, mainly because I'm wearing a narrow skirt and some stupid shoes that Eva lent me, which have ill-fitting sling-backs and absurdly-high heels. The female presenter, Mindy Something-or-other, says my dancing's the funniest thing she's ever seen, but she doesn't think we'll do it on camera, after all.

She's not finding me even remotely funny by the time my phone starts to ring, just as the recording lights go out after the show.

"Someone wasn't listening when they were told to turn their mobile off, were they?" she says.

I assume that's a rhetorical question, so I don't answer and race outside to answer my phone instead. Albert sounds almost as out of breath as I still am, once he starts to speak.

"Don't panic," he says, an entirely futile instruction which works as well as you might expect. "Your aunt's just had an accident."

I open my mouth but no sound comes out (probably due to the combination of too much dancing, combined with panicking), so then I rummage in my bag for the Rescue Remedy, but the bottle's empty. I remind myself that Eva said it doesn't work anyway, then I concentrate on breathing through my nose as Albert explains what's happened to Pearl. Apparently, she tripped over an oar when she arrived at the lake, and landed so awkwardly that Albert thinks her ankle's broken.

"Clearly, the problem with oars runs in the family," he adds.

I ignore that provocative statement, even though I'm finally capable of speech now I know Pearl's not likely to die.

"Where is she now?" I say, so croakily that Albert has to ask me to repeat the question twice, before he replies that she's in hospital.

"The warden took her there in the minibus, once I got her back to Abandon Hope," he adds.

I've no idea how Albert managed to get Pearl anywhere, given how rough the terrain is in that area. There's no way you could drive a vehicle right down to the waterside, or not an ordinary one. Also, I can't see an eighty-year-old man carrying out a fireman's lift without dropping dead from the strain. I'm exhausted just from happy dancing, but Albert says the whole thing was a doddle.

"I used to be a logistics expert, don't forget," he says. "So it was easy, actually. I just rolled Pearl onto my coat, then dragged it by the sleeves while she laid there reclining like Lady Muck. A very bossy Lady Muck."

A very bossy Lady Muck who was only at the lake because I'd asked her to go, so now I feel consumed with guilt, even more than I did when I hacked Dan's *No-kay Cupid* account and then sat by while Eva deleted all his messages. I've probably brought all kinds of bad karma upon myself, so I need to start compensating for all the awful things I've done of late, before anything else happens to someone I love. Joel's accident-prone at the best of times, and he's travelling back from Dan's in Birmingham later on today!

"I'm on my way to the hospital now," I tell Albert.

I'm about to ring off, when he says,

"No hurry, Hannah. Take your time, and make sure you drive more carefully than you row."

No hurry, when Pearl's in a hospital, all by herself? I'd tell Albert exactly what I think of that inconsiderate comment if I had time, especially as it's all too easy to imagine being old, unwell and alone myself since Dan walked out on me.

★ ★ ★

Karma's going to add yet another thing to my list of misdemeanours now: falsely accusing Albert of being inconsiderate. I should have known he wasn't the type, but I wasn't thinking straight.

He's sitting at Pearl's bedside, keeping her company, when the nurse shows me into her cubicle in A&E. Even under the harsh lighting, she looks pretty good for someone with a broken ankle, which is probably because she hasn't got a broken ankle. An X-ray's just confirmed it's intact, but badly sprained.

"You didn't think I'd leave her alone, did you?" asks Albert, when I express astonishment at finding him there. "She'd have done a runner if I had, seeing as she didn't want to come here in the first place. Said old people never get out of hospital alive, but she looks all right to me."

He winks at Pearl and she blows him a kiss, which may

be due to the fact that she banged her head on a log when she fell. One of the nurses explains that's the reason she'll have to stay in overnight.

"Just for observation," she adds. "But we will need to sort out who's going to take care of her after that. She can't go home if there's no one there to look after her, because she won't be fully mobile for quite some time."

"But there *is* someone there," I say. "Pearl lives in a very fancy retirement home, which has a warden and on-site nursing staff. Otherwise, she'd be welcome to come home with me, of course."

Never say things that you don't mean. Karma really doesn't like it, though it would help if it would chop your tongue off before you finish saying profoundly stupid sentences like the one above.

"I'll stay with you, in that case, Hannah," says Pearl, "because I can't stand that bloody warden. She talks about old people as if they're not there."

She gives the nurse a baleful look, which is all the proof I need that she's perfectly *compos mentis*, suspected head injury or not. I wish I could say the same for me.

★   ★   ★

It's almost 10pm by the time I get home from the hospital and recall Eva's text about Will. I read it again, but I'm so knackered I can't be bothered to start Googling emojis, or sexting, or anything else I've never heard of. I can't see the point, anyway, as I'm never going to have the privacy to date someone new once Pearl is here as well as Joel. Talking of Pearl, I suppose I'd better go and check I've got clean sheets for the spare bed for when I bring her home tomorrow. I'll just rest my eyes for a moment or two before I do.

★　★　★

I have no idea how long I sleep for, but it's long enough to dream I'm in the middle of a desert, all alone, with no idea in which direction civilisation lies. There's a shimmering haze along the horizon, and when it finally starts to thin, I see Dan standing a short distance away, surrounded by scantily-clad women in impossible yoga poses. They've all got sucked-in cheekbones and pouty lips, too, just like the real Pamela Anderson. He seems unaware of me, but he's smiling at them, while holding a laptop. Each time he taps one of the keys, another super-flexible beauty pops up and adds herself to the growing crowd of his admirers, while I become more and more consumed with jealousy.

When I wake up, sweaty and shaking, I decide enough is enough, which means deleting my *No-kay Cupid* account, as soon as possible. If I don't, I'm always going to be tempted to check out Dan's profile, and to stare at those weird gold flecks around the deep brown of his eyes, while imagining him looking at someone new the way he used to look at me. I know this for sure, because it's the first thing I've done every morning since I discovered his picture on the site.

It's also the first thing I do when I log on to *No-kay Cupid* to delete my account tonight – and that's an even bigger mistake.

Chapter 21

I do *try* to exert self-discipline, I honestly do. I only look at Dan's profile for a second before I force myself to click back onto mine, in order to work out how to go about deleting it. That's when Dan's photo pops up in one of those instant-message boxes, and almost gives me a heart attack. For one long and highly-traumatic moment, I think it's a Skype box and that Dan can actually see me, so I duck so fast I almost knock myself out on the wooden arm of the couch. I lie flat-out, rubbing my head for a minute or so, before I realise my mistake.

Finally, I sit back up, and peer at the instant message Dan's just sent.

Nice hat. I used to have one just like that.

Why, why, why am I such an idiot? This is how I end up responding to Dan's comment about the hat:

It probably suited you better than it does me.

That's it. That's all I say before I hit *enter*.

I don't know what is wrong with me. It took two hours to decide upon the content of that literary masterpiece, and yet, for some totally unknown reason – like my being certifiable – it still manages to omit the fact that my real name isn't Pammy, or that Dan and I are married to each other. I just make it sound as if we're both talking about the self-same hat, which of course we are. The men in white coats can't be far away.

★ ★ ★

My stupid Pammy comment can't have been as stupid as I thought it was, because Dan replied to me straight away, or rather, *Dannyboythesaxman* replied to Pammy.

What are you hiding under that hat? I'm intrigued.

Eva says that's a polite way of asking whether I'm hideously disfigured, or over ninety, when I text her at midnight to tell her what I've been up to. She calls me back, because she's lost her glasses and can't read a word of what I've written.

"How's Pearl?" she says, after I've finished telling her that I have somehow ended up talking online to my ex-husband, but as someone other than myself.

"Coming to stay with me when she's released from hospital," I say.

I try to sound as if I'm looking forward to it, but Eva isn't fooled.

"Having Pearl and Joel living with you's hardly going to make dating a lot of fun, is it?" she says, slurping at something that must be very alcoholic, judging by the hiccups it then brings on. "Being chaperoned by them, I mean. You're probably better off having a virtual affair, even if it is with your own husband, you absolute muppet. I can't believe you've got yourself into such a mess."

It's all very well for Eva to laugh, but some of us just seem to attract chaos and calamity. We can't all plan our lives with logistical expertise, no matter how much Pearl keeps praising Albert's. She wouldn't stop going on about him, once he left the ward to go and fetch her some toiletries and a nightgown. She's getting quite boring on the subject now, especially for someone who couldn't stand the man until he rescued her.

Anyway, I digress, which also demonstrates a lack of planning ability, I suppose. Back to Eva, agony aunt extraordinaire – by which I mean someone who's nosy, but no help at all.

"I can't keep on talking to Dan online, though, can I?" I say. "There's nothing to be gained from it, and he'd go mad if he found out it was me."

"I reckon you can get away with it for a bit longer," Eva says, once she's thought about it for a while. "That's if you *want* to carry on, of course, though for God's sake don't ask Dan to tell you what went wrong with his marriage, if you do. Eavesdroppers *never* hear anything good about themselves."

Eva's always so certain about everything, isn't she? And her advice always ends up being wrong. I take it when I compose my first reply to Danny, which says:

What am I hiding under my hat? That's for me to know, and you to find out ;-)

Then I recall that Eva's hardly an expert in the marriage stakes, so I do the opposite of what she told me to do when I draft my second reply.

What's your situation, by the way? I know you say it's complicated in your profile description – but that could mean absolutely anything.

I'm not sure which of the two messages is worse when I read them back to myself: the first one with its agonising attempt at flirting and that terrible, winky-faced emoticon; or the second, with its shameless nosiness. Whichever it is, I bet I'll never hear from *Dannyboy* again.

Chapter 22

I don't get to bed until gone 2am when I finally stop talking to Eva on the phone, but then I can't sleep for fretting about what Dan's going to say when he finds out that I am Pammy. I toss and turn for hours and eventually give up at about 5:30am and come downstairs, just in time to crash into Joel, who's blundering about in the dark hallway while trying to locate the light switch. I assume he's struggling with that simple task because he seems so drunk, and it soon becomes clear that he's unlikely to make it safely upstairs by himself. He's too big for me to help him, in case he overbalances and takes us both down, so I lead him to the sofa in the living room and tuck him up under a blanket there instead.

"Thanks, Mum," he says, slurring his words. "Come and talk to me – let's bond."

Why is it that the only time adult sons ever want to talk to you is in the middle of the night when they're roaring drunk? Joel's been so uncommunicative recently, though, that I don't like to turn down any opportunity to find out what's going on with him, however crap his timing is.

"Hang on a sec," I say, then I head to the kitchen and return carrying a glass of water, two paracetamol and a water-soluble Vitamin C tablet, which I drop into the glass and swirl until it ceases fizzing.

Joel's eyes are now closed, but he fumbles the paracetamol capsules into his mouth after denying that he needs them. Then he slurps the liquid down and passes the glass back to me. He doesn't even open his eyes to work out where I'm standing, or check that I've taken hold of the glass properly before letting go of it himself. Imagine feeling you can rely on someone else to that degree! It makes me feel a lot less grumpy about Pearl needing to come and stay with me – as well as bringing back that feeling of dread that I'll end up facing illness alone when I'm as old as her.

"Why are you drinking so much at the moment, Joel?" I say, not really expecting an honest answer. "Are you okay?"

One of Joel's eyes flickers open, then closes again.

"Yeah, I know I'm overdoing it," he says. "I'm just a bit fed up, I guess, and there seems to be something on every night recently, so I suppose I'm bound to be drinking more."

I can see the logic in that to a certain extent, but Joel never used to go out every single night when he was dating Izzy, or not straight from work and continuing through until the early hours, anyway. Even if he did have something planned for the evening, he'd almost always have dinner with me and Dan before he went out. Now he's hardly ever at home.

"Well," he says, when I mention it, "it's not as if it's a bundle of laughs being here these days, is it, Mum? It doesn't feel like home at all with Dad not here, and you looking like a rabbit in the headlights most of the time. It's even weirder when I go to Dad's, especially now he's in a different city. Nothing feels like it used to and it gets me down, so it's better if I'm not around so much. Makes it easier to ignore how much things have changed."

I'm lost for words, and I assume Joel is, too, until his hand reaches out for mine.

"I'll always love you and Dad, Mum," he says. "No matter what happens. This is just a bit tougher than I thought it would be, but I suppose we'll all get over it. Eventually. It would help if you two were talking to each other, though."

I don't trust myself to reply, because I can't tell him that Dan and I *are* talking to each other, but Dan doesn't know we are. I squeeze Joel's hand instead – so hard, it makes him yelp.

★   ★   ★

Joel can't recall anything he said last night, when he finally wakes up, but the Vitamin C and paracetamol combo seems to have done the trick. His hangover isn't too bad at all, so he offers to come with me when I go to the hospital to pick up Pearl.

When we get there, I'm expecting to see her lying in bed, still looking a bit frail and out of her depth, like she did when I left her yesterday, but there's been a transformation overnight. She's a hundred per cent back to her old self now: up, dressed, and ordering the nurses about.

"Don't you go forgetting about that old lady in the corner bed again," she says to one of them. "And don't go thinking no one will notice what happens to her, once I've gone. I'm going to put in a complaint and make sure they don't."

The nurse doesn't reply, though I'm pretty sure she must have heard. She merely sighs as she watches Joel test out the wheelchair intended for Pearl by doing wheelies around the ward. Pearl refuses to swap with him until I insist, and as soon as we exit the lift down from the ward and wheel her into the lobby, she demands to get out of the chair again. Joel and I hover on either side of her as she makes her way slowly towards the main exit on the elbow crutches that she's been loaned. She's rubbish at using them so far, apart from as an imperious pointing device, but not half as rubbish as I turn out to be when she sits down briefly and I give them a try.

I set off along a corridor and almost take a passing phlebotomist out, before a security guard orders me to give the crutches back to Pearl. Then he supervises us closely until we're almost off the premises, while drawing my attention to a poster proclaiming A&E a "zero-tolerance zone".

"That includes zero tolerance of anti-social behaviour, Miss," he adds, which comes as a bit of a shock.

It's been twenty-seven years since anyone called me "Miss", and I can't say I'm too keen on it.

"Ms," I say, at which the guard gives a patronising nod, as if that's exactly what he'd expect someone like me to say.

"Did you see that?" I say to Pearl, but she's not listening.

She's busy telling Joel that we're to take her home to Abandon Hope, because she isn't coming to stay with us after all.

"I can manage perfectly well by myself," she says, "and it'll be much less boring than staying with you two when you're both out at work all day."

"You must be mad," I say, butting in. "You can't be by yourself, not while you're on crutches."

I hand those back to Pearl, who immediately stands up and marches off, as if to prove she can.

We argue about it all the way to the car, but it's only when Pearl's settled in the front seat and I've started the engine that she finally tells me what's going on.

"I won't be on my own," she says. "Albert came by first thing this morning to say he's arranged for the nursing staff at Abandon Hope to help me get up and go to bed, and he's going to keep me company for the rest of each day until I'm mobile again."

I'm so stunned, I don't say anything. I just drive, while Pearl tells us the nurses ignored the cries of a distressed woman with dementia for most of the night. Pearl ended up getting up and hopping across to the old lady's bedside herself, remaining there until it got light.

"I'd be frightened to go back into hospital myself, after witnessing that," she says. "If I didn't have you and Joel to rely on, that is – oh, and Albert, of course."

I wish I could say, "and Dan, of course", when listing the people I could count on to look out for me.

★　★　★

When Joel and I get back from settling Pearl in at Abandon Hope, he throws himself onto the sofa for a "post-hangover nap", so I open my laptop and log on to *No-kay Cupid* and nearly give myself yet another heart attack. Danny's face pops up in a chat box straight away, so now I'm having to talk to him while my laptop's half-closed in case Joel wakes up and spots his dad's photo on the screen.

Danny doesn't bother with my first message, the flirty one. He just answers the nosy second one instead.

I'm recently separated.

It feels horrible, reading that, but at least he's being honest, so I reply in kind.

So am I. How are you finding it?

Silence. Total bloody silence. Danny takes so long to respond that I'm about to give up waiting and go and make something to eat instead, when he finally begins to type again.

Difficult.

There's a short pause, and then the *ping* of another message.

What with all the shagging it involves.

What the fuck? I sit in front of the computer, gawping at the screen in disbelief, until – eventually – this arrives:

Bad joke. What I really meant to say was that you're with people who aren't your family, and you have no real privacy. You either feel you have to go out all the time and leave the house to them, or you end up joining in with their social lives even if you don't like them much. It's either that, or lock yourself in your room to get away.

If Dan keeps this up, I'll soon be feeling sorry for him, even though he's the one who left. I'm already feeling guilty for pretending to be someone else when he seems to be being honest with me, so that's why I make my vow: Pammy will only lie to Danny when it's a hundred per cent unavoidable. Otherwise, she will tell the truth – and she'll start now.

That sounds shitty. I'm still living in the family home, so maybe I've been luckier than I thought.

Chapter 23

It's amazing how the virtual world can stop you feeling lonely in the evenings. I haven't phoned Eva for a couple of days, and I opted out of a lecture on life coaching that Esther wanted me to join her at tonight, because I'm so busy now I've got Dan to talk to – or Danny, anyway.

We continue discussing his living arrangements when I log back on to *No-kay Cupid* straight after work. Joel's watching the Formula One highlights, so the *neeaw-neeaw* sound almost makes it seem as if Dan's right here, rather than talking to me online as *Dannyboy*. He carries on our conversation about his new living arrangements, as if it hadn't been interrupted by sleeping and doing a full day's work at all.

I hated sharing a house at first. It was a struggle trying to keep some shape to my life and not let it spiral out of control.

Out of control, in what sort of way? I hope he doesn't mean he's in danger of becoming a sex addict or something equally horrible to imagine, because imagine it I will – probably between the hours of midnight and 3am. That's normally when the worst Dan-related scenarios occur to me.

I ask *Dannyboy* what he means, then wish I hadn't, until he sends me his reply.

Oh, you know, when you start feeling lonely, and then you think, "Fuck it, I'll just go down the pub for some company, because it's sociable". Then you find yourself propping up the bar like one of those sad old gits you always swore you'd never become.

What, the ones who chat up the barmaid, while telling her their wives didn't understand them?

So much for Eva's *don't-ask-about-Dan's-marriage* instruction. I figured if I approached the subject elliptically, it wouldn't count.

Dan doesn't seem to think it counts, either, because he doesn't answer my question. He's already moving on.

Motivating yourself to do less-destructive things in your spare time is hard, when you don't have anyone specific to do them with. But I'm getting better at it now.

I start to type, "I wish I was", but then pause to consider. I did swear I'd tell the truth as Pammy, after all, even when doing so involves creative thinking, like when Danny asked for a photo of me without the hat last night. I said I couldn't send him one, because I couldn't risk being identified, in case it led to anyone discovering where I worked. That was entirely true, if you change "anyone" to "him" but, anyway, I digress.

Am I getting better at doing things by myself? I suppose I am, though "by myself" is a bit misleading. Most of the things I do are either with Eva, Esther or Pearl in tow, or with Albert, of course, where rowing's concerned. Drawing and gardening are the only activities I engage in when I'm completely on my own, apart from showering, sleeping and sitting around feeling sorry for myself – and messaging Danny as Pammy, of course.

At least I've got friends in real life now, though, haven't I? That's a definite improvement on when Dan and I first split up. And I've even been known to spend whole evenings socialising, rather than watching TV. All I need now is to start enjoying them.

I cross out, "I wish I was", and then tell Danny I think I'm getting better at doing things by myself, though not by much. Then I ask what made it easier for him, and that's when he astonishes me.

Oh, I don't know. Finding new interests, I suppose, or making plans to do things I've always wanted to, like going to China.

China? Dan wants to go to *China*? That's news to me, as he's never mentioned it to me, not once in all the years we spent together. What with the fact that he's talking about how he feels, and that he's also someone with dreams and interests I'd either forgotten he had, or never even knew about, I'm starting to wonder if he and Danny are one and the same.

Unless married Dan isn't the same as the unmarried version. A not-exactly-comfortable thought.

★   ★   ★

I've spent so much time talking to Danny over the last week or so, that I haven't been concentrating on anything else, but I'm trying to be more focused today. I'm having lunch with Esther in the courtyard of a cafe just down the road from HOO, because she doesn't want the Fembot to know that I'm helping her with the top-secret mission she's still working on: *Project Get Esther Promoted ASAP*. She's trying to come up with ways to attract more *Halfwits* users, but it's proving a bit of a struggle so far, probably because our existing users are so bonkers they put prospective new ones off.

"I asked the rest of the team to email me their suggestions privately," says Esther, as she starts to munch an "artisan" scotch egg, "but none of them bothered to get back to me. Honestly, they're such a bunch of shits."

"Ah," I say.

The rest of the team aren't too keen on Esther, not least because they know she thinks they're a bunch of shits, but I can't exactly tell her that.

"I'll think of some suggestions now," I say, "while I eat."

I do intend to follow through, but it's such a lovely day that I get a bit distracted. After I've eaten my Caprese salad, I sit basking in the sun that's flooding the courtyard and it makes me feel so relaxed that my mind just starts to wander – to *Dannyboy*, and how much he seems to like talking to Pammy. Before I know it, I've closed my eyes, so I can concentrate on picturing his profile photo, and then I start humming a song he recommended I download a few nights ago.

"You're not even trying," says Esther, interrupting my reverie. "I don't know what's the matter with you, this last few weeks. You seem absurdly happy for no good reason, as far as I can tell. You never seem to want to go out in the evenings any more, either, even though I keep suggesting things for us to do."

I haven't told Esther about Danny, because I *know* she wouldn't approve, so formulating a reply to what she's just said proves quite beyond me. Luckily, she only paused for breath, and doesn't notice.

"You haven't even had any more dates since that emoji guy, have you?" she continues. "I don't know what you're playing at."

I don't either, seeing as I've just realised that she's right: I haven't had a single date since Mr Insulting Fruit and Veg.

★   ★   ★

I can't stop thinking about what Esther said earlier while I'm driving over to Abandon Hope for my rowing lesson tonight. She's made me realise I'm concentrating all my energies on someone who has no idea who I really am, and who wouldn't dream of talking to me if he did. And a virtual relationship isn't the same as a real one, is it?

Talking of relationships, I have no idea what's going on between Pearl and Albert, but every time I go round to her flat these days, they're sitting there together, just like they are when I arrive tonight. They look really happy, too, though Pearl tells me to mind my own business when I ask her if they're dating, during one of Albert's frequent visits to the loo.

"We oldies like our privacy," she says, "so mind your own business, Hannah. We don't feel the need to share our every thought with the world via that silly social media that you lot are so addicted to."

She's got a point, now I come to think of it. That's another of the reasons the rest of the *Halfwits* team aren't keen on Esther, because she once held forth about how "moronic" they were on her Facebook page, without realising she'd set her posts to "public".

★   ★   ★

Albert obviously shares Pearl's view about oversharing being undignified because, later, when I try to sound him out about how things stand with Pearl once we're alone together at the lake, he's having none of it. In fact, he tells me to "shut up and concentrate".

"You can't afford to talk *and* try to row, Hannah," he adds. "Not when you still spend every lesson going round in circles."

That's a metaphor for my life, isn't it? I keep spotting *those* everywhere at the moment – and getting distracted by them, too. Now I've dropped my bloody oar.

"Not again," says Albert, reaching for the boathook to pull the oar back in. I apologise and assure him that I'm determined that, one of these days, I'm not only going to learn to row forwards, I'm also going to keep hold of both oars while doing so.

Albert clearly doesn't think that's going to happen today, as he says I seem too distracted to row, so he suggests we call it a day and have a coffee in the cafe by the lake instead. I can see why he likes it so much once we take our seats as, although it looks really run down, the location's gorgeous. How many retirement homes have a lake like this close by? The Abandon Hope lot have no idea how lucky they are. I'll be broke when I retire, not least because the management of *Halfwits* pride themselves on running such a young and "vibrant" company that no member of staff would be seen dead asking for a pension scheme. I'd been relying on Dan's for when I retired, but that's out of the window now, and I doubt Danny could give his to Pammy, even if he wanted to – not when she doesn't exist.

I'll probably end up living in a tent by the time I'm Pearl's age, and relying on soup kitchens and handouts for my basic needs. Mind you, I'd prefer the tent to taking my chances in some of the old people's homes you hear about on the news: the ones where cruel, stupid "carers" abuse vulnerable old people who haven't got anyone to look out for their interests. That'll be me, if Joel doesn't remember he's supposed to visit me occasionally, and I bet he *will* forget. Meanwhile, as I rot away, alone and unloved, *Dannyboy* won't know I'm there, Dan won't care, and I won't have met anyone new, because I've been concentrating all my energies on an online romance that can't ever become reality.

A wave of sheer terror washes over me and I become breathless and start to cry. In front of Albert, Mr Dignified.

"I thought splitting up with Dan might be liberating, once I got used to it," I wail, in-between hiccuping and sniffling while Albert sits back and sips his coffee, patting my hand occasionally. "But it isn't at all, it's just scary. When he first left me, I was almost too frightened to get out of bed, and I still have days like that now. What if I'm going to be alone for the rest of my life? I don't think I can cope with it."

"That's because you're behaving as if you're helpless, Hannah," says Albert, then – just as I'm about to glare at him – he adds, "I felt like that when my late wife died."

That stops me in my tracks. What a pathetic, self-obsessed idiot I am. Albert's wife is dead. Dead. And Dan is very much alive, unless *Dannyboy* is a ghost with access to a home computer. I should be ashamed of myself for being so crass, and how on earth did I forget that Albert is a widower? People like me deserve a slap.

I start grovelling, but Albert brushes my apologies aside.

"How do you cope?" I ask, when he's finished reassuring me that I haven't mortally offended him.

He stares out across the lake, while he considers my question. His expression is inscrutable, and he takes so long to reply that I'm starting to wonder whether he ever will by the time he eventually starts to speak.

"I suppose I haven't given up hope of being happy again," he says. "And nor should you. But in the meantime, maybe you should concentrate on getting your confidence up, so you'll believe you *can* be independent, and maybe even enjoy it a little, too? I know that would make your Aunt Pearl happy. She worries about you, you know."

"Does she really?" I ask, watching as a huge white swan swims into view, followed by a brood of fluffy, grey swanlets, or whatever they're called. Crying always reduces my brain to toast.

"She does indeed," says Albert, following my gaze. "Much more than you might think. She just doesn't show her feelings much. Now shall we feed those swans?"

★ ★ ★

The sun is setting by the time I walk back from the lake with Albert and pop in to say goodbye to Pearl, who confirms she really has been worrying about me recently.

"Joel says you're spending a lot of time online in the evenings," she adds, "which can't be good for you, or him."

"He's a fine one to talk," I say, stung by Pearl's criticism of my mothering skills. As if it's not enough to have failed as a wife, is she saying I'm a crap mother, too?

Pearl denies the accusation, as soon as I've finished making it.

"No, of course I'm not saying that," she says, while patting me on the shoulder – a bit tentatively, as if I'm a dog that might all too readily bite her hand. "I just think you're a bit oblivious to what's going on with him, because you're so bogged down in your own problems."

I don't know what to say, so there's a brief silence, which is not a comfortable one.

"Not that I blame you for that, my dear," adds Pearl, some-what hastily. "It's been a difficult time for all of you. I just think you ought to keep an eye on Joel, as he seems to be going a bit off the rails to me. First he gets rid of that lovely girlfriend of his and then he says relationships are for idiots, or something like that."

"I think the word he actually used was 'suckers'," says Albert, from his place in the wingback chair nearest the window. It's turned towards the view and obscures its occupant so thoroughly that I'd forgotten Albert was even here.

I don't know if that *is* what Joel said, but I feel as if I've been sucker-punched. I knew all of this stuff, of course – and I *have* worried about it occasionally – but I didn't think Joel wanted to talk to me about it, except the other night when he was drunk, so I haven't tried to persuade him to.

I sigh, then apologise to Pearl for snapping at her.

"You're right," I say. "I am worried about him, especially how much he seems to be drinking, though what can I do? I can't make Dan come back."

My voice wobbles a bit, which Pearl and Albert both politely pretend to ignore, then Albert goes off to fetch something from his flat, presumably to give me time to get myself back under control.

When I stop crying, Pearl passes me a tissue, and then she says, "No, you can't make Dan come back, my dear – much to my regret, as well as yours – but has it occurred to you that Joel might cope better if he could see *you* were? He's a good boy, really, and he loves his mum."

He is, and hopefully he does, so I promise Pearl I'll make an effort and then I change the subject to what's going on with her.

"So, talking of getting back into the swing of things, how's your internet dating going?" I say.

Pearl looks a bit uncomfortable for a second, and then she says, "I thought I'd told you. I've given it up."

Honestly, talk about "don't do as I do, do as I say"!

I accuse Pearl of being hypocritical, and then she tells me she got tired of all the men she encountered on the dating site.

"They all seemed content to just sit in their chairs and fade away," she adds, "but I've got a bit more life left in me than that, and I wanted a man in the same position."

"Albert seems to fit that bill," I say, to which Pearl makes no comment other than to raise an eyebrow, and then she passes me a slice of the cake Albert brought round for her yesterday.

It's coffee cake, which I love, so my "get fit" plan goes out of the window, and by the time I've finished stuffing my face, Pearl's brought the conversation back round to me.

"Don't give up, like those sad old men," she says. "Not with what you and Dan have put yourselves through in order to be happier. You can't expect things to improve overnight, but one thing's for sure, they won't ever improve if you keep spending all your time on a computer."

I know she's right, but that's what's so annoying, so I decide to leave before she can share any more irritating pearls of wisdom. I take the dirty cake plates through to the kitchen, wash them up, then kiss Pearl and pick up my coat.

"Things change when you least expect them to, Hannah," she says, as I walk towards her front door. "If being married to a diplomat taught me anything, it taught me that."

I open the door before I can be subjected to any more United Nations-style efforts to resolve my problems, especially if they involve giving up Danny to date other men.

Chapter 24

I've been trying to think of the positive things in my non-virtual life since my pep-talks with Pearl and Albert, but Eva's not making it easy tonight. I'm right in the middle of describing a narrow escape Pammy had when she made a comment to Danny about his son's age (which Danny was positive he'd never told her), when she interrupts.

"Talking about yourself in the third person is the first sign of madness, Hannah," she says, unscrewing the cap of the bottle of wine she's brought with her and pouring us both a generous glass.

She insists we take those upstairs to my bedroom, where I sit on the bed while she flings open the doors to the wardrobe.

"Talking of madness," she adds, "we'd better get down to business if you want me to help you choose what to wear for this stupid supper club idea you've had."

I can't see why it's such a stupid idea, but Eva says supper clubs are a complete and utter waste of time for single women. That sounds like the voice of experience, but I ignore it, anyway. If I'm to make Joel feel better about the situation with Dan, I need to start being more independent, socialising by myself, and coping with it. That's why I've banned both Eva and Esther from coming with me to my first supper club.

Eva was very happy to be spared the bother, Esther far less so.

"But I need to meet men, too, Hannah," she said, when I told her about it at work earlier on today. "And you're more outgoing than me, so it's easier if I go to things with you."

"Didn't exactly pay off for us when we went clubbing, did it?" I said. "Not when everyone kept calling us Siamese twins. I still don't understand how we both ended up wearing the same dress."

Esther changed the subject when I mentioned the identical dress mystery, so that got me off the hook. Now all my clothing's about to be in much the same position, as Eva's pulling everything I own out of the wardrobe, and piling it onto the bed.

When she's finished, she stands back to survey the result.

"You need to chuck out half your wardrobe, Hannah," she says, and then she informs me that I need a makeover, asap.

I ask what that would involve, exactly, but she's not listening. She's staring at something propped up on my dressing table instead. Oh, bugger, it's the photo frame.

Eva picks it up, studies it closely for a split second, and then says, "Who's this, Hannah? Secret lover?"

I roll my eyes, defiantly, and refuse to answer her. She knows perfectly well who it is, even though she's never seen him before. It's Dan, of course.

"It's Dan, isn't it?" says Eva, when it becomes clear I'm

refusing to admit it. She contemplates the photo for a moment or two, and then she adds, "I can see what you saw in him, but what's he doing on your bedside table, for God's sake? You two split up."

"Don't you think I know that?" I say, making a grab for the frame but missing when Eva jerks her hand away. "I just forgot it was there. Give it to me and I'll get rid of it, if that'll make you feel better."

"It's you who ought to feel better after putting it out of sight," says Eva. "I thought you were supposed to be moving on?"

She raises a reproachful eyebrow as I yank open the bottom drawer of the bedside table and put the frame inside. I'll reinstate Dan tonight, when Eva's gone. I occasionally blow him a kiss, just before I go to sleep.

"I *was* moving on," I say, "I mean, I *am*. Now can we please not talk about Dan any more?"

Eva agrees and changes the subject as we make our way downstairs. We spend the next hour or so sitting curled up on the sofa, singing along to my old "Soul Weekender" CDs, and trying to work out what sort of haircut I should have, as part of the makeover that she's planning. It's much harder inserting a photo of yourself into those online hairstyle templates than it looks, and eventually Eva loses patience with my failed attempts and takes over the process herself. She hands me a magazine to read to keep me occupied while she does it, the latest edition of *Viva Vintage*.

God knows how someone as undomesticated as Eva can edit a magazine that seems to glorify all the skills from which Pearl and my mum were so desperate to disassociate themselves in the

1970s, when they were raising their consciousnesses and burning their bras all over the place. (Mum got away with the bra-burning as she had a minuscule bosom like mine, but Pearl says the Women's Lib movement should have warned members the effects gravity would have on bosoms as pronounced as hers.)

The magazine's content may be a bit puzzling to someone my age, but the overall effect is aesthetically pleasing. In fact, the photography manages to make the most mundane household objects appear beautiful, and the shots of cupcakes are really enticing. The *Halfwits* cupcake crew are going to have to up their game to compete with those.

I read the magazine from cover to cover, while Eva messes about slotting my head into various templates. There's even a garden section, which surprises me. I haven't told Eva how much I've been getting into gardening recently, because I'd assumed she'd disapprove, but now I pass her my latest drawing of the violas, as a test.

"Nice," she says, tilting her head this way and that, as she studies it. "Reminds me of a vintage botanical print. Can you draw any kind of flower, or just violas?"

"I don't know," I say. "They're the only ones I've tried. Doesn't gardening make me sound old and tragic, though?"

"No," says Eva. "It makes you sound young and hip. Gardening's taking off in a big way among the young, you know."

Maybe that's why Joel tried to persuade me to give him a flowerbed for his personal use. I refused, because I assumed he wanted to grow cannabis.

★　★　★

"Join our singles' supper club and enjoy delicious food while finding love," the advert said. It should have added, "But only if you're a lesbian."

Fifteen women – and only three men. *Three* of them, for goodness' sake! I may as well have left my hair unwashed.

The hostess tries her best to make a joke of it, though none of the other women present seem to think it's very funny. There's a fair bit of muttering about taking people's bookings under false pretences, and someone even mentions the Trade Descriptions Act.

"Oh, let's not lose our sense of humour," says the hostess, in an attempt to quell dissent. "We'll have one man per table, and then they can swap seats between each course. It'll be fun, like musical chairs."

Even the men look uncomfortable with this idea, and I can't think of anything more humiliating for the women. If this is what socialising by yourself as a single, middle-aged female is going to be like, then it's the bloody pits. No wonder Eva said I was being stupidly optimistic about the supper club. The only highlight is the food, as the conversation's so dull it makes me want to rip my own ears off and dip them into the cheese fondue the hostess described as "something to get everyone to interact".

The men aren't interacting at all. They don't need to. As the wine flows, they just sit back in their chairs, smiling benignly, while the women try harder and harder to earn their undivided attention. Honestly, what with some of them trying to look as if they're fellating chunks of bread dipped in cheese, and others trying to feed them to the men, it's getting more and more nauseating by the second. By the time the main course is served, the air's so thick with sexual innuendo that I can hardly breathe.

I just keep quiet and eat my way steadily through each course, while drinking too much wine and doodling caricatures of the other guests on a pile of spare paper napkins I found lying around on the end of my table. I've got enough material for a whole Hogarthian series of paintings by the time I get careless about covering up the evidence with my arm, at which point one of my table-mates spots the sketches and then shows them to everyone else.

It's an awkward moment, to say the least, one that demands a convincing reason to make a rapid escape. I can only think of a wholly-unconvincing one, but luckily, all the guests are so absorbed in arguing about which doodle represents whom that none of them notice I'm answering a phone that hasn't rung. They don't even react when I ask my imaginary caller, "So it's definitely an emergency?"

The only person who shows any interest in me at all is the hostess, and she seems almost pleased when I apologise and tell her I have to leave immediately. Maybe she's worked out that the half-naked table-dancing doodle is of her.

Chapter 25

God, this single life involves a lot of drinking *and* a lot of hangovers. I'm almost late for work this morning, because it takes me so long to get going, and then I make it into the Fembot's presentation just in time, only to realise I've left my sunglasses at home. The rest of the team have all remembered theirs, except for Esther, because her team didn't tell her they're essential for whenever the Fembot dims the lights.

As soon as she switches the projector on, her over-whitened teeth fluoresce. The effect hurts your eyes after a while, so by the time the meeting finishes, Esther's are streaming with tears.

"Why didn't you warn me?" she says, as we help ourselves to some of today's batch of cupcakes: more breasts in frilly half-cup bras.

"I meant to phone you last night," I say, "but then I ran out of time to get to the supper club."

Of course, that leads Esther to demand the whole story, by which time the Fembot's joined us, so she gets to hear all about my latest disastrous foray into the dating world as well.

"I'm never going to find a new man," I say, biting into another pink-iced breast.

The Fembot stands back, hand on hip, and looks me up and down for what feels like hours. I'm squirming under the scrutiny by the time she nods, as if she's finally worked out something that's been bothering her.

"What about Botox, Hannah," she says, "or a face lift? Have you considered either of those?"

"I'm not filling my face full of poison, and going all shiny," I say, "and I can't afford a face lift."

I don't add that I wouldn't get one, even if I could. I'm pretty sure no one thinks people who've had loads of plastic surgery are younger than they really are. They just think they've obviously had plastic surgery, so they *must* be older than they look.

"Well, what about a boob job, then?" says the Fembot. "I can recommend my surgeon."

Looking over her shoulder, I can see some of the staff high-fiving each other, and money changing hands, as yet another Fembot-related bet is settled. I shake my head: No. Dan never liked big boobs, and surely he can't be the only one?

The Fembot never gives up once she gets started on something. She twirls a couple of times, while clicking her pen against her teeth, which probably accounts for her next suggestion.

"Teeth-whitening?" she says.

★　★　★

I'm trying not to chat to Danny so much these days, especially while I'm at work, so I spend this lunchtime answering questions on *Halfwits* instead, though the quality of those isn't getting any better. The first ten I check out are variations on a theme: "What's a cute thing to say to a woman on a first date?"

"Can't these idiots think of anything for themselves?" I ask Esther, who's also spending her break answering questions in the hope that'll help her get promoted.

She's now *Halfwits'* self-appointed allergy specialist, and is munching through her sandwiches while inspecting photos of other people's skin complaints.

I don't know why she's bothering as, not only are the pictures repulsive, but the Fembot almost always goes to the gym at lunchtimes so she won't have a clue whether Esther's working overtime or not. I point that out, but Esther's taking the whole thing so seriously that she just shakes her head to shut me up, then returns to the answer she's been working on.

"You're no fun any more," I say, spinning my chair round and round, and circling my ankles while I try to recall my first date with Dan, and what he said.

To be honest, it wasn't supposed to be a date at all, seeing as we were just friends at the time, and not the kind with benefits. We'd first met in life-drawing class and got on so well, we often ended up hanging out together late at night in the art school bar. Dan made me laugh, and he wasn't precious about his work like so many of our classmates were.

"It's only sculpture," he'd say. "It's not as if I'm saving the world, or anything useful, is it?"

He was a good sculptor, though, but even better at playing the sax. That's where we'd been when things changed between us: at a gig he and his band were playing. If you want to blame anything for what happened afterwards, then blame the saxophone. It ought to be called the *sexophone*, given the effect it had on me, though Dan always ascribes the whole thing to the new dress I was wearing.

It was one of those back-to-front mid-'80s dresses, a simple, fine-knit jersey shift in midnight blue, with buttons all the way down the back.

I thought it was fantastic, which was a good job as it had cost most of the money I'd earned from painting a highly-flattering portrait of the (really ugly) local mayor, but Dan didn't say anything about the dress all night – not until he'd walked me back to my flat, where we drank a bottle of wine while lying on giant floor cushions and listening to Van Morrison. (*Inarticulate Speech of the Heart*, in case you're wondering.)

Anyway, when it began to get light, Dan said he ought to be going, but then we stood talking for ages in the hallway, still making far more eye contact than had ever been normal for us in the past. I couldn't seem to tear my eyes away from his, and he seemed to be having much the same problem, but eventually I turned around to switch off the light (because by then the sun was fully-risen), and that's when he said, "God, that dress." Then he kissed me on the nape of my neck and just kept on going – downwards.

The rest, as they say, is history, achieved without the so-called "help" of *Halfwits* users.

I type, "Say, 'God, that dress'" into the answer box on the screen in front of me, and then hit *post*.

★ ★ ★

When I get home from work, I tell Joel all about how stupid today's questions were, and – naively – expect some sympathy. He listens fairly attentively (for him) but, when I've finished, he just looks bewildered.

"So, let me get this straight, Mum," he says, as if he has no idea about the company I've worked at for the last God knows how long. "It's a website. People log on and ask complete strangers to answer a question, and that's it?"

"Um, yes," I say, not quite sure where this is going, but not much liking the sound of it.

"Well, then, why the hell don't these halfwits, as you call them, just ask someone they know for the answer?" says Joel. "Or, even better, Google it?"

I spot some weeds in the garden that urgently require pulling up, so I rush outside, and close the back door firmly behind me. That was the one question I've never worked out the answer to, despite Googling it myself. Clearly my love life isn't the only aspect of my existence that could best be described as utterly futile.

★ ★ ★

I do wish the Fembot wouldn't appear from nowhere so often – especially when I'm in the ladies' toilets. Today, she comes click-clacking across the floor on her Louboutins and then raps on the door of the cubicle in which I'm mulling over what to do about my love life, now I've decided it's as futile as my job. She's obviously been considering exactly the same thing for the last few days, since I ruled out her suggestions for self-improvement.

"I've been thinking about what we were talking about the other day, Hannah," she says, through the door. "You know, about how you're going to find a new man. Have you thought about blind dates, at all?"

I sigh, then open the door so I can see the Fembot's face, just to check if she's being mean and implying only a blind person would be willing to date an unreconstructed me. Her expression is uncharacteristically kindly, though, so I try to avoid assuming the worst on the basis of past experience.

"No, I haven't thought about it," I say, eventually. "But only because it hasn't occurred to me before. Why are you asking, anyway?"

"Because I know the perfect man for you," says the Fembot. "Shall I arrange a date?"

There's no time to think because, at that moment, someone else comes in and starts spraying vanilla Impulse everywhere and the Fembot motions that we should leave. It's not as if there's much to think about, anyway. I'm not getting anywhere by myself.

I take as deep a breath as the choking clouds of body spray permit and then I say, "Yes, please. Go for it."

I ignore the image of *Dannyboy* that immediately springs to mind.

Chapter 26

Maybe I *can* find romance without having to go online: I've got a date tomorrow night! The Fembot lives up to her motto that if you want something done, you should ask a busy person. Late this afternoon, she informs me that it's all arranged. I'm to meet the guy she's set me up with at 8pm, at a new restaurant in town.

"I think it's called *Orgasmic*," she adds, loud enough for my entire team to hear, so now I'm never going to live *that* down.

I do my best to rise above it, anyway, mainly by pretending I can't hear the snorts of stifled laughter coming from behind the screen that separates my side of the long desk from where the majority of my team have been ordered to sit today, as part of the Fembot's hot-desking experiment.

"Is the food there any good?" I ask, hoping it won't involve anything too messy, like spaghetti in a sauce or anything containing bits of spinach. I always get those stuck between my teeth.

"I don't know," says the Fembot. "*Orgasmic*'s pescatarian, I think, but the Paleo diet's what I'm on at the moment."

That shuts me up completely as I have no idea what the Paleo diet is, so I turn back to my computer and Google it, while everyone else packs away their belongings and then says goodbye. When the search results pop up, they prove more interesting than I'm expecting, because the Paleo diet promises to improve your libido. I know I don't need that at the moment, because sex is the one thing talking to Danny in cyberspace still doesn't involve, other than in the dreams I sometimes have about him afterwards, but maybe this date will turn out to be someone I *can* use my libido on, whether it's been improved or not.

Christ, it's possible I may have sex tomorrow! I'd better go home, right now. I've only got this evening to shave and/or wax everything in sight, paint my toenails *and* get an early night. I need all the beauty sleep I can get.

★ ★ ★

Is there no end to the indignities of growing older? I'm trying to shave my bikini line – an activity that's getting ever-more hazardous as my eyesight gets poorer, along with my flexibility – when I spot a clump of prickly white hairs sticking out, and at very peculiar angles, too. *White* hairs, for goodness' sake! Now not only do I risk inflicting female genital mutilation on myself every time I need a tidy-up down there, due to the vision problem, but I also need to find out whether you can dye your pubic hair without getting chemical burns.

I phone Eva to check, and she tells me to "go to a beauty salon and get the whole thing waxed, like any normal person would". I say that I see nothing normal about stripping off in front of a judgemental and probably spotty teenager wielding instruments of torture in the form of waxed strips, and Eva informs me I'm being "even more ridiculous than usual".

"No one has pubic hair these days, you idiot," she adds.

"What, *none*?" I ask.

How ridiculous must that look on someone of my age? There you are, all smooth and bald as a pre-pubescent down below, but with an obviously-middle-aged face looming above. Disturbing isn't the word for the image I've just conjured up.

"Well, put a bag over your head if you're so paranoid about the discrepancy," says Eva, who is the most unsympathetic person I have ever met. "Or grow your head hair even longer, so you can cover your face with it during The Act."

Only Eva can capitalise spoken words, as well as written ones, and I'm not going to take her advice, anyway. I'm *not*. I don't even need to be worrying about any of this stuff just yet, now I come to think of it, as it would be stupid to sleep with my blind date on the first night, however "perfect" the Fembot says he is for me. I'm going to take the whole thing slowly, and see what happens.

Also, I always swore I would never sleep with a man whose name was Nigel. *Nigel!*

★   ★   ★

I haven't been able to concentrate all day today, and I'm a nervous wreck now I'm back at home. Tonight's the night, to quote Rod Stewart. (I don't even like Rod Stewart, which only goes to prove the state I'm in.)

I've tried Kalms, gallons of Rescue Remedy, and I've also been muttering "Om" every few seconds since I began to get ready, but none of those things are calming me down effectively. In fact, the "Om" thing's just making me hoarse, but it's safer than the alternative, which would be to hit the gin. I can't afford to do that, not only because I can't risk alcohol-induced palpitations to add to the anxiety-induced ones I've already got, but also because I need to look as if there's nothing to be nervous about. I haven't told Joel I've got a date, and he's hanging around the house and watching me like a hawk.

"Where are you off to tonight, Mum?" he asks, when I tell him that I'm going out.

"Cinema with Esther," I say. "Won't be late, though I suppose we might have a couple of drinks afterwards."

I cross my fingers while I'm lying to my beloved (but annoying) son, but get punished for it anyway. Joel chooses that moment to mention Dan.

"You should see the film Dad was telling me about the other night when I was on the phone to him," he says. "He said it was brilliant, so bear that in mind, if you haven't already decided what to see."

I nod, but am incapable of speech. The last thing I want is to bear in mind *anything* to do with Dan tonight. Not when I'm about to go on a date with another man, let alone another man whose name is Nigel. Dan would really take the piss, if he knew, and so would Danny, if Pammy told him about it – which she's not going to.

If things go well tonight, and Nigel and I end up being an "item", he's going to have to change his name entirely, seeing as diminutives won't solve the problem. In fact, they're worse. Imagine Joel saying to Dan, "Mum's new boyfriend's name is Nige," or, even worse, "Nidge"! I'd rather not imagine it, actually, as I can already visualise Dan's expression.

I say a few more "Oms", and tell myself the best thing to do is wait and see how Nigel and I get on. If we end up becoming a couple, I'll choose an appropriate nickname for him (preferably one that doesn't contain any of the letters that make up *Nigel*), and then I'll refer to him by that.

Now my taxi's here, so I'd better go. Ouf. Deep breaths, Hannah – deep, deep breaths.

Chapter 27

I get to the restaurant before my date has arrived, so I pop to the loo and spend a few minutes collecting myself and breathing into a paper bag, because the deep-breaths thing seems to have caused me to hyperventilate. Then, I chew three pieces of Wrigleys Extra simultaneously, while I sort out my windblown hair, then spit them into the bin and squirt myself generously with Rive Gauche. Then I remember Dan bought that for me, so I wash it off again, and walk out scentless and half-witless into blind date land.

The waitress shows me to a table and I sit and wait. My hands become clammier with every second that passes, until finally, someone approaching the table from behind me says, "Hannah?"

I turn round, and there he is. Nigel. In all his glory.

You know how I said I was going to choose a nickname for him? Well, now I have. It's Gandalf.

"Don't judge people on their looks, Hannah," I instruct myself — in my head, obviously. I'm not *that* bonkers, though I am almost shocked enough by my date's appearance to say it out loud. Nigel's got a ponytail. Not even a proper pony-tail, but one of those stupid ones that looks as if he decided to start cutting his hair himself, got all the way around the sides, then couldn't quite reach the bit at the back. It's tragic.

He sits down opposite me, which is an improvement as now I can't see the thing coming out of the back of his head, though I still can't forget it's there. Maybe a double gin will help, though Gandalf looks a bit surprised and disapproving when I order it.

"I thought we'd be drinking wine," he says. "I'm a bit of a connoisseur, so I was looking forward to recommending something you'd enjoy."

I'd enjoy taking scissors to his hairy protrusion, but I don't mention it. Instead, I change my order to a single gin, which I describe as "an aperitif", and then I allow bossy boots Gandalf to choose the wine. I'm pretty sure he'd like to tell me what to eat as well, but there's only so much I'm willing to do to placate his ego. And what an ego it turns out to be.

We spend the first hour talking about his exciting career in teaching. The *exciting* bit was Gandalf's description, not mine, and if he bores his students half as much as he bores me, I should think he's singlehandedly responsible for the UK's truanting problem. In fact, I'm not entirely convinced Gandalf doesn't think he's teaching a student while he eats, as the way he speaks to me is so self-important and full of certainty. I try not to compare him with Dan, but I do keep praying for just one amusing comment, just *something* that will make me laugh and imply I'm not just here to provide Gandalf with a captive audience. What was the Fembot thinking when she described this tedious man as "perfect" for me? Am I as boring and pompous as he is, or something? No wonder Dan left me, if I am.

I've been eating the whole time Gandalf's been talking, so I finish my meal ages before he does, which thankfully makes him shut up for a bit while he catches up. The sudden silence brings its own problems, though, as now I have to talk to him and I can't think of a word to say.

I excuse myself and visit the loo, where I phone Eva, as I promised I would if Gandalf turned out to be a serial killer. I'm not one hundred per cent certain he isn't, as he's certainly killing the art of conversation, and if he does the same thing to every woman he meets, then that's the "serial" bit sorted, too.

Eva doesn't answer, so she's obviously forgotten she's on bodyguard duty. I leave a message.

"If you can die of boredom, then you need to get me out of here," I say.

She doesn't call back in the next five minutes so eventually I have no choice but to head back to the table, where Gandalf's studying the dessert menu, and being rudely offhand to the waitress. I hate people who treat waiting staff like that. They've obviously never had to do the job themselves, unlike me and Dan. We both worked our way through art school by waiting tables, and we still remember what it was like. That's why we always insist on tipping, even though Joel keeps making us watch that scene in *Reservoir Dogs*, the one where Mr Pink asks why he should tip waiters when he's not expected to tip the guy who sells him shoes. (Joel claims it's the general principle he agrees with, and that it has nothing to do with selling shoes himself.)

"Zabaglione, for both of us," says Gandalf to the waitress. I haven't even looked at the menu yet, but I love Zabaglione, so I don't object. Maybe I have more in common with Gandalf than I thought, so I resolve to be nicer to him, even though he still seems incapable of saying "please" or "thank you" to waiting staff.

"What do you do in your free time?" I ask, while we wait for our puddings.

I wish I hadn't. Gandalf's obsessed with the works of Tolkien. Oddly appropriate given his new nickname, but even more boring to listen to than his droning on about school inspectors and the hours he spends marking homework has already been. I wonder aloud whether the Tolkien thing is why the Fembot set us up: she once called me a hobbit, because I'm so short.

"Oh, didn't she tell you?" asks Gandalf, in response. "My son's her personal trainer, and I think she's got a soft spot for him, since she offered to go round and cook him dinner while I was out tonight."

I'm pretty angry when I hear that, but I get even crosser when I pick up the menu in an attempt to calm down by pretending to study it. Turns out the restaurant is only willing to make Zabaglione if the order's for two people or more.

I don't mention it, as Gandalf's already back on the subject of *Lord of the Rings*, so I hand him payment for my half of the bill, along with my pudding, which has just arrived. Then I tip the waitress excessively, and call a cab. No way am I dating a man who claims that orcs are real.

Chapter 28

The Fembot's not speaking to me because of what happened with Gandalf last night. I overhear her telling Esther he came home "in a foul mood" and "at an inopportune moment", which may have cost her a second date with his personal trainer son.

"I may have to get you to date Nigel next," she says to Esther.

It's obvious from the Fembot's tone of voice that she's joking, but Esther still says she might consider it. She must be *desperate* for that promotion.

She even tags along with the Fembot when she goes to lunch, and the two of them come back the best of friends, which makes me feel a bit left out, though not enough to pretend I've changed my opinion of bloody Gandalf – or of the Fembot for suggesting I go on a date with him.

For the rest of the afternoon, all I can hear is the Fembot holding forth (mainly about the "awesome" Paleo diet and the importance of positive thinking), and Esther agreeing with every word she says. I can't ignore their tedious conversation because the stupid hot-desking rota means I'm seated between the two of them this week.

"You're acting very pally towards the Fembot all of a sudden," I say to Esther, when the Fembot finally shuts down her computer, then gets up from her desk to fetch her coat.

"No, I'm not," says Esther, "I'm acting the same as I always do."

That claim is rapidly disproven when the Fembot shouts, "Bye, all!", then turns to leave.

Everyone grunts a non-committal reply, apart from Esther, who really goes for it.

"Bye, hun," she says.

There's a sudden, very noticeable silence as the rest of the staff stop talking and wait to see what happens next. The Fembot likes underlings to know their place, which is something Esther clearly hasn't learned about her yet.

We don't have long to wait before she does.

First the Fembot turns round, and freezes Esther with a single look, and then she says, "Pardon, Esther? I don't think I heard you properly."

"Goodbye," says Esther, in a very small voice.

★   ★   ★

I feel awful for having to turn down Esther's invitation to go for a drink to calm her down after the "hun" debacle with the Fembot, but Eva's already on her way round to mine. She's coming for a debriefing of the Gandalf date, though judging by the gifts she's bearing, she's already got a pretty good idea of how it went.

She passes me a bottle of Prosecco and a hand-tied bouquet, and then pulls a box of lavender-scented tissues in vintage-style packaging out of her bag.

"Blind dates really tell you what the person who organises them thinks of you, don't they?" I say, once I've thanked her for the gifts. Then I query how she knew a box of tissues would be required.

"Just a feeling," she says. "Mainly because your boss is an idiot, so anyone she recommended was likely to be an idiot too. I assume things did not go well?"

I shrug in the face of understatement of the year, and then rummage around in the kitchen cupboards, trying to find the only vase Joel didn't manage to shatter when he was still a teenager and Dan bought him that stupid BB gun. (We lost a lot of lightbulbs that way, too.)

"Where are you, you bloody thing?" I say, as I give up on the kitchen cupboards, and head for the understair cupboard instead. (Talking to vases is another worrying new habit I've developed, along with talking to myself.)

I rack my brains to recall the last time I used the vase, but when I do, it's not much help. It was for some gerberas Claire and Theo bought me as a thank you for looking after their cat while they were on holiday, just before Dan and I split up and I became *persona non grata* at their dinner parties, but I can't remember where I put it after that. I eventually find it outside the back door, streaked with mud and stained with bright green watermarks, the now-mouldy gerberas still inside. Joel must have put it there when the flowers died, while I was in my newly-separated state of *not giving a shit about anything.*

I bring the vase inside, squirt it with washing-up liquid and then dump it into a sinkful of hot water. The whole process takes so long that Eva loses patience, and decides to open the Prosecco herself.

"I've got a feeling you could do with some of this," she says, handing me a glass. "Now tell me what happened on your date, and don't leave anything out."

I do as I'm told while I clean the vase and finally put the flowers in water, and she shudders appropriately at all the worst bits of the Gandalf saga. I save the part about his pony-tail until last, to go out with a bang (unlike the date).

Eva winces.

"Jesus," she says. "A semi-pony? That *is* traumatic. And did he really have ears like Gollum's or did you make those up?"

"No, I didn't, and yes, he did," I say. "Now change the subject. I'm feeling sick at the thought."

Another glass of Prosecco helps the nausea a lot (who knew?), and then Eva starts to tell me off.

"You are an idiot, agreeing to that date," she says, rearranging the flowers I seem to have mangled during my attempt to fit them into the vase. "If I'd known you were desperate enough for high-risk dating, I'd have suggested someone who'd be a much better option."

"Who – a child?" I ask, thinking of Eva's penchant for Marlon, and her fake one for Joel, too. I hope it is a fake one, now I come to think of it. Imagine having Eva as a daughter-in-law!

There's no chance of that, though, not with Eva so dead-set against marriage. She's always telling me the single life is best, especially when I get a bit maudlin about Dan – which usually happens when I drink too much Prosecco. That could happen any minute.

"Cheer up, Han – I know a man who'd be ideal for you," says Eva, stopping my wobble in its tracks.

She goes on to say that she's just employed someone she knows to come and work at *Viva Vintage*, and he doesn't know anyone in the UK because he's been in the US almost as long as Eva was. She adds that he doesn't have a ponytail, does have normal ears and – most importantly – does *not* believe in orcs.

"He's also unbelievably handsome," she says, making her closing argument. "I mean the stop-you-in-your-tracks kind of handsome."

I'm not stupid. I do ask Eva why she's not snaffling this man for herself, if he's such a catch, but she changes the subject and I forget to bring it back up again before she leaves. I don't forget to agree "in principle" to go on a date with him though, once I've had the makeover Eva's promised me. My normal self might be good enough for the Gandalfs of this world, but it won't do for the super-handsome.

Chapter 29

Time flies when you're having fun, but it goes even faster when you're not. It's Dan's birthday in two days' time, and are you supposed to send your husband a birthday card when you and he are separated? What's the protocol? I don't want him to have a happy birthday – not without me – but I don't feel I can ignore it either, not when he *knows* I know that it's his birthday. That would just seem petty, wouldn't it?

I spend most of the day dithering, but when I go into town after work, I decide the best thing to do is send a joint card from me and Joel.

More hours of indecision later, I finally choose a card featuring a Terry Frost painting (one of Dan's favourite artists). It's lovely, and also blank – so there are no embarrassing verses that could be misconstrued. When I arrive home and show it to Joel, he informs me he bought a card for Dan "ages ago", and has already posted it.

This has never, *ever* been known to happen before. Even on the very rare occasions when Joel remembers to buy someone a card, he always forgets to post it and sometimes he doesn't even get round to writing it. That last part comes in quite useful, actually, as it means there's usually a spare card or two somewhere in Joel's bedroom, perfect for birthdays you've overlooked.

I probably could have used one of those, and saved myself the trip to the shops, but now I sit and stare at the card that I've just bought. Should I send it to Dan or not? And, if I do, what the hell should I write in it? I've been scrawling the same thing every year for twenty-seven years, but it won't do now. "I still love you as much as I always did," doesn't seem appropriate any more, even though it may be true.

In the end, I just write, "Happy birthday, Dan. Hx."

Then I start worrying about the x, so I try to obliterate it by making it look like an extra-large full-stop. That results in the pen puncturing the card and making a total mess of it, so I throw the whole thing into the bin and use one of Joel's spares instead. It says, "Happy Birthday" on the front, so I just scrawl "H" inside.

* * *

Bloody Pammy finds everything easier than Hannah does. On the morning of Dan's birthday, she just chooses a really cool animated e-card, then signs it "P" and adds a heart right next to it. I'd kill her, if she wasn't me.

Danny doesn't bother to thank me for the card I sent him, but he does tell Pammy that he loves hers.

I could read what you wrote on it, too, which was a bonus, given the one I've just opened from my son.

I ask what was wrong with that (or rather, Pammy does), so then Danny explains.

I had to get it translated by a Chinese triad who runs my local takeaway. He's an expert in UK gangsta-speak.

★　★　★

Once Pammy's finished sucking up to Danny about his birthday, I take myself off to Abandon Hope for a rowing lesson.

I row about 200 yards without dropping an oar but, as 190 of those yards are in circles, Albert eventually suggests we give up and go and get a cup of coffee.

"While we still can," he adds. "Someone's bought the cafe, so I bet they'll ruin it when they do it up."

I sit wondering if *that* will also be the effect of the make-over that Eva's planning to give me, while Albert phones Pearl to suggest she joins us.

"Watch out you don't fall over any more oars on the way, my dear," he adds. "Hannah's been throwing those around with gay abandon."

Not on *land*, I haven't, so Pearl makes it to the cafe in perfect safety. She sits down next to me while Albert goes to the counter to order her a drink.

"Did you remember it's Dan's birthday today?" she asks,

which is such a stupid question that I don't bother to answer it. I ask if she's got any news instead.

That's one of those polite enquiries you make when you're trying to deflect attention away from yourself, isn't it? Usually without any expectation that there will be news, or none that's interesting, anyway – but this time, news there is, though I'm not sure "interesting" is the word for it. Astonishing's a better one.

"Yes, we have got some news," says Pearl, using that "we" that's been creeping into her conversation more and more often since she had her accident and she and Albert became such friends, if friends is all they are. I'm not at all convinced of *that*, not least because Pearl still changes the subject whenever I bring it up.

Her "good friend" Albert's arrived back at our table now, carrying a flat white for Pearl, along with Danish pastries for all of us.

"You told Hannah yet?" he asks, but Pearl shakes her head.

"I thought I'd wait until you joined us," she says to Albert, as he settles himself into his chair. Pearl adds sugar to her coffee and then she makes her shock announcement: "Albert and I are off to China next week," she says.

I'm so stunned I accidentally take a bite of Albert's pastry instead of my own, and then apologise. He tells me not to worry, and to finish the rest, but I'm too stunned to eat any more – or to speak. He and Pearl sit and share her pastry, while they wait for me to react. I wish they weren't watching me so intently.

"Did you say, 'China'?" I say, eventually, my mouth so dry

that it's tricky to form the words. "Or did you say a Chinese restaurant?"

Albert laughs as Pearl pats my hand and says, "China, of course, you daft girl. We're going for six weeks as retiree volunteers, to teach English in a school a few miles from Beijing. Albert's idea, but it's a good one, isn't it?"

I hope my manic nodding convinces them, even if it doesn't convince me. Pearl's going away, and for six whole weeks? I thought she was dependent on me, but now I've got a horrible feeling it could easily be the other way round.

Summer

Summer

Chapter 30

Danny signed off last night by saying that Pammy reminds him of his wife, "but in a good way", and when I tell Eva what he said, she isn't any help at all.

"So?" she says, giving what I'm wearing a more disparaging glance than usual.

I was gardening when she turned up, so why would I dress up for that? I stick my tongue out at her, then carry on dead-heading, which is what I'd quite like to do to her and Dan.

"Well, what d'you think Dan meant?" I say, as I decapitate a mass of ox-eye daisy flowers with such force that they fly everywhere.

"I don't know," says Eva, picking dead flowers off her dress and flicking them back at me. "I *can't* know, can I? Not when I've never met Dan, or Danny, either – but maybe that's the point. He probably just pictures Pammy differently to how he sees you."

I snip particularly violently at a browning rose and accidentally cut off several healthy ones.

211

"Fuck it," I say, contemplating the damage I've just wrought. Then I add, "Well, whatever it is, he's not interested in me at all, now he's so enamoured of her."

I chuck the secateurs into my new gardening basket and sit down huffily next to Eva.

She gives me a kiss on the cheek, then says, "Look, Han — there is no polite way to say this. Why don't you stop wasting time on Dan and concentrate on the date I've arranged for you? Preferably by coming into London with me tomorrow, so we can shop for this bloody makeover you keep putting off?"

Joel walks into the garden at that moment, which completely freaks me out. I hope he wasn't lurking indoors, listening to Eva going on about my forthcoming date. Or about Danny, for that matter.

"What makeover?" he asks, at the same time as I say, "I can't afford new clothes. Not at London prices."

Eva says, "You can if Joel pays you a fair rent."

She fixes Joel with the same look she gave my outfit earlier, and then she adds, "Your mother needs new clothes, Joel, to make her feel better about herself. So why don't you stop making excuses and pay up? She's a single parent now and you are a working adult. One who's still living in her home, at her expense."

I should have tried that line myself, because Joel doesn't argue, he just says, "Fair enough. I'll do it now."

Then he goes online and transfers me half the outstanding money straight away.

"I'll give you the rest of what's owing as soon as I get paid again," he says, when he rejoins us in the garden. "If that's okay with you, of course?"

He's addressing Eva when he asks that last question, judging by the fact that he's looking at her, not me, but I answer, anyway.

"That'll be fine," I say.

A split second later, Eva adds, "You better had."

Honestly, what with Eva being so much better at running my life than I am, and Pammy being so much better at *being* me, I might as well resign from both.

★ ★ ★

"Do we really need to do this?" I ask, as Eva and I arrive in London and begin our mission to make me over.

I'm already feeling intimidated, and this is only the first shop that Eva's taken me to. The assistants are all even more stylish than she is, as well as decades younger, and I'm sure one just whispered something about me to her colleague, who smirked, then laughed out loud.

Eva gives them both one of her most withering glares, which shuts them up immediately, and the whispering one starts to fidget nervously when Eva gives me a big smile and a wink. Then she takes my arm and starts guiding me around the rails, as if she was a guide dog with more fashion sense than usual.

"We do need to do this, Han," she says, "if only to make you feel better about yourself, and because I don't want you to let me down by wearing that bloody shift dress for your date with Stefan."

His name is Stefan? Oh, my God. That's cool. It's at least ten times better than Nigel, or Nige – and a hundred times better than Gandalf. Now I'm even more nervous about this date than I was before.

I sneak a Kalms tablet out of my bag, stuff it into my mouth, and chew it rapidly. I don't think Kalms are designed to be chewable, as now my mouth tastes so foul I need a swig of water. I don't dare try that in here, though, not with Misses Whisper and Smirk following my every move.

I return to the subject of the shift dress to distract myself from the horrible taste.

"I couldn't wear it again, even if I wanted to," I say to Eva. "I gave it to the Oxfam shop to avoid any more Siamese twin disasters, though Esther said I should have given it to her, for when hers gets worn out."

I don't mention the other thing that Esther said when I told her Eva was going to help me choose a new wardrobe today: that Eva "enjoys having an unattractive friend". I don't mention it, because I don't agree with it. If that was the case, Eva would be only too happy for me to continue to wear my old clothes, wouldn't she? Mind you, she obviously liked my shift dress a lot more than I thought she did.

"You gave that to Oxfam?" she says, in an incredulous voice. "It was the best thing you own, by miles."

After making that wildly exaggerated statement, she orders me to wander around the shop and to pick up anything I think would suit me, then bring it back to her.

"After that, you can try it all on," she says. "Let's see how you get on by yourself."

214

For a second I wonder if Esther might have been right, but then I agree to do as I'm told, on condition that Eva doesn't let those snooty saleswomen anywhere near me once I start. They still scare me even more than the prospect of my date with Stefan does.

Half an hour later, I've finally managed to choose a few things, so I take them over to where Esther's waiting, dealing with emails on her phone. She inspects my choices, one by one, before rolling her eyes and walking over to the nearest rail where she dumps the whole lot, before rejoining me.

"They don't belong there," I say, horrified – God knows what Whisper and Smirk will say about this anarchic behaviour, but it won't be good. "And, anyway, what was wrong with them?"

Eva informs me that all the clothes I've succeeded in choosing are the same as the ones I already have.

"We're trying to update your look," she adds. "Not duplicate the damn thing. Now sit down, and leave this to me."

She gestures at a chair in one of those seating areas that are usually reserved for elderly people whose legs are a bit tired, while she goes off to choose my clothes. I don't argue as my feet are already hurting, and I know I'm hopeless at this stuff. I can appreciate style in other people – and could even achieve it for myself, decades ago – but now the best I aspire to is practicality. In natural fabrics, worn in plenty of layers so that I can put things on, then take them off again. (Often repeatedly, to cope with these bloody hot flushes, or whatever they are.)

Eva's gone over to the far side of the shop by now and all

I can see is the top of her head, so I take out my sketchbook and begin to draw the other customers, all of whom look amazing to my untrained eye, regardless of their age. None of them are following the other part of my normal dress code: always wear black, because it makes you disappear. These women are wearing every colour of the rainbow, along with the most amazing accessories and even more amazing shoes. I love shoes, which is probably where Joel gets his obsession with trainers from, though I'm not responsible for the abusive socks.

"What are you drawing?" asks Eva, who's reappeared from nowhere with Whisper and Smirk in tow. They're staggering under the weight of the mountain of clothes that Eva's somehow persuaded them to carry on her behalf.

"Her shoes," I say, pointing to a woman who must be in her sixties, but whose shoes wouldn't look out of place on one of Joel's brunettes.

This grey-haired woman is getting away with wearing them because she carries herself so well, and seems so confident, too. I wish I could look like that.

"Nice," says Eva, following my glance. "Now come with us, and hurry up. It's time for you to try things on."

I get up and walk dutifully to the changing rooms, slouching along as slowly as I can behind Eva and her attendants. *They* seem to have experienced a major change in attitude.

"If there's anything else you need, just give us a shout," they say, once they've hung all Eva's selections on an extra-long clothes rail, and wheeled it into position outside a luxurious changing room.

"Thanks – I shall," says Eva, ushering me inside.

Once there, she whispers that all she had to do to effect Whisper and Smirk's transformation into decent human beings was to "casually mention" that she's the editor of *Viva Vintage*, which is their favourite magazine, apparently. Then she passes me the first series of outfits she's chosen, and goes to wait outside.

I stare in disbelief at a dress with such a complicated construction that I've no idea how to put it on, which may explain why I have one arm left over, once I've put the other into the hole next to what I *thought* was the larger one for the neck. I wrestle my way out again under the glare of the halogen lights. They work miracles for my appearance, but do nothing for the flushing thing. I'm already as hot and bothered as it's possible to be.

"How are you getting on?" calls Eva, through the curtain.

"Fine," I lie, moving on to dress number two.

I can tell which bits of me are supposed to go where with this one, so I'm making progress of sorts, but it's not my colour, seeing as it's not black. It's a soft, dark grey instead, and the fabric feels amazing. It looks pretty amazing, too, when I finally zip it up and look at my reflection in the mirror.

"Not bad," says Eva, yanking the curtain across and stepping inside the cubicle without warning. "Though it might look better if you hadn't left your jeans on underneath."

"I didn't want Whisper and Smirk to see me in my pants," I say, "if they also came barging in here, without waiting to be invited, like you just did."

Eva takes no notice, and simply instructs me to "stop being a wuss, and get on with it".

Four hours later, "hot and bothered" has given way to "dying of heatstroke", even though I abandoned my jeans and my modesty more than three hours ago, along with much of my apparently "tragic" underwear. I have to give it to Eva, though, she knows what she's doing with this styling business. Thanks to her, I am now the proud possessor of what she describes as a "capsule wardrobe", by which she means a series of separates and dresses that I couldn't put together badly, if I tried.

I stand in the changing room, and take one more look at the last outfit she's selected, which includes a pair of jeans that actually suit me and which don't resemble Pearl's, for once – but without looking like those worn by Joel's young female friends, so there's no question of anyone thinking "mutton" when confronted by the sight of me wearing them. They fit in all the right places, and the colour of the top Eva's chosen to go with them makes my skin look ten years younger. My arse seems to have achieved the same feat, when Eva angles the mirror to prove it to me. I don't recognise myself.

"Bloody hell," I say and then I start to smile. "Now shall we go and look for shoes?"

Chapter 31

It's three days since Eva and I went shopping, and I still haven't worn any of my new clothes to work. Joel asks why, while he's preparing our pasta sauce tonight.

"You were chuffed with them, when you got back from London the other night," he says, "so why haven't you worn them since?"

I pull one of those faces that's supposed to warn people you feel too stupid to answer their question, but it doesn't work. Joel doesn't give up easily, unless you're talking about the essays he should have written when he was still at school. Those took him so long to start that, by the time he'd eventually begun, the deadline would then be so close he'd immediately decide he might as well give up again. It drove Dan and me nuts, especially when Joel began to use his self-diagnosed "learning difficulty" as an excuse not to go to university.

He could have gone to catering college instead, on the basis of tonight's performance in the kitchen. His cooking's improving all of a sudden, whereas mine is not.

"Answer me, Mum!" he says, chopping an onion at dizzying speed, thanks to a YouTube instruction video Marlon sent him.

I close my eyes, in case any fingers get chopped off, but then open them again in a panic, in case I give Joel the same idea. It would be just like him to test whether he can chop at speed while his eyes are closed.

Thankfully, he doesn't, so once he's finished wielding the knife, and is still the owner of all ten digits, he repeats the question, and I answer it.

"I can't wear them," I say. "Not to go outside the house."

Joel looks incredulous as I explain I put a new outfit on on Monday morning, but then felt so conspicuous I took it off again before I left for work.

"Why the hell did you do that?" he says. "I thought you looked good when you modelled your new clothes the other night. So did Pearl."

I *did* look quite good, but so different from how I usually look, I couldn't face walking into work and everybody noticing and commenting on it. I don't like people looking at me at the best of times.

"Oh, for God's sake, that's pathetic, Mum," says Joel, giving the sauce a vicious stir.

It splatters all over the cooker, so I decide it's time to head for the sitting room and message Danny instead. I'm sure he won't say I'm being stupid, because he understands me, unlike everybody else.

Just as I open my laptop, Joel comes marching into the room and thrusts my phone at me.

"Someone for you," he says, before turning round and walking out again.

"What's this Joel told me when he answered your phone?" says Eva. "That you're too chicken to wear your new clothes?"

"Um, no," I say. "Well, yes, but I'm not being chicken. I just don't like drawing attention to myself."

Eva points out that my hideous old clothes drew plenty of attention, "just not the right kind". Then she says that, if I haven't sent her photographic evidence that I'm wearing my new clothes at work by tomorrow lunchtime, she's cancelling my date with Sexy Stefan. Those are her exact words.

★   ★   ★

It's the hottest day of the year so far, especially in the office, which has floor-to-ceiling windows – and I am sweltering in this bloody coat. I Google "heatstroke", which makes it pretty clear I'm going to have to take the damn thing off, so I fight my way out of it without standing up and drawing attention to myself. Phew. That's a relief, though I'm still too hot.

I make a fan from a piece of printer paper then sit hunched forward over my desk, waving the fan up and down as fast as I can. It doesn't help, probably for the same reason that Joel says it never does: because you burn so much energy fanning yourself, it raises your temperature instead of lowering it. I need to find some other way to cool down, before I blow a fuse.

A nice long drink would do it, from the water cooler.

Always beware of overheating, then allowing yourself to

think about water. It makes you do stupid things like standing up and walking the full length of the office in search of a drink, and then walking back to your desk again – all while wearing your new clothes.

There's a round of applause as I sit back down.

"Lookin' good, Hannah," says the Fembot, in what doesn't sound like her sarcastic voice.

She looks me up and down, then orders me to stand up and do some Fembot twirls.

"Very nice indeed," she says, fingering the fabric of my skirt as I grind to a halt, somewhat dizzied by the twirling. "Did someone help you pick it out?"

"Yes," I say, though I'm a bit wounded that the Fembot doesn't think I'm capable of choosing my own clothes.

She walks around me once more, then orders the rest of the team to stop wolf-whistling, which I'm assuming is ironic anyway.

"Whoever helped you did a good job, didn't they?" she says, turning to Esther who's just passing on her way back from the loo, having missed the catwalk show I've just given everyone else by accident.

I'm not sure she would even have spotted me now, if the Fembot hadn't pointed me out, because she always looks down at her feet when she walks. She says it's due to low self-esteem, which is something I can understand all too easily, given what she does next.

She stops dead, looks up at the Fembot, then slowly turns her head in my direction. Then she just stands still and stares, in total silence.

"Well?" says the Fembot, after the tension's become too much, even for her.

"Oh, sorry," says Esther, and then she says, "Hmm."

There follows another protracted silence until, finally, she nods and says, "Very nice, but you haven't got much room in that for when you get bloated, have you, Hannah?"

★　★　★

"She's jealous," says Eva, when I call her at lunchtime to tell her about Esther's reaction, and to check she got the photo of me sitting at my desk while wearing my new clothes.

"No, she isn't," I say. "Esther's not like that at all and, anyway, she's my friend. The Fembot just caught her by surprise: by being nice to me, for once."

Eva says they'll both need to prepare for an even bigger surprise after she and I get back from where she's taking me tomorrow night: to see a friend of hers.

Her announcement throws me into a state of total panic in case she's sneakily brought my date with Stefan forward to stop me losing my nerve – like I lost my nerve about my new clothes – but when I accuse her of doing so, she denies it. Then she explains that we're going into central London after I finish work, to visit a session hairdresser she uses for photo shoots at *Viva Vintage*. After that, Eva's going to give me a make-up lesson, and then she says I'll finally be "Stefan-ready".

"So it'll be a busy evening," she adds, "but then your head will live up to your clothes, if that's what's been bothering you."

It isn't, as the thought hadn't occurred to me, until now. Now it has, I'm tempted to ask Eva what she's going to do about making my body live up to my clothes as well – in case Stefan decides to check *that* out.

Chapter 32

When I tell Esther I'm going to have my hair cut tonight, she says, "That's brave. What are you having done?"

I can't answer that, because Eva says I'm not going to have any say in it. This session hairdresser sounds as if he may be even more of a control freak than she is, the way she describes him when we're on the Tube this evening. I bet he'll think it's a complete waste of his time to cut my hair, anyway, when he's used to working on models every day.

"Don't be silly," says Eva. "I just mean he's better placed to decide on the best style for you than you are, Hannah. What the hell are you doing, by the way?"

I don't answer, as I'm trying not to make it obvious that I've just bent forward in an effort to put some distance between my nose and the sweaty armpit of the man who's standing next to me. I have no idea how Eva copes with working in central London, when that means she has to ride the Tube home from work each night during rush hour. I can hardly breathe, everyone's standing so close together, and I don't like being in a tunnel, either. *That* reminds me of how I felt when Dan first left.

"Next stop," says Eva, which comes as a major relief, given the armpit man has just moved closer.

We walk to the hairdresser's flat, which turns out to be in a converted Georgian house in Islington. The front garden is filled with Mediterranean plants and puts mine to shame, and the house does too. I swallow, hard, to control my nerves.

"Eva, darlin'," says a man who looks just like Will Smith. A slightly camp Will Smith, admittedly, but one who probably shares his lookalike's personal trainer. "Come in, come in!"

He and Eva kiss each other on the cheek a number of times, but both clearly know when to stop, as they manage to do so simultaneously, unlike me and Mr Nordic. Then Will Smith turns to me.

"Frankie," he says, extending his hand, "as in Goes to Hollywood, not that I'm ever working *there* again. You wouldn't believe how bitchy some of those people can be."

"You're just annoyed that they were better at it," says Eva, to which Frankie replies, "Ouch, my precious – but *touché*."

They're both sitting down on Frankie's squashy pale sofas by now, but I'm still standing, overwhelmed by the scale of the room that we're in. It's huge, and the ceiling takes my breath away.

"Wow," I say, looking up at the elaborate plasterwork. "Your ceiling is amazing, and it's so high!"

Frankie laughs, then says, "Essential, when you're six foot four, not that you'd know much about that, would you, Hannah? You're even tinier than Eva said you were, especially under all that hair. But that's soon dealt with, don't you worry. We'll just have a quick drink before we start. Ooh, and help yourself to nibbles, girls."

A drink turns out to mean round after round of cocktails, all made by Frankie using herbs and flowers he picks fresh from his garden, and all even nicer to look at than they taste. I'm starting to get a bit worried about what's going to happen to my hair, though, if Frankie's going to be legless by the time he gets around to cutting it, but then he puts down his glass and says,

"Right, Hannah. Time to reveal what lies beneath – a terrible film, by the way, though La Pfeiffer's as gorgeous as ever. Pop yourself up on this and we'll get started."

He gestures towards a bar stool that he's just dragged into the middle of the room, while Eva re-positions herself for a better view.

"This is going to be good," she says, looking miles happier than I bet I do – or than Frankie does. He wags his finger at Eva, reproachfully.

"Now, my sweet, you know better than that," he says. "I will *not* have you giving me your so-called helpful comments while I work my magic, so bugger off into the other room and look at the test shots from last week's shoot while I transform our little Hannah."

I don't like the sound of "transform", particularly when I've just remembered that Dan prefers my hair long.

"Frankie, what are you going to do?" I say, but now it's me he wags his finger at.

"Just wait and see," he says.

An hour and a half later, Frankie and I have become friends for life, mainly because of Edith Piaf. Frankie's an even bigger fan than I am, though I'm hoping I'll also be regretting *rien* when I finally get to see what he's done to my hair. There seems to be a lot of it lying on the floor, but I can't see into a mirror from where I'm sitting. Frankie's just tweaking what's left, by now.

"That's it," he says, a few minutes later, so I climb down from my stool and walk towards the large mirror over his enormous fireplace. I think trepidation's the best word for what I'm feeling.

Oh, my God. I look *wonderful*. Frankie's cut my hair into a really edgy, choppy bob, and he's done something masterful with the colour, too. The grey has disappeared completely and my hair's far brighter, but without looking artificial at all.

"Wow," says Eva, walking into the room and stopping dead as soon as she sees me. "You could be Keira Knightley's mum, Hannah – if she looks like an older version of Keira, that is – or Kylie's mum, given your height. I should think *she's* shorter than Keira's mum, isn't she, Frankie?"

I interrupt before Frankie can answer that burning question.

"Can we please stop talking about people's mums?" I say. "I'm less than ten years older than Kylie, thank you very much."

"Ah," says Frankie, "but let's face it, darlin', Kylie's had a *lot* of help, and there's only so much a haircut can do."

★　★　★

It takes me ages to get ready for work this morning, because I'm trying to follow Eva's make-up instructions. The strobe cream she gave me is *amazing*. For once, my skin's glowing in a good way – rather than from yet another hot flush – when I arrive at the office on time, but only just. When I walk towards my desk, it's like the moment when I revealed my new clothes all over again, this time because of my hair.

"What's the hairdresser's name?" demands the Fembot, while everyone else is making thumbs-up signs. "He must be *seriously* good, because you look at least ten years younger. That'll help, now you're single."

I try to take the last two comments in the spirit in which they were intended, while explaining that there's no point telling her Frankie's name, because "he doesn't cut just *anyone's* hair".

I didn't say I *succeeded* in taking the Fembot's comments in the spirit they were intended, just that I was trying my best, and I have to try even harder when Esther finally gives her reaction to my hair. I've just realised that she was the only one who didn't give it the thumbs-up when I arrived.

"Hmm," she says, putting her head on one side, while staring intently at my hair. Then she moves her head to the other side, and says, "Hmm," again. Finally, she asks me if *I* like it.

"D'uh, yeah," I say, wondering why she's even bothering to ask, given what I look like now compared to how I looked before.

"Why d'you ask?" I add, but Esther doesn't answer. Instead, she announces that she's got an appointment to have *her* hair done at lunchtime today.

"Such a coincidence," she says, when I raise my eyebrows. "Although I booked mine weeks ago."

In which case, it's a bit of a mystery why she didn't mention it yesterday morning when I told her about Eva's Frankie plan. I'm about to say so, when the Fembot gets in first.

"You'll be lucky if yours turns out as well as Hannah's," she says, making the situation worse, though not as bad as it becomes.

★　★　★

I get back from lunch – most of which I spend searching for a rare Andrews Sisters album to give to Frankie, as a thank you for my amazing new haircut – but there's no sign of Esther for another hour or more. The Fembot's unimpressed by this "dereliction of duty", and she keeps muttering about poor timekeeping being the sign of a disorganised mind.

Eventually, she loses her temper completely and says, even louder than she normally speaks, "How can it take hours to do someone's hair when it's as thin as bloody Esther's?"

The rest of us keep quiet and just shake our heads to confirm that we don't know, but then Esther slams the door behind her as she walks in, and it becomes blindingly obvious why her haircut's taken so long. She hasn't had much cut off – mainly because her hair was quite short, anyway – but now every individual hair has been gelled, or moussed, to within an inch of its life, so that each one sticks out in a different direction from the others. She looks as if she's been electrocuted.

The rest of us are so stunned that we probably look as if we've had much the same experience. We've even lost the power of speech, except for the Fembot, to whom that would never, *ever* happen.

"You're late," she snaps at Esther. "And when I said you'd be lucky, you clearly weren't."

Chapter 33

Frankie's right, there's only so much that a haircut can do and it doesn't help when everyone you love is leaving you. I've got to drive Pearl and Albert to the airport this morning – very early – ready for their trip to China. Joel was supposed to be coming with me, but he claims he's too hungover when I wake him up at 5am. That's probably because he's only just got home after yet another wild night out with Marlon, one which probably involved more half-naked brunettes.

I'm pretty hungover myself. I took Esther out drinking straight after work last night to cheer her up about her haircut. She insisted I stay out longer than I'd been intending to, so I hope I'm not still over the limit now.

I try to walk a straight line with my eyes closed and manage it with ease, except when I fall over a pair of Joel's trainers. (That could happen to anybody, given he leaves them in such stupid places.)

Reassured by the line-walking – if not by the falling-over – I leave for Abandon Hope, confident I'm fit to drive to Heathrow, if utterly miserable about the reason. I've got a horrible feeling I'm going to miss Pearl much more than she'll miss me, seeing as she's got Albert to keep her company. If it weren't for Joel, I wouldn't have any of my loved ones living nearby, now Dan's away on this stupid secondment, not that I love Dan any more. There'd be no point when he clearly likes Pammy far better than he does me.

I drive along, sticking carefully to the speed limit while stewing about my situation, which suddenly doesn't seem much improved by the fact that I have great new hair and clothes. Once Joel leaves home, I'm going to end up as one of those women who'll go to the opening of a browser window rather than face yet another lonely evening eating boil-in-the-bag fish and talking to herself. I'll probably develop a penchant for leaving vitriolic anonymous comments on strangers' blogs, or referring to women I don't like as "hunny" or "lovely", like Esther does. I might even start dabbling in obscure religions. Paganism would be good. I could learn to read a crystal ball so I can work out how many years it's going to be until I'll have sex again.

I'm still thinking about sex – or the lack of it – when I pull up outside the main entrance to the Elysium building, where Albert's waiting with his baggage.

"Exciting times," he says, as he opens the car door and climbs into the back.

"For you and Pearl, maybe," I say, as I drive the few hundred yards towards the front door of Pearl's flat. "I'm going to miss my lessons while you're gone, and I dread to think how bad my rowing will have become by the time that you get back."

Albert laughs and then tells me that taking a few weeks

off won't do much harm. He doesn't clarify whether that's because my continuing obsession with learning to row is completely pointless, because I never get any better at it.

"If you do go down to the lake while we're away," he continues, "keep an eye on what's going on with the cafe, will you, Hannah? I'm still worrying about it being sold to someone who will ruin it."

"Ruin what?" says Pearl, as she pulls open the other door and clambers in. "Not your hair, Hannah – that looks great!"

I smile, until I realise that I'm sitting in the front of the car by myself, like a chauffeur, while those two are both in the back.

"Drive on, Jeeves," says Pearl, reading my mind, as usual. "We can't afford to miss our flight and let those little Chinese children down. They're depending on us to teach them English, don't forget."

"I don't know how much English you're going to manage to teach them in the few weeks you'll be there," I say, which is stupid, given that it plays straight into Pearl's outstretched hands.

"More than you've learned in months of rowing, I should think," she says.

★ ★ ★

I make a right idiot of myself at departures when I wave Pearl and Albert goodbye, then promptly burst into floods of tears. They keep dripping intermittently during the whole time I'm at work, and I'm still a bit wobbly when I get home, especially when I discover Joel has gone out again.

I cheer up when I realise that his absence gives me the perfect opportunity to catch up with Danny.

We've hardly spoken for the last few days, because we've both been so busy: me with Eva's "re-make Hannah" initiative, and Danny with work, or packing to go somewhere, or something like that. To be honest, I couldn't concentrate on a word he was saying last time we "talked", because Joel kept coming in and out of the room, but tonight he's got my full attention.

Talking of Danny, it's weird, but he's becoming more Dan than Danny, if you see what I mean. He's like a new Dan, or even the old Dan I fell in love with all those years ago. More alive, somehow, and much more interested in things, as well as more communicative, too.

It's not just the wanting to travel, and the cycling, either. He still loves listening to music, and so do I, now I come to think of it – so why the hell did we end up spending all our evenings watching the news or reality TV, instead of going to gigs or listening to albums like we used to do?

I'm also a bit surprised by what Pammy tells Danny that she enjoys.

It turns out that she still loves dancing, still wants to live by the sea – or overlooking some form of water, anyway – and she also wants to learn to windsurf before it's too late, as well as to row. She's also just recalled how good at table football she used to be, so now she's planning to order her son to get his old tabletop version down from the loft. I mean *I'm* planning to order *my* son to do that, not her. Leading this double life will give me an identity crisis soon if I'm not careful, especially when Danny says he wants to take things up a notch.

He adds that the reason he wants to is because his landlady keeps saying that Pammy's a figment of his imagination, one he uses to get out of dating all the women she suggests. It's a view that's dangerously close to the truth, so maybe Bonkers Alice isn't as bonkers as I thought, though I have no idea why Dan's still talking to her now he's living in a hotel in Birmingham, instead of in her house.

Pammy cracks and asks him the same question, and gets an answer straight away.

I'm still having to pay Alice rent, so she's still my landlady. I need my room kept free for when I come back from my secondment.

I'm about to ask when that will be, when Danny continues typing, and freaks me out.

We should talk on the phone, you know – or text, at least. What d'you think? You up for it?

I panic so much that I don't stop to think. I just type, "No". It sounds a bit harsh when I read it back.

Being accidentally horrible to Danny makes me feel even more panicky, which probably explains the lunatic thing that I type next.

I can't, not won't. I'm in China, you see.

China? *China?* For fuck's sake, what the hell is wrong with me? I'm committed now, though, so I may as well go the whole hog. Apparently, Pammy's in an unspecified part of China without telephone access because she's working on a "top-secret and very sensitive project". Probably better known as "How to keep digging when you've already dug yourself a bloody great hole". All the way to China, I presume.

Chapter 34

Pammy may have been in China yesterday, but she won't be staying there much longer. Not when she may have been guilty of libelling the Chinese government today.

It's all Danny's fault, or the fault of his latest suggestion, anyway.

We could Skype each other. It's about time I saw what you look like without that hat.

There is *no way* that Danny's seeing a hatless me, so that's why I get a bit carried away when I reply, or rather, Pammy does.

We can't. China's a repressive state, remember? They don't like it when you try to communicate with the West – and anyway, my being here is supposed to be top secret.

I add that it's such a secret that even the people I live with have no idea that I'm in China, though I don't explain that's because I'm not.

Dan doesn't sound one hundred per cent convinced. First he asks if I'm pissing him about, and I assure him that I'm not, and then he sends me this:

You'll have to tell me all about it when you get back, instead. How much longer will you be away?

However long it takes until he tires of waiting to meet up with me, I suppose. How long is that?

Not for the first time, I ask myself what the hell I think I'm doing, spending every spare moment corresponding with my husband, when I can't even tell him that my husband is who he is. I just don't seem to be able to stop messaging Danny because his replies make me see the world quite differently – just like drawing does. Before, I used to walk to and from work without noticing my surroundings at all, looking down at the pavement the whole time, to avoid tripping over, but now I really notice things. The other day, I even registered how beautiful everything looked after rain, just like it did on the very first day of art school when I got caught in a torrential downpour on my way to register. The day I first met Dan.

I don't want to go back to being oblivious to the world around me, so I can't stop talking to Danny any more than I could stop drawing now that I've finally started again. Not voluntarily, anyway. That's why I keep Pammy's reply to Danny's question about how long she'll be away as vague as possible.

It's not decided yet. Could be a couple of weeks, or a few months. I'm not sure.

Danny doesn't respond, so he obviously still doesn't believe a word of this China stuff. I suddenly feel sick and breathless, because I know what he's going to say if and when he does reply. Better to get it over with.

You'll have found someone else you want to meet by then, I suppose.

As soon as I've sent that message, the bloody tears start again, along with the odd snort-cum-hiccup. One of those is so loud, it almost makes me miss the ping of Danny's reply when it finally arrives:

Let's see how it goes.

Chapter 35

Danny obviously doesn't believe Pammy's China claim because he's taken his own advice to change his life – by ceasing to talk to her. She hasn't heard from him all day.

"Good job," says Eva when she phones at lunchtime, "seeing your date with Stefan is tonight."

"Well, now I come to think of it, Dan did say he's been really busy this week," I say. "So maybe that's all it is."

Eva sighs in an exaggerated fashion, then tells me to shut up about Danny and concentrate on "a real man".

"I mean that literally, as well as figuratively," she adds, and then she breathes in deeply, as if preparing herself for one of her long lectures on why I'm wasting my time on Danny when I should be moving on.

I tell her that Joel's blown the house up to give me a reason to get off the phone. It's a credible excuse, as if he doesn't turn his bloody music down, he's going to blow up part of it at least, or the speakers, anyway. Honestly, you couldn't make it up. My great plan was to spend most of today calmly choosing what to wear, and experimenting with my new make-up. By now, I'm *supposed* to be luxuriating in a scented bath before running the pubic hair-removal gauntlet and then doing other stressful stuff, like eyebrow plucking (hazardous when you go blind whenever you close one eye), all without Joel-shaped distractions.

He should be at work, like me. The only reason I'm not, is because of Esther, the absolute sweetheart. She offered to write the report the Fembot ordered me to produce when I told her I'd like to work from home today, and added that she'd email it to me later on tonight so I could print it out and take it into work with me tomorrow, ready to prove to the Fembot that I wasn't just pretending to be working. That way, I won't get into the twirling one's bad books – and all I have to do to repay Esther is do the same for her one day.

The plan would have been a work of genius, if Joel hadn't woken up with a migraine this morning. He phoned his boss to say he might be late, and for some unknown, and totally infuriating reason, his boss told him he might as well take the whole day off, as everything at the shop was under control, for once. I wish I could say the bloody same for the situation here, but now I'm trying to get ready while a fully-recovered Joel is driving me nuts.

I'm in the middle of plucking my eyebrows when he comes barrelling into my bedroom to offer me some Haribos. He startles me so much, I end up plucking out a big chunk of loose eyebrow skin, and now the damn thing won't stop bleeding. I'm not even going to attempt any more hair-removal procedures under these hazardous conditions.

This decision is proved wise when Joel comes barging back

into the bedroom just as I'm trying out a fancy new mascara, one with a wand that curves upwards and sideways, and promises to create an alluring cat's eyes effect. Not with Joel around, it doesn't, unless some cats have one red eyeball from being poked with a mascara wand, or bloody great black splodges underneath said eye from where supposedly water-proof mascara has run during the ensuing waterfall of tears. It's a really bad idea to site a mirror just inside a bedroom door.

"For God's sake, Joel," I yell. "Can't you just leave me alone for a minute? My head feels as if it's going to explode."

"That's a thing, you know," he says, flinging himself onto my bed and stretching out, as if preparing for a long and leisurely conversation. "Exploding heads, I mean. I Googled it when you said you've been hearing loud bangs since Dad moved out, every time you're about to drop off to sleep. It's called Exploding Head Syndrome, funnily enough. You'd never have found that out by using *Halfwits*, would you, Mum?"

I refuse to admit I've even tried, but I am sufficiently interested in Joel's discovery to put up with him for a little longer. I've been getting quite worried about what was going on with these bangs in my head, as I keep thinking I must be about to have a heart attack or a stroke or something, or that I'm losing my mind and imagining the whole thing, which would be just as bad.

"So, if it's a known condition, then what the hell is causing it?" I say. It'd be great if I could find a way to make it stop.

Joel sits up, and grabs my Tangle Teezer from the bedside table.

"Stress," he says, as he begins to brush his beard with it.

★   ★   ★

I somehow survive the Joel-related stress and make it to the restaurant on time, only to discover that Eva wasn't lying: Stefan really is "unbelievably handsome", just like she said he was! He's a composite of every bit of every film star you've ever fancied, all seamlessly blended together into a toned, olive-skinned, slightly exotic, heavy-lidded, sexy-voiced *beautiful* man. And he sounds intelligent, too, and cultured, and … oh, my God, I've gone all Mills & Boon.

I'm handling myself better than the waitress, though. Every time Stefan speaks to her she loses the plot and starts wriggling and giggling, and generally making an idiot of herself. She kept it together long enough to remember what he ordered to drink, but she's had three attempts at fetching me a G&T so far, and she still hasn't managed to bring tonic, let alone gin.

Despite the lack of alcohol, this is a great cafe-bar, much better than stupid *Orgasmic*, which was about as far from being orgasmic as anywhere could be, though that could have been due to the Gandalf effect. Stefan could make a tent look good. A big tent in the desert, with servants waiting on you hand and foot while you lounge on tons of cushions on a rug-strewn floor, and eat with your fingers by candlelight. It'd be like something out of *Lawrence of Arabia*, with that really handsome actor in it, the one whose name I can't quite recall, but who Stefan looks exactly like. A young Omar Sharif, maybe? God knows, and I don't care. I'm mad with lust.

Thank Christ for that. Dizzy Gillespie's finally got my order right, so I down my G&T in one and order another straight away, while there's still a chance that she'll retain such hard-won information.

Stefan leans back in his chair and looks at me appraisingly. He doesn't even try to pretend that he isn't, and when I raise one eyebrow quizzically, he just laughs. He laughs again when I ask him if he's hypnotised the waitress.

"No, of course I haven't," he says, as she comes back with my second drink. She spills it all over the floor because she's too busy looking at Stefan to bother to ascertain the exact location of the table before letting go of the glass.

I raise my eyebrow again as she runs off to get a cloth, and Stefan says, "Well, maybe I have – just a little. Want me to try it on you?"

"Good God, no," I say. "And anyway, I'm far too sceptical to be hypnotised."

Now it's Stefan's turn to raise an eyebrow, but he doesn't seem to be spinning any objects around and his eyes aren't oscillating like those of the snake in *The Jungle Book*, so I think I'm safe, until I look across the bar and see a familiar profile silhouetted against one of the windows. It looks an awful lot like Dan, but the bar's so busy, I can't see properly as too many people are in the way, and I also can't see who he's with.

It can't be Dan, anyway, not when he's still in Birmingham on secondment, so I give myself a virtual shake, then turn my attention back to Stefan. He's still staring at me with that appraising look.

"You're a very beautiful woman, Hannah," he says, "though your energy's far too high. We could work on that."

"What do you mean, it's a bit high?" I say. "That's a good thing, isn't it? My boss seems to think it is."

I think it's a good thing when applied to waitresses, too, now I come to think of it. There's still no sign of our food, and I am starving.

"No, it's not a good thing," says Stefan. "Our systems need to be in balance, so what you need is something to ground all that energy. You're living completely in your head."

Which keeps on going *bang*, along with my heart. I could drown in Stefan's hooded brown eyes, and I'm about to get even more carried away when, thankfully, our food arrives, so now I can sort out my low blood sugar by eating at last. It must be about to go through the floor, which is probably why I feel so weird.

I say much the same thing to Stefan as we begin to eat our *moules* with *frites*.

"It isn't because of lack of food," he says, "but a lack of something else. Everything's so high in your system, you'll feel a whole lot better if we can get you grounded."

"And how do we do that?" I say, transfixed by watching him eat, and fascinated by the way he extracts each mussel by using a discarded shell as if it were a pair of tongs. "What exactly does it take to ground a person whose energy is too high?"

Stefan looks at me, long and hard, then says, "Sex. That's what reconnects you to the earth."

I've never felt so disconnected in my life, so I have another gin. And then another, and then another – until, before I know it, I'm feeling a bit woozy and I have a sneaking suspicion that Stefan's leg isn't brushing mine by accident.

"I really can help with that, you know," he says, fixing his suspiciously-hypnotic eyes on mine. "The grounding process, I mean. Have you ever had a full-body orgasm, Hannah?"

I don't answer, as I'm suddenly feeling extremely peculiar. It's like a hot flush, but not from the same place as usual. I excuse myself, and head for the loos, to give myself some time to think. I thought all orgasms were full-body ones. Has Dan been doing something wrong?

There's a massive queue for the toilets and it reaches out into the corridor, so I stand there for ages, swaying slightly and trying to decide what to do about Stefan and the prospect of sex with someone other than Dan. I close my eyes to see if that stops the room from spinning, then open them again when I feel a warm hand on my back.

"Are you okay?" says a very familiar voice, and I open my eyes to see Dan's concerned ones regarding mine. I stagger a bit from the shock, at which he puts his arms around me to hold me up. He's so comfortable to lean against, but when I rest my head against his chest, he moves backwards a little and looks me up and down.

"You look great, Han," he says. "Really ... great. Gorgeous, in fact, if a tiny bit pissed."

I giggle like an idiot, then say, "So do you – pissed *and* gorgeous. Especially your eyes ... and, oh, you smell so good."

The volume of the conversations taking place around us has suddenly become much louder, along with the clattering and banging from the kitchen close to where we're standing, and Dan shakes his head, then says, "I didn't hear that. Can you say it again?"

I lean towards him aiming to speak directly into his ear, but he turns his head at the last minute and suddenly our mouths are closer than they've been for months and months ... and getting closer by the second. I shut my eyes, lift my chin and wait.

"'Scuse me, pal," says another familiar voice. "I can manage the lady from here on in, though your *generous* help was much appreciated."

There's a distinctly sarcastic tone to what Stefan's just said, but he hasn't finished yet.

"Come to your favourite sex therapist, Hannah," he says, "and let's get on with that healing process."

Presumably he doesn't mean the healing process that he's just comprehensively buggered up.

★   ★   ★

By the time I've made it into the loo, thrown up, and finally staggered out again, there's no sign of Dan but Stefan's still waiting in the corridor, so I allow him to lead me back to our table like a wobbly-legged foal that's just been broken-in by a sadistic trainer.

I sit still, alternately groaning and sipping water, while first he tries to continue flirting and then goes on about his CV.

"I genuinely am a sex therapist, Hannah," he says. "Ask Eva if you don't believe me."

I do believe him, as that's probably why Eva's employed him to write a column giving relationship advice. I just hope he doesn't offer any to separated couples like Dan and me, who might otherwise have reconciled. I need to get out of here and find Dan, quick, but when I stand up I feel so dizzy and breathless, I have to sit back down again.

Stefan orders a brandy from the waitress (who still appears to be under his spell), but he accepts my slurred assertion that I don't require any more alcohol tonight. We sit in silence until his drink turns up, at which point he knocks the whole thing back in one, waves across to his apron-clad fangirl for another, then goes back on the attack.

"As I was saying," he continues, his voice even more slithery and Kaa-like than it was before, "Eva can definitely vouch for my abilities, if you get my drift."

He smiles a long, slow, self-satisfied smile, one I'd probably have described as sensual before my encounter with Dan, but which now looks smug, and seedy, too.

"Are you saying what I think you're saying?" I say, my voice sounding borderline hysterical. "Have you and Eva slept together?"

"Of course we have," says Stefan. "That's why she knew I'd be good for you."

There's a five-second delay while I sit there, mouth wide open in astonishment, but then I get a grip and gather speed. In fact, I've already made it out of the restaurant *and* stolen someone else's cab by the time Stefan's parting shot sinks in: "I've had a lot of happy customers."

★ ★ ★

I turn my phone back on as soon as I settle down in the taxi, ready to call Dan and explain, but then I see that I've already had a missed call from him. Oh, and he's left me a voicemail, too. I take a deep breath, and dial 121.

"If that's the kind of sleazeball you find attractive, Hannah," he says, "then I have no idea why you ever wanted to be with me. But don't worry, if it wasn't over before tonight, it bloody well is now, so do whatever the hell you like."

I dial his number immediately, but his phone goes straight to answer phone. I have no idea what I'd say even if he did answer, so I try phoning Eva next. She's not answering either, so I start typing a text to Dan, but that makes me feel so car-sick that I have to stop. By the time I get home, I'm feeling so awful I spend the next few hours throwing up, and then I crawl shivering into bed and cry myself to sleep.

I wake a few hours later when I hear a girl's voice on the landing, but I feel too ill, and too despairing, to get up and check if it's Ruby or a new brunette.

Chapter 36

Dan doesn't respond to any of the texts I send him this morning, before I phone in sick. *That* doesn't go down well with the Fembot at all.

"So, Hannah," she says, "working at home yesterday and then off sick today? What an interesting combination. I'll meet with you first thing tomorrow, then."

I'm so distraught about Dan, and so furious with Eva, that I don't even care if I've pissed the Fembot off. And I *am* sick, anyway. This can't just be a hangover, so I bet those bloody mussels were dodgy – almost as dodgy as what Eva did, setting me up with someone like Stefan. I'm about to tell her what I think of that, but there's no answer when I call her number, so I send her a text instead.

Call me asap!

I wait a few minutes for her to do as I've asked, but she doesn't bother, so I turn my phone to silent and crawl back into bed. Joel doesn't even check on me before he leaves for work.

★ ★ ★

I must have slept all day, as it's getting dark by the time I wake up when I hear the front door slam. It's Joel, and there seems to be someone with him as I can hear talking coming from downstairs. Maybe it's Dan, and he's forgiven me? I check my phone, quickly, just to see if there are any messages from him, but there aren't, so he's hardly likely to come round here if he's still too cross to reply to a text.

I'm about to turn over and go back to sleep when Joel shouts upstairs.

"Mum! Mum! Where are you? There's someone down here to see you, but I have to go out again straight away."

It *is* Dan – oh, bloody hell. Look at me! And God knows what my breath is like. I jump out of bed, regret the sudden movement and walk slowly to the bathroom to clean my teeth and brush my hair.

"Hello, Hannah," comes Eva's voice.

Oh, sod it, it's only her.

"Down in a minute," I say, but then I take as long as possible to pay her back.

It doesn't seem to work, as Eva looks totally unfazed by the time I get downstairs. She passes me a weak cup of tea she's just made, then says, "Hangover, or food poisoning – or both? Stefan says he thinks the mussels you two ate last night were off."

"That's not all that was bloody well off," I say. "How could you, Eva? I thought you were my friend, so I didn't expect you to pull a stunt like that."

252

"I *am* your friend, you idiot," says Eva. "Now tell me what you're so angry about."

That process takes a while, and Eva seems no wiser by the end than she was at the beginning.

"I thought it'd do you good to get over your paranoia about having sex with someone new," she says. "Then you'd get your confidence back, and be able to move on from Dan. Stefan's really good at what he does, and you've got to admit he's gorgeous, too."

"He's a sleazeball," I say. "And good at what, anyway? Is he your ex-boyfriend or a gigolo?"

"A bit of both," says Eva, giggling. "I've never paid him, though, and he wasn't intending to charge you either. He draws a firm line between work and pleasure."

I say nothing, and just sit there, scowling, while Eva starts questioning me about how the date actually went. She's like one of those celebrity lawyers once she gets started. (Or a Rottweiler.) First she gets me to admit that I did think Stefan was handsome and sexy, and then she forces me to admit that he made me feel quite sexy, too.

"So he was basically a warm-up act for you and Dan?" she says, with the sensitivity she ought to be so famous for.

"No," I say. "That was just Dan, and me, and raw chemistry – until Stefan came along and blew it."

Eva frowns as if she's considering what to say next, but then she comes right out with it.

"Bullshit!" she says. "You and Dan hadn't reacted to each other like that for ages before you split up, according to you. So is it at all possible – I mean, even remotely possible – that

Stefan managed to make you feel you were sexy again, and then you communicated that to Dan?"

I don't answer. I hate admitting it when other people may be right.

★   ★   ★

"So, Hannah," says the Fembot this morning. "Where's the report that Esther wrote? She says she emailed it to you, and you were going to show it to me today. You know, the report *you* were supposed to be writing yourself? I hope yesterday's sickness was more genuine than your so-called working from home?"

I'm so nonplussed that my mouth falls even wider open than it did when Stefan released the Eva bombshell.

"Um," I say, when I realise that time's been passing while I've been too stunned to think. How does the Fembot know that Esther wrote the report? That's not how the plan was supposed to work – and anyway, Esther's version was rubbish, so I had to spend most of last night re-writing it after Eva left.

I try to put that as tactfully as I can, and end up managing to make it sound as if Esther producing the first draft was the intention all along.

"I see," says the Fembot, looking unconvinced. "And the sickness? Was that real or due to alcohol?"

I don't know the answer to that question, either, and I am rubbish at lying, so it's a gift when the Fembot's phone begins to ring.

"We'll continue this later," she says, as she waves me away as if I was a nasty smell.

I head back to my desk and mouth, "What the fuck?" at Esther. She sends me an email.

From: Esther Wood
To: Hannah Pinkman
Subject: Misunderstanding

Tell you during coffee break.

Esther does try to follow through on her promise when we take our mid-morning break, but her explanation doesn't really make sense, except for her claim that the Fembot bullied her into telling the truth about who was writing the report. I'm still not quite clear about what made the Fembot suspicious in the first place, though, but Esther's moved on by now and is demanding to know every detail about my date with sex-fiend Stefan. She's not half as shocked by his occupation as I was, and seems to think it's a good thing that Dan and I were so rudely interrupted.

"I don't want to encourage your fantasies that you'll get back with Dan one day," she says, "because that's not what friends should do. I think you were both so drunk you would have fancied anyone."

I glare at her, as this is not something I want to hear, which probably means it's true.

"And neither of you was in any condition to make sensible decisions, by the sound of it," adds Esther, pressing home her advantage. "Otherwise why would you even consider getting back together with a man who annoys you as much as Dan?"

I don't remember saying Dan annoyed me *that* much, though the not-listening was irritating, plus the sighing and the eye-rolling whenever I said something he thought was stupid – like Formula One being really tedious. And the lack of interest in sex, now I come to think of it. He must have been as pissed as a fart last night to fancy me again.

"You're right," I say to Esther, as she passes me a cupcake that looks like the Cookie Monster. "Thanks. I feel better now."

I mean better in the sense of feeling angry, rather than sad, but there are no such distinctions required to describe how I feel about the apology the Fembot offers me when she returns from lunch. That makes me feel better in every way.

Apparently, she spent her lunch hour reading my report, and then a copy of the local paper, which contained a short piece about the number of people who'd been taken ill after eating at the same cafe-bar that Stefan and I were at, on the very same night. The article says that Environmental Health has slapped a temporary closure order on the owners, and the Fembot says she feels so bad about falsely accusing me of faking my illness that she wants me to take the rest of the afternoon off.

"If you can write a report as good as this when you're not feeling one hundred per cent, Hannah," she adds, "then imagine how effective you'll be when you're fully recovered. Now off you go, and rest up at home. Then you'll soon be fighting fit."

The words, "fighting" and "fit" remind me I had been planning to become exactly that, so I do two sit-ups as soon as I get home. Then I get back under the blanket on the sofa, and revert to feeling sorry for myself.

Chapter 37

It's becoming increasingly obvious that Dan's never going to reply to any of the texts I've been sending him.

Esther made it sound a good thing that he didn't actually kiss me, while she was lecturing me about it at work yesterday, but now I'm not so sure. Maybe nobody will ever kiss me again, except in the pecky, tentative way I sometimes kiss Pearl on her powdered cheeks – unless I change my mind about a gigolo. I'm not going to, though, no matter what Eva says.

She phones just as I am leaving work for the day and when I tell her how I'm feeling, she does her best to persuade me to reconsider my decision never to date Stefan again.

"No," I say. "I may be hopeless at flirting in clubs, and shit at blind dates with orc fanciers and sex maniacs, but I am *never* going to pay someone to sleep with me, or sleep with someone who usually gets paid for it, even if I would get a "session" free as a favour to you."

I drop my voice when I realise this is probably not a conversation I should be having at full volume while walking around Tesco and trying to think of something to cook for tea. People are definitely giving me funny looks, so I tell Eva to hold on a minute while I find a quiet corner in the Healthy Options section.

"It wasn't a favour to me," she says, once I confirm it's safe to continue. "Stefan really fancied you. And you shouldn't turn your nose up at the chance of whole-body orgasms, I can tell you."

I ask Eva what other kinds there are, but she refuses to elucidate, although she does say her opinion of Dan has just improved "dramatically". That doesn't help at all, so then she apologises for the Stefan idea and for its effect on me. That doesn't help much, either, and nor does the fact that someone else has just turned into the aisle I'm hiding in. Is there nowhere in this shop to hold a private telephone conversation, for goodness' sake?

"I've got to go," I say to Eva. "The walls here all have ears."

"But I'm worried about you," she says. "What are you planning to do?"

I don't know, do I? First I'm going to escape from here and go home, but as for what I'm going to do for the rest of my life ... that's anyone's guess.

"I'll probably join a convent or something," I say, before I hang up.

That's when I notice the elderly woman who's contemplating me from across the aisle. She's weighing two different-sized bags of quinoa in her hands, is smiling enquiringly, and seems to be a full-blown nun.

★　★　★

When I get home from Tesco, Joel confirms that Dan's secondment is over, but that's all he says, and anyway, it's too late for the information to be of use. Not when I've already encountered Dan while on a date with a gigolo. As a result, I just grunt at Joel as if I'm not interested, then sneak off upstairs to call Dan again, but there's no reply so I leave a message begging him to call me back. When my phone begins to ring five minutes later, I answer it so quickly it stuns the caller into a protracted silence. I have to say hello three times before Eva finally starts to speak.

"Continuing on from when you hung up on me earlier," she says. "I'm sorry about Stefan and Dan. I really am. Will you forgive me, Han?"

"No," I say, to which Eva replies that I'll change my mind, once I know what she's just bought us for my birthday.

"*Us?*" I ask.

I'd rather think about the "us" part of the sentence than the other bit. I have no desire to do anything for my fiftieth birthday, other than to go and hang myself. I don't care what Pearl says about never knowing what's round the corner: sometimes you do, and it isn't swanning off to China with a new man, it's just more crap. What with Stefan screwing up my one chance to get back with Dan, and Danny having gone totally silent since Pammy claimed she was in China, I can't see that the next half-century gives me a whole lot to look forward to.

Eva succinctly sums that view up as "utter bollocks", and then she adds, "I'm taking you to France for the weekend. To an arts residential thing. Come on, you know you want to go."

"No, I don't," I say, at which point Eva demands to speak to Joel.

I don't know what she promises him, but he does a much better job of arguing her case than her. First, he makes me look at the centre's website, and then he shows me endless photos of French beaches and cafes. By the time I go to bed, I've agreed I'll go – though I haven't admitted I'm looking forward to it. I'm holding out on that.

★   ★   ★

Phew. Danny hasn't disappeared forever, which is good, but what he says when he contacts Pammy tonight is definitely *very* bad.

I didn't renew my contract for another three-month secondment, because I thought if I moved back home, you and I could finally meet up – and then we'd know if this thing between us would survive reality. The thing I thought we had.

Pammy hasn't even started to reply before Danny carries on typing.

I guess when you decided to claim you were in China so you didn't have to phone or Skype me, that told me all I needed to know. So how about we just stay friends?

I can't see any alternative, especially not after the Stefan incident, so I've got no choice but to agree.

"Just friends" is better than nothing, isn't it? That's what Pearl and Albert keep claiming to be, though I'm not convinced. They're sitting very close together in the photos they've just emailed me from Beijing, and if their smiles were any wider they'd obscure the view.

"We're having a fantastic time," Pearl adds. "China is a wonderful country."

"I know," I say, in my reply. "A close friend of mine has always wanted to visit, and he goes on and on about it."

I cross out "close" before I hit *send*. After all, Danny just said "friends".

Chapter 38

I'm driving Eva mad, while she's driving us through France to this arts weekend, or so she claims.

"Can you please quit phoning Joel every five minutes?" she says. "You haven't stopped since we left home, and now you're distracting me when I should be concentrating on driving on the wrong side of the road."

I apologise and switch to texting instead. I wrote Joel a massive list of do's and don'ts last night, but I forgot to leave it on the kitchen counter when Eva picked me up in the early hours. Then I dropped it down the loo while we were at a service station. Eva says that proves you shouldn't try to text and sit down for a wee at the same time, not when you've got an important list in your back pocket.

"You need to trust Joel a bit more, Hannah," she adds, after she's finished tackling a particularly complicated intersection. "That is, if you ever want him to get around to leaving home."

I've got mixed feelings about that prospect, if I'm honest, so I just keep quiet and slide my phone back into my bag. Joel was so unhappy that I was going to be away for my birthday, I'm feeling quite guilty enough about him already.

"But I was going to throw you a party, Mum," he said, when I told him about Eva's plan, when she first mentioned it a week ago.

"You were leaving it a bit late, weren't you," I said, "given my birthday's this coming weekend?"

Joel asked me whether I'd never heard of the word, "impromptu", and then said maybe he'd have the party anyway – at our house, and without me.

"Seeing as you'll be away," he added.

Recalling that worrying development, I take my phone back out of my bag and send him yet another text.

If you even think *of having a party in our house, I will kill you when I get back.*

I'm just adding some kisses to soften the blow, when Eva lets out a manic "whoop!"

"See that?" she says, gesturing wildly over towards our left and swerving dangerously in the same direction. "There's the sea, and it's blue!"

I glance up, then back down at my phone to check if Joel has replied.

My signal's disappeared.

★   ★   ★

Well, we've finally arrived, and Eva's right – this place is beautiful. No wonder she's been here so many times before.

It's a 17th-century *manoir* in the Charente-Maritime on the Atlantic coast near Royan. It sits in its own grounds, which look quite spectacular in themselves, but the best part is that the estate leads down through a small wood onto a sandy beach fringed with pine trees. The air smells incredible when I step out of the car – fresh and salty, but overlaid with the scent of pine and lavender. I take so many deep breaths that I make myself quite dizzy, so then I have to get back in the car for a few minutes, until the spinning stops. Then we get our bags out of the boot and make our way from the gravelled car park along the path towards reception.

"Those are the studios where the classes are held," says Eva, pointing towards some restored stone barns and outbuildings in the distance, "and some of the self-catering accommodation, too – but I've booked us into the house itself, even though I could only get a shared room at such short notice. Hope you don't mind? It seemed worth sharing to have a restaurant and bar on tap."

I don't mind at all, as long as Eva doesn't snore as badly as Dan did. What an incredible place to spend a birthday, especially one you'd otherwise prefer not to have, and what an incredible gift she's given me! This must have cost a fortune and I'm suddenly so overwhelmed by Eva's generosity, that I have no idea what to say to express my gratitude, so I give her a big hug instead. That ends up going on for so long while I try to prevent myself from crying, that eventually she shakes me off.

"It's your fiftieth," she says. "So it needed to be memorable. Now will you please put that bloody mobile away or, even better, give it to me?"

I was only checking if my signal had returned – which it hasn't – but Eva insists, even though I argue that I need to keep the phone on me in case of emergencies. Eventually, I give in and hand it to her on one condition: that she warns the staff at reception to put any calls from Joel Pinkman through to our room, *tout de suite*.

"Here, you are going to behave like someone who is young, free and single, Hannah," she says, as we collect our room key and then head up a wide, sunlit staircase towards the first floor. "Because youngish, free and single is what you are, so you might as well start enjoying it."

As Eva opens the door to our room, and reveals a floor-to-ceiling window with a balcony and a view of the sea, I start to think that I just might.

★　★　★

When Eva and I eventually walk back into reception, after we've unpacked and taken showers, the doors to the dining room are open and the room is packed with really stylish, arty people and, all of a sudden, I lose my nerve.

As Eva walks across the threshold into the room, I hang back behind the open door and pretend to be searching for something in my bag. It's not our room key, because Eva insisted on taking charge of that. She must have anticipated that I might do a runner, and now she's obviously realised that that's exactly what I'm about to do. As soon as she turns around and spots that I'm no longer beside her, she heads back towards the door while I hide behind a potted palm.

"Come out, Hannah," says Eva, lifting a palm leaf away from my face. "I am hungry and I know you are, too. Now get a bloody grip."

She frogmarches me across the room to our table, orders me to sit, then calls the waiter over.

"*Une bouteille de vin*," she says, then adds "*Et dépéchez-vous, s'il vous plaît. C'est une urgence!*"

He raises his eyebrows, and then says, "*Comment?*"

Clearly he has about as much idea of what Eva's going on about as I do, which is none. I sit and fidget with my napkin, while Eva continues to speak to the waiter while gesturing towards me.

"*Elle est une épave nerveuse,*" she says, which seems to do the trick.

The waiter smiles, then nods and rushes across the room.

"What the hell did you say to him," I ask, "to make him hurtle off like that?"

"Nothing," says Eva, passing me the menu. "I just told him we needed wine immediately, because you're a nervous wreck."

"*Merci beaucoup,*" I say, mainly because that's pretty much all the French I know. It sounds nicely sarcastic to my ear.

Chapter 39

I'm so horribly hungover this morning when our classes start, that I don't have the energy to panic any more. We were almost the last to leave the bar last night, along with some guy called Sean that Eva picked up. That woman can pull at the speed of light.

"See you later, alligator," she said, as she headed off to his ground-floor room with him "for one last drink".

"I'll believe it when I see it," I said, rolling my eyes, and preparing to climb the stairs, which were shifting about a bit. They must have fixed them during the night, because they seem fine now. Probably after Eva finally came in and climbed into bed, just as it was getting light.

She's learning silversmithing today, while I've got a life-drawing session first thing. I thought I'd enjoy that, seeing as I always used to love drawing from life when I was at college, but that was before I saw the model. She's young, beautiful, and very shapely: all the things that I am not. I draw her anyway, but – right at the end of the class – I give her an enormous wart on her chin, and then another on her arse.

"Interesting addition," says someone, from behind me.

Someone male and extremely attractive, once I turn round to have a look, so then I pretend the warts are accidental smudges and rub them out again. *That* makes a horrible mess, due to the charcoal, and now I'm covered in it. There's no point in worrying about it, though, because now I've sneaked a second, closer look, this guy is way too young for me, which is a tragedy. He's got amazing eyes.

"Jude," he says, extending his hand, which isn't half as dirty as the one that I put into his.

"Hannah," I say, as the woman supervising the class announces that it's now over, and everyone begins to pack their things away. I stand up and cross the room to wash my hands, and by the time I come back from the sinks, Jude has gone.

★ ★ ★

"Silversmithing's not for me," says Eva, when we meet for lunch. "Just look at this!"

I have no idea what the tangled mass of silver wire that she shows me is supposed to be, so I agree she might be better off switching to textiles this afternoon. I'll be doing landscape painting, which I'm looking forward to, not least because the light is so fantastic here.

"Eva, please can I have my phone back?" I say, as the waiter brings our drinks. "I just want to check if Joel's okay."

Eva rolls her eyes, and then refuses.

"No news is good news, Hannah," she says. "So just relax.

He hasn't called you, because I've already checked, and you'd hear soon enough if something was wrong."

I know Eva's right, but that doesn't stop me worrying, which she says is probably why Joel's still at home, and also why Dan isn't.

"Joel's wonderful, but you mollycoddle him so much you might as well tell him you think that he's incompetent," she adds. "No wonder he hasn't got the confidence to move out, and things might not have got so bad with Dan if you and he had put each other first occasionally."

That's a bit harsh, isn't it? Especially on my birthday. My *fiftieth* bloody birthday.

I make a *moue* with my mouth to denote that I'm upset – I'm in France, after all, and *moue* sounds better than pursing your lips. It works better, too, because Eva notices and apologises straight away.

"Take no notice of me," she says, "I'm probably just jealous because I can't have kids. Happy Birthday, to my best friend!"

She clinks her glass against mine, then takes a large swig of wine, while I'm still taking in what she just said. Eva can't have kids?

"I didn't know," I say, after an awkward pause. "I'm sorry, Eva. That's really sad."

Eva shakes her head, as if she doesn't want to talk about it any more, and then the waiter brings our food. By the time he's finished serving it, Eva's swigged back the rest of her wine, has poured herself a second glass, and the moment for confidences seems to have passed. She drinks steadily through the rest of the meal, nagging me occasionally to keep up with her. I do my best, which turns out to have been inadvisable when I join the landscape class. Who knew that alcohol turns you into an impressionist painter, even when you didn't intend to be?

★ ★ ★

When I get back to our room after classes have finished for the day, it's already early evening, but there's no sign of Eva. I'm about to phone her when I recall that she's still got my mobile, so then I take a shower instead, after turning the dial to "cold". One of the tutors told me earlier that it's been the hottest day of the year so far, and the temperature's showing no sign of dropping, even now. There's no breeze at all, and when I step out of the shower, my skin feels warms again almost instantly, probably because of the heat the room has been storing all day, even though we left the blinds closed when we went out this morning.

I open them now and look out across the terrace and the lawns, and over to where the sea is just visible through its screen of pines, shimmering and almost impossibly blue, and then I realise why I feel so odd. I'm happy.

I stay that way while I change into a cool silk dress, and then I head back downstairs to look for Eva. I find her in the bar, and I'm pretty sure she's already drunk.

"How was your textile class?" I say, but she isn't paying attention to me.

Instead, she's listening to the sound of Euro disco coming from a marquee that's been set up outside.

"They're getting ready for the Saturday night 'Get to know you' party," she says. "So we'd better hurry up and eat. I hope you're wearing your dancing shoes?"

I haven't got any "dancing shoes", as far as I'm aware, but my new sandals will do just fine. I'm more concerned about the state of Eva's legs, which look as if they'll be getting wobbly pretty soon if she doesn't slow down with the alcohol consumption. She's already slurring her words a bit.

She assures me that she'll "sip more slowly" during our meal, though I'm not sure she keeps her promise while I go to the loo. She certainly doesn't seem any more sober by the time we finish eating, but she brushes me off when I ask if anything's the matter.

"Nothing making the most of being young, free and child-less won't sort out," she says, pushing back her chair and standing up. "Let's go."

We make our way outside to the marquee as dusk is falling and tiny white fairy lights are lighting up all around us. The effect is magical, and so is the now-familiar smell of lavender and pine that's drifting through the still-hot air. If you could bottle that, you'd make a fortune. I pause and sniff a few times while Eva weaves her way through the marquee and then stands at the bar, next to a familiar face. It's Sean, the man she went off with last night, and he's definitely wearing his dancing shoes. I'm still on my way to join them when he drags Eva over to the dance floor, and that's the last I see of her.

I take Sean's vacated seat at the bar, order a drink and stare at my reflection in the mirror above the optics. Fairy lights are much more flattering than I realised, and I don't look half bad, for once. I take one last look, give myself a wink, and then swivel round in my seat to observe the room.

"Do you always wink at yourself in mirrors?" says a voice, presumably from the seat that's next to mine – the one I've just turned my back on while swivelling myself around. "Not that I blame you: you're a sight for sore eyes."

Oh, my God. It's a cringe-making line, but nothing like as cringe-making as being caught winking at yourself, like a narcissistic idiot. Well done, Hannah, you've made yourself a laughing stock.

I groan, then swivel in my seat again to confront Mr Sarcastic face to face. I recognise him from somewhere, though I don't know where.

"More of a sight for sore eyes than a woman with a gigantic wart on her nose and another one on her arse," he says, then raises his glass to me, by way of a toast.

Chapter 40

After about half an hour, it doesn't seem as though Eva's got any intention of returning to the bar, which is probably a good thing in one way – the *minimising her drinking* way – but not so good in another. It means I'm stuck here like a spare part at the bar. Jude's gone off to try to locate the colleague he's supposed to be spending the evening with and I'm just staring into space, wishing I could disappear. I seem to be the only person here on my own – and it's my birthday, too! That's probably what the next fifty years are going to be like, now that I'm such a mature single person.

I glance outside and notice that the sun is finally starting to go down, though the temperature still hasn't dropped by much. Maybe I'll go and watch the sunset from the beach, and then come back. I can sit on the sand, wallowing in my loneliness while pretending to be Princess Di sitting outside the Taj Mahal. Minus the photographers.

I'm pushing my way through the crowds of people thronging around the entrance to the marquee, when someone calls my name. It's Jude.

"Where are you off to?" he says. "I was just on my way back to find you."

I shrug, then give him a sceptical look. I hate insincerity.

"Honestly, I was," says Jude, following me out onto the terrace. "I was just trying to tear my drunken mate away from the woman he's dancing with first, before he makes a twat of himself, but he didn't want to be torn, as you can see. He's as pissed as a fart."

"So's my friend, I think," I say, "though I haven't seen her for ages. That's why I thought I'd take a quick walk to the beach."

Jude looks absolutely horrified.

"It can't be that bad, can it, Hannah?" he says, grabbing my arm. "*Nothing* can."

Honestly, talk about being melodramatic. He thinks I'm going to drown myself. Not in this silk dress I'm not. It cost a bloody fortune.

"Oh, for goodness' sake," I say, as I shake his hand off, then set about reassuring him before he decides to call for the men in white coats. I wonder if white coats are what shrinks wear in France.

Jude has no idea when I ask him, but now he thinks I'm barking mad on top of being suicidal.

"Well, whether they do or they don't," he says, taking hold of my arm again, "I think I'll tag along, if you have no objection. Just in case."

★   ★   ★

"I wish I'd brought my camera with me," says Jude, almost an hour later when we're lounging on the sand together,

274

talking about ourselves and watching the darkening red circle of the sun as it sinks slowly towards the sea. The regular *shu-u-ush*, *shu-u-ush* of the waves as they come sliding into the shore is making me feel weirdly relaxed, almost hypnotised, unless that's just the drink – or the company.

Did I say, "hypnotised"? That makes me think of Stefan, and how people aren't always what they seem, which then makes me wonder if Jude could be a serial killer. One with whom I've just walked along a deserted path to sit on an equally deserted beach. Good work, Hannah. Right up there with winking at yourself in terms of sheer stupidity.

I panic and sit up, dislodging Jude's arm from its position along the base of my spine, where he seems to have sneaked it when I was still in a hypnotic trance.

"I wish I'd brought my sketchbook," I say, sitting bolt upright, and then shifting along the sand a little to put some distance between me and the potential serial killer. (If I keep making polite conversation, I doubt he'll realise that I suspect him.)

"Would you give the sun warts on its surface, if you drew that?" says Jude.

I ignore him and concentrate on pretending to frame the scene, which would definitely make a better impressionist painting than the landscape I did earlier. I could even sneak Jude into the picture when he wasn't looking. If he is a serial killer, he's a very attractive one, so he'd add a certain *je ne sais quoi*. I wonder how old he is. He still looks awfully young to me: under forty, at a guess, though I'd better check. The police will want to know his age if I end up reporting him for anything, like being too good looking while on a beach near a woman who hasn't had sex in …

I don't want to think how long it is, and nor am I going to think about having sex with a teenaged serial killer, even if it is my birthday.

Now I'm just being silly. Jude is not a teenager, nowhere near. In fact, he could be in his mid-forties, couldn't he? In a bad light, and if fate was smiling on me. Less than five years wouldn't be too big an age gap for whatever it is I'm refusing to think about.

Jude shifts position beside me, and then he breathes out long and slow, as if in satisfaction.

"Mmm," he says, and I turn and look at him out of the corner of my eye, expecting to find him still looking towards the sun.

Oh, shit. He's looking at me instead.

"You're very lovely, Hannah," he says. "I'd like to take your picture sometime – but, now, I think I'd rather do this instead."

He leans over and kisses me as the sun finally collapses into the horizon, and both sea and sky glow purple, orange and red.

★   ★   ★

I should have realised that very few serial killers try to prevent their intended victims committing suicide by accompanying them to beaches. Now that that's become blindingly obvious, even to me, I kiss Jude back, once he's finished kissing me. It's just as nice the second time around, but then his mobile starts to ring.

"Shit," he says, reaching into his pocket for his phone.

He stabs at the screen several times in an attempt to cancel the call, but only succeeds in answering it.

"Shit," he says again, then "What?"

He sounds so horrified that – for one dreadful moment – I think he must be taking a message for me: one saying that Joel's been in a hideous accident, or has burned the house down while throwing a party. I'm just reaching out to take the phone, when I realise I'm acting like a lunatic, so I pretend to scratch my nose instead.

Jude doesn't seem to notice, because he's still listening to the caller, while mouthing, "Sorry, sorry" at me.

I take deep breaths and wait for him to finish, so we can get back to what we were doing, but it's not to be. When Jude eventually hangs up the phone, he raises both hands in an appropriately French-style shrug of resignation, and then he says, "I'm really sorry, but I've got to go back to the party. Sean's got into some sort of ruckus at the disco, and the staff want me to come and deal with him."

He stands up, then extends a hand to pull me to my feet, while I wonder whether there can be two Seans staying at the *Manoir des Beaux Arts*. If not, is Eva still with him, and is she all right? You don't leave your friends when they're drunk, not if you're any sort of proper friend, which I am obviously not.

"Wait for me," shouts Jude, as I turn and start running flat-out along the path, away from the sand and the hypnotising sea.

★   ★   ★

Sean's sitting on the floor next to an upturned table, amidst a pile of broken glass, when Jude and I arrive at the marquee. It's almost empty now, apart from some staff and a small cluster of rubbernecking guests.

"Mate," says Jude, crouching down next to Sean. "What's up?"

Sean's so drunk that most of what he says is incomprehensible, other than "frigid bitch".

He can't be talking about Eva, which is a relief, but I still can't see her anywhere. More worryingly, this is definitely the Sean she was with earlier, and yesterday evening, too.

"Where's my friend Eva?" I yell at Jude. "The one he was with last night, as well? A tall blonde – a very attractive one."

"Thasser," says Sean, fighting off Jude who's trying to lift him to his feet. "Thass the bitch."

After that comment, Jude can leave Sean on the bloody floor as far as I'm concerned, but now he's making excuses on Sean's behalf, about how difficult it is when your long-term partner leaves you without warning.

I don't say anything in reply. I just aim a kick at Sean's leg, then run to the barman and demand to know where Eva is. It takes a while to get an answer, even though his English is far better than my French, but eventually I discover that Mademoiselle Fraser *"est dans sa chambre"*.

"Merci," I say, several times, and then I head for the exit.

When I get there, I look back, and when I do, Jude is also looking at me. He mouths, "Sorry" again, but I turn away and start running again, to find Eva.

★ ★ ★

Eva is in tears when I reach our room, as well as full of self-reproach.

"I never get so drunk I make bad decisions," she says, "and then I go and do it on your birthday, of all the days to choose. I'm sorry, Han. That's what happens when I talk about subjects that depress me, like infertility."

I give her a big hug which she seems to appreciate, and then I reassure her that I had a lovely time, anyway, but without going into any detail. I'm more interested in hearing about what happened with Sean.

Apparently, he got even drunker than Eva did, and ended up shoving his hand down her bra while they were on the dance floor, while yelling, "Come on love, you look up for anything."

When Eva told him to fuck off, he lost his temper and said she didn't seem "half so frigid" the night before.

"I'd only bloody snogged him that first night, anyway," said Eva, "and he was a perfect gent when I said it was time to leave. Tonight was a totally different story."

After the "frigid" allegation, Sean then told everyone at the party that all women were bitches who didn't know a good thing when they saw it, and then he went to slap Eva across the face when she told him to calm down and stop making an idiot of himself. She stepped out of range, and he crashed into a table piled with drinks.

"That's why I don't usually date men my own age," Eva continues, once she's finished crying and I've pointed out that we should really get some sleep. "Even when they're not drink-fuelled madmen like bloody Sean, they have way too much emotional baggage. Young ones haven't accumulated any yet."

On that note, she crashes out while I lie awake for ages, wondering whether Jude is likely to be baggage-free before I eventually manage to doze off. I don't come up with an answer to the Jude question, but I do work out that Eva snores when drunk.

Chapter 41

When Eva wakes this morning, she says she feels too fragile to make it to the screen-printing class we're both supposed to be attending, so I set off on my own. I'm secretly hoping that Jude will be there, but there's no sign of him. I take a very roundabout route back to our room afterwards, but I still haven't encountered him anywhere by the time that Eva and I carry our bags to her car, ready for the journey home.

"You never told me what you got up to last night," she says, as she struggles to re-set the satnav, largely due to the dark glasses that she's wearing. "But you look pretty pleased with yourself about it, so come on, Hannah, spill the beans!"

I do. I figure if Eva knows what a great time I ended up having without her, then maybe she'll stop beating herself up about leaving me alone last night, so I opt for maximum spillage with nothing held back.

Eva can't believe her ears, especially when she discovers I didn't get Jude's number in all the chaos. She can't believe her eyes, either, when he appears on the top step of the *manoir*, just as we are driving towards it. He spots me through the car window and gestures at us to stop, but there are other cars behind us, so we can't. The French aren't slow to beep their horns.

As we continue driving past, Jude runs down the stairs towards us, still waving his arms and mouthing something incomprehensible. As he does so, Eva glances over at him and says, "My God. I didn't know *he* was here."

Oh, shit. This is going to be another Stefan moment, isn't it? I knew last night was far too good to be true.

"You *know* him?" I say, in an outraged voice.

We've reached the end of the driveway by now, so Eva doesn't answer me. She's too busy negotiating the tricky junction with the main road, the one with a convex mirror on the far side that you're supposed to use to check if the road is clear before you pull across. I reach over and take off Eva's stupid glasses as she prepares to turn, then – once we've made it across the junction – I hand them back and repeat the question, and finally she answers me, though I'm none the wiser when she does.

"No, I don't *know* him," she says, as she straightens the wheel and accelerates. "But I know who he is. Don't you?"

"Well, obviously, *I* know who he is," I say. "He's Jude, like I told you earlier. So what?"

Eva throws both hands up in the air, which is a very bad idea when driving, and then she says, "So what? I'll tell you what: you forgot to mention your Jude was Jude Morley, better known as *Morley*."

My expression must be blank, so then she adds, "Morley the photographer, you ignoramus! The one known to everyone who works in the creative industries, apart from those who design thumbs-up icons for a living, apparently."

I don't reply, mainly because there's no denying *that's* my job.

★   ★   ★

Eva keeps huffing about my "general cluelessness" all the way back to England, at which point I finally admit I'm an idiot in exchange for her giving me back my phone. I immediately check it for messages from Joel, but there aren't any, so then I spend the next part of the journey trying to get hold of him – increasingly frantically – but all my calls and texts go unanswered.

I even log on to his Facebook page, but apart from more photos of unidentified brunettes in various nightclubs and bars, there are no clues as to what he's been up to for the last three days.

"He'll be fine," says Eva. "Young guys never update their Facebook statuses or reply to texts on time."

She's probably right, so I calm down and take a look at the rest of my timeline, which mainly comprises Esther's status updates. I don't think she's been having half as relaxing a time as me, poor girl.

"This year is about my career," she said on Friday night but by Saturday, she'd decided it was about her health, instead. This morning, she'd apparently given up on both.

"I am not worthy of my dreams," she announced, but by this afternoon she was fighting back: "I'm telling my doubts to sit in the corner and be quiet."

"Gordon Bennett," says Eva, as I read the series of statuses aloud. "Bit melodramatic, our Esther, isn't she?"

I don't respond, mainly because my own doubts about what Joel's been up to are getting stronger and stronger the closer that we get to home. By the time Eva drops me off at my house, I'm relieved to see that it's still standing, though I still feel a sense of trepidation as I open the front door and step inside. The hallway looks remarkably tidy, and so does the living room, when I glimpse it through the part-open door.

"That you, Mum?" shouts Joel, sticking his head out into the hallway from the kitchen.

I drop my bags and rush towards him and he scoops me up in a big hug.

"Happy belated birthday," he says, as I kiss him on the cheek and then step back to begin my inspection.

No obvious signs of any accidents, no bloodshot red eyes, and all the dirty dishes I didn't have time to do before Eva and I left for France have now been washed and put away.

"Have you been staying somewhere else this last few days?" I ask, as Joel gestures for me to sit down at the table.

"No," he says, looking a bit puzzled, and then he asks if I'm hungry, because dinner's nearly ready.

"Pasta," he says, which sounds familiar, but in a positive way for once. I had a great time in France, but it's lovely to be home.

It's even lovelier when Joel's pasta dish turns out *not* to be the one that we've been eating every night since Dan left home.

"Asparagus and crispy bacon in a rosemary cream sauce," he says, when I ask him what it is. "A Gordon Ramsay recipe."

I ask for seconds as my phone beeps with a message from an unknown number.

Sorry I missed you this morning. It's taken me until now to get home and recharge my phone – after I finally managed to persuade those jobsworths at le manoir to give me your number. Fancy meeting up again?

The sign-off simply says, "Jude", so while I'm on a roll of mega-good fortune, I text him back a *yes*.

★ ★ ★

After Joel and I have finished eating dinner, I check my emails to find that Danny sent Pammy a virtual birthday card while she was away. Pearl sent me one, too, promising a "proper card and present to follow when Albert and I get back from Beijing".

I put off replying to either of them tonight, as now I'm feeling pretty tired, but I do open my real-life cards and gifts.

Dan hasn't sent me any kind of card, whether proper or not, but Joel has. He's also bought me a present, and some flowers, too. I'm delighted with the gift – a voucher for the store from which Eva and I bought most of my new clothes – but I'm unnerved by the flowers, though I try my best not to show it. They're freesias and roses, both in white, my favourite kind. That's why they're the flowers I chose for my wedding bouquet.

I'd think Joel was up to his *reconcile-your-parents* trick again, if I wasn't so sure that he can't possibly know that I've met someone new.

I have, haven't I? I've *actually* met someone new …

Chapter 42

I haven't heard any more from Jude all week, not since he sent me the text about meeting up again, but I've been too busy to fret about it much. I've been spending most evenings with Esther, partly to make up for her having missed out on the arts weekend, and partly to persuade her to give internet dating another try.

"I suppose that's the only option left for me, isn't it?" she says, when we're having yet another quick drink after work tonight. "Seeing as not all of us can go to France and pick up a younger man, and you'll be too busy to spend time with me now you have."

I reassure her that I've got no intention of abandoning my friends and ending up as a Billy-No-Mates again, and then I apologise and say that I really should go, but I'll phone her tomorrow to check if she's finished her dating profile. I'm determined to keep tonight's drink as quick as it's supposed to be, because Joel's getting annoyed with me for being late home for dinner every night, since he turned into a hipster-bearded Gordon Ramsay.

"Don't write me off as coupled-up yet, Essie," I say, downing my gin in one overlarge gulp, and spilling half of it down my front. "I doubt I'll hear from Jude again."

Esther doesn't even have time to respond before my phone starts to ring, and it's the man himself.

"Sorry," he says, by way of introduction. "Been shooting in Italy all week and this is the first chance I've had to call."

"Oh, hi, Jude," I say, apparently much to Esther's disgust.

When I stand up and go to kiss her goodbye, she moves her cheek out of the way.

Jude's talking again now, though, so I just grimace an apology at Esther and then walk out of the bar. It's too noisy to hear properly in there, given that I thought that Jude just said he wants us to meet up *tomorrow night*.

"You don't live far outside London, do you?" he adds. "Though I can come to you if that's easier."

Joel would kill me if he thought I was seeing someone other than Dan, so I think I'll go to him instead. Jude, I mean. A forty-mile trip from Bracknell into London's a small price to pay to keep your son happily in the dark.

★　★　★

Remember that fantasy date I had when Dan first left, the one with Mr Suave? Well, that's almost exactly what my first date with Jude is like, minus the pretentious wooden chopping boards. And Jude looks even better in a candlelit restaurant than he does in an art class, or on a beach at sunset.

He meets me off the train at Victoria station and then we

walk the short distance to a small, family-run Italian restaurant in the heart of the City of London. The maître d' doesn't make much fuss of me, as per the Mr Suave scenario, but he's very effusive in his greeting to Jude, kissing him several times on both cheeks. Then he shows us to a table in the window where we spend the next four hours staring into each other's eyes and talking about ourselves. It's wonderful, apart from the bit about Jude's age. He's only thirty-five, for goodness' sake, which is even younger than I thought he was, and which may account for why I get hiccups as soon as I find out.

Once I've finally got rid of those by drinking a glass of water upside down, I change the subject before Jude can ask how old I am. Later on, it becomes apparent that I don't need to worry half as much about the age difference as I have been doing.

We're the only ones left in the restaurant by now, but the waiting staff don't seem to mind. They're buzzing about unobtrusively in the background, while the music's still playing and our second candle is still burning. Then the chef/patron comes out and joins us at our table.

"*Amico mio*," he says to Jude, slapping him on the back. "When I 'ear you are in tonight, I finish early so I come sit with you."

"Hannah," says Jude, "meet my old friend, Salvo. The best chef in London, by a mile."

"Pfft!" Salvo waves away the compliment, then adds, *"Ciao, Bella"* as he begins the cheek-kissing ritual with me. Once that's been completed, he orders Sambucas all round and he and Jude chat for a bit, mainly about Jude's trip to Rome earlier this week.

I watch as the flame flickers from the coffee bean in my glass and then burns itself out. It reminds me of the sunset Jude and I watched together when we first met.

I'm about to say so, when Salvo asks Jude, "So, you take *una foto* of Hannah today?"

Jude looks over at me and says, "No, though I may take pictures of her one day, if she'll let me. Hannah is my date tonight."

He smiles as he says it, but Salvo seems overcome by embarrassment for some unknown reason. He slaps himself on the forehead, then stands up while apologising profusely for interrupting.

"*Sono un idiota*," he adds, then, "I go back to kitchen now, give you *po' di* privacy."

"What was that about?" I say, glancing at my watch.

Shit, I need to leave now if I'm to catch my train, so Jude says he'll explain what Salvo was talking about in a second, once he's got the bill.

That proves a bit more difficult than it sounds, as apparently, Jude isn't *allowed* to pay the bill and nor am I, though I offer to, repeatedly. Salvo comes back out from the kitchen to tell us that he won't allow it.

I ask Jude why, after Salvo's finished another kissing ritual, and we're finally walking towards the door.

"It's complicated," he says, "but basically, I used to pay him in photos when I was an art student and had no money. Now he says their value's gone up so much, I overpaid."

He glances towards a photograph on the wall and I follow the direction of his eyes. I've been so busy looking at him that I haven't taken a blind bit of notice of my surroundings, until now. All the walls at *Salvatore*'s are covered in photographs, and they're all of beautiful women. Not just young women, as you might expect, but women in their forties, fifties and sixties – and some even older than that. All their faces show laughter lines, and past sadness too.

I raise my eyebrows, and Jude says, "I see beauty in women of all ages. Always have. My mother and grandmother taught me that, though I sometimes have trouble seeing it in my annoying sister. Now shall we walk? I thought you wanted to catch your train."

I get less and less sure of *that* as we stroll arm in arm, towards the station, stopping to kiss every few minutes under the stars. It's easy to forget how beautiful London can be if you normally see it from the Tube.

Chapter 43

It's horrible, dating someone in secret. There's no one I can talk to about my date with Jude, apart from Eva, and she's abroad for the next few weeks and only contactable in the middle of the night. I can't tell Joel, Pearl's still in Beijing falling in love with Chinese children, and Esther's internet dating isn't going well. Pammy can't even tell Danny about Jude, even though they're now "just friends". She'd feel uncomfortable doing that in case he then told her that he was dating someone, too. Mind you, Esther's first internet date sounds as if it was even worse than that horrendous prospect would be.

She tells me about it when we run into each other in the stationery cupboard first thing this morning. Apparently, we're both trying to avoid the Fembot, who's harassing people into signing up for an awayday of some sort. The last one was bad enough, so I have no intention of going to another, and Esther never goes to staff events "on principle".

"So?" I say, as we load up with Post-its and other non-essentials. "How's the dating going?"

"I've decided it's not who I am," says Esther, somewhat

incomprehensibly. "I've never had a typical life path and I guess I never will."

I make a sympathetic face, then sit down on a box of printer paper. It sounds as if this may take a while.

"The guy met me at the station," Esther continues, making me think back to Jude, which is so enjoyable that I get distracted, until Esther coughs to attract my attention.

"With me so far?" she says, and then continues, "He looked me up and down as if I was something for sale on eBay, and then told me I didn't look like my profile picture."

I say I bet he didn't either, as Esther groans, sits down on another box and puts her head into her hands.

"No, he bloody didn't," she says. "Not without the six inches that had mysteriously gone missing from his height."

That seems to be a common problem, given Pearl's experience when she was catfishing, but Jude's exactly the right height for me.

"Ergh-ergh-hm."

Esther's doing that *cough-hint* thing again, so I force myself to stop thinking about Jude and to concentrate on her instead. It's difficult, though, as now the Fembot's yelling my name somewhere further down the corridor, and Esther's started sneezing. Hayfever season lasts all year for her, so I wait while she rubs her eyes, which turns them bright red, and then she scrabbles in her sleeve for a tissue and starts trumpeting so loud the Fembot's bound to hear us soon, if she hasn't already.

"Hush!" I say, in a panic, so Esther whispers the rest of her story, which starts with the moment the waitress brought the bill and Mr Short got out his calculator.

"Then he proceeded to add it up and divide by two," says Esther, in a disgusted tone.

I can't see what's so bad about that, myself. Wasn't the independence of paying our own way one of the things feminists fought so hard to achieve? Esther agrees it was, but says she didn't expect Mr Short to then point out that she needed to pay an additional £3 to cover the extra coffee she'd had.

"I didn't expect him to calculate twenty per cent of £3 to add to the tip, either," she says.

"Holy shit," I say. "Nothing could be worse than that."

Famous last words. The Fembot's just opened the door.

"Get out here *now*, you two," she says. "I knew you were in here because of Esther's wheezing. So I'm volunteering you both for the HOO awayday. We're going to do extreme sports."

I can definitely hear panic-stricken wheezing now, but this time, I'm the one it's coming from.

★   ★   ★

Time flies when you're having fun, doesn't it? I've had two more wonderful dates with Jude by the time that Eva returns from the States, so now there's someone I can talk to about him, at long last.

"So," she says, as she opens her front door and ushers me in. "Slept with him yet?"

I make a non-committal noise as I follow her into her living room, but it doesn't put her off.

293

"You haven't, have you?" she says, chucking a bright orange box towards me, just as I am sitting down.

It misses my head by about half an inch.

"Gift from the US," Eva says, by way of explanation. I thank her profusely, to buy some time, even though I've always hated peanut butter cups.

There follows quite a long silence, during which Eva stares at me, while she waits for me to answer the dreaded sex question, and I stare back at her. Finally, I'm the one who caves.

"No, I haven't slept with Jude," I say, "and I don't think I ever will. I'm shit scared by the thought of it."

I was doing fine when we first got back to Jude's flat in Shoreditch the other night, after he'd taken me out for another meal, and I was even looking forward to taking things further for about five minutes, until the disrobing started. Then I recalled that I haven't slept with anyone but Dan for donkey's years, and my body looks nothing like it did when he and I first started having sex. After that, I got a migraine, which lasted all the way home on the train. I've got a horrible feeling that if Jude ever manages to get all my clothes off, he'll end up ordering me to put them straight back on again.

He's being very patient, but Eva says I'm being an idiot and should "just get drunk and go for it".

"Talking of drink," I say, "can we have a glass of wine, if we're going to keep talking about having sex with Jude? I'm going to need one, if we are."

★ ★ ★

Turns out I need three glasses, as Eva spends so long trying to reassure me that sleeping with Jude will be "a piece of piss". Her efforts prove so ineffectual that I'm still totally unconvinced by the time she calls me a cab, though I'm well on the way to being pissed. Even so, I'm still capable of registering her parting shot: "And get a wax before you do it," she yells, as I stagger down her garden path. "Don't forget these younger guys grew up on porn."

I sit in the back of the cab, feeling thoroughly sick, and wishing I still didn't have anyone to talk to about Jude. Talking to Eva made things ten times worse.

★   ★   ★

I'm too busy to think about sleeping with Jude today – or getting waxed – because I'm collecting Pearl and Albert from the airport, now they've come back from Beijing.

"It's so good to see you," I say, hugging Pearl so hard I'd be worried about her bones cracking, if she didn't insist there was no chance she could have osteoporosis, due to all the sit-ups and planking that she does.

"It's wonderful to see you, too, darling girl," she says, "though don't get too used to it. Albert and I'll be off again, as soon as we can arrange our next bout of voluntary service overseas. It's changed my life!"

Danny's talking about changing his again, too, when he and Pammy catch up when I get back from dropping Pearl and Albert off at Abandon Hope.

The Council's having to cut jobs, so now I've been offered a redundancy package. I think I'm going to take it and do something different with my life – probably one of the things I've always wanted to do.

Pammy never thinks before she replies, that's her trouble. She just types this:

Well, don't move to China. It's really shit.

Even when you think you may have been caught out in a lie, you have to keep it going, if you don't want people to despise you. Then you need to change the subject, so I ask Danny what he's considering and he says he's not sure yet, but it might be something to do with food.

I need some good recipes, given that now I'm pulling myself together, I can't let Joel do all the cooking, every night. He says he's getting bored with it, and it's "taking too much time away from the brunettes". The continuing use of the plural form of brunette worries me, but I don't think Joel's changed his position on commitment yet. He still says it's a waste of time, if people can "just get bored with each other and give up trying".

I think that may be what Danny's getting at when I decide to ask him what happened with his marriage. Surely we can discuss this stuff, now that we're just friends?

Apparently not. This snaps back, straight away.

I'm not really comfortable talking about my wife.

I note that Danny didn't say, "ex-wife", so I repay him for that by apologising. I add that I didn't mean to pry, and then I suck up a bit, to help me get over the guilt I'm suddenly feeling about Jude.

You seem such a lovely, considerate, funny guy. I can't understand why you and your wife split up.

There's quite a long delay before Danny replies this time, and I'm not a hundred per cent sure how to respond when he does.

Let's just say that maybe you stop seeing each other when you've been together for a long time. Not that there was much of me left to see. I'd become pretty grey and boring, I think.

I hope that doesn't mean he's taken to using Grecian 2000. Joel would never let him get away with that, though maybe it'd work for pubic hair. If it did, I wouldn't need a bloody wax.

★   ★   ★

Oh, dear God. Never, ever get a wax. They're *agonising*. On top of that, now I've got a horrific red rash which looks like syphilis or something equally off-putting, so I definitely won't be sleeping with Jude until it wears off – if it ever does.

Eva promised me the whole thing would be a doddle, which is why I arranged to have it done during my lunch break, but now I can't walk properly, because it feels even worse than it looks. I'm walking like John Wayne when I waddle back into the office.

"Where'd you leave your horse, Hannah?" shouts Geoff, one of the irritating "wits" I have to work with, day after infinitely-boring day.

I try to kill him with one of Joel's death-stares to shut him up, but it's too late, because the Fembot's already spotted me. She gives my bandy legs a funny look, and reminds me that the HOO awayday is tomorrow.

"I hope you're not thinking of faking an injury to get out of it," she adds. "Like Esther has. A partially-slipped disc, my arse. She sounded far too cheerful for that when she called in sick this morning."

She probably was cheerful, because there's nothing wrong with her, except fear of making an idiot of herself. I told her that would be my role when she called last night to tell me her plan, but she wouldn't listen. She's even more terrified than I am of doing these bloody sports, even though she's so much younger than me, and even when chickening out isn't likely to help her chances of promotion. I don't care about mine, so maybe I could claim to be sick as well. I'm sure a nasty rash would count.

Judging by the Fembot's expression when I enquire, it seems it won't.

Chapter 44

I *knew* Albert was wrong about my ever being able to learn to row a boat. I can't even handle a kayak.

It's time for the first set of activities at the awayday centre, which turns out to have been set up for adrenalin junkies who like all things coastal and insane – and I get to have first go. That's thanks to the Fembot, who is both in charge, and a sadist. Lucky me.

I sit on a rock, shivering with terror as the instructor finishes his lecture on what to do if anything goes wrong – which isn't exactly reassuring – and then he helps me into my kayak. I think I'm seasick already, judging by how nauseous I feel.

"You can do it," he says, when he sees my face. "Now off you go!"

I think he's right, for the first five minutes, as it goes surprisingly well, until the Fembot decides to intervene. I'm rowing along quite nicely – or paddling, or whatever you call it – when she suddenly yells, "Go, Hannah! Show the rest of us what oldies can do!"

That load of nonsense ruins my concentration – and my

rhythm – and before I know it, I'm underwater, thrashing about like a newly landed fish.

I can hear the Fembot yelling something else, probably more helpful instructions about how to prove I'm not completely past it, but her voice is muffled by whatever's banging in my ears, which is why it takes me a while to realise that the instructor's appeared and is trying to help me get upright again. By the time he succeeds, I'm freezing cold and I've swallowed so much salt water I'm sure I'm dying of dehydration.

"Never mind," says the Fembot, marking me down as a fail on her chart. "You can restore your honour on the zipline."

Honestly, Esther had the right idea, didn't she? She insisted she was still too unwell to come with us this morning, even after the Fembot sent her an email questioning her commitment to her job, and to any idea of being promoted. Getting a better job isn't likely to be much comfort if you die in the process of achieving it, which is probably what's going to happen to me if I get on this zipline. Even the thought of it's enough to give me a heart attack.

I stand at the very back of the queue, watching the rest of the team fly past one by one. Their expressions range from elation to agony, and I start to wonder if I can sneak off into the bushes before it's my turn.

"Yee-ee-ha-aah!" shrieks the Fembot, as she goes whizzing past.

Her mouth's so wide open with excitement, hopefully a seagull will mistake it for a cave and fly inside. That would shut her up.

I throw a small pebble towards the nearest seagull, to give

it a hint, but it just gives me a look of intense disdain, and then returns to pecking at the remains of one of the energy bars the Fembot doled out when the HOO team boarded the coach at stupid o'clock this morning.

"Wake up, Hannah," she shouts, having landed safely on the ground and removed her harness. "You should have climbed up to the platform by now, so get a move on, will you? We're all waiting to have our lunch."

She's welcome to the energy bar the seagull thought too disgusting to eat, if she's so bloody hungry, so I wave the wrapper at her, but she just shakes her head and gestures for me to hurry up.

I stare hopelessly up into the trees at the platform, which is so high that I can barely see it, while contemplating the stroke I'm bound to have on my way there, if I manage to avoid the aforementioned heart attack. After that, I think of my whole team, all watching me from down below, and all believing I'm too old to manage anything, and finally I recall Eva telling me the other night that age is just a number, when I said I couldn't sleep with Jude. I start to climb.

* * *

Fail, writes the Fembot again on her chart, next to *zipline* and *Hannah Pinkman*.

Age may only be a number, but terror is exactly what it says on the tin. I only got halfway up to the platform when a gust of wind scared me so much I spent the next five minutes stuck where I was, clinging to a flimsy wooden ladder that was swaying like mad, no matter what the instructor and the Fembot kept claiming from the ground. When people say they're paralysed by fear, they really do mean paralysed. I couldn't move in any direction, and it was only when the instructor climbed up behind me, linked me to his harness and then wrenched my fingers away from the ladder that I agreed to follow him back down.

I'm so embarrassed I wish I could just disappear. There's no escape, though, so I do the next best thing. I carry my phone up the slope behind the cafe where the rest of the HOO team are lunching on full English breakfasts, until I find a signal, and then I call Eva and tell her that I want to die.

I have a bit of a self-pity-fest, actually, given that I go on for at least ten minutes about how I can't do anything, and how I must be an idiot to think I can. It's almost a match for Esther's current Facebook status, which says, "Everything I have ever wanted has been denied to me." I know that, not because I'm checking Facebook, but because Eva's just read it out to me.

"You've gone back to being more of a bloody wuss than Esther is," she adds. "I thought you'd grown some balls over the last few months, Hannah – and started to believe you're as good as anyone else – but now you're wimping out again. What would Pearl say if she saw you acting like this? And God knows what Jude would think."

He'd think I was being pathetic, so Eva's right, but that doesn't make the situation easier. I was hoping she'd help me think of an excuse to avoid this afternoon's suicidal activity: abseiling down a cliff.

★ ★ ★

302

"It isn't a cliff," says the instructor later, when he's trying to persuade me to walk towards the edge. "It's just a steepish slope."

Like an idiot, I trust him, only to find out that he tells lies. It's definitely a cliff, and now I'm supposed to be jumping off it.

"Shall I just write *fail* now, Hannah?" asks the Fembot, from further along the edge of the cliff-cum-slope. "Save us all the bother?"

My eyes begin to prickle as I fantasise about pushing her off the damn cliff or whatever it is, but then something weird happens to me: the last nine months flash before my eyes and I decide I won't give up before I've started. After all, I didn't think I could survive Dan leaving, but I somehow have, and I didn't think Joel could manage without me while I was in France, but he did. I also thought Pearl would die on the flight to China – from a DVT or something – but she looked better than ever when she returned. Now she wants "an even greater adventure" next time she and Albert go away.

Abseiling can be my great adventure. It's only a slope, after all, albeit a very cliff-like one.

I allow the instructor to help me into my harness, adjust all the ropes and talk me through what's going to happen, all without panicking once. I even manage to smile and nod when the Fembot says, "You're really going to do it, Hannah?"

We Pinkmans are made of sterling stuff – until we find ourselves walking backwards over a cliff edge above a hell of a drop. Then we almost shit ourselves.

I take several deep breaths in through my nose and make

wild promises to any gods that are likely to be listening, if they'll just allow me to get through this nightmare in one piece. Then I start letting the rope out and begin to descend. It doesn't get any better at that point – not if you're stupid enough to look down, which I am.

I stop dead about thirty feet below the edge of the cliff, and hang there, swaying for what feels like quite a while. It's the zipline ladder experience again: I can't go up, or down.

"Don't stop – keep going!" shouts the Fembot, who must have been a cheerleader when she was at school. She's jumping up and down like a maniac further along the cliff, and waving her arms about.

I don't respond, as I'm trying to breathe through my nose while looking out towards the sea, rather than at the ground below. That's a very long way away.

"Get on with it!"

The Fembot's yelling even louder now, and she even threw a star jump in just then, for emphasis. Glaring at her is a useful distraction, which is why I spot what happens next.

She does another few star jumps while she shouts, "Go, Hannah! Go, Hannah! Hannah, g –"

The rest of the word "go" is lost as she loses her footing and disappears off the edge of the cliff.

★ ★ ★

Everyone falls silent in horror as they contemplate the section of cliff where the Fembot slid off, and then they rush, en masse, to look over the edge.

I don't need to, of course, because I'm still dangling on the line below, which is why I can see the Fembot already. She's fallen onto a small outcrop of rock that seems to be covered in prickly yellow-flowered gorse. She's groaning and her face is almost as white as her teeth.

"Don't move, Kristin!" shouts the instructor, and for a moment, I wonder who he's talking to. I'd almost forgotten the Fembot has a proper name.

I watch, trying not to think where I'm watching from, while the instructor throws a rope down to the Fembot and instructs her to tie it onto the harness that she's already wearing, but she's panicking so much, it doesn't help. Every time the rope comes near her, she freaks out and bats it away again by accident, destabilising herself further and further. Now she says she thinks she's broken something, so the instructor gives up on the idea that she'll ever be able to pull herself back up, even if she could stop shaking long enough to grab the rope.

"Just stay still!" he shouts. "I'll be down to get you, as soon as I've configured my equipment. I'll be as quick as I can."

Then he starts messing about with ropes and slings for what seems like ages. I glance over at the Fembot again, just as a piece of rock detaches itself from the ledge she's lying on and slides down the cliff with an ominous rattle. Eventually, it falls onto the rocks at the bottom and shatters into pieces. Oh, God, she's going to fall if she doesn't stop thrashing around in such a panic, isn't she? And I'm much closer to her than the instructor is, and on her level, too.

I take an extra-deep breath, and then I push my feet against the cliff face, experimentally. The action shifts me outwards a bit, so then I push with my feet again, harder this time, while leaning my body to the side. I swing outwards by what feels like a terrifying distance, but when my feet finally make contact with the cliff again, I've moved a couple of feet closer to the Fembot. This could actually work, as long as I make sure my rope doesn't catch on anything as I bounce my way along the cliff.

"Don't try it, Hannah!" shouts the instructor, who's just spotted what I'm up to. "I'll get to Kristin as soon as I'm fully equipped."

That's going to be too damn late if the Fembot doesn't stop shaking soon. Another few pieces of rock have just detached themselves from the ledge she's on, so I continue bouncing in and out. I'll be fine, as long as I don't look down.

Push out, swing sideways, bounce inwards again, and then repeat.

"Go, Hannah!" shouts someone from above. I think it's Geoff, but I don't look up at him, or down.

Push out, swing sideways, bounce inwards again – and then repeat. Push out, swing sideways, bounce inwards again – and then repeat.

It's slow, but effective, as eventually I finish up right next to the Fembot's ledge. She looks even more terrified close up.

Her face is drawn with pain, and she's still shaking with fear, so I tentatively take one hand off my rope and stretch it out towards her. She takes hold of it, and grips it, hard.

"It's okay, Kristin," I say, "Don't panic, and try not to move. I'll stay with you 'til the instructor arrives."

"Promise?" she says, staring at me as if her life depended on it. Her eyes are like those of a wounded puppy.

I nod, to reassure her, but she doesn't take her eyes from mine – or let go of my hand – until the instructor finally abseils down on his rope to rescue her. He tells me to "get clear" while he attaches her to his harness, and then I watch as they drop slowly towards the ground, while roped together. I get the rest of the way down by myself. It feels like nothing, after sideways bouncing along a cliff.

Chapter 45

The Fembot's in hospital having a pin put in her broken collarbone, but everyone else at work spends the morning congratulating me on "saving" her yesterday. Everyone except Esther, that is. She hasn't said a word about what happened so far, even though she must know what we're all talking about, and she didn't even react when she answered the office phone to Joel, who asked to speak to "Supermum". (He only wanted to know what I wanted for dinner, but I was chuffed by my new nickname, all the same.)

When I get home, I'm just about to phone Jude and tell him how much I surprised myself by my "heroics", but then I realise I can't, seeing as I've been pretending to be both fitter and younger than I really am to him, so I decide to tell Danny, instead. Pammy confessed her anxiety about extreme sports to him the other night, and he was very sympathetic.

Eva isn't, when she calls just as I'm logging on to my computer.

"You've got no excuse not to sleep with Jude now," she says, when I get to the end of the saga of the HOO awayday accident. "Not when you've just proved you're as good as people half your age. Better, seeing as it wasn't you who fell off a ledge in the first place, now I come to think of it."

"Don't be so unsympathetic," I say. "The Fembot only fell off because she was trying to encourage me."

Eva huffs loudly down the phone. She might as well say I'm an idiot, right out loud.

"That's what I'm trying to do, too," she says, in that tone which tells you immediately that someone's rolling their eyes at you. "So just get on with it!"

She's no more sympathetic when I mention the dreaded question of porn, and what's expected of everyone these days, including geriatrics, judging by that Kinky Sex booklet I found lying around at Pearl's. The one she claimed was tucked inside one of those free gadget catalogues.

"You said young guys grow up on porn," I add. "And I know you're right, because it's everywhere these days, even in retirement homes. I'm not sure I can live up to any of it, not even with that stupid wax."

Eva laughs and asks me if my rash has gone (which it has, but only to be replaced by itching, thank you very much). I'm getting a bit upset by now, which must be apparent in my voice. Sex with someone new is in no way comparable to rescuing someone from a cliff. It's ten times scarier, which is what I tell Eva, along with the fact that I don't think I can live up to the competition. That's when her sympathetic side kicks in, at last.

"Yeah, I know, Hannah," she says, in a much more serious tone of voice. "It *is* a challenge, competing with what these young guys look at every day online. But what else can you do? Become a nun? That's no role for Supermum!"

I pretend we've been cut off at that point. No one wants to think of themselves as mum when they're already freaked out about having sex with someone younger then them.

*   *   *

Several hours later, I'm having yet another conversation about bloody porn, and it's all Pammy's fault for starting it.

She's talking to Danny about how younger people just don't get our generation's cultural references, when he says that landlady Alice found porn on her desktop computer the other day. Porn that didn't belong to her.

Pammy asks the obvious question before she can stop herself. Or before I can stop myself, to be more accurate.

Was it yours?

I'll give him his due: Danny doesn't hesitate before he answers.

No. It was Aasim's, believe it or not. Anyway, getting back to cultural references, I don't think he's ever seen Fawlty Towers – and nor has Alice! They both looked at me as if I was mad when I put on a Spanish accent and said, "I know nothing" about the porn. How many people don't know a quote from Manuel when they hear one?

I haven't got a clue, but I do wonder if Jude might be one of them. Then another question occurs to me – or to Pammy, which is far more dangerous. She comes right out with it before I can apply the *subjects-not-to-discuss-with-Danny* filter.

Why do men use porn, anyway, instead of having sex with their wives?

Apparently, Pammy's decided that now she and Danny are just friends, the *only* thing they can't talk about is his wife. He doesn't seem quite so sure, as there's quite a pause before he replies.

Lots of reasons, I suppose. Laziness, or for a quick release, or –

He must have hit *send* mid-thought, but Pammy doesn't wait for him to type the rest of his reply. (That could be exactly the sort of interruption men are trying to avoid when they opt for "quick releases", now I come to think of it.) She just dives in with another of her tactless questions:

What? Are you saying men prefer porn to sex because it's easier, or that they just prefer the women they're looking at to their wives?

Neither. They're two totally different things. Why can't women ever understand?

Because we're not men. Explain it, then.

I can't believe Pammy's asking Danny about this at all, let alone demanding further explanation, especially when I hardly ever mentioned it to Dan. Porn didn't bother me when I was younger, or not much, anyway – but now, it really, *really* does.

Danny says there's no reason why it should.

It's different because you don't have the feelings you do when you're with a real person – and you don't imagine yourself doing it with the women in the magazine, or online. They're just images, that's all.

I think about what he's claiming, for a while, but I still can't make sense of it. They're not images that look like me, are they? Or not as far as I'm aware. I can't see there being much of a market for double-chin porn.

You still there?

Oops. I've been so busy mulling over how different my body looks to those of the women on the porn sites I came across while clearing the cache on the computer a couple of years ago, I'd forgotten that Danny was still waiting for a reply. I type as fast as I can, to compensate.

Well, if what you say is true, and images are all they are, then it seems a shame they cause such a loss of confidence for real-life women, especially as they age, isn't it?

Danny's simple answer is that they shouldn't.

They're unrelated, as I keep telling you – and have you ever considered men might worry about how appealing they are to look at, too? Images don't judge you if you have middle-aged spread, but women do.

I don't know what to reply to that, and neither does Pammy, as it's never occurred to either of us, until now. And could Dan mean *me* when he says, "women"?

Autumn

Chapter 46

I stood naked in front of the full-length mirror in my bedroom when I got up this morning, and – for once – I didn't want to scream at my reflection. In fact, I can't believe how much better Danny's explanation about porn has made me feel, though I do feel guilty for not realising that Dan was feeling just as unattractive as I was, most of the time.

The Hannah/Dan sex-life meltdown was probably as much my fault as his, now I come to think of it. I've got a horrible feeling I mentioned middle-aged spread to him more than once, and he did start hiding his torso from me whenever he was naked after that. My usual response was to take the piss by comparing him to bathers in the 1950s: you know, the ones who could strip off their swimming costumes and get fully dressed, all while hiding every inch of flesh under garish patterned towels.

Maybe I'll apologise if we ever meet up again, which we probably should if we're ever going to make Joel feel better about the situation, now that he knows I'm seeing Jude. I told him about that late last night, but he didn't look happy about it, and he's been abnormally quiet ever since.

He's so quiet that even Pearl comments on it during the visit we make to Abandon Hope this evening, though Joel denies it's because he doesn't like the Peruvian-style sweater that she's just knitted him. (She says she's taken up knitting again to "fill the time" until her next trip abroad with Albert. Apparently, they're off to Peru next year.)

"I love it, Pearl," says Joel. "Honestly, I really do."

He doesn't sound very convincing to me, but Pearl believes him, and offers to knit another one.

As soon as we drive away from Abandon Hope, Joel takes the sweater off.

"Thank God for that," he says, adding something about jumpers never making it as streetwear, ever. Then he brings up the subject of Dan and me.

"You two were friends, before you got together, weren't you?" he asks, to which I nod.

It's true, we were, though I can't see what that's got to do with Peruvian jumpers.

"Then I don't understand how you can just cut that bit off as well as the romantic stuff," Joel says. "It'd make me feel a lot better about things if you could still be friends at least."

He looks so forlorn, that before I know it, I've agreed to call Dan later on this evening, once I've arranged my next date with Jude. (I need to sleep with *him* as soon as possible, before my new-found ability to get naked without screaming begins to wear off.)

★ ★ ★

I wait for Joel to go round to Marlon's before I phone Jude, or Dan.

Jude gets so overexcited when I hint that sex may finally be on the cards, he tries to persuade me to stay over at his flat, and for the whole weekend, not just one night.

"Don't be daft," I say. "Just because Joel knows I'm seeing someone now, I'm still not shoving it in his face like that. He seems a lot more depressed about me and his dad splitting up since I finally told him about you, and I only got round to doing that last night. It took me 'til then to pluck up the courage."

I don't mention that I wouldn't even have told Joel at that point, if I hadn't decided that real Supermums don't deceive their sons.

I shiver, suddenly, probably at the thought of Joel's expression when he heard that I'd met Jude, unless it's just because I'm cold. France seems a long time ago now that it's September. There's definitely a chill in the air tonight, so I put Joel's abandoned Peruvian jumper on. It's almost as itchy as my waxed unmentionables, so then I take it off again.

"Can you hear me, Hannah?" asks Jude, who's been silent for what seems like ages. His voice sounds as if it's a long way away, and it's tinny, too.

My headphones must be loose, so I go to push them back into my ears, then realise that they're not there. Shit. Jude's obviously been talking the whole time I've been shoving my head in and out of jumpers, losing my headphones in the process. They've completely disappeared.

"Hold on!" I shout, in the direction of the tinny voice,

which seems to be coming from somewhere further along the sofa.

A few minutes later, I find my headphones inside the now-discarded jumper, put them back into my ears, and apologise.

Jude laughs, and tries again.

"Who's that hairdresser you're friendly with?" he asks. "Frankie, isn't it? The one who lives in central London. Maybe you could tell your son you're staying with him, if you don't want to admit you're staying with me."

Frankie did offer to put me up any time, almost as soon as we'd bonded over Edith Piaf and the Andrews Sisters, so it wouldn't be a total lie – except it would, because I've just remembered that he'll be in the States this weekend.

Jude says that's not the point.

"If you pretend that's where you're staying, then you won't have to rush back the same night like you usually do. There's a private view on Saturday night I want to take you to, followed by an after-party, which you'll miss if you have to get the train. Then we could chill out together for the whole of Sunday, preferably in bed."

I promise I'll think about it before Jude rings off, but I don't need to. Joel made me ask Frankie to pick up a pair of trainers for him from Niketown in New York, and he's so excited about those, he won't have forgotten that's where Frankie's going this weekend – and I've got no intention of lying to him, anyway. He's going to need plenty of time to get used to the idea of Jude if the two of them are ever going to get along – and that'll be important, won't it, if Jude turns out to be a keeper?

In the meantime, I'll just do my best to improve things with Dan, for Joel's sake. If all he wants is for us to be friends like Danny and Pammy, that doesn't seem too much to ask.

I dial Dan's number, before I change my mind.

"Can I talk to you about something, Dan?" I say, as soon as he answers.

He sounds so surprised to hear from me that I start gabbling like a maniac, though he listens patiently while I spill out my concerns about how much Joel's drinking, and how depressed he sometimes seems. I don't mention Jude, but I'm about to suggest that Dan and I try to be on more friendly terms, when he starts to speak, at last.

"I know," he says. "I'd already noticed Joel seems a bit low, so that's why I've just phoned him to suggest he comes away with me this weekend. It'll give us quality time together and we can chat about stuff, man-to-man. Maybe that'll help a bit."

It turns out that Dan's separated flatmate, Aasim, talked Dan into accompanying him on a European mini-break ages ago. Now he's pulled out at the last minute because his wife's agreed to a trial reunion.

"I did offer to bow out and let them go together, but Aasim said his wife hates flying," adds Dan. "So now his ticket's going free, and the accommodation's booked and paid for, too."

I'm so choked up by the notion of trial reunions, all of a sudden, that I forget to ask Dan where he and Joel will be going, until just before he ends the conversation.

"Amsterdam," he replies.

Obviously, I must have forgotten to mention Joel's excessive dope consumption being another of the things that I'm worried about. And, forgive me if I'm wrong, but isn't Amsterdam the capital of porn? I'd call Danny a bullshitter, if I was Pammy. I call him one myself, after I've hung up and sworn at him for making me lose my nerve about sleeping with Jude. Under my breath, obviously, because Joel's just come home.

Chapter 47

The Fembot comes back to work today, and is full of gratitude for what I did to help her when she fell off the cliff.

"Oh, it was nothing," I say. "Anyone would have done the same."

"Not when they were as scared as you were," says the Fembot, giving me a one-armed hug, which is a strange experience, more akin to being strangled.

I'm still getting over that when she hands me a present, "as a small thank you". It's a beautiful new sketchbook, along with a much better drawing pen than the one I've got.

"Now tell me all about this new man of yours," she says, as she walks towards her office. "Geoff mentioned you'd met someone when he visited me at home."

He's always had a big mouth to match his stomach, has Geoff, but I'm saved from answering by Esther, who's just arrived. She's carrying a bouquet of flowers which she presents to the Fembot, to "welcome" her back.

They don't quite seem to do the trick, if they were supposed to make up for bottling out of the awayday experience. The

Fembot's thank you is brief, and sounds entirely insincere, but Esther doesn't get the hint. She follows us into the Fembot's office and sits down, uninvited, on the sofa. She's still there when the Fembot brings up the subject of my "new man" again.

Esther corrects her, which is always inadvisable.

"You mean Hannah's toyboy," she says, clearly expecting a reaction, but not the one she gets. That surprises me, too, if I'm honest.

"I think it's exciting that Hannah's found someone," says the Fembot, chucking Esther's flowers towards her desk. She misses and they overshoot, probably because it was a one-handed throw. I pick the flowers up and am just about to go in search of a vase when the Fembot carries on.

"I know I wish I could get a new man," she says. "My biological clock's ticking away like mad."

Maybe it's the thought of hers that makes Esther do what she does next, or at least I hope it is. She snatches the flowers out of my hand and then she says, "Good job men's don't do that, isn't it, Hannah? Otherwise Jude might think twice —"

She stops talking, and puts her hand in front of her mouth, horrified at what's just come out of it.

"Oh, my God," she says. "I'm sorry. That's not what I meant at all."

I tell her repeatedly that I know she didn't, but she doesn't stop apologising for the next two hours *and* she brings me my own bouquet when she comes back from lunch. It's even nicer than the Fembot's.

★   ★   ★

Dan and Joel left for Amsterdam last night, and now I'm on the train to Jude's, along with my overnight bag. It's now or never.

I try not to lose my nerve when Joel posts a photo of a giant penis in Amsterdam's Sex Museum onto his Facebook page, but I do wonder if Danny ever lies to Pammy. I'm sure he told her this trip would be "mainly cultural".

"You can't go to Amsterdam without going to the Sex Museum," says Jude, when he meets me off the train.

I bet they've got a spot waiting for me in there, in the "relics" section – or they soon will have, if I don't hurry up and have some sex. Jude seems to feel much the same way, given that he goes for it as soon as we arrive at his studio.

None of his assistants are there, presumably because it's a Saturday – we're only here to collect Jude's spare keys, ourselves – but as soon as he closes the door behind us, he takes me in his arms.

"Hello, gorgeous," he says, and then he kisses me.

An hour later, I'm lying naked on the leather sofa in the corner of the studio, and so is he. *And* I'm not embarrassed. It's a miracle.

"Comfortable?" says Jude, as I glance up at him, then kiss him on the cheek.

"Very," I say, as he trails his fingers down my back.

I'm lying, but I don't want to move just yet. Leather sofas make a hell of a noise when you try to unstick them from bare skin.

★ ★ ★

"Fuck!" says Jude, packing away his cameras and other equipment. "Look at the time! We've got to go or we'll be late."

I take another look at the photos he's just taken of me – very arty nudes, in which I look surprisingly attractive, thanks to good lighting – and then I shrug. I'm not in any hurry to leave.

"Does it matter if we are?" I say, stretching and then lying down again. "Late, I mean? Last time I went to the opening of an exhibition, people were still arriving ages after the time it said on the invitation."

Jude gives me a funny look, as he searches for his boxers in the pile of clothes we abandoned in a trail across the studio, after I undid the top button of his jeans when he first kissed me. He looks so good without clothes that he could make quite a name for himself as The Naked Photographer, if he wasn't already well known, of course.

"Um, yeah, actually, it does matter a bit, Hannah," he says, fighting his way into a T-shirt without turning the arms out the right way first. "It's my exhibition we're going to."

★ ★ ★

There are hundreds of people at Jude's opening and I even recognise some of them, though not because I know them personally. They're just even more well known than Jude.

"Morley's surpassed himself with this exhibition, hasn't he?" says a woman more usually seen presenting the culture show on late-night TV. She's standing next to me contemplating one of Jude's latest portraits of ageing women. (The best one, in my opinion.)

"Yes, he has," I say, while making a mental note to get the memory card out of Jude's camera before we go to sleep tonight, the one containing naked shots of me. Imagine if he put *those* up on the wall, for everyone to see? I'd die of shame, and I can't think why I let him take the damn things, now I'm fully-dressed again. I must have temporarily lost my mind, unless another of the joys of menopause is becoming an exhibitionist when you least expect it. I'm pretty sure I'm blushing now just at the thought of an exhibition featuring me, unless I'm having a hot flush.

I fan myself with the programme, but it doesn't help.

"You okay, Hannah?" asks Jude, walking up behind me and kissing my neck. "It's almost over, not long now. I hope you're not bored? I know these things can be a drag."

I'm not sure he thinks they are, given how much he seems to be enjoying posing for all the press photographers. No wonder he took so long in the bathroom when we were getting ready earlier, and I'm starting to suspect his eyelashes aren't naturally that long and black.

I stare at them when he looks away from me for a second but, before I can come to a definitive conclusion about male mascara, someone from *The Times* calls him over.

"Back soon," he says, with an apologetic smile.

There are so many journalists still waiting for quotes that a quick return seems unlikely, so I walk out into the corridor off the main gallery and sit down on a chair. It's cooler out here and these shoes aren't as comfortable as I hoped. Also, I really should check my messages. God knows what Joel and Dan are getting up to in Amsterdam by now.

There are no more pictures of penises on Joel's Facebook page, whether giant or not, but Eva has sent me a sex-related text, nosy as ever.

Have you DONE THE DEED?

I reply that indeed I have and leave it at that – or, at least, I think I do – but then Eva replies with another question. An even nosier one.

How was it?

I move my bag off the seat next to me to allow an elderly man to sit down, and then I put Eva out of her misery.

It was all right – surprisingly.

There's no pleasing some people, especially not Eva.

Only all right? What the hell was wrong with it?

I'm not replying to that, because I'm too busy trying to answer the question in my own head. How should I describe having sex with Jude? More than "all right", obviously, but it wasn't as good as sex with Dan, which is a surprise. More exciting initially, maybe – probably due to the novelty factor – but less so by the end.

Maybe it's always like this the first time you sleep with someone? I don't know, mainly because I can't remember, but there's definitely something to be said for familiarity. When you've spent decades with someone, you both know exactly what the other one likes, even if you don't do that thing anywhere near often enough.

I sigh, thinking of all the times Dan and I went for months without having sex, only to do it again and then ask each other why the hell we didn't do it more often, given how good at it we were. We never learned our lesson, though ...

Maybe Jude and I will get the hang of having better sex together if we keep trying? At least now I know I can take my clothes off in front of a man without him looking at me in horror, and then telling me that he's changed his mind. *That* scenario features in far too many of the dreams I've been having since Dan and I split up, all those that don't involve me and Joel drowning on the *Titanic*, that is.

"Ouch," I say, as someone steps on my feet and then trips over those belonging to the man sitting next to me. We're both in the way now that everyone seems to be leaving, so I move through to the gallery in search of Jude. I finally find him in the office at the back, smoothing his eyebrows and applying something that looks suspiciously like bronzer to his face. I wonder if I should be doing much the same thing, but I can't be bothered, so I adjust the straps of my shoes and then sit down to wait.

Eventually, Jude has finished grooming himself and now he's saying goodbye to the staff, one of whom hands him our coats. "You ready, Hannah?" he asks, wrapping mine around my shoulders. "Time to go to the after-party!"

I hope it doesn't last too long. I'd prefer to get more practice in.

Chapter 48

A fifteen-year age gap seems twice that size sometimes. The music at Jude's after-party is absolutely shit, apart from one session by a DJ who plays some of my all-time favourite songs.

I smile over at Jude, who smiles back at me so broadly that he's obviously relieved that I've finally stopped moaning about how much I hate Radiohead and making sarcastic remarks about his generation's musical taste.

"This guy's good," I say, gesturing towards the stage. "Who is he?"

"That's DJ Retro," says Jude.

It turns out that he isn't being sarcastic, so I go to the bar for another drink. When I rejoin him, he's standing in the middle of a crowd of male friends, all discussing their latest scores on *Call of Duty*. Joel springs to mind for a second, but I banish that thought and concentrate on joining in. It's a bit difficult as I've always thought computer games were for children, but I do my best.

Eventually, someone asks the dreaded question, "So what

do you do for a living, Hannah? Are you a photographer, like Jude?"

"No," I say, but that doesn't seem to be enough, so then I have to explain about HOO.

I try to make it sound amusing, but I'm not sure I succeed. Jude's friends all seem as clueless about *Fawlty Towers* as Danny's flatmates, judging by their reactions when I say the *Halfwits* users *know nothing*, in a Barcelona accent. One guy even asks me if I'm Spanish, though Jude claims to have got the joke, when I ask him about it later on. He looked blank at the time I said it, though, so I'm not convinced he isn't fibbing. Now he says he's starting to feel "too pissed" and am I ready to go back to his place?

I jump at the chance, not least because the latest DJ's playing something I've never heard of, and never want to hear again.

"I'll just go to the loo before we leave," I say, to Jude. "Meet you out front."

There's a huge queue for the ladies' toilets, and I'm almost at the back of it, so it takes ages before I make it into a cubicle. When I do, I lock the door behind me and then start that crazed hopping thing that you do when you think you're about to wet yourself while struggling to pull down your tights. It works, and I sit down and breathe a sigh of relief, and it's then that I hear someone mention Jude.

"Who's that woman with Morley tonight?" she says. "I've never seen *her* before."

"God knows," says a different voice. "But whoever she is, he obviously hasn't got over his mummy thing yet. She must be twenty years older than him."

That's not even true, but I don't know what else the women says, due to the roaring in my ears. I stay in the cubicle until it ceases, and I hear the main door to the ladies' close. It's only then that I come out.

Chapter 49

Jude and I didn't get any more practice in last night as we were both too knackered for sex – or rather, I was too depressed by those bitchy women, and Jude was way too drunk. He's got a shocking hangover first thing, so I open his bathroom cabinet looking for paracetamol, but there isn't any. There are stacks of male grooming products, but those won't cure Jude's "headache from hell", so I keep looking. Eventually, I find a part-used packet of ibuprofen in a drawer in the kitchen, and take that to him, along with a large glass of water. He thanks me and then goes back to sleep.

At noon, he wakes up again and decides he now feels well enough to make it up to me for last night's lack of sex. He's doing a pretty good job of it, too, which means that practice *is* all it's going to take, but then someone rings the doorbell, and keeps on ringing it for the next few minutes.

"Oh, shit!" says Jude, reappearing from under the bedclothes and looking at me wildly, his hair on end. "That's my sister – I've just remembered I invited her to lunch today before I knew you'd be staying over. I'm sorry, Hannah, I'll have to go and let her in."

He throws on last night's clothes and runs to the door, while I retreat to the bathroom and get dressed there. London life is super-busy, isn't it? Jude and I haven't spent any time just chilling out and doing nothing, not since that evening on the beach in France. It's lovely to have a social life, but the occasional bit of downtime is nice as well. I don't know how he keeps going, actually, given how hard he works. He calls me most evenings when he finishes at the studio, and he always says he's got two or three things to go to later that night, usually one straight after the other. He never seems to spend any time at home, except when he has people round, like now.

People being the operative word, rather than just one person. There are two small children having a fight in the middle of Jude's living room when I walk in.

"Quiet, Harry!" says a very attractive woman in her early thirties. "And you, too, Phoebe. *Shush!*"

Neither child takes a blind bit of notice, so then the woman looks at me and smiles apologetically.

"Hannah, meet my sister, Kate," says Jude, scooping both children up in his arms, and then spinning around like a top until they shriek for mercy.

Kate seems nice, and so do Harry and Phoebe, contrary to first impressions, though that may have less to do with innate good behaviour than to the fact that Jude keeps them so well entertained while Kate and I drink tea and chat politely about very little. The *very little* part suits me fine, as I'm not risking any more missed references to TV series, or disagreements about music, and I'm not keen to talk about my job — or my age.

Kate has the grace not to mention *that*, though I've got a feeling that she's inspecting me closely when I turn away from her to pass Jude a juggling ball that he's just dropped. In case I'm right, I mould my face into a manic smile before I turn back to face her, to throw her off the scent.

"Jude's so good with kids," she says, giving him a fond glance as he goes off to rummage about in his kitchen cupboards for something, and then returns with a giant bubble-blowing kit.

"He is," I say, also looking over at Jude, who blows me a kiss.

"Aw," says Kate. She puts her hands to her chest and pulls a soppy face at how "sweet" we are together.

"It's a shame Jude hasn't got any children of his own yet, though — isn't it, Hannah?" she says, lowering her voice a bit. "He's not getting any younger. Have you got kids?"

I nod, though I bet Kate's next question will be how old Joel is.

★ ★ ★

"Kate liked you," says Jude, when he comes back from showing her and the children out.

I wave to Harry and Phoebe through the window, and they wave back, while I buy myself some time to think. Kate looks up at me and gives a small, tight smile.

There's a *click* from Jude's espresso maker as he switches it on.

"Did you hear what I said about Kate?" he asks, as I turn away from the window and look at him. "I said she likes you."

"Yes," I say, "but she also thinks I'm far too old for you."

Jude starts to speak but I gesture at him to let me continue. This is hard enough, without being interrupted.

"She's right," I say.

Jude stops dead, mid-way through frothing some milk. The steam nozzle hisses angrily as he says, "But why? What are you talking about? I decide who I want to date, not Kate, so it doesn't matter what she thinks."

I take the milk jug out of his hands and replace it under the hissing nozzle.

"It does to me," I say.

★ ★ ★

Four hours later, I still feel exactly the same, even though Jude's been trying his best to change my mind. I just keep thinking of all the things that separate us, not just the obvious (like a decade and a half), but the more subtle things, too, like those shared references that Danny and Pammy keep talking about. Jude says that those don't matter, but that's only because he doesn't notice their absence. I do, and then there's the thing about children, too.

"I don't even know whether I want kids yet," says Jude, when I bring that up again. "So I can't see why it's relevant."

It is to me, in case I fall in love with him (despite *Call of Duty*, Radiohead and his tendency to check himself out in mirrors when he thinks that I'm not looking), and then he decides that of course he does.

Better stop now, before that can happen.

★ ★ ★

Jude insists on walking me to the station to catch the last train, even though he's still upset about my decision that we should stop seeing each other. I think he finally understands what I've been saying, though. Not only do we not have enough things in common, but we can't possibly have a long-term relationship (which I still want again one day), because that would cost him the chance to have kids of his own.

"Part of me knows you're right," he says reluctantly, as he opens the train door to allow me to board, "but as for the other part –"

He shakes his head and I reach up and wrap my arms around his neck, before I kiss him one last time. Then I board the train and don't look back. I can't, because there's something in my eye.

Whatever that something is, it vanishes as the engine starts and the train begins to pull out of the station, leaving my mascara a total mess. I scrub at my eyes with my knuckles, then glance out of the window and wish I hadn't. Jude's walking alongside the train, looking in at me, and he keeps that up until my carriage finally clears the platform and he disappears from view.

I get another something in my eye, which doesn't go away for at least the next ten minutes, and then I spend the rest of the journey wondering if I've made the right decision. As we pull into the station and I get up from my seat and reach for my bag, I notice a couple of the other passengers giving me sympathetic looks. They must think I've just been dumped!

I smile, even more brightly than I smiled at Kate when she was trying to work out how old I am, and I'm still grinning madly when I get off the train and join the queue at the taxi rank.

My fake smile lasts until I arrive back home and open the door to an empty house. It's then that it starts to waver a bit.

Chapter 50

It's Monday morning, though it still feels like the middle of the night when I get up for work. That's probably because it *was* the middle of the night when Joel got back from Amsterdam and woke me up by shouting goodbye to Dan in what I assume was pidgin Dutch. I rolled over and tried to go back to sleep once he'd gone to bed, but without success – unlike Joel, who's still out cold.

Danny's wide awake, despite his lack of sleep. At 7am he messages me for the first time since he left the UK on Friday.

I missed you more than I thought I would.

I bet he did, spending his days wandering around the Sex Museum, though I doubt he's going to mention that. Not when he's the one who claimed watching porn is different from having sex with real women. Real women just like Pammy – I mean, *me* – the sort of women who ask people who've just been to Amsterdam if they visited any museums while they were there, as a test.

Danny tells Pammy that he did.

The Rijksmuseum. It was great.

Pah. Neither Pammy nor I can think of anything polite to say to that obvious load of bull, but it doesn't matter, because Danny's still adding to it.

I had a hell of a job persuading my son to come with me, though. He only agreed when I traded it for a trip to the Sex Museum. Afterwards, he said he preferred the Rijksmuseum.

"Like hell," types Pammy, but then she recalls that she and Joel have never met. She changes the sentence to, "Oh, good," before hitting *send*.

★　★　★

Joel backs Danny's wild claim up when I get home from work. In fact, he says he *loved* the Rijksmuseum, and he doesn't mention the giant penis once.

"You going rowing with Albert tonight, Mum?" he asks. "I'll come with you if you are. I haven't seen him or Pearl since she gave me my jumper."

Normally I have to bribe Joel to visit "the wrinklies", so this is unusually enthusiastic for him – and he becomes even more so when I tell him that Jude and I have split up, while we're on the way to Abandon Hope.

That's probably not the best place to be going now that I'm newly single, come to think of it, though I don't say so to Joel. My expression must do all the talking though, because he immediately asks if I'm okay.

"I'm fine," I say.

I'm not sure I believe that's true but Joel does, which is the main thing, I suppose. I don't want to lower his mood when he's looking so much happier than before he went to Amsterdam.

"I'll just pick myself up and move on again," I continue, as I indicate left, then park directly in front of the living room window of Pearl's flat.

She waves to us as Joel says, "Glad to hear it, Mum. There are plenty of fish in the sea, as I've been proving ever since I split up with Izzy."

"Ah," I say, reduced to a monosyllabic response by my amazement that Joel didn't take the opportunity to suggest that Dan and I get back together, I'm still in shock about that by the time I start my rowing lesson with Albert at the lake.

There probably aren't plenty of fish in *there*, not by the time I've finished thrashing my oars about, and we can't even have a coffee instead, as the cafe's now closed for renovations. (That's a pretty good metaphor for how I feel.)

Chapter 51

It's still a bit weird not chatting to Jude on the phone in the evenings when he finishes work, even though it's been over a month since we split up now. Tonight, Eva and Frankie are going to a fashion show (where Frankie's cutting the models' hair), and Esther's visiting a psychic to try to discover whether she'll ever get a promotion — or a boyfriend. Joel's planning to go round to Marlon's, so I'm out of options if it's company I need.

It is, which is why I accept the Fembot's unexpected invitation to go with her to the cinema after work. We have a surprisingly enjoyable time, mainly discussing what a great actor DiCaprio is, but I probably should remember to call her Kristin from now on, if we're going to repeat the exercise as regularly as she suggests.

She drops me off at about 10pm, which feels far too early to go to bed and far too middle-aged, as well. Maybe I should reactivate my online dating profiles, otherwise how will I find someone new to keep me company when my friends are busy? I can't see Eva taking me back to France on a man-hunt, not when she still thinks I'm an idiot for finishing with Jude.

When I first told her that's what I'd done, she said failing to share each other's cultural references wasn't a big deal, especially when set against the benefits of younger men being "emotional baggage-free zones". Then she ordered me to change the subject when I mentioned the children thing.

Anyway, now I'm home alone, and so bored that I could scream.

I wander around the house, shivering. It's cold, even for mid-October, so I change into a nightie and a dressing gown, which Eva would have a major objection to if she saw them. When I say nightie, I don't mean *negligée*, and when I say dressing gown, I don't mean silk. What I do mean is thick fleece for both items, which is lovely and warm but bulks you out. When I glance at my reflection in the mirror, I'm not sure whether I'm looking at the Michelin Man or a middle-aged woman. If it's the latter, she doesn't look much like the improved, made-over Hannah, and she doesn't look anything like a woman who was shagging a famous photographer only a matter of weeks ago.

I decide made-over, photographer-shagging Hannah would drink gin, not cocoa, so I make myself a G&T, and then I take it to bed with me, along with my laptop and my reading glasses. Once there, I log on to *No-kay Cupid*.

Up comes a message from Danny asking how Pammy got on with cooking the recipe he sent her the other day.

Great, thanks. My son loved it.

I don't mention that he also noticed that it was exactly the same meal he'd eaten at Dan's house the previous night. I got away with blaming *that* on coincidence, but Pammy needs to work a lot harder at keeping her real life separate from her virtual one, and so do I.

For safety's sake, I change the subject away from Joel and onto the film I saw with the Fembot, which Danny and Pammy both rate exactly the same. They also agree on music, especially their hatred of Radiohead, and on their love for Scandinavian crime thrillers, as well. Both things come as far less of a surprise to Pammy than they do to Danny, somewhat *un*surprisingly. He's amazed by how much they have in common.

I thought I'd never find anyone like-minded again, after I separated from my wife.

Pammy's on her second large gin by now, and losing her already-too-few inhibitions.

Why did you? Separate from your wife, I mean.

There's a pause, and then Danny says he's still not comfortable with discussing his wife, but it wasn't his choice to split up with her. Pammy's so gobsmacked by that ludicrous statement that she's only capable of a one-word answer.

Really?

I'm pretty sure *that* conveys the full spectrum of outraged sarcasm that it was intended to, but Danny manages to miss it, anyway. Instead, he seems to think further explanation is all that's required.

Yes, really, though I still don't know why my wife wanted to. It's not that we weren't getting on, because we still were, most of the time, but I think we'd just stagnated. We hadn't thought about splitting up, though, or not as far as I was aware. It just happened.

There's a pause, during which neither Pammy nor I can think of a single word to say, so we both wait until Danny starts up again.

You stop noticing, I suppose. It's the same with things you've always wanted to do with your life: you stop thinking about them as you get older and just coast along instead, but sometimes that can be the easiest way to miss out on doing them – and to lose the people you love.

People you love, or loved? Now I'm even more lost for words.

★   ★   ★

I promised Eva that I'd give internet dating another try, but Esther tells me not to bother, because of the nightmare bloke she met last night.

"So much for that bloody psychic I saw," she says, as she

tries to squeeze an imaginary spot in the mirror, while we're both in the loo at work this morning. "She promised me this guy would be The One."

"I'm not sure there *is* only one The One," I say, though I lack the evidence to prove it, so far.

To be fair, Jude did come close, even if he was a bit too young for me, or "much too young", according to Esther. I wash my hands while she abandons the non-spot squeezing and dabs Hide the Blemish on the giant red lump she's just created. As a result, she now has an equally-large beige lump on her chin, so I spend the next five minutes reassuring her that it's not as noticeable as she thinks.

"I give up on this stupid spot," she says, eventually. "Anyway, as I was saying, this guy definitely wasn't The One, or even one of The Ones, though I thought he might be until the end."

The hand dryer isn't working, and there are no paper towels, so I start waving my hands about and blowing on them, while Esther wipes hers on her skirt, leaving several streaks of beige.

"What happened at the end?" I ask, in the gap between breathing in and blowing on my hands again.

Esther starts to tell me, but then stops and shrugs, as if she can't bear to go on. I'm getting really curious now, as well as dizzy from blowing out far more air than I'm breathing in.

"Just tell me!" I say. "Before the Fembot fires us for spending too much time in the loo."

That threat seems to do the trick.

"When we got outside the restaurant," Esther says, "he

hugged me and said he was relieved everything had gone so well with me, because his last date had accused him of rape."

I'm so stunned I don't say anything for at least the next ten seconds, and not just because I'm all blown out. Poor Esther!

When I get my breath back, I try to persuade her that not everyone you meet online is destined to be an idiot, or a prospective rapist, but she refuses to be convinced, even when I add that normal men like Dan do internet dating, too.

"I'm surprised to hear that," she says, "though he's probably the exception that proves the rule. You didn't exactly meet many normal men when you last tried it, did you, Hannah?"

That's true, but if Esther keeps this up, my mood's going to end up as negative as hers before too long, so I'd better do something to cheer her up. Asap.

I suggest we have a girly night in at her house tonight, if that will help, and she says she thinks it might. In fact, she's thrilled.

"I've always wanted to have a girly night in," she says. "Because I was never invited to any when I was at school. I haven't got much food in the house, though, and I'm also not the world's most confident cook. So are you sure?"

"You won't need to cook," I say. "We'll stop off at a super-market after work, on the way to yours, and buy ready-meals we can bung in the oven. And we'll get some snacks, as well, for when we get the munchies watching films."

That idiotic snack idea is why I almost run into Dan when I'm least expecting to, and when I look like shit, thanks to a genuine spot that's just come up on the end of my nose – one much, much bigger than Esther's non-spot lump.

She and I are wandering around the deli section, debating the respective virtues of sour cream and chive dip versus guacamole, when I spot something familiar out of the corner of my eye. I don't register who or what it is at first, but something makes me raise my head and look over towards the "special selection" shelves. Maybe it's the way Dan moves (or even his silhouette) that's still so familiar it triggers recognition even when I'm not actually looking directly at him, but whatever it is, it's the only thing that's familiar about him now.

As I stare across the aisles to where he's standing looking down at the display, it's as if he's a stranger who just looks a bit like Dan. A very attractive stranger, wearing such stylish clothes and shoes that even Eva would approve of them. Dan's never been interested in clothes or shoes before, or in how he looks, and this is exactly the wrong moment for him to start.

"Duck!" I say to Esther, as Dan turns slightly, and then I bend down and lean as far into the chilled cabinet in front of me as I can get.

"Why?" says Esther, not ducking at all.

Instead, she's staring around in all directions.

"It's Dan," I hiss, yanking at her arm in another futile attempt to persuade her to stop drawing attention to us. "Over there, wearing that navy jacket and the really nice jumper."

Esther looks at me as if I'm mad. I'm certainly freezing cold.

"What, your husband, Dan?" she says. "Bloody hell, I thought he was quite nice-looking when I saw the photo of him on your desk, but he looks a lot better in real life."

"Exactly," I say. "And I look crap, so the last thing I want is for him to notice me."

It's not the last thing I want, actually. The last thing I want is to notice how great Dan looks in the flesh, at exactly the same time as realising that I'm never going to be able to touch that flesh again.

I head for the exit nearest the alcohol section, when we make a run for it.

Chapter 52

I narrowly miss running into Dan again when he comes to pick Joel up from the house this morning.

"Should I invite him in?" asks Joel, who's clearly still on a mission to make me and Dan behave like friends.

I was so unnerved by our last encounter that I refuse, on the basis that I'm in a hurry. I've got a busy Sunday planned, so it's not much of a lie.

"Next time, maybe," I add, which is.

I have no intention of hanging out with Dan drinking coffee and making polite conversation, ever. That would just be weird.

He's taking Joel to another exhibition, this time at the Design Museum, so Eva's invited me over to her house for Sunday lunch once I've finished my rowing lesson.

"What have Dan and Joel gone to see?" she asks, after I show her the drawing I made of Albert when he was attempting to punt us back to the shallows using the sole remaining oar. "Not Jude's exhibition, I hope?"

I raise my eyebrows at the thought.

"No," I say. "Thank God. It's *Shoe Design Through the Centuries*."

Eva says we should go and see it ourselves sometime, then carries on preparing lunch while I fill her in on what Danny said to Pammy about his wife being the one who wanted to split up. After that, I tell her about when Esther and I almost bumped into Dan in Tesco the other night.

I end up going on so much about how great he looked, and how horrible it felt not to be able to touch him, that I almost bore Eva to greater tearfulness than the smoke emanating from her oven is already causing.

"For God's sake," she says, giving up on the burnt chicken and chucking it out of the back door into the garden before it can set off the smoke alarm.

I suggest that we go out for lunch.

★   ★   ★

We spend most of the meal planning what we should wear to Eva's forthcoming birthday party, which is to be in fancy-dress because she was born at Halloween. Esther described that birthdate as "oddly appropriate" when Eva mentioned it to her once, which is probably why Esther hasn't been invited.

"She wouldn't want to come anyway," says Eva, when I ask her to reconsider. "She's your friend, not mine, and she doesn't like me, either. Look at the latest sarky comment she left on my Facebook page, if you don't believe me."

I promise I will, but then I tell Eva that I'm sure she and Esther would get on better if they spent more time together in real life.

"It's pointless you two pretending to be friendly via social media," I say. "That's one thing I've learned this year: virtual friends aren't the same as proper ones."

The waitress comes over and takes another order for drinks, so I pause while Eva orders more wine and I choose another bitter lemon. That seems appropriate seeing as I'm the lemon who ended up volunteering to drive us to the restaurant and therefore cannot drink.

"Carry on," says Eva. "You were telling me about real-life versus virtual friends."

Maybe I was, but now I can't seem to recall why or what, which is happening rather too often these days. I even asked *Halfwits'* users what causes brain fog, but when they all answered, "The menopause", I decided to ignore them and not give in to it.

"Virtual friends ..." I say, still without any clear idea of where I'm going with this, so I work it out as I go along. "Oh, yes. I was saying that I spent more time communicating with virtual friends on Facebook than I used to spend actually talking to Dan – and a fat lot of good they turned out to be when he left."

"That's *not* what you were saying," says Eva, looking smug, "or not the bit about Dan, anyway, but you can't leave the subject of him alone today, can you, Han? In fact, you never stop talking about him and bloody Danny. Which brings me back to why you don't just meet up with him, and come out as Pammy."

At least Facebook "friends" don't tell you harsh truths you'd rather not hear. That's a *huge* point in their favour.

★　★　★

When I get home from dropping Eva off, I think about what she said about coming out to Danny, and then I phone her to discuss it further. I can't bore her any more than I've already bored her today, and anyway, she can't just suggest something like that without explaining how to make it work. That's when she comes up with her mad idea, the one I end up agreeing to. Eventually.

"You need to start off by meeting Danny as Pammy, and then reveal you're you once he's made a move on her," says Eva, who's clearly still drunk after what turned into a boozy lunch, though only in her case.

I'm still stone-cold sober, so one of us retains some common sense.

"And how the hell am I going to pull that off?" I ask. "Force him to wear a blindfold for the first half of the date?"

That's something I once suggested he should do during sex, after I got paranoid about what I looked like naked, but since the porn conversation with Danny I finally get why Dan refused. It probably *was* unnecessary if he really wasn't comparing me to young porn stars during the act.

"No, you dipshit," says Eva, interrupting that disturbing line of thought. "You're forgetting about my birthday party. You invite Danny to meet Pammy there, and then she turns up in fancy-dress."

That's *such* a stupid idea, even though Eva's party is being held at the offices of *Viva Vintage* so Danny wouldn't be able to guess who Pammy is from its location. It's the fancy-dress part that I'm not keen on, especially with a theme like

Halloween. Zombie Pammy would look more rotting corpse than femme fatale.

Eva groans and then points out that the dead person look isn't what she's thinking of, because "zombies aren't compulsory".

"You wear some sort of super-sexy masked costume, then take the mask off once Danny makes his move on Pammy," she explains. "Preferably after he's had a few drinks, so that'll numb the shock when she turns out to be you."

"Thanks a bunch," I say, to which Eva replies that she meant, "nice surprise, not shock".

Then she says she's already thought of the perfect costume.

"Catwoman," she says. "With a half-face mask, with built-in ears. You can easily get away with wearing a latex catsuit, too, now your sit-ups and rowing are paying off."

"Thanks," I say, again – this time in a genuinely appreciative tone of voice. Who knows, this might just work.

★　★　★

Joel's back from the exhibition by the time that Eva rings off, and he doesn't shut up about shoes for the next half-hour, so eventually I decide I'll go for a walk. I need some peace and quiet to consider the pros and cons of inviting Danny to Eva's party before I commit a certifiable act by actually doing it.

I walk on and on, without a clue as to where I'm going. It's been a beautiful day, though cold, but the sky remains cloudless and blue, and there are still plants flowering in some of the gardens that I pass. Probably thanks to global warming, but I dismiss that thought as being negative when I'm trying to think positive, for once. As a result, instead of fretting about whether we'll be in the middle of a new Ice Age by the time Joel gets married and provides me with some grandchildren, I look ahead down the long, tree-lined street that I've just turned into. It stretches out as far as the eye can see, and there's something so familiar about the quality of the light bouncing off the tops of the large Victorian terraced houses on either side, that suddenly I'm back in time.

I'm the same age as Joel is now, just twenty-two, and I'm on my way to my first job, while feeling absurdly happy because Dan and I have just moved in together. Our flat's a poky ground-floor conversion in the building I'm passing right this minute: a damp, cold space with black mould growing on the bathroom walls and hideous 1970s patterned carpets. It was also flooded with light, due to the floor-to-ceiling windows that made it so perfect for painting in. They still retained their original full-length shutters, the ones Dan used to kick shut whenever we became over-whelmed by passion.

When did we become *underwhelmed* by passion, and why? And can Dan and Hannah reverse the trend, as well as Danny and Pammy? I guess it has to be worth a try.

* * *

I've gone and done it now, or rather, Pammy has. She's just invited Danny to Eva's party, and Danny says he'd love to come! He also says something else, something that almost freaks me out.

I can't wait to meet you, though I already feel I know you really well. It's weird how familiar you seem.

★   ★   ★

Why do ideas sound eminently reasonable one day and insane the next? The word "meltdown" was created for how I feel when I wake up this morning and recall that Pammy's intending to meet Danny at Halloween.

I phone Eva, ignoring the fact that it's 6:30am. Emergencies don't wait for more sociable times of day.

"Fuck off, whoever you are," she says, by way of greeting, but she does at least listen while I regale her with my anxieties.

"Just get into Pammy mode and refuse to come out of it until after the party," she says, when I've finished. "And now let me go back to sleep."

"But what if Dan says he likes Pammy, but he doesn't like me?" I say, contemplating taking up smoking again after a decade of self-restraint.

I *bet* Pammy smokes, probably seductively, while waving a 1930s tortoiseshell cigarette holder around and purring in a voice sexier than Marlene Dietrich's.

Eva sighs, extremely loudly, then points out that it's not being Pammy that's made me more interesting, it's because I've widened my horizons since Dan and I split up.

"How can gardening have widened my horizons?" I say, looking out of the window as the sun begins to rise. "I don't think talking to flowers counts as conversation. It's pretty one-sided, in my experience."

"That's not the point," says Eva, "and that applies to drawing, as well, before you bring that up. I just meant you're doing stuff you enjoy now, and not expecting Dan to make you happy with no help from you."

It's really annoying when someone's capable of being right, as soon as they have woken up.

"If you're so smart, how come you're still single?" I ask.

"That's *why* I am," Eva replies, before the line goes dead.

I consider calling her back but rule it out on the basis that, while she's undoubtedly the smartest of my new best friends, she's definitely not a morning person.

Instead, I drag myself out of bed and approach the dressing table mirror, where I stare at myself unenthusiastically. I may be more interesting now, but I definitely don't look it. Not unless you're an anthropologist researching the effects of rough cotton sheeting on ageing faces. Maybe I should buy one of those silk pillowcases that Eva keeps going on about. I need to do something because, while the Catwoman mask will hide half my face, the other half will be on show.

Frankie's comment about there only being so much a haircut can do rings in my ears as I pull my slack jowl skin up and hold it behind them to see if Marlene's face-lift technique would work, but then my mobile starts to ring.

I pick it up with my left hand, letting go of that side of my face in the process. My cheek plummets downwards, giving me an odd resemblance to Pearl when she gets tired, though the effect looks far worse on me than it does on her. Then I realise that I still haven't answered the phone, so I drop the other side of my face, swipe the screen and say, "Hello."

Eva continues our earlier conversation as if it hadn't been interrupted by her falling back to sleep.

"You're being stupid, worrying about Pammy being more appealing than you," she says, "because you *are* Pammy, you idiot. She's just the creative side of you – the one who notices the positive, and who thinks about the good things, not just the bad."

"Have you spent the last ten minutes reading a self-help book?" I ask. "No wonder you dozed off again."

Chapter 53

It's Halloween tonight and I'm a nervous wreck. Why is it you can always get what you don't want, but so rarely what you do? If a genie popped out of a bottle and gave me one wish right this minute, I know exactly what it would be: for Eva's party to be over and for Danny-and-Pammy to be Dan-and-Hannah again.

A genie pops up after lunch, but in the guise of the Fembot – sorry, Kristin – and she's all out of wishes, though she *has* got something I don't want. When she calls me into her office she offers me a new job as Project Manager of User Experience, whatever the hell that means. I refuse, but now Esther's barely speaking to me.

Apparently, she overheard some of my discussion with the Fembot while she was on her way to the photocopier, though not enough to realise that I turned the offer of promotion down. She missed that bit because Geoff spotted her lurking outside the door and threatened to tell the Fembot she was eavesdropping if she didn't "move her arse". It's not all bad, though, because at least it means she won't know what I said to the Fembot next: that she should consider Esther for the job, "because she's better at administration and more committed to her career".

I'd prefer her to think that was the Fembot's idea, so I have no intention of mentioning what I said, even when she accuses me of "stealing her promotion" as I'm walking past her desk. By the time I reach my own, I don't need to tell her, anyway, because Geoff already has. Turns out he only made her stop eavesdropping so he could do it himself.

Now Esther's blaming the whole thing on what she describes as my "showing off" by going to the Fembot's rescue.

"You know my job's the only thing I've got!" she adds, before she swivels her chair around so I can only see her back.

I'm about to say that it's the only thing that I've got, too, but then I recall that Esther hasn't got a Joel, or a Pearl – or a Danny to her Pammy – so I count to ten, repeatedly, until I calm down a bit. Then I spend the next few hours grovelling like mad, but nothing works until it's almost time to leave for the day. At that point, the Fembot calls Esther in, offers her the job, and Esther accepts. She's all smiles when she comes out of the Fembot's office and suggests we "bury the hatchet",

Geoff mutters that she'd probably like to bury it in my skull seeing as the job was only offered to her on a trial basis, unlike when it was offered to me.

"Why?" I ask. "That makes no sense. Esther's more than up to it."

"Not as far as the Fembot's concerned," says Geoff. "She was going on about Esther showing a lack of courage and commitment by bottling out of attending the awayday when I just happened to wander past the door."

I groan before making Geoff promise he won't ever mention that to anyone else. Then I ask Esther how I can make things up to her.

"Come out with me to celebrate," she says. "Tonight."

★ ★ ★

Esther's unimpressed when I tell her I can't go out with her tonight, and even more unimpressed when I tell her why.

"I've got a fancy-dress party to go to," I say. "And Eva will kill me if I'm late."

"Ah, *Eva*," says Esther. Her expression changes completely and then she continues, "I'll find someone else to celebrate things with in future, Hannah. Don't worry about it."

Now her tone has changed as well. It's so chilly you'd think it was December instead of late October, and it makes me worry quite a lot, contrary to instructions.

I start to protest that I'm only asking for a rain check, but Esther cuts me off in mid-sentence.

"I'm sorry I bothered you in the first place," she says, and then she stalks out of the office without even saying goodbye.

I consider running after her, but I'm not sure I want to continue the discussion now. Not when I should try to calm down ready for the Danny/Pammy reveal and, anyway, I can't spare the time. There's a lot to do if I'm to turn a Hannah sow's ear into a Pammy silk purse by 9pm.

I power walk home, thinking about ways to make it up to

Esther tomorrow, and then I head straight for the bathroom to take a shower.

The door's not locked, but that turns out to be misleading. The room's already occupied by Joel and Marlon, who've already started getting ready for tonight. I'd forgotten they always dress up for Halloween.

I order them to hurry up and then Joel demands to know why he and Marlon haven't been invited to Eva's birthday party.

"There are bound to be hot models there," he adds.

I hadn't thought of that, so I forget about gaining access to the bathroom and message Danny instead, for reassurance.

He claims he'll only have eyes for me, then refuses to tell me what his costume's going to be, though he adds that his plan to sweep me off my feet should give me a clue. It doesn't, but the general idea's so wonderful that I spend ages visualising it, while Joel and Marlon continue to faff about in the bathroom. The swearing level seems to be increasing with every minute that passes, so eventually I go back upstairs, to investigate.

"Fuck's SAKE," yells Joel, as I step into the bathroom.

"Don't you swear at me," I say, stopping dead in shock. "You're not too old to be grounded, you know."

Joel corrects this erroneous assumption in no uncertain terms, but then apologises and explains he wasn't swearing at me anyway.

"It's these bloody contact lenses," he says. "You were right, Mum. It *is* stressful putting them in."

Why do young people never listen to a word you say until

they've proved the value of your advice by experiencing the consequences of ignoring it? I *told* Joel he and Marlon would regret basing their entire Halloween outfits on the concept of *less is more*. They insisted they didn't need any costumes because wearing ordinary clothes with weird, red slitty-eyed contact lenses would represent a "mindfuck of epic proportions" by messing with people's expectations. I put that load of nonsense down to laziness at the time, and now Joel admits that I was right.

He and Marlon both look wrecked: their hands are shaking and sweaty, and their faces pale as they explain that they've only managed to insert one lens each so far. The eyes that are still contact-less are now so bloodshot, they're redder than the ones that aren't.

"The list of things that can go wrong when you use these lenses is a bit of a worry, too," says Joel, to my amazement.

He's always claimed that reading warning notices is a waste of time, so I point that out.

"It *is* a waste of time," he replies. "The warnings are what stressed us out so much, we'd lost our nerve before we even started putting the bloody things in."

It's almost 7:45pm by now, but when I yell at the boys to get a move on, it doesn't help to speed them up. First Joel drops his other lens onto the floor, which means it has to be cleaned and soaked again, and then Marlon succeeds in inserting his second one, only for it to migrate to the back of his eye. Cue more swearing from all parties, including me.

"Let's go for make-up instead," says Joel. "Mum, lend me yours?"

No chance, not now I own the expensive kind. I shake my head, and then Marlon has his bright idea.

"Face paint, Joel!" he says. "The stuff we bought last year's still at my house, so let's go there!"

When Joel agrees, they both rush for the front door, while yelling goodbye. It's time for Catwoman to take centre stage.

★　★　★

Shit, shit, shit, shit, SHIT!!! I'm sorry, I know that makes me sound like Joel, but this is justified. How the hell are you supposed to put on a latex bodysuit? I can't seem to pull mine up further than my calves before it gets stuck. I text Eva in a panic and, thankfully, she replies immediately.

Talc yourself first. Then ease it on, and take your time.

Time is exactly what I haven't got, along with talc, so now I'm going to have to race round to Tesco Metro and see if they've got some there. Talc, I mean, not time.

I pull the Catwoman suit off and kick it under the bed, in case Joel decides to return home while I'm out. Then I pull on a grotty old pair of jogging bottoms and a hoodie that once belonged to him, throw my coat over the top and rush out of the door. It's dark, so hopefully I won't bump into anyone I know, or get run over by a bus, seeing as I'm ignoring Pearl's rule about never leaving the house without wearing decent underwear.

I run all the way and it only takes me ten minutes to get

to the junction of the street where Tesco is. I can see the store from the pedestrian crossing where I stand, waiting for the lights to change.

It's drizzling, I'm out of breath and a bit lightheaded, too, partly from the running, and partly from worrying about how things are going to turn out with Dan tonight. Maybe that's why I don't spot the 4x4 that's about to jump the red light, until I step out.

Chapter 54

I can't see anything at all, so I have no idea where I am, or even which way up. Then I hear a voice close by.

"I'm putting a blanket over you," it says. "Don't move, the ambulance is on its way."

I try to reply, but the words sound oddly muffled and then I realise I'm face-down in the road. That's when I pass out again.

★ ★ ★

I don't know how many times I come to, only to pass out again, but it must be quite a few. One minute I find myself in a brightly-lit ambulance, then everything goes black, until I regain consciousness while being wheeled at speed along a corridor.

After that, I have no idea what happens until I come to again, this time in a curtained cubicle surrounded by people wearing uniforms.

"You're in A&E," says someone on my right.

She's leaning over me and cutting Joel's hoodie off. "Can you say your name again?"

I do my best to oblige, though the words sound muffled.

"I thought she said her name was Pam, last time you asked her," says a man in a white coat.

He's just appeared on my left-hand side.

"Have a look at her phone. That should tell you," says yet another person, in the background. "Check for ICE numbers, too. Now let's take her down for a CAT scan, asap."

"Cat? I'm supposed to be Catwoman," I say, before everything returns to black.

★　★　★

At an unknown point in time, I regain consciousness but immediately assume that I must have died.

I'm lying on some sort of bed or trolley, surrounded by a giant white halo. Beyond that, everything else within my limited field of vision is also white: walls, ceiling and low storage cupboards – and the room is silent, except for a low hum in the background.

I panic and try to get off the trolley, only for a disembodied voice to say,

"Just a little longer, Hannah. Try to lie completely still. We're running the scan one more time."

I do try, but I'm now so anxious that I can't help shaking and, by the time that I'm wheeled back into my cubicle, the shaking has become so severe that someone wraps me in a foil blanket.

"Your temperature's a bit low, so this should help to warm you up," says the nurse, the one who wielded the scissors on

Joel's jogging bottoms. "You were lying in the wet road for quite some time, apparently."

I still can't recall exactly what happened, and I'm about to ask when Joel comes hurtling through the curtains of the cubicle.

"Mum!" he yells. "Oh, my God! What happened to you?"

"Never mind me," I say, mumbling a bit because of whatever's buggered up my ability to move my mouth. "What happened to you? Nurse, can you please help my son?"

Joel's cheek is split by the most horrendous bleeding cut, which looks as if someone's taken an axe to his face. I have no idea why everyone's still fussing around me when there's someone with much more serious injuries standing right in front of them, until Joel realises what I'm freaking out about and wipes half the "cut" off on his sleeve.

"Face paint, Mum," he says. "Nothing for you to worry about."

That soon proves not to be one hundred per cent accurate, as a consultant arrives and says there *is* something for me to worry about. Several things, actually, the most pressing of which is the damage to my head.

"You've got multiple skull fractures, I'm afraid," he says. "In fact, your skull seems to have cracked all over, like an eggshell, so we'll need to keep you in for a while and make sure nothing sinister's going on inside."

It's a funny old business, being a worrier. You fret and fret over *what-if's* and *what-might-have-been's*, but when someone confronts you with something genuinely worth worrying about, you barely react. I feel calmer now than I have since the day Dan walked out. I don't know why, but maybe being

369

totally powerless to influence anything just makes you roll over and wait to see what happens next. That's what I do, anyway.

★ ★ ★

If I *have* died, then Heaven's not too bad so far. Not if it involves waking up to find Richard Gere at your bedside, holding your hand.

I blink the one eye that's capable of blinking. (The other one seems to be permanently closed, though no one's offered me a mirror so I'm not sure why.)

"Hello, you," says a familiar voice.

It's Dan – wearing a full dress uniform, just like the one Richard Gere wears in *An Officer and a Gentleman*. Now I get what he meant about sweeping me off my feet, though I hope he didn't *intend* for that to happen via a 4x4.

"I can't leave you alone for five minutes, without you getting yourself into trouble, can I?" he says, pressing his lips to the hand he's holding, while his eyes seem to be either twinkling or watering a bit. It's hard to tell in the weird half-light of the trauma unit, to which he says I was moved a little while ago. Probably while I was unconscious again.

"Where's Joel?" I ask.

The last thing I remember is him saying, "I love you, Mum," when we were still in A&E.

"I sent him home to get changed once the doctors said you were stable," says Dan. "He was causing too much of a stir with all that face paint on."

I try to nod, but give up when I'm almost poleaxed by a

sudden increase in the pain in my head. Dan notices my distress and asks a nurse for more pain relief, then turns his attention back to me.

"I'd have been here sooner if I'd known, but apparently you've only got Joel's number listed under 'in case of emergency' in your phone these days," he says. "If he hadn't called me while they were moving you from A&E, I still wouldn't have had a clue what had happened to you."

He clamps his lips shut, as if he'd like to say more on that subject but doesn't dare, and then the nurse arrives with painkillers and a flimsy paper cup of water. Dan looks away while she manoeuvres a straw into my mouth to enable me to drink, and by the time he looks back again, his expression is unreadable.

I don't remember deleting his number from where it was stored under the ICE acronym, but I suppose I must have done, maybe when I was in a fury at him for walking out on me. I don't remember a lot of things at the moment, actually. I just want to sleep, though the nurse seems determined not to allow me to, or not for more than fifteen minutes at a time.

Every time I doze off, she rouses me and starts asking annoying questions like what date it is and which government's running the country, for goodness' sake. I get quite stroppy about it until I realise she's ascribing that to my head injury, too, instead of to being asked daft questions while overtired. After that, I answer as best as I can each time, then squeeze Dan's hand and go back to sleep.

My insomnia seems to have disappeared now he's sitting

next to me, though the Exploding Head Syndrome's a whole lot worse.

★ ★ ★

When morning comes, Dan hasn't moved from his position alongside my bed, though he's fast asleep in the chair. I lie still and stare at him, until he senses me looking and wakes up.

"How do you feel?" he asks, rubbing his eyes, then taking hold of my hand again.

"I'm not sure," I say, though "Weirdly happy you're here" would probably sum it up.

I'm not letting myself think about the fact that, when he does go home eventually, it will be to the house he shares with Bonkers Alice rather than the one he used to share with me. Pretending that's not the case gets even easier as the next couple of days pass in a haze of tests and further X-rays, all of which Dan insists on being present for.

He breathes a big sigh of relief when the maxillofacial surgeon says there shouldn't be any permanent damage to my sight, as my eye socket looks as if it's still intact.

"Why does my mouth hurt so much?" I mumble. It's like talking through a mouthful of pebbles, and as uncomfortable as that sounds.

Dan informs me I bit through my lip when my face made contact with the bonnet of the 4x4.

"The police said you left a perfect imprint of a kiss embedded in the metal," he adds. "That's why you've got a pout like Pamela Anderson's at the moment, though she probably paid for hers."

I fix him with my one good eye, but he just looks back innocently, so I conclude his reference to Pamela Anderson must have been a coincidence. That's a relief, as I've only just remembered about his date with Pammy. He's bound to think she stood him up.

He doesn't seem too bothered about it, if he does, which is a good job given I'm nowhere near a computer so I can't send him an email to apologise. Even if I could, I couldn't, if you see what I mean. I'm not allowed to use any sort of screen until I'm fully over my concussion. I'm also not allowed to use the phone, which is why I have to rely on Joel to tell Pearl what's happened, and Eva too, though I request that they don't visit until I'm back at home. I don't feel like talking much, and anyway, I'm perfectly happy being with Dan – and Joel, who takes over periodically, so Dan can get some sleep.

Joel's the one who's with me when the neurologist appears at the end of my bed late on Sunday afternoon.

"I was called in for an emergency," he says, "so I thought I'd pop by and see how you're feeling while I'm here."

Doctors never trust a patient's judgement, do they? When I say I'm fine, the neurologist double-checks this with the nurse.

"How's Mrs Pinkman been doing?" he asks. "Any more signs of confusion since I last examined her?"

"Not really," says the nurse. "Though she did say she was in China on one of the occasions when we asked her where she thought she was."

★ ★ ★

Joel says me thinking I was in China is "trippy", but he finally agrees not to tell Dan about it when I say there's no point worrying people about something that happened in the early stages after the accident, not when I'm making good progress now.

"Fair enough," he says, as Dan walks back onto the ward.

He takes the chair that Joel's just vacated, then smiles at me. I feel lightheaded when I look back at him, though I'm not sure if that's the concussion or the relief of him acting like my husband again. It's a nice feeling, whichever it is, and Dan seems happy about it, too. He spends the evening telling me about his plans for the future, the redundancy that's now taken place, and a new project that he's been working on. He won't tell me what that is, as he wants it to be a surprise, but he does say he'll be self-employed.

"So I'll easily be able to spend time with you while you're recovering, Han," he adds. "Then you won't have to be on your own while Joel's at work."

The mention of work seems to remind him that I'm supposed to be at *Halfwits* in the morning, though I've forgotten about work altogether while I've been in hospital. The only time anything *Halfwits*-related occurred to me at all was when one of the nurses told me that her daughter uses HOO to get other people to do her homework for her.

"I'll let your boss know what's happened," says Dan, standing up and getting ready to leave for the night. "But is there anyone else I should notify that you're in hospital? Anyone important?"

He says *important* in a very meaningful way, and seems relieved when I say no.

"When you phone work, though," I continue, "can you ask to speak to someone called Esther rather than the Fembot, please? Esther's just been made a manager, so she'll be keen to be treated like one."

Dan agrees but makes no further comment. Instead, he kisses me goodbye, though this time he puts his lips to mine rather than to my undamaged cheek, as he's been doing up 'til now. It doesn't seem to hurt at all, so I get him to do it again, to make sure.

Chapter 55

I'm going to be allowed home tomorrow and I can't wait to tell Dan about it. I just wish he'd hurry up. He's usually here much earlier in the day than this, unless now I'm getting better, the staff are insisting he sticks to designated visiting hours?

Those are almost over by the time that he finally arrives, bearing a couple of bags containing clothes and toiletries, but he doesn't answer when I ask why he's so late.

"God knows what's in that bag," he says. "I told Joel to pack whatever he thought you'd need."

"Well, I doubt I'll have much call for sun cream," I say, opening the sponge bag first. "Or beard oil, either."

Dan doesn't laugh, and nor does he sit down. He doesn't take my proffered hand either, not even when I waggle it hopefully in his direction.

"Work said you're not to worry about however long you have to be off," he says, "and they all send you their love. Are you positive there's no one else I should have contacted?"

"No," I say. "No one else."

Dan gives me a quizzical look, then turns to leave, even

though there are still ten more minutes until visiting time is officially over. I reach out to detain him, then ask if he can drive me home from the hospital tomorrow, but he says he can't.

"Can someone else come and get you instead?" he asks. "I've got places to go and people to see tomorrow, I'm afraid."

"I suppose so," I say, after a pause during which I try very hard not to cry. I'm not successful, but Dan doesn't seem to notice the tear that rolls out of my undamaged eye.

"Sleep well," he says, and then he walks away.

He doesn't kiss me goodbye, he doesn't look back – and no, I do *not* sleep well.

★   ★   ★

"Sorry, Mum," says Joel when he arrives at the hospital to pick me up in Marlon's psychedelic camper van. "I know you'd probably have preferred me to order a taxi, but Marlon offered. He's trying to make it up to me."

"Make up for what?" I ask, though I don't much care.

I'm too busy worrying about what the hell is wrong with Dan. Has he worked out that I am Pammy? Or has he just remembered that, if he's in love with either of us, it's with her, not me?

"Marlon abandoned a bro for the sake of a woman," says Joel. "Which is *so* not cool."

He goes on to explain that Marlon got together with someone at Halloween when he and Joel gatecrashed Eva's birthday party, which is the first I've heard of it.

God knows what would have happened if I'd been at the party dressed as Catwoman to Dan's Richard Gere and then Joel had turned up. I give a brief lecture on why you shouldn't go to anything to which you haven't been invited, and then Joel says he didn't make it to the party proper, anyway. Apparently, he and Marlon had only just walked into the lobby at *Viva Vintage* when Joel got the call from the police saying I'd been in an accident.

"Marlon had to go to the loo while I was still on the phone," he continues, "so although he knew something had happened to you, I didn't wait to tell him I was leaving. I just went. Now he's claiming that he only got off with this woman because he 'over-celebrated' when I texted him to say that you weren't dead. He's been spending all his free time with her ever since, so he hasn't used his van for days."

Joel wheels me out onto the forecourt of the hospital and gestures at Marlon to drive towards us, while I blink my good eye in a shaft of weak sun. The bad eye still can't blink, so that just waters.

"I thought this van was Marlon's shag-pad," I say, trying to take an interest in someone other than myself. "So you'd think he'd be using it more, not less, if that's the case."

"It used to be," says Joel. "But this woman's got her own place, and Marlon says it's great. He says *she's* great, as well. I don't know what's got into him."

Whatever it is, Marlon's looking happy about it. He beams at me as he pulls up in the van, and even offers to pull out the bed so I can lie down on the way home, if I like. I refuse and remain upright all the way, though my head's spinning a bit by the time that we arrive, which could be due to the fact that the van's psychedelic on the inside as well as the outside. It's like an abstract representation of my state of mind.

★　★　★

Marlon drives off tooting his horn after Joel helps me out of the van and up the path. He's still patting his pockets down in search of the keys when the front door opens from inside.

"Surprise!" says Pearl.

She hugs me so hard that I wince, then plumps the cushions on the sofa and orders me to sit down. It's only when I've dropped clumsily into a half-prone position that I notice Albert.

"How are you doing, Hannah, my girl?" he says. "Been in the wars a bit, haven't you?"

Kindness is such a bitch. Before I know it, I'm sobbing and hiccuping until my head hurts almost as much as it did on the day of the accident.

"It's the shock," says Pearl to Joel, who's looking completely freaked out now.

I try to blow my nose as gently as possible and make a concerted effort to get a grip. It almost works, apart from the odd rogue sob.

"Shall I phone Dad?" asks Joel, as yet another one escapes.

I don't trust my voice, so I just shake my head. If Dan cared about me he'd be here already, wouldn't he? Everyone else who does is in this room, apart from Eva, and Joel says she's coming round as soon as she's finished work, now I've lifted my ban on visits by anyone other than him and Dan.

Even my *Halfwits* colleagues seem to care more about me than I thought they did, as there's a huge bunch of flowers in the middle of the coffee table and a card signed by everyone including Esther, and the Fembot, too.

"They look nice," I say, "though that's a weird scent they're giving off. It seems to be making my headache worse."

"It will be," says Pearl. "I hate bloody lilies. The smell always makes me think of funeral homes, which is not something you want to be reminded of at my age."

She looks over at Albert, who laughs and says, "Too true. Not when there's still so much living to do."

For him and Pearl, that may be true. For me, lilies seem the perfect choice, if they also symbolise the death of other things – like Dan-related hopes and dreams.

* * *

Eva arrives, just as Pearl and Albert are leaving, so it seems as if everyone's come to an agreement to make sure I'm not left alone during my first day back at home. Everyone apart from Dan, that is. Joel says *he* phoned earlier to check whether I'd got home okay, but didn't want to "bother" me by speaking to me himself.

"Oh," I say.

"I'm sure he'll come round tomorrow, or the next day, Mum," says Joel. "Or soon, anyway."

Joel doesn't sound any more convinced by that than I am, so when he goes out to collect the takeaway he's ordered, I ask Eva to log on to Pammy's *No-kay Cupid* account. Maybe

Dan's been more open with the pint-sized one about what is going on with him.

Eva can't understand why I haven't checked Pammy's emails already. She says she'd have done it "as soon as Dan started behaving like a weirdo".

"I couldn't," I say. "I'm still not allowed to look at screens, though I'm not sure why. I assume it'll cause long-term brain damage if I do."

"It's arguable *that* took place months ago," says Eva, as she picks up my laptop and opens it.

That's when I discover that, if I hadn't clicked that thing that remembers your passwords when I first set up my *No-kay Cupid* account, no one would be able to access Pammy's emails ever again, as I can't recall my log-in details.

"It's probably temporary amnesia," says Eva, "due to the accident. I wouldn't worry, if I were you."

I'm reassured for all of thirty seconds, until she opens Pammy's inbox, and scrolls through the contents.

"There's nothing new in here," she says, after a cursory glance at the screen. "The last thing Danny sent Pammy was just before my party, when he was going on about sweeping her off her feet – or you off yours."

Eva's not supposed to be actually *reading* the messages, but that doesn't matter half as much as the fact that Dan's dropped Pammy, as well as me. I'm not sure who's taking it hardest, me or her, and I'm still trying to deal with this latest blow when my mobile rings. It's Joel, calling from Nando's.

"My money-off voucher's expired, Mum," he says. "So it's going to cost more than I thought. Can I use your card to

pay for it, as I haven't got enough cash on me? I've just realised I've still got it from when the hospital gave me your
belongings to look after."

I tell him to go ahead and am just about to remind him
to get me a portion of savoury rice when I realise that he's
already begun the transaction. In the background, someone
says, "Please enter your PIN."

"Joel," I say. "Stop! I can't remember the number!"

There are four beeps and then Joel says, in a low voice,
"Don't be stupid, Mum. It's the same PIN you use for
everything, including the parental controls on the TV. I worked
that out years ago."

If he's so clever, then maybe he can also work out what's
gone wrong with Dan. Eva's only halfway there. She says she
has no idea why Dan's being so cold to me, but it's obvious
why he's cross with Pammy.

"She stood him up," she says. "You should have seen the state
he was in at my party. I recognised him from that photo you
keep beside the bed, so I was watching him, though he didn't
realise who I was. He kept pacing around the room looking at
his watch, and then, all of a sudden, he got his phone out,
listened for a few seconds and went hurtling out of the room."

If Eva spotted Dan at the party, on the basis of a barely-seen
photo, then Joel would definitely have recognised him, and
Catwoman, too. Thank God my accident interrupted his
gatecrashing plan.

I'm in the middle of saying so to Eva when Joel walks
through the door and demands to know why we're talking
about him.

"I was telling Eva what a good son you are," I say, "and how fast you got to the hospital once you heard what had happened to me, especially when you should have been partying instead."

"That's me," says Joel, "devoted to my dear little Mum."

He's not even being sarcastic, so I blow him a kiss which is harder work than it sounds, what with my puffy Pammy lips. I'm not sure it compensates Joel for missing the party, though. Eva says that was *really* good.

Chapter 56

The concussion must be wearing off, as things are coming into clearer focus now. That's probably why I spend my second day back at home in a state of abject misery.

Pearl's bewildered by how fed up I am, as she says I'm lucky to be alive, and Joel seems to feel the same. He calls me after he's finished work to say he's going round to Dan's to return a witch's hat he borrowed from Bonkers Alice during his last-minute fancy-dress emergency, which reminds me I've forgotten to deal with my Catwoman suit. That's still under the bed.

I've only just packed it into its box and hidden it safely from view when Joel comes home and starts regaling me with supposedly funny anecdotes about Dan's flatmates in an attempt to cheer me up. As these all involve marital break-downs, his good intentions misfire a bit.

Aasim's wife has thrown him out again. She caught him smoking an e-cigarette behind the garden shed.

"I can't see why that's a problem," I say. "Surely e-cigs are better than cigarettes?"

"Not when you're filling them with cannabis oil," says Joel, who enjoys Aasim's catastrophic attempts to reconcile with his wife much more than I've enjoyed my equally disastrous ones to get back with Dan. Maybe that's because Joel's still so anti-relationships, especially now that Marlon's "so loved-up".

"He's busy tonight and tomorrow evening, too," says Joel, in disgust.

Presumably being too busy is also why Dan still hasn't been round to visit me. Maybe this new project's taking up all of his time, seeing as Pammy isn't.

"Talking of busy, how's your dad doing, Joel?" I ask. "What's he been up to this last few days?"

"Oh, for God's sake, Mum," says Joel. "You two really get on my nerves, trying to use me to find out what the other one's up to all the time. I had to tell Dad to cut it out when I was round at his house earlier."

"Cut what out?" I say.

I can't imagine why Dan would be asking what I'm up to as he must know it's nothing exciting, unless he'd find moving from bed to sofa and back again a lot more thrilling than I do. Not being able to use a computer or watch TV is leaving me with too much time on my hands, and my anxiety levels are through the roof. I've got weeks of this ahead before I'm allowed back to work, by which time I'll probably be a halfwit myself.

"Cut out asking if you've got a boyfriend," says Joel, who's finally decided to answer my question, despite it being against his ridiculous "parental engagement" rules. He pauses, then

385

adds, "A *serious* one. Were you telling me the truth when you said that you'd split up with Jude?"

I promise I was, and even invite him to look into my eyes if he doesn't believe me, but he's too distracted to take up the offer. He's contemplating the side of his thumb, which is bleeding because he's just chewed a hangnail. That's not the only thing wrong with his hands, as now I can see that his fingernails have been bitten right down to the quick.

I'm about to ask when this destructive new habit started when he returns to the subject of Dan.

"Even when I broke my rule and told Dad you hadn't got a boyfriend, he still refused to believe me."

Having just looked into a mirror for the first time since the accident, I can't see why. I'm not a pretty sight.

★ ★ ★

The evenings are really drawing in since I got out of hospital, and I've been sitting in the dark feeling sorry for myself ever since Pearl went home at 4pm today. She did offer to stay longer, as Joel's got to work late this evening, and Eva can't come round to take his place, but I told her I'd be fine. I just can't be bothered to turn on the light.

There's a cold draught coming through the window behind the sofa that I'm lying on, so I pull myself upright intending to yank the curtains closed, but then there's a loud bang, followed by a shower of golden sparks forming glowing seed heads in the sky. It's Guy Fawkes' night, which I'd forgotten about until now.

I prop myself up more comfortably and watch the fireworks light up the sky, as I recall the first time Dan bought Joel a packet of sparklers and taught him to write his name by waving them about in mid-air. I love sparklers, far more than fireworks that are often more loud noise than spectacle. There are a lot of that type going off around the house tonight, which is why I don't immediately realise that someone's banging at the door – until they really go for it.

I get up and make my way warily across the room, as I still haven't switched on the light, and I've been prone to dizziness when standing up since the accident. There's another volley of banging at the front door as I open it, at which point Eva comes flying inside as if she's just been fired from a cannon.

"Have you heard from Dan?" she asks, as another series of rockets start to go off nearby.

"No, I haven't," I say. "Why?"

My voice is almost drowned out by the noise outside, so Eva turns and shuts the front door I've accidentally left wide open.

"Because I've just seen him out on a date with someone," she says.

She reaches out to steady me as I stagger, and then almost fall.

★   ★   ★

I'm back in the living room now, though getting here wasn't without incident. First I stubbed my toe on the foot of the sofa and then I tripped over the coffee table while I was still hopping on one foot due to the pain in the big toe of the other one. At that point, Eva asked me why the hell the light wasn't on, and then – once she'd remedied that oversight – she went into the kitchen to get ice for my toe, and to search for alcohol.

Now she's just walked back into the living room, carrying a sandwich bag of crushed ice in one hand and a bottle of vodka in the other. I can only assume the latter belongs to Joel, as it certainly doesn't belong to me.

"You saw Dan out with someone?" I say, as Eva puts the sandwich bag on my foot and then sits down facing me. "Are you sure?"

"Unfortunately, yes," she says.

She opens the vodka, pours a generous shot into a rather grubby-looking glass, then takes a slug. Then she repeats the pouring process, but this time hands the glass to me.

"Drink that," she says. "You're going to need it."

I shake my head and pass the glass straight back to her.

"I'm not supposed to drink alcohol yet," I say.

"No, well, lots of things aren't *supposed* to happen," says Eva. "But they still fucking do."

She downs the second shot of vodka almost as if she's unaware that she's doing so, then tells me that, not only has she just seen Dan out on a date with someone, but "that someone was someone we both know".

As the firework display outside reaches its crescendo, she adds, "It was Esther."

Chapter 57

Initially, I don't believe what Eva's just told me, and then I decide that, if it's true, Esther must have run into Dan by accident and now she's probably trying to talk him into getting back with me. The one thing she couldn't *possibly* be doing is trying to steal him away from me, if you *can* steal someone who's already chosen to leave you of his own accord.

"Esther wouldn't do that to me," I say to Eva. "She wouldn't. I know she was a bit upset about the job thing and not being invited to your party, but she's still my friend. She knows I still love Dan, and how much I miss him, too. I told her that after we ran into him in Tesco before my accident."

"You're too nice for your own good," Eva replies, drinking yet another glass of Joel's vodka. "That woman knows exactly what she's doing. I waylaid her in the ladies' loo."

It turns out that when Eva questioned Esther about why the hell she was out with Dan, Esther told her to mind her own business because Dan's not interested in me any more.

"Then she said he's a really nice guy, who you were 'obviously

389

too selfish and stupid to appreciate'," says Eva. "That's a direct quote, in case you're wondering."

I risk a swig of vodka myself, without bothering to use a glass.

"What did you say to that?" I ask, handing Eva back the bottle.

"I called her a prize bitch," she says, "which I now think was far too moderate."

I agree, especially once Eva tells me that when she asked Esther how she proposed to go on working in the same place as me while making a play for my husband, Esther corrected her and said, "ex-husband". Then she said it didn't matter what I thought as, if I didn't like it, I could leave my job.

"She even claimed you wouldn't be missed if you did," says Eva, "which I'm sure is a big fat lie."

Eva's so angry, she's almost in tears by now. I'm already there.

"I'm glad someone thinks I'm still worth something," I say, searching my pockets for a tissue.

There isn't one, so I resort to wiping my nose on my sleeve. I'm past caring about social niceties, and anyway, Eva doesn't notice. She's far too busy ranting about Esther's treachery.

"I even thought about appealing to her better nature," she says, "but then I realised I couldn't tell that absolute witch that you and Dan were on the verge of a reconciliation, without telling her that you'd been talking to him as someone else online. And I didn't think you'd want him to find out about that from her!"

I don't know *what* I want any more, other than for everything to go back to how it was at the end of last year, before Dan and I had that stupid argument. Now my *Titanic* dream is coming true: he's rowing away from me and Joel, as fast as he can, and with Esther sitting next to him in the bloody lifeboat. She's probably cheering while we drown.

Eva looks at her phone then says, "Shit! I'm sorry, Han, I have to go outside for a moment. That was my date asking how much longer I'll be. I forgot he'd brought me here, so he's been waiting up the road since I arrived."

She hugs me hard and I hug back, even though it hurts a bit. My shoulder's still sore from when I bounced off the bonnet of the 4x4 and into the road.

Eva notices my sharp intake of breath and releases me, pulling back to look into my face.

"I'd ignore him and wait until he buggers off," she says, "but I really like this one –"

"Don't be silly," I say. "You go. I'll be fine. Honestly."

I think I make that sound convincing, even though fine is the opposite of how I feel. Not only have I lost Dan, but I've lost him to one of my closest friends – Esther, that two-faced bitch from hell – and now I'm going to lose Eva too, if she's finally met someone she likes so much. I'll be back to Billy-No-Mates before you can say Jack Robinson.

"I'll come back tomorrow evening, and we'll work out a plan," says Eva. "We'll find a way to sort this out in the long run, I promise you. We'll kill Esther if we can't come up with a better idea."

We don't need a better one, as far as I'm concerned.

★   ★   ★

I spend the next half-hour walking round and round the house in circles, like a lioness in a zoo. A dizzy, wobbly, half-blind lioness, admittedly, and one that keeps driving herself mad by envisaging her mate getting it on with another member of the pride. I just don't know what else to do, though that doesn't stop me racking my brains in an attempt to find a quick solution.

First I decide to get a taxi to the pub where Eva saw Dan and Esther together, and to create a major scene when I arrive, but then I decide I can't humiliate myself like that. Not in public, anyway, and not when I've still got the world's most hideous black eye.

Next, I consider going round to Dan's house and lying in wait in a bush again, ready to jump out wielding an axe if Esther should come home with him. But what if Dan goes to hers instead, and then I end up lying in the bush all night? I could be dead of hypothermia by the time the morning comes.

Each new solution is more problematic than the last, so eventually I stop pacing and sit down on the sofa.

I'm paralysed by indecision, hurt and jealousy. And I *cannot* understand how any of this could have happened. I thought my only rival was Pammy, but maybe there are hundreds of the buggers? It's time to renege on my no-snooping rule, even if that does mean risking brain damage from using a screen.

I turn on my laptop and then log into Danny's *No-kay Cupid* account; thankfully he hasn't changed the password. Probably because he's been too busy dating every woman on the planet to worry about internet security, all while pretending to be solely devoted to *PintSizedPammy*.

392

I open his inbox and scroll upwards past all his messages until I reach the latest ones, and that's when I find something I wasn't expecting. Yes, it's an email from someone new, with a thumbnail of her profile picture attached, which I sort-of *was* expecting. But despite the fact that the photo's been taken from an angle, I wasn't expecting to recognise the woman in it. The only reason I do, is because it's Esther.

She's pouting as if her life depended on it, and I'm temporarily overwhelmed by the force of the hatred that washes over me when I look at her, but then I take some deep breaths and open the email she sent to Dan. At that point, everything becomes crystal clear.

The date on the email shows it was sent on the same day I asked Dan to contact Esther to inform her of my accident, later on that same evening.

From: Esther Wood
To: Dan Pinkman
Subject: Hannah

Hi Dan,
Nice to speak to you earlier today, despite the circumstances. I was so shocked to hear about Hannah I forgot to ask you something, so I was glad to find you on this site. Has anyone told Hannah's partner about what's happened yet? I think he's abroad at the moment …

What partner? Apparently Esther knows this mystery man well enough to have his number on her phone, even though he

393

only exists in her imagination. Her *warped* imagination, not that mine's much better. I seem to have doodled a tombstone with "RIP Esther" inscribed on it while I've been reading through her message to Dan, and I'm just about to scribble it out when I notice her P.S.

If you ever fancy meeting for a drink, just give me a call. I'm sure we've got loads more in common than our match percentage indicates!

She finishes with a stupid smiley face, but I'll soon wipe that off her duplicitous, Hide-the-Blemished one. I pick up my phone and hit speed-dial.

Chapter 58

"Hi, Hannah," says Dan, though he's hard to hear over the hubbub of noise in the background. He and Ms Ultimate Betrayal are obviously still in the pub.

"Ask Esther to give you my so-called partner's number," I say. "Do it now!"

"What?" says Dan.

His tone's changed from concern to hostility, so it's now a pretty good match for mine.

"I'd have thought you'd have that number already," he adds. "So why play games?"

"Oh, *I'm* not the one who's playing games," I say. "But Esther is. Go on, ask her for the number."

I can hear Esther saying something to Dan now, though I can't make out what.

I do hear what he says in reply: "Hannah wants to know her partner's number, for some unknown reason."

There's a pause, and then Dan adds, "Though I don't know why she didn't ring you, instead of me."

That thought seems to get the cogs spinning in his brain,

even if they're not exactly whirling round at the speed of light, because then he says,

"Hannah – how did you know Esther would be with me this evening?"

He sounds so confused, I'm almost feeling sorry for him by now. Almost.

"Never mind that," I say. "What does Esther say the number is? Tell her to hurry up."

I wait for what feels like hours while Esther starts mumbling again, but finally Dan comes back on the line.

"She says she can't find it," he says.

"That's because she never had it in the first place, Dan," I say. "Imaginary partners tend not to be contactable by phone, and I ought to sue the bloody woman for slander for saying I have a boyfriend when I don't. For libel, I mean. Seeing as she *wrote* it down."

Dan remains silent, presumably while his cogs do a bit more whirring, so I wait a few seconds and then I add,

"Can you come round now, or do I have to come to you? If you choose the latter option, you'd better warn Esther to make herself scarce before I arrive. I don't like people who lie, or stab their friends in the back."

I don't know who's more surprised by Rambo Hannah: me or Dan. I quite like her, though.

★   ★   ★

Dan's definitely scared of Rambo Hannah. He turns up less than half an hour later, probably to avoid my threat to go to the pub and punch Esther if he kept me waiting. I'm not sure I'd really have gone through with the punching part, but it seems as if Esther believed I would.

"She admitted she lied just before I left," says Dan, as I open the front door and usher him in. "Though God knows why she did, or why she asked me out. I only agreed to meet her because I wanted to find out about your secret partner."

I'm still letting *that* information sink in, when Dan asks a tricky question.

"How did you know she'd written something about him down?" he says.

Oh, God. Now's not the time for Rambo Hannah to lose her nerve, but I think she might be going to. I swallow, hard, then try to position my face so Dan can't see my swollen eye.

"I will tell you in a minute, I promise," I say, "but first, there's something else."

Dan looks across at me and, all of a sudden, his face looks lined, and almost as anxious as I bet mine does.

"What now, Hannah?" he asks. "I'm not sure I can take much more. It's been a very stressful week already, what with thinking you might die."

I didn't know that was even a possibility, but it's nice to hear he wasn't too keen on the idea, even though he'll probably change his mind once I've told him the awful truth.

"I love you, Dan," I say, gabbling the words and looking down at my feet to avoid meeting his eyes. "I still do, as much as I ever did. More, probably, now I've realised how much I was taking you for granted before you decided we ought to split up."

"*You* decided that," says Dan.

This is hard enough already without hairs being split all over the place, so I give him a reproachful look to silence him.

"And I wish you'd come back," I continue, still gabbling in case of further interruptions. "Though you definitely won't want to, once you know how I found out what Esther wrote. I hacked your *No-kay Cupid* account."

I glance at Dan's face, which looks incredulous, and then I reach over and grab the vodka bottle that's still on the coffee table where Eva left it, hours and hours ago, or so it seems.

"How the hell did you know I was on *No-kay Cupid*?" Dan asks, as he snatches the bottle from me and takes a swig.

I make a variety of noises, ranging from "Erf" to "Um".

This next bit's going to be even trickier, and I'm not sure where to start.

Eventually, I try another "Erm", and then I add, "Because I'd already hacked it once before."

Now it's Dan's turn to make unspellable noises, while his colour fades to a shade halfway between grey and pistachio green. It'd make a popular addition to Farrow and Ball's heritage paint colour chart, but it isn't a particularly flattering choice for the complexion.

"So you know about —" he says.

Then he stops dead, and takes another giant mouthful of vodka. He can't even say her name, can he? Unsurprisingly, I can.

"Pammy, you mean?" I say. "Oh, yes, I know about her. *All* about her, actually."

Dan looks so guilt-ridden that I feel terrible. He starts to speak, but I put my fingers to his lips.

"Hang on a sec," I say. "I ought to show you something, before you explain."

I go out into the hallway, and rummage about in the cupboard under the stairs where I almost succeed in giving myself a new head injury. I'm tugging at a box overhead when I dislodge one of Joel's old skateboards which falls down, missing me by millimetres. It makes a hell of a crash, and Dan shouts to ask if I'm all right.

I won't know until I've shown him what's in the box I'm trying to reach, so I don't answer. I just tug at it some more and, eventually, it jerks free, just as Dan comes into the hallway to look for me.

"Are you okay?" he asks, again.

"You tell me," I say, as I pass him the box. "Go and sit back down, then open it."

He does as he's told, and I sit right next to him. That's why I can only see one side of his face when he finally lifts the lid of the box to reveal a folded black latex costume, with a Catwoman mask on top.

*　　*　　*

Dan spends what feels like ten minutes staring at the Catwoman costume, and then he says, "It's you?"

His expression's so inscrutable I'm lost for words, so all I do is nod.

If I was expecting a big romantic ending at this point –

which I wasn't, though I *was* keeping my fingers crossed – I'm disappointed. Dan doesn't take me in his arms, he just stands back up again.

"You lied and said you were Pammy, for all that time?" he says.

It sounds terrible, when he puts it like that.

"Yeah, I did," I say, eventually. "I'm sorry."

Dan shrugs, so then I start to jabber.

"It was an accident," I say. "To start with, anyway, and then I fell back in love with you. But, by then, you seemed to be falling in love with Pammy and wanted to meet her, which is why she had to go to China. By that point, I was too scared to tell you I was her, because you liked her so much better than me."

Dan sits down again, heavily. I don't like to mention that he's parked his bottom on top of my tucked-up feet.

"I *was* falling in love with Pammy," he says. "She reminded me of you when we first met. The you I fell in love with back then, the one I thought was gone forever."

He probably feels like adding, "To be replaced by Rambo Hannah," but he doesn't. He takes my hand, instead, and starts to spin my wedding ring on my finger, round and round.

"Did you lie about *everything* when you were being her?" he says, as we both watch the ring rotate. "Not just about her name, I mean?"

"No, not everything," I say. "Just the name, being in China ... and working for MI6 while I was there, of course. The rest was true."

Dan makes a really strange noise, and for one horrible moment, I think I may have made him cry. Then it dawns on me that he's laughing.

"It *is* you," he says, and then he kisses me, hard, on my puffy, pouty Pammy lips.

★　★　★

Dan and I stop kissing when we hear a cough. One of those "Ahem, someone's watching you" coughs – emitted by Joel, who's come into the house without slamming the door for the first time in his entire life.

"Don't mind me," he says, when we turn to face him. "I'll go and see if Marlon's around, and give you guys some privacy."

He starts to walk out of the room, then ducks back in, quickly, just to make a thumbs-up sign.

"*He* seems pleased," I say, to Dan. "Though I'm not sure how we're going to explain to him how all this came about."

"Well, you're the one with the most explaining to do," says Dan. "So I'm leaving that bit up to you. Now how about if I help you put this costume on, then take it off again?"

I agree, on condition he tells me what he learned at the Sex Museum while he's at it.

★　★　★

Next time Dan and I attempt to have sex, I think we'll do it round at Bonkers Alice's house. That way we can't be interrupted by Joel returning home less than an hour after he went out.

"Bloody hell," he shouts, as he comes in and reverts to his usual form by slamming the door. "Mum, you won't believe what I've just found out!"

It's a good job Dan's already removed my Catwoman outfit, as otherwise I might have died of a heart attack from the stress of trying to explain to Joel why I was wearing it. As it is, I just pull on my dressing gown in a hurry, while Dan dons his trousers and shirt, and then we head downstairs.

"You'll never guess who Marlon's dating," says Joel, pulling the world's most disgusted face.

I match that, though with a shocked one, when Joel answers his rhetorical question.

"Eva," he says. "Your cougar mate!"

"No! She promised me she wouldn't go there," I say, bewildered by why Eva would betray me, too.

Can't I trust *any* of my new friends? Next Albert will probably turn out to be a retired gangster or something equally out of character.

I dial Eva's number, and she answers on the first ring.

"I was just going to phone you," she says. "I know you're going to want to kill me, but there are mitigating circumstances, honestly."

These turn out to have something to do with the hazards intrinsic to pulling someone while they're unrecognisable, due to face paint and fancy-dress.

"By the time I realised the sexy zombie was Marlon," Eva says, "things had gone too far to stop. You get that, don't you, Han? It's a bit like what happened to you with Pammy, isn't it?"

It is, annoyingly, so I shut up. It's not up to me to judge who people fall in love with, after all – unless it's a purely one-sided obsession like the one Esther seems to have developed for Dan. Eva's chuffed I've dealt with *her*, but now she wants to know what I'm planning to do as my next step.

"I assume you're going to resign?" she says. "Seeing as you can't carry on working alongside that bitch."

I haven't even thought about that yet, but now Eva comes to mention it, the idea of resigning's very tempting. I can't do it, though, not without another job to go to, and not when Dan and I have just agreed we're going to take things slowly and date until the contract expires on his room at Alice's. Even if he *was* moving straight back in, he couldn't afford to keep me unless his redundancy package is a lot bigger than he's letting on, and I wouldn't expect him to, anyway. I need a job to keep my brain from atrophying. Once it's recovered from being hit by a 4x4, that is.

"I can't see why your brain's a factor," says Eva, when I explain my reasons for not telling *Halfwits* to stuff their job immediately. "It's not as if you've been using it while you've been working there. Not your creative brain, anyway."

"Good point," I say, although some of the suggestions I got from *Halfwits* users in answer to my question about how to take revenge on Esther were inventive, to say the least. Most of them were probably illegal, too.

"I know my job's not right for me," I say, "but it's not as if anyone's offering a better option."

As usual, Eva proves me wrong.

★   ★   ★

There's no greater feeling than resigning from your job because you've got one a million times better, is there? Especially not when it allows you to tell your new line manager to go fuck herself at the same time.

I do the sweary part by sending a text to Esther, so as not to punish anyone else at *Halfwits* for her sins. Then I write a perfectly polite email to the Fembot, suggesting that we stay in touch, and saying how much I've enjoyed working for her (a bit of a fib, at least until recently), and with my team (largely true, apart from Geoff).

I end the email with a bang.

As soon as I'm declared fit to work again, I'll be starting my new job as an illustrator for **Viva Vintage.**

Winter

Chapter 59

It's fab, Dan being able to take time off whenever he likes now he's working for himself, though he still won't tell me what he's up to. He says he'll be ready to make the big reveal by New Year, just after he moves back in with me. In the meantime, he's booked us a long weekend by the sea to celebrate us getting back together, and my new job.

We're sitting in our rented apartment looking out across the ocean. Even though it's December now, the sun's just come out from behind the clouds, and it's glinting off the waves breaking onto the beach below the apartment block. I'm still not supposed to look at flashing lights, but I'm hoping that sparkles on water don't count.

They're difficult to sketch in pencil, though, so I'm just rummaging around for my watercolours when Dan says, "You've explained yourself, but you still haven't asked about *my* reasons."

"Your reasons for what?" I say.

"Why I acted the way I did after we had that stupid row."

I push my sketchbook aside as Dan explains how things

panned out, from his point of view. It's a revelation, to say the least.

"I spent the next few days waiting for the blow to fall," he says, "with the tension building up and up. Eventually, it got to the point where I couldn't take it any more, so I thought it'd be easier to bring the hammer down myself."

"Well, that was a bit drastic," I say. "Wouldn't talking to me about it have been a better option? Or even apologising?"

Dan gives me a warning look, which scares me a bit, but then he winks and carries on.

"If you weren't going to eat humble pie, I sure as hell wasn't going to," he says. "And, anyway, I was shocked."

It seems we both were, mainly at how an argument can become serious so quickly, especially when it starts with something as ridiculous as half-naked Brits staggering about in Spain.

"But you're the one who said you didn't fancy me," I say, thinking back.

That was the killer, as I recall.

Dan rolls his eyes, then says that no one fancies their wife in the middle of a shouting match.

"Except in films," he adds. "When they go from hating each other's guts to shagging each other's brains out within a split second."

There should be a law against scenes like that, if they're so misleading.

"But you implied you hadn't fancied me for ages before we had the argument," I say, after a pause. "You know you did."

Dan strokes my shoulder as if to acknowledge that statement might – just *might* – be true.

"But we'd been doing nothing but snap at each other about stupid, petty things for ages by then," he says, in mitigation. "And you'd go mad whenever I asked, 'What's the point?'"

I move my shoulder out of stroking reach. I always hated it when Dan said, "What's the point?" He might just as well have said he wanted to split up, there and then.

He sighs, pulls me back towards him, and resumes the stroking. Then he says that nothing sums up the difference between men and women better than this.

"When I said, 'What's the point?' I was asking what the point was in having such a stupid argument," he says. "But you always heard, 'What's the point of our relationship?', didn't you?"

"Um," I say.

I did, but I hate it when I'm in the wrong. (That's who Joel gets it from.) There must be some way to defend myself against Dan's accusation, which is seeming more unfair by the minute, now I'm making an effort to find it so.

"But –" I say, only for Dan to interrupt.

He seems to know exactly where I'm going to accidentally go with this, if I'm left to my own devices.

"Let's go for a walk, or something," he says, "before we end up having another row. That's what we should have done last time."

He's right, which is why we spend the rest of the afternoon in perfect harmony. Not because we go for a walk, as per his suggestion, but because we end up in bed, as per mine. You can't let a man win every round.

★　★　★

"So, did you have as much fun as this when you were single?" I ask, hours later, as I watch Dan walk across the bedroom naked, on his way to make us both a cup of coffee.

All the exercise he's been taking has certainly paid off, as has mine, to my surprise. I didn't even wait until I was under the covers before I took my clothes off this time. I'd thank Albert for his contribution to my improved fitness – and thus my sex life – if I didn't think he'd be appalled by the excess of information.

"So how *did* you spend most of your free time?" I add, because I haven't forgotten I'm still waiting for Dan's answer to my original question, the one about whether he had more fun when he was single.

"Swimming, cycling, getting pissed," he says, answering both at once. "Oh, and shagging everything that moved, of course."

He ducks, but not quickly enough to avoid being hit in the face with a well-aimed pillow. I may take up throwing the discus as my next hobby. I could become the shortest discus thrower in the West.

"I'm only joking," he says, mopping up the coffee he's just spilled with the pair of boxer shorts he discarded earlier. "Though, in the beginning, I used to try to make it sound to other people as if I was having fun, mainly to prove to myself that I was fine, instead of falling to pieces."

"That's what I kept trying to do, as well," I say. "Why the hell didn't you tell me how you were feeling, though?"

"Why didn't you tell me?" Dan replies. "I kept hoping you'd say something that would allow me to say what I was feeling, too."

I get out of bed, wrap myself in my dressing gown and walk into the living room of the apartment, thinking about what would have happened if one of us had cracked and admitted to the other how miserable we were all those months ago. The sun is setting over the sea, and the gorse and bracken on the cliffs are glowing a fiery orange in the reflected light. The scene would make such a great painting that I grab my camera to record it.

"Maybe the time we've spent apart wasn't entirely wasted," I say, as I take the first of a series of photographs. "If we hadn't, I wouldn't have started drawing again, or getting fit, and I wouldn't have met Albert, or Eva –"

"Or Esther," says Dan, sailing dangerously close to the wind again, given there are plenty more cushions within reach.

"You're right, though," he adds. "I'd still be stuck in my tedious job, and so would you. And we'd probably still be spending our free time arguing over nothing and watching our lives diminish, little by little. Instead of which –"

He makes a broad, sweeping gesture towards the view, but I know what he intends it to represent.

Chapter 60

It's mid-afternoon on New Year's Eve and everyone's at *Viva Vintage*, getting excited about Pearl's party tonight. That's being held here at the office, once we've cleared up after the photo shoot that's about to begin. The location for the party was all Eva's idea, but the photo shoot was hers and Joel's. Mainly Joel's, actually.

After Amsterdam, he decided to get a portfolio together and apply to art school, and when he mentioned his plan to Eva, she offered him some work experience as an intern. Now she says he's "a natural", and yesterday he heard he'd been offered a place at Cordwainers on their shoe design course next year. Dan and I are very proud of him, as well as relieved he'll be moving out. (We've done our best to keep the relief part secret.)

Anyway, Joel first had the idea for today's photo shoot weeks ago, during a family Sunday lunch, when someone mentioned it's almost the end of Pearl's first year at Abandon Hope, and Eva suggested celebrating with a party at *Viva Vintage*. (I know Eva's not *technically* family, but she qualifies in other ways, like being loyal, and getting almost as angry with people who stab you in the back as you do yourself.)

"That's a great idea," I said, assuming I was speaking for everyone else around the table.

I was, except for Pearl.

She objected, because she assumed the location would mean the other residents of Abandon Hope couldn't attend, but Eva told her not to be daft: of course they could.

"All right, then – it's a deal," Pearl said, "as long as you young ones don't make us oldies feel out of place."

That's when Joel had his eureka moment.

"Actually, the residents are what vintage really means," he said. "So couldn't we use them in a feature for the magazine?"

Eva thought that was a brilliant idea, which is why we're all standing around outside the offices now, watching a crowd of elderly people being helped out of the purple bus that belongs to Abandon Hope.

They're all dressed up, and they've brought bags of old clothing with them, as per Joel's instructions. They're also very excited about having an excuse to "get their glad rags on", and to have their hair – or what remains of it – restyled by Frankie. Once that's been done, Joel wants "the wrinklies" to be included in the photographs, standing next to professional models wearing the vintage clothes.

I can't take any credit for the effort that's gone into any of this, as I've only just been declared fully fit. Today's the first day of my new job and I'll be working this evening, too. Eva wants line drawings of scenes from the party, "to capture the spirit of the event".

"You know, like the sketches you did at that fashion exhibition we went to," she explains, "or the ones court artists do."

With Pearl in charge of the aged contingent, war artists seem more appropriate. She's already threatened a mass walk-out if my sketches make any of the residents look too old.

★ ★ ★

I've never been able to handle champagne, and I think I may be a bit pissed already, even though midnight's still a fair way off. It's the first time I've drunk alcohol since the vodka I swigged on the night that Dan and I got back together. The same night that Esther almost succeeded in preventing *that* from ever happening.

"Have you heard anything from her at all?" asks Eva, as we stand and survey the room together.

It's full of candles in tiny glass lanterns, and the flickering light is reflected in all the mirrors that Eva's had temporarily fitted to the walls. The Abandon Hope women are loving the effect as it's so flattering to their complexions, which is exactly why Eva chose it.

"Have I heard from who?" I say, turning to look at her.

"Your friend Esther," she says. "Though I always thought she was more of a frenemy, myself."

I don't even know what a frenemy is until Eva explains, and then I grimace in recognition. Sometimes my naivety amazes me, though never as much as it amazes Eva. We clink our glasses to real friends and lifelong friendships, and then Eva tries again.

"So, *have* you seen Esther?" she asks.

"No," I say. "And I hope I never do."

Eva looks at me as if that wasn't the answer she was expecting, though I'd have thought my response was entirely predictable.

"You're so uncharitable, Hannah," she says. "I, on the other hand, am filled with goodwill to all men, thanks to this one in particular."

She waves her glass in the direction of Marlon, who's standing close by, locked in conversation with Dan.

Being in love is totally changing Eva's personality, which is not a good thing as far as I'm concerned. I liked her just the way she was, as hostile to duplicitous so-called friends as I still am.

"I even sent Esther a Christmas present," she continues. "Stefan's business card. The one for his 'sex therapy' service."

I laugh, though I'm not sure if that was cruel or kind. It could be either, but maybe goodwill's contagious, as now Dan's moved closer and put his arm around me, I'm starting to feel a bit sorry for Esther myself. If Stefan can give her her confidence back, the way this year's given me mine, then maybe she won't feel she needs to shaft any new friends she makes in future. Or become their *frenemy*.

I raise my glass to that imaginary scenario, then turn my attention to Dan, who's whispering something into my ear.

"Don't get too drunk," he says, which I take to mean that he has designs on my person for when we get back home tonight, though apparently that's not the reason he's calling for restraint. It's because he wants me to be in a fit state to meet him at the lake at noon tomorrow.

"Why have I got to meet you there?" I say. "Surely we can go together?"

Now he's finally moved back home, there's no point taking two cars when one will do. I'd have thought Dan would be the first to object to that wasteful idea, given he's still got a membership card for Greenpeace in his wallet, but he says travelling together "won't be feasible".

"Just bring Joel and make sure you're there on time," he adds. "I've got something important to show you both when you arrive."

If we're going to the lake, then maybe I'll have something to surprise Dan with, too, if I can borrow Albert's boat. It doesn't do to be too predictable if you want your relationship to last, or so Stefan said in his most recent article for *Viva Vintage*. For once, I'm taking his advice.

"Talking of Joel, why is he so late?" I ask Dan, as someone starts banging a knife on a glass and calling for everyone "to shut up a minute".

"God knows," says Dan, as the room falls silent, and then someone turns a spotlight onto Pearl, who's looking extremely beautiful tonight, though all she said was, "Pfft," when I told her so.

"Ladies and gentlemen," she says, her clear, beautifully modulated voice perfectly audible to those of us at the back of the room, even without a microphone. "I have a brief announcement to make."

For once, I can imagine Pearl as the diplomat's wife she

used to be. Everyone's paying attention to her, waiting to hear what she says next. There's no shuffling about, no muttered conversations, just a captive audience.

She's wearing the beaded vintage dress that Eva gave me, which only goes to show that Eva's rule about not wearing "vintage" when you could have owned the clothes from new is shit advice, if you look as good in it as Pearl.

"Come here, please, Albert," she says, then waits for him to join her in the spotlight.

"Oh, my God," I say, to Dan. "Are they getting married or something? I thought they might be more than friends, but they always told me it was none of my business whenever I asked."

Dan says he has no idea, but then Pearl confirms it, to a degree.

"I bet you all think we're going to announce we're getting engaged or something," she says, "but I'm afraid we can't be bothered. Been there, done that, as my nephew Joel would say. We're just going to live in sin at Abandon Hope, which we're renaming "Hope Regained", so let's all raise our glasses to that."

There's an enormous round of applause, and quite a bit of cheering, too.

"*We* could get divorced and live in sin," I say to Dan, as we watch the oldies clustering around Pearl and Albert to offer their congratulations. "It sounds more fun to me."

"No, you bloody well don't," says Joel's voice, coming from somewhere on my left-hand side. "You've only just got back together, and I couldn't handle it if you split up again."

"I'm only joking, darling boy," I say, turning to give him a hug.

I don't notice the girl that Joel's brought with him until Dan says, "Hi, son. Who's this?"

"Ah," says Joel. "Dad, meet my girlfriend. Mum, I think you two have already met?"

I nod, at exactly the same time Ruby does.

Epilogue

I've got the hangover from hell *and* I'm in the middle of a lake. All I need now is for my *Titanic* dream to come to pass, and today will end almost as badly as New Year's Day last year.

"Keep going, Mum," says Joel. "I'm freezing my arse off, sitting here."

"At least you're not having to use your hat to bail," I say. "Though you will be in a minute, if you don't shut up and let me concentrate."

All I've got to do is dig deep, stay calm and keep on keeping on. If I've managed to get halfway already, then surely I can get all the way across?

"Make every stroke count," says Joel, who's obviously watched the Boat Race once too often. "Now *hammer* those legs, and don't forget to breathe."

"I wish *you* would," I say.

How am I supposed to concentrate on keeping my shoulders perpendicular to a square, or whatever Albert always tells me to do, when I've got an over-excitable passenger who keeps

419

standing up and waving towards the people on the shore? I can't, so I'm going to have to get a grip some other way.

I know, I'll motivate myself by visualising the moment in my dream when Joel and I were about to drown, and Dan started rowing away from us. I'm not ever going to let myself be put in that helpless position ever again, so this is where I prove I won't.

Pull, I tell myself, then *pull* again. Over and over, while the distance from the bank we launched from gets further and further away and – hopefully – the bank I'm aiming for gets nearer and nearer. I really don't like this business of rowing with your back to where you're heading. It gives you a hell of a crick in your neck, if your navigator's as hopeless as Joel is. Now he's claiming to be seasick, which I don't think is possible on a freshwater lake, but at least the nausea's rendered him incapable of further speech.

Pull – and – pull – and – pull.

I'm tiring now, and I feel quite like giving up, but then I remember what Albert said when he agreed to lend me his boat last night:

"If you want to prove something to yourself, Hannah – when you get close to exhaustion – rise to the challenge and go beyond yourself."

It all sounded a bit self-help-bookish at the time, but it seems to do the trick now that I'm attempting it, especially when I envisage the *Titanic* scene again. Then I start ploughing through the water like a madwoman, and soon I can hear shouts of encouragement, which seem to be getting closer and closer.

With a few more deep pulls that make my wrists and shoulders burn, I finally reach the shore to loud cheering from all around. Take that, you horrible recurring dream. This time Hannah Pinkman didn't drown. She didn't even drop an oar.

Dan steps forward to catch the rope that Joel throws towards him, then ties the boat – very firmly – to its mooring. After that, he waits while Joel and I clamber out and stand wobbly-legged on the shore.

"Well done, Han," he says, pulling me to him. "I'm proud of you, and relieved you didn't tip yourself into the lake like you did when I proposed. Talking of which, I hope you think *this* is more romantic than that."

He turns and gestures to where a crowd of customers are sitting at tables outside the lakeside cafe. Their faces are familiar as they're all our friends and family, but the cafe itself looks totally different from how it used to when Albert first began teaching me to row.

"It's been revamped since I was last here," I say, in astonishment. "It looks wonderful."

"And it's ours," says Dan. "Do you like the sign?"

He's watching me closely for my reaction, but it's a confused one, when it comes. Tears and laughter at the same time. The cafe's new name is *Danny and Pammy's*.

The End

Meet Molly Bennett.

*Married to Max, and mother to two warring teenagers,
she's what Bridget Jones would call a 'smug married'.
But smug's the last thing Molly feels, especially after the birthday
she's just 'celebrated'. . .*

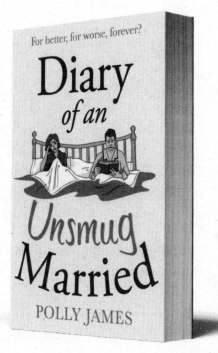

If you crossed *Bridget Jones's Diary* with *The Thick of It*, this
book is what you'd get.

A funny and perceptive book about real relationships, and
what happens to love when life gets in the way.

Perfect for fans of **Sue Townsend** and **Helen Fielding**.